GOODBYE PICCADILLY

Patricia Burns was born in Essex. After a variety of jobs, she decided to train as a teacher, which she now combines with writing novels. She is happily single and lives with her youngest son, a cat and a delinquent tortoise. This is her fifth novel. Her previous four, *Trinidad Street*, *A Step From Cinnamon Alley*, *Keep Safe for Me*, and, most recently, *Packards* are all available in Arrow.

PATRICIA BURNS

GOODBYE PICCADILLY

Packards At War

ARROW

Published by Arrow Books in 1998

1 3 5 7 9 10 8 6 4 2

Copyright © Patricia Burns 1998

First published in the United Kingdom in 1998 by Century
Arrow Books Limited
20 Vauxhall Bridge Road, London SW1V 2SA

Random House Australia (Pty) Limited
20 Alfred Street, Milsons Point, Sydney
New South Wales 2061, Australia

Random House New Zealand Limited
18 Poland Road, Glenfield
Auckland 10, New Zealand

Random House South Africa (Pty) Limited
Endulini, 5a Jubilee Road, Parktown 2193, South Africa

Random House UK Limited Reg. No. 954009

A CIP catalogue record for this book
is available from the British Library

Papers used by Random House UK Limited
are natural, recyclable products made from wood grown in
sustainable forests. The manufacturing processes conform to
the environmental regulations of the country of origin

ISBN 0 09 916452 3

Typeset by SX Composing DTP, Rayleigh, Essex

Printed and bound in Germany by
Elsnerdruck, Berlin

1

October 1913

It was far too beautiful a day for a funeral.

Golden sunlight shone down from a deep blue sky, turning the yellow brick of Tatwell Court to a mellow honey, glowing on the autumn leaves of great oaks and chestnuts and hornbeams in the park, glancing off the still waters of the lake. It was a day for galloping over the wide grassland and trotting through the woods, or for a shooting party that might bag a record number of birds, a day for bonfires and the making of vast vats of fruit preserves. Instead, the busy, ordered world that was Tatwell was stilled. Even the smoke from the many chimneys hung motionless in the sky.

On the gravelled sweep before the house, the estate workers were gathered, weather-beaten men with leathery hands, uneasy in their Sunday best, unable to keep their eyes from straying to the carriage at the foot of the Palladian stairway. It had been there for fully ten minutes, a hearse of high Victorian magnificence complete with six black horses with plumed heads. There was the sound of motorcar wheels on gravel. The heads of the men turned. A gleaming maroon Rolls-Royce purred round the corner of the house, the head of a procession of vehicles. It drew up behind the hearse. The great front doors of the house swung open.

First came the house staff. They processed out of the doors and lined the steps, the men in black jackets, their heads bare, the maids with black ribbands in their caps. They stood with clasped hands and bowed heads. Then came the coffin, borne on the shoulders of four of the footmen. The men waiting outside snatched off their hats. Down the steps it swayed, to be slid into the hearse and surrounded by banks of wreaths. Sir Thomas Packard, the man who had come to London at the age of fifteen with three shillings in his pocket and founded the greatest department store in the Empire, had embarked on his last journey.

The mourners followed. Sir Thomas's widow, Lady Margaret Packard, leaned on the arms of her daughter Winifred and son-in-law Bertie. Both women were dressed in black crêpe and heavily veiled. They stepped into the Rolls-Royce. Behind them came the eldest grandson, Edward Amberley Packard, his wife Sylvia on his arm, his expression suitably sombre, his dark eyes lowered so that nobody could see from the gleam in them that this was the happiest day of his life. They boarded the large green Renault that was next in line. After them came Thomas's other two grandchildren, Amelie Rutherford, obviously pregnant, with her husband Hugo, and Perry and his wife Gwendoline. All four got into Hugo's Austin.

Amelie had not realised that grief was such a very physical pain. It was a tangible presence within her, as real and hard as the baby that drummed its sharp little heels under her ribs. She knew its colour, this pain; it was black shot through with red. It spread through her and clawed at her with its talons. She could keep it in check in public, if she concentrated very hard, but now,

2

sitting staring ahead at that gross monstrosity of a hearse, it reached up and clutched her round the throat.

Her brother Perry patted her hand.

'Bear up, old thing.'

She turned on him, raging through the tears.

'Bear up! What do you care? You never loved him. He was just a source of money to you, that's all. Well, I shouldn't hope for too much from his will, if I were you. He saw through you. He knew just what you are.'

'Really–' Gwendoline began, offended.

Hugo put a restraining hand on Amelie's arm.

'My dear, control yourself.'

He hated public displays of emotion.

Amelie shook him off.

'Don't touch me!'

She felt rather than saw the men exchange glances over her head.

'She's upset,' Perry murmured.

Upset. It was such a feeble term that she almost laughed. Then the motor began to edge forward, silencing her. With the immediate family all present, the cortege was moving off, led by mutes in black frock coats and crêpe-swathed top hats. Other motorcars were drawing up at the steps to take the more distant relatives, the political figures, the founders and current chairmen of other great London stores, the senior management of Packards.

With excruciating dignity, the procession crawled through the park. Halfway up a grassy slope, the herd of fallow deer raised their heads and watched, ears flicking nervously, ready to run. Thomas Packard had loved those deer, enjoyed watching them roaming on his land, enjoyed even more eating their succulent flesh. Most of all, he took pleasure in embarrassing his daughter by telling her Society guests that when he was a lad he had been shot at by gamekeepers for snaring rabbits, and now here he was eating his own venison. It never failed to mortify poor Winifred.

Hugo was staring not at the hearse but at the Renault immediately in front of them.

'I cannot think what possessed Edward to buy that French motor. There are plenty of good British models for him to choose from.'

'I thought the Froggies were our allies. Entente cordiale and all that, what?' Perry said.

'Indeed yes. They're the only truly civilised nation,' Gwendoline agreed.

Hugo snorted.

'Believe me, we're much closer to the Germans. Their thinking matches ours in a great many ways. They've just got a bit above themselves, that's all. Need teaching a lesson on who's really in charge.'

Amelie ignored him. She had long ago given up trying to understand her husband's opinions and beliefs. None of them stood up to close analysis; it was best to just let him get on with it. At least he had given up trying to persuade her to take an active part in propagating them. Except when it came to producing children, of course. On that there was no moving him. She rested her hands on top of her belly. Her fourth baby in under five years. She had hoped for a daughter this time, after her three sons. But now, gazing at the black and silver hearse towering above even the massive Rolls-Royce, she wanted another boy. They could not call him Thomas, for her eldest already bore his great-grandfather's name, but he would be the one who would carry his spirit on into the future. The thought was oddly comforting.

The church contained a satisfyingly important roll-call of names. Mr Lloyd George was there, and Mr Gordon Selfridge, Mr John Lewis, Sir Ernest Maple and many other great men from the world of retailing. But more important to Amelie, and, she was sure, to her grandfather, a contingent from the store had been invited. Her mother had been horrified when Amelie had suggested it, but she had fought fiercely for their inclusion. For once, her brother Edward had agreed with her.

'This is not a Society event, Mother. Of course there must be representatives from the staff.'

Winifred had been outnumbered.

The store itself was closed today. The great Oxford Street landmark that Thomas Packard had built from a job lot of mourning apparel in a tiny rented shop on the Tottenham Court Road was silent and still, the counters and cabinets swathed in dust sheets, blinds covering the dazzling window displays for which Amelie was responsible. Amelie stared at the coffin just feet away from her in the packed church. Tomorrow she would turn those windows into memorials to her grandfather. She had commissioned large copies of the portrait photograph of him in his prime, and would place one in the centre of every display, draped in black ribbands.

She held on to this idea through what felt like an interminable service. The prayers and the readings seemed to go on and on. She could only mouth the words of hymns for fear of breaking down. Her eyes kept coming back to the coffin. There lay the man who was dearer to her than her mother, far dearer than her husband. He had been such an all-important presence in her life that at times she still could not really believe that he was gone for ever.

Edward got up and walked to the lectern, produced a sheet of notes from his inner pocket, paused. A deeper quiet settled over the church. Edward read well, his voice carrying easily, his tone suitably respectful. As long as he spoke of his grandfather's achievements, Amelie was all right. Here they were in the realms of fact. But when he started speaking of Thomas's qualities, of his own sense of loss, she churned with a sick rage at such hypocrisy. She wanted to leap up and accuse Edward of gloating beneath that smooth mask. For gloating he certainly was. With Thomas gone, the store was his. And with Edward in charge, everything would change. Unless, that was, Thomas had left behind some bombshell in his will. There was always a chance of that, a chance that kept Amelie sitting with her hands folded in front of her, outwardly brave and controlled. She stroked the bulge. There at least she had the better of her brother. Edward had fathered just one child, a girl. She allowed herself a ghost of a smile.

At last it was over, and they were all processing out for the interment. The previous owners of Tatwell had been laid to rest in a family vault in the church, but Thomas had left strict instructions about this. He wanted no stone mausoleum. He was to lie on the earth of the churchyard.

They gathered round the open grave. Amelie's head swam. She caught hold of Hugo's arm, glad for once for his physical strength. He glanced down at her.

'Are you all right?'

Amelie nodded.

'. . . our brother Thomas . . . dust to dust . . .'

She threw the rose she was holding into the gaping hole.

People were moving, she realised. The rector was talking to her grandmother, holding her hand in his. That was it. He was gone. She stared down.

'Amelie–'

Her mother's voice, low and urgent, close to her ear.

'Amelie, who are those people over there?'

'Where?'

Dazed, Amelie looked about. There were people everywhere, family, official mourners, folk from the village and the estate come to pay their last respects.

'Over there, by the cherry tree—'

Then she saw who Winifred meant. A woman and a young man, both in deepest mourning, were standing together, isolated from everyone else. It was hard to tell how old the woman was, for she was heavily veiled, but it was obvious that she was deeply distressed. The young man's arm was round her shoulder and he was trying in vain to comfort her. Amelie was about to tell her mother that she had no idea who they were, when the man looked up, looked right at her. She caught her breath, stared and stared again. It was as if she were looking at a younger version of that photograph she planned to use in the windows of the store. It was not just the features, it was the expression, that look of fearless determination. She wrapped her free arm protectively round her unborn child.

'Well?' Winifred asked.

Amelie swallowed.

'I – I have never seen them before in my life.'

'Nor I, so why are they here?'

Amelie dragged her gaze away and faced her mother. It was obvious from the sharp suspicion in her face that she had made the same guess.

'Why don't you go and find out?' she asked.

'Speak to that person? Certainly not,' Winifred retorted, predictably.

Amelie stopped short of suggesting sending someone else to speak to them. Her mother might just take up that idea.

Winifred glanced again at the strangers.

'I wonder if your grandmother—?'

'For heaven's sake, Mother! The last thing we want to do is to draw her attention to them. We must make very sure that she doesn't see them.' Amelie looked to where her grandmother, supported by Edward, was still receiving condolences from a long line of mourners. There was plenty to distract her there.

'Of course I wasn't going to do anything of the kind. The very idea! If they are who they appear to be, then I think it the very depths of bad taste that they should show their faces here at this time. But then I suppose that is all one can expect from those sort of people.'

'I quite agree,' Hugo said.

Amelie stole another look at them. She had heard the rumours, of course, and it was hardly unusual for a man to have a mistress. But her grandfather had been eighty-one when he died. Surely that was a trifle old? Or had it all been a long time ago? The son, if he was indeed her son, was at least twenty. The woman's shoulders were heaving with sobs. He began to lead her away.

'She must have loved him very much,' she mused out loud, with a stirring of sympathy.

Her mother snorted.

'Disappointed at having her source of income removed, I should imagine.'

People were moving over to speak to them. Amelie lost sight of the unknown pair as she shook hands and nodded and said all the things that were expected of her. Through the formal words the genuine feeling reached out to her, comforting.

'. . . a fine man . . .'

'. . . a true innovator . . .'

'. . . will be much missed . . .'

Her sister-in-law Sylvia appeared at her side, impeccably turned out as ever, upright and apparently totally in control. Her veil hid not a face ravaged with grief, but one as calm and cool as if she were hostessing a tea party. Once, Amelie had been sorry for Sylvia, married to her brother and abominably betrayed within weeks of their wedding. But now she was beginning to feel that they deserved each other.

'Your grandmother is very tired. We are taking her back to the house now.'

Sylvia's tone was suitably sympathetic. Amelie looked at her. Perhaps she was genuine. She was certainly being considerate of Lady Margaret's welfare. Who could say what was going on behind that impassive expression? It could be anything or nothing. Amelie rested a hand on her belly, unconsciously drawing attention to her pregnant state. She saw Sylvia stiffen.

'I was surprised to see you here at all, in your condition,' she said.

'You mean it's not entirely *comme il faut*? I would have thought that a reminder of new life was a comfort at a funeral.' Between the heads of two distinguished businessmen, she saw her brother escorting her grandmother towards the Rolls-Royce. 'Hadn't you better join Edward?' she asked.

Sylvia left, leaving Amelie feeling more raw than ever. With the departure of the widow, everyone headed for their motorcars. Perry and Gwendoline appeared and climbed into the Austin with Amelie and Hugo.

'Well, that all went as well as could be expected, didn't it? Old boy would have been pleased with the turnout,' Perry commented.

'Yes,' Amelie said.

'I say, did you see those rum coves in the graveyard? Young chap looked the spitting image of the old boy. Gave me quite a turn, it did. And the old boiler blubbing fit to burst. I—'

'Thank you,' Hugo said repressively. 'I don't think we need your views on the matter.'

'Well, you're going to get them all the same. Do you think Edward saw them? That'd stir him up a bit, wouldn't it? Just think, he's our uncle, after a fashion. Half-uncle or something. Do you think Grandfather's left them anything?'

'Perry!' Something snapped inside Amelie. 'For God's sake! We've only just buried him. Don't you care at all?'

Unexpectedly, Gwendoline sided with her, putting her arms round Amelie and turning on her husband.

'Yes, be quiet, Perry. Haven't you got *any* sense?'

The tears that Amelie had held back all through the service spilled forth, scalding her throat, racking her body with sobs. Ignoring both men, she gave herself up to her grief.

2

Close to, the Packard family were even worse than Alexander Eden had imagined. He had always loathed and resented them, the acknowledged ones, living their lives of ease and splendour in the full glory of the Packards empire while he, his father's only son, did not even bear the Packard name. He sat at the rear of the small church, his mother's arm tucked in his, patting her hand automatically every now and again as she wept silently beside him. Up in the church tower, a single bell tolled. Eighty-one chimes, one for every year of his father's life. If he shifted a little to the right or left, he could see the backs of all their heads. He knew who they all were.

Right at the front, bedside the flower decked coffin, was the small, bowed figure of his mother's rival, Lady Margaret Packard, or simply Her, as she had always been known in his household.

'Your father can't come today, he's got to go somewhere with Her,' was one of the statements he most dreaded in the days of his childhood. It always heralded a spate of bad temper and sulks from his mother.

Even now, at the end of his father's life, She had triumphed, for there she was next to his coffin, receiving

11

the sympathy and condolences of this entire churchful of people, while his mother was here at the back, alone and ignored but for him.

Alec looked along the front pew. Next to Her, he could just see the top of the elaborate hat belonging to his half-sister, Winifred. The discrepancy in age between himself and the rest of his father's family was another thing that vaguely disturbed him. Winifred was a good few years older than his mother, while her children, his half-nephews and -niece, were older than him. All the same, he felt superior to Winifred. From what his father had let drop, she was a stupid woman, concerned with nothing but appearances and furthering her place in Society. She was not a true Packard.

The same applied to Perry, her younger son. There he was, with all the opportunities he could wish for to make his mark in the Packard organisation, and all he did was fool around. Alec had often seen his name mentioned in the Society columns of the newspapers, but never as having done anything remarkable. He was just there, a member of that privileged set that did absolutely nothing to justify their existence on earth except spend huge amounts of money. As Alec looked to Perry, his wife leaned forward. He could see very little of her, swathed as she was in the obligatory black veil, but he knew from a photograph he had seen in the *Illustrated London News* that she was a very pretty woman. When you had the Packard fortune behind you, you could marry beauty.

The service started. Alec half listened to the prayers, helped his mother to her feet for the hymns. A sense of unreality crept up on him. This was his father's funeral. Thomas Packard had always been the ruling force in his life. The rhythms of the household were attuned to him. He was his mother's reason for existence. And yet he had been absent so much of the time that it was hard to believe that this time he really was not going to return.

While the congregation was standing, he caught a glimpse of his half-niece, and experienced a sour kick of jealousy. Amelie was the one his father loved. His little girl, he called her. Amelie only had to ask, and she got what she wanted. She should have been a mere debutante, graduating to a Society lady, and therefore no threat. But no, she had wanted to be part of Packards, and his father had let her, despite the fact that she was a girl. She had set up and run her own department when she was only eighteen, then she had been given responsibility for display and advertising, and now she had shares of her own, a place on the board and a real say in the running of the store. Everything was easy for her, everything was possible. And on top of that she had provided his father with more male heirs. Three of them, and another soon to come. And all of them acknowledged.

His mother pulled at his arm. He bent his head to listen to her.

'All these . . . people, come to . . . see him off.'

She could hardly speak for sobbing.

He was not quite sure what response was expected from him.

'Yes.'

'Very . . . important people.'

'He was well respected, Mother. He was a very important man himself.'

She nodded. He thought she had finished, but she was just gathering breath.

'But it was . . . it was . . . me that he . . . he loved.'

'Yes, Mother. Only you.'

She broke down again, weeping into her sodden handkerchief. Alec produced another from the supply he carried in his pocket, rather spoiling the line of his black jacket. Black-bordered handkerchiefs, from

13

Packards. He handed it to her, and she pushed it up under her veil to cover her red and swollen eyes. He didn't see Her crying like this.

The congregation settled into their seats once again. At the front, a tall figure stood up and walked to the lectern. Edward. The enemy. More than Amelie, more than any of them, Alec hated Edward.

He paused for a moment while the shuffling died down, then he began to speak, clearly and with authority, his voice carrying easily to the furthest corners of the church. Alec stared at him, his face a stony mask. That was his place that Edward was taking. He was Sir Thomas Packard's son. Edward was only his grandson. He should be the one standing there telling these people what a great man Thomas Packard had been. What was more, he knew that he could make every bit as good a job of it. He sat willing Edward to make a mistake, but his delivery was smooth and faultless. Too faultless. He spoke of his own loss and sorrow, but Alec did not believe him. Hadn't his father often said that Edward was heartless? A cold fish, that's what he had called him. But despite that, it was Edward who was heir to the Packard empire.

The service drew to an end. Sir Thomas Packard's remains were borne out of the church by his grandsons and sons-in-law. His son stood and watched the procession pass. He should be there as well; he should carry the weight of the coffin, feel it cutting into his shoulder. The rest of the family passed, sombre and black clad, eyes downcast. Alec hated their hypocrisy. Parading their grief like this, when no doubt they were looking forward to hearing just what they had inherited. He took his mother's arm and guided her out after the VIPs, ignoring the disapproving looks of those whose place in the procession he had usurped. Let them glare. He had a right.

14

Out in the churchyard the sun shone down out of a perfect blue sky, making him blink after the darkness of the church. He guided his mother towards a tree close to the open grave, where they could watch the interment without being noticed by the family. If he had been there by himself, he would have shouldered his way to the graveside, but he did not want his mother to be insulted. The occasion was proving to be quite enough of a trial for her as it was.

A close-packed phalanx of black-clad mourners came between Alec and his mother and the grave. They could see hardly anything, but the rector's sonorous voice carried across the churchyard, bringing them the words of the committal.

'. . . dust to dust . . . in sure and certain hope . . .'

Alec put his arm round his mother's heaving shoulders and suddenly wished himself a thousand miles away. He had been absolutely determined to come to pay his last respects to his father, and nothing on earth would have kept his mother away, but after all, what good did it do? His father was dead. He didn't know who was there to see him laid to rest. And his mother was getting more distraught by the minute.

'It's all right,' he said, knowing just how inadequate that sounded. 'It'll all be over soon.'

But that only made her weep the more.

The mourners began to move away from the grave. Through their thinning ranks he caught sight of Amelie. She was holding tightly on to her husband's arm. As he watched, she threw a single red rose into the open grave. Fascinated despite himself, he stayed watching her, unwilling to believe that here might be one member of the acknowledged family who truly cared about his father. She was approached by Winifred, then what he had half hoped for, half dreaded happened. They both turned and gazed at him and his mother. He could not

15

see their expressions behind those veils, but he could guess at their outrage. Defiantly, he gazed back, staring them down until they looked away.

Winifred still appeared to be talking urgently to Amelie, but she did not look at him again, neither did she seem to be agreeing with her mother. Other members of the family were talking to the mourners, conferring with each other. He intercepted other curious glances directed his way, some coldly disapproving, some openly hostile, none sympathetic. It confirmed only too well what he had known all along: he was the outsider, the pariah. He was not wanted. He stood his ground. They were not going to force him to leave. He had as much right to be here as any of them.

Edward assisted Her into the huge Rolls-Royce. It was the signal for everyone else to move. There was an almost visible haze of relief as the rich headed for their motorcars, glad that it was all over.

'They're all off to stuff themselves at the big house, I suppose,' Alec remarked.

His mother did not reply.

The poor folk, estate workers, Alec supposed, and shop assistants and people from the village, dispersed more slowly. Some of them came up and laid bunches of garden flowers beside the heap of florist's wreaths.

'Come along,' he said to his mother.

He led her up to where the gravediggers were already at work filling in.

She stood shaking so much that he had to hold her up. Between her sobs, he could just about make out what she was trying to say.

'Tommy – Tommy – I love you –'

He took from her hands the wreath she was clutching, and laid it with the others, glancing at the black-bordered card attached to it.

'To my darling Tommy from your ever loving Dora

16

and your devoted son Alexander.'

Let the rest of the family read that and choke on it.

He gazed into the grave. Only one shiny corner of the coffin could be seen. Even as he looked, it was covered up.

'Goodbye, Father,' he said. 'Rest in Peace.'

Somehow, the tried and tested words seemed to be the best.

Then he led his mother away to face the journey back to London.

In the days that followed, Alec began to dread coming home to St John's Wood each evening. The white-painted house in the tree-lined street that had been home to him all his life was entirely given over to mourning. His mother kept the blinds down all the time, had the pictures and looking glasses covered over, forbade him to play the piano or the gramophone.

'How can you even think of it, with your father not cold in his grave?' she would cry as he shuffled through his collection of ragtime records. 'Come and talk to me, darling.'

Alec would sit down beside her and try to entertain her with stories of whatever had been going on at the office that day, but she hardly seemed to listen. He might be halfway through a tale of how Ambrose had tried to get the better of Levison but had been foiled, when his mother would heave a great sigh and remark that his father would have been proud to hear how well he was getting on, and it would be the signal for the start of another long round of reminiscence.

'He was a wonderful man, wonderful. Always so kind and so generous. Some of them aren't, you know. That Mona Bigley down the road never knows where she is with hers. Always worried she is, that he's gone off and found someone else. Never knows whether she might be turned out of house and home. But your father wasn't like that. I was the love of his life, you see. He always said that to me. "Dora," he said, "you are the love of my life." And of course there was you. None of the others gave him a son. Not Her, and not any of the other women he had before me. He was so proud the day you were born! You should have seen this house. A bower, it was. A real bower. Flowers everywhere. And do you know what I found wrapped up in tissue paper in the middle of a sheaf of three dozen red roses?'

Alec did know, because he had heard the story a hundred times before. But he knew that she liked to tell him all the same.

'No, what?' he dutifully asked.

'A diamond necklace!'

Alec was suitably impressed.

'It was beautiful. I put it on then and there, sitting up in bed in my nightgown and bedjacket. I couldn't bear to take it off. I was still wearing it when he came to visit me. You should have seen his face when he saw me wearing it!

' "I don't know what I've done to deserve this," I said, and do you know what he told me?

' "You've given me something more precious than all the diamonds in the world," he said, "you've given me a son."

'He did, he did really. That was what he thought of you, you know. And I wore those diamonds to go out. Oh, we went to some lovely places . . .'

Alec let her ramble on while he turned over what she had said. He had to make allowances for her exaggeration, of course. It was quite possible that his father had never said anything like that on the occasion of his birth. Whether he did or not was hardly material now. The fact was that he was not precious enough to be given a part of the store. When he had left school at eighteen his father had found him a place in a merchant bank.

'Learn all you can about how money works, my boy,' he advised him. 'That's where the power is. Money and land. Learn how to control it and you can hold them all in your hands – tradesmen like me, the aristocracy, politicians – they all need loans at some time. I had to learn about it the hard way. You get in on the inside. Believe me, it's the right place to be.'

Alec had not believed him, but he had very little choice. His father held the household purse strings, and his word was law. Despite all the romantic stuff about being the love of his life, he knew that his mother was worried about being replaced by someone younger. After all, that was what she had been at first, a replacement, and now she was beginning to look middle-aged, despite lavishing every attention and all the beauty aids known to woman on her face, hair and body. If he had rebelled against his father's wishes, it could have rebounded upon his mother. Of this she was convinced. So Alec went to work at the bank, and would have found it interesting had he not felt that he had been fobbed off.

The feeling was even stronger now.

'If he had really cared about me, he would have left me an interest in the store,' he said, voicing his thoughts out loud.

'What?'

'Nothing,' he said hastily. There was no point in upsetting her further. She was not actually crying at the moment, which was a real improvement. But she had heard him, and after a few seconds the meaning filtered through to her brain.

'Alec!' Slowly, her face crumpled and reddened. 'How can you say such a thing? Whatever your father did, he did for your own good–'

Alec sighed.

'Yes, Mother, I'm sure he did,' he temporised.

But it was too late. She broke down in tears.

'Oh Alec,' she sobbed on his shoulder, 'how am I going to live without him?'

He did not know how to cope with her grief. If there was anything he could have done to bring his father back, he would have done it. Beyond that, he did not know how to console her. There was nothing else in her life.

When the storm had subsided a little, he rang for the maid to take her up to bed, and once she was settled, took her a glass of brandy and water himself and made sure she drank it. He hoped it would help her to sleep.

After that he wandered restlessly round the house. The heart, the point of it had gone with his father. It was still home, but it was empty at its centre. He stopped in the dining room. Here, during the last two or three years, he had begun a new, adult relationship with his father. They had talked about money and trade and politics. His father had taught him to appreciate a good cigar and a fine port. He had learnt about his father's own youth, about how he had come to London with three shillings in his pocket, about his early struggles and the growth of the shop that was to become the greatest department store in the British Empire. Slowly, Alec pulled out a chair and sat down. The terrible ache in his heart seemed to be choking him. His father had been a unique man. He thought with deep regret of all the lost years, the time when he had hated his father. All through his adolescence he had loathed him because it was his fault that they were not the normal happy family he had assumed them to be in his childhood. He was different, marked out, a bastard. He had to tell lies and make excuses to his friends in order to cover up the shameful truth. He had hardly spoken to his father during that time, beyond the bare demands of good manners. Now he was overwhelmed with sadness at so many wasted opportunities. There was so much he would never know about the man who had been Thomas Packard, and now it was all too late. Alec lowered his head into his arms as his body was wracked with harsh sobs.

It was some time after midnight when he made his way upstairs. Emptied of emotion, practical worries came back to possess him. He was the man of the house now. He fervently hoped his father had made some provision for his mother's future. The house might be quite modest by Tatwell standards, with only four bedrooms and three servants, but his salary would not cover the rent and the servants' wages, let alone the food and his mother's clothing bills. If they had to move, his mother would be devastated.

Alec stood at the window of the frilly guest bedroom which had never been used and looked out into the darkness of the garden. One thing he did know: he was not going to let his father's other family get it all without a fight.

3

May Hollis stood at the kitchen door. Her mother was stirring porridge on the stove. Even her back, thin and resolutely straight, spoke disapproval.

'I'm ready now, Mum,' May said.

A selection of May's younger brothers and sisters jumped up and hurled themselves at her, the smallest ones sniffling. Mrs Hollis turned slowly.

'You'd best be off, then. Don't want to miss the train.'

Tears pricked at the back of May's eyes. She walked across the tiny room and leaned forward to kiss her mother's unyielding cheek.

'I'll be a good girl, Mum. Honest I will. I won't get led astray or nothing. I'll go to chapel twice every Sunday and I'll write to you every week.'

Mrs Hollis made a non-committal noise in her throat.

'That's the least I expect of you, my girl. I still don't see why you got to leave your family and go to that wicked city. You could have got a job at the big house same as your sisters.'

May sighed. They had gone over this argument so many times before.

'It's not that much different, Mum. I would've been

living in there. And I'm still working for the family, only at the store, not the big house.'

'It ain't the same at all.' The two lines running down from Mrs Hollis's nose to the sides of her mouth deepened into furrows. 'If you was up at the house, you could come home on your half day. Up in that evil London, you'll be open to all sorts of temptations in your spare time. I've heard about what happens to young girls there.'

'It won't happen to me, Mum. I'll be strong. I'll stand up to the Devil, I promise.'

Mrs Hollis only snorted.

May blinked back the threatening tears.

'I got to go, Mum.' And as her mother still made no move, she begged, 'Won't you just give me your blessing?'

Mrs Hollis hesitated, then gave her a quick peck on the cheek.

'Be strong in the Lord.'

May hugged her resisting body. Her big brother Silas appeared and picked up the stout wooden box that held all her belongings.

'Ready, Sis?'

'Yes.'

Surrounded by an assortment of brothers and sisters, May walked down the muddy village street. All her life she had lived here in Tatwell. Her friends lived here, in these cottages. She had been educated there at the elementary school. She had run errands for her mother to the baker's and the butcher's. She had worked since leaving school at the general store, until the owner's daughter was old enough to take over her job. She had attended the little corrugated iron chapel twice every Sabbath without fail ever since she could remember. Now that the time had come, she could hardly believe that she was leaving home. She felt both exhilarated and afraid.

23

People came out of cottages and shops to call out and wave. Her friend Mabel, who had started school the same day as she had, ran over to give her a hug.

'You off to the big city, then? Lucky thing, you! Wish it was me as well. Here,' – pressing a small object wrapped in a twist of paper into her hand. – 'this is to remember me by.'

'Oh, Mabel, thank you . . . Oh, you shouldn't have . . .'

At the end of the village stood the smithy, now doubling as a garage for the motorcars that passed through their way to the big house. Jim the apprentice straightened up and pushed his cap back on his head. He stared at May but said nothing. She felt a blush flooding her face. She and Jim had had words over her going away. She took a deep breath and marched up to him, holding out her hand.

'Won't you part friends, Jim?'

Jim held her eyes for a moment. Then, slowly, he wiped a large paw on his trousers and shook hands.

'Bye, May.'

'Goodbye, Jim. The Lord be with you.'

Then they were out of the village and passing the few outlying cottages. In the fields the plough teams were out, and two ancient men were at work cutting and laying the hawthorn hedge by the side of the road. There was a wide silence, but for the stirring of the wind in the remaining November leaves, the chattering of the children, and the distant whistling of the ploughboy. Soon she would be in the great city, where there was noise and bustle and excitement day and night.

'Don't you wish you was coming with me, Silas?' May asked.

Her brother shook his head.

'Not me. I've no mind to be gallivanting off. No more would you, if you had any sense.'

May shrugged.

'You're an old stick-in-the-mud, you are. Don't you want to see the world?'

'Tatwell's good enough for me,' Silas said. 'Should be good enough for you, too.'

'I want to better myself. I don't want to be no skivvy.'

'There's nought wrong with honest labour.'

It was no use arguing with him. He was just like their mother and father. None of them understood her desire to get out of the confines of the village. Why, there were people in Tatwell who had never been further than Hertford in their whole lives, who thought going to Sawbridgeworth was an adventure. She did not want to be like that, nor did she want to be a housemaid, and since that was the only job open to her now that her place at the general store had been taken over, she had taken her courage in both hands and approached Sir Thomas Packard, just a week before he died, and asked him if there were any positions available in his famous store. Pleased with the service she had given him when he'd called at the village shop, he had said that he was sure he could find something for her. And sure enough, he did. It must have been one of his last acts, for just three days after the funeral, a letter had come for her, offering her the post of junior assistant.

Getting the job was the easy part. Then came the task of persuading her parents to let her take it up. There were great consultations amongst the elders of the chapel. In the end, the fact that Sir Thomas was now dead swayed them: it gave the offer more authority, coming as it did almost as his last wish. Much thought was given to May's moral safety. Conditions inside the store were perfectly acceptable. She would be well supervised and kept busy all day long. It was her leisure hours that caused the anxiety. Packards no longer provided bed and board for employees. They had to find their own lodgings, although the store had a list of approved places they could apply to. This was not good enough for the chapel elders. They contacted a sister establishment in Clerkenwell and arranged for May to stay with one of their members. Only then were they satisfied that she would be properly watched over. May had no choice but to go along with all these arrangements. It was that or not go at all. Besides, even though she wanted to get out into the big wide world, it was a frightening step, and it was quite nice to have something familiar to go to.

So now here she was, on her way at last. Silas and the little ones tramped the mile and a half to the station with her and joined the collection of people gathered for the London train. Stiff in her Sunday best black jacket and skirt, a plain felt hat anchored firmly to her scraped back brown hair with a steel hatpin, May stood clutching her brand-new umbrella. A small figure with a resolute expression on her face, she looked younger than her eighteen years, an impression heightened by the dusting of freckles across her snub nose.

Silas, never one to chat, fell silent, and May felt too sick with nervous excitement to say anything. Only the children chattered and played round them.

'It's coming!' one of them called.

Sure enough, there was a puff of smoke in the distance. The small crowd stirred, gathering up parcels, checking tickets. Suddenly, May did not want to go. But it was too late to back down now, and besides, she had her pride. She swallowed, and held on to her umbrella just a little more tightly as the train steamed into the station. Silas climbed into the third-class carriage with her and put her box up on the luggage rack. May put her hands on his shoulders and planted a swift kiss on his cheek.

'Thanks, Silas. The Lord be with you.'

Silas flushed. They were not given to displays of affection in their family.

'And with you,' he replied gruffly and retreated to the platform.

The guard blew his whistle. May let down the window and hung out.

'Goodbye, goodbye!' she called, blowing kisses to the children.

The train started. Silas stood rock still on the platform, but the little ones ran as far as they could then gathered in a little group at the end, jumping up and down and waving. May watched them until they were out of sight, then sank down on to the hard seat. She felt very alone.

For the first part of the journey May hardly noticed the countryside rushing by outside. She was too overwhelmed by what she had done. This was it; she was on her way. There was no going back now. From now on, she must rely upon herself. It was a daunting thought for one who had always been surrounded by family, chapel and the force of village opinion to order her life. But as the train ran into the outskirts of London, her eyes were drawn to the window. Terraces of new brick houses with slate roofs ran down to the track. From the carriage, May could look down into neat gardens with lines of flapping washing, rows of cabbages and leeks, and spindly new fruit trees. Through gaps between the houses, quiet streets and parades of suburban shops could be briefly seen. Utterly absorbed, May caught little glimpses of other people's lives: a woman rocking a baby, a man digging potatoes on the bank of the cutting, a baker getting down from his van with a big basket of bread over his arm.

As they drew nearer to the centre of the city, they left behind the gardens and trees. Now the houses were packed together under a pall of smoke from factories and engines and hearths. The streets here were cobbled and crowded with traffic, the buildings blackened and dilapidated. Then it changed again, and they were running between tall office buildings four and five stories high, edifices of Portland stone and polished granite. Through the rows of gleaming windows, May caught sight of clerks bent over desks, while on the pavements strode men in black coats and shiny top hats. The train was slowing down now, until it rattled under a vast canopy and drew to a halt.

A spurt of panic forced May to turn to one of the other occupants of the carriage, a middle-aged woman dressed entirely in black.

'Are we here? Is this it?'

The woman gave a ghost of a nod.

'Yes. This is Liverpool Street.'

May saw disapproval in her eyes.

'Thank you,' she said stiffly, and struggled to get her box off the luggage rack.

'Here, let me.'

A rough-looking man reached up and lifted it down with ease.

'There y'are, Miss. Just you step down on to the platform and I'll pass it to you.'

His voice was reassuringly burred with a country accent. This, surely, could not be one of the wicked London people everyone had spoken about. May thanked him and took the awkward box under her arm, supporting it on her hip, then, armed with her umbrella, allowed herself to be swept along with the tide of people making for the end of the platform. Once through the barrier and washed up on the steps outside the station, she was truly on her own.

She stood for a few minutes, bemused by what she had embarked upon. Everything was so big, so loud, so fast, so smelly. The street was packed with all sorts of vehicles – cabs, vans, drays, buses, motors – the fumes from the petrol engines overpowering the familiar country smell of horses. The clatter of hooves and iron-bound cartwheels competed with the chugging of engines. People called for cabs, street sellers cried their wares, and everyone seemed to be in a hurry. This was London, this was the bustle and excitement she had come for, and it was frightening.

'You look a bit lost, my dear.'

May jumped. There beside her was an expensively dressed woman with an impressively corsetted figure.

'Up from the country, are you?'

May nodded, swallowing. Why was this person speaking to her?

'London's a big place for a young girl to be on her own. You need someone to look after you. Do you have somewhere to stay?'

She might look rich, but she spoke with a Cockney accent. And was that rouge on her cheeks? And surely hair never grew quite that colour naturally? May's mouth went dry. This was just what she had been warned against.

'No, yes, I mean I have somewhere, thank you. Goodbye,' she gabbled, and plunged into the throng on the pavement, her heart pounding in her chest.

She had memorised what she had to do next, which way to go, which bus to catch, but even so, she longed to get out her letter of instructions once again and reassure herself. But she dared not stop. The woman might catch up with her, might drag her away to who knew what den of depravity. Panting, she scanned the numbers at the bus stops. There were so many. All these routes, all these destinations, and all of them as foreign to her as China. With a great rush of relief, she spotted the right stop, and joined the end of the queue, dumping the box at her feet. Was the woman following her?

29

She shuffled up close to the person in front of her, and was profoundly glad when a solid couple joined the queue behind her. Now that she was enclosed by people, she felt less threatened, though apprehension still churned in her stomach. She didn't feel really safe until the bus came and she climbed on board and sank into the nearest seat. She had escaped.

She paid her fare and sat holding her ticket, absurdly proud. She had foiled the woman, she had found the right bus, she had asked for her destination just like a real Londoner. Everything was going to be all right

Half an hour later, she was still feeling buoyant. She had found the right road, a little back street with terraces of houses opening straight on to the pavement, and now she had only to get to the correct house. She looked at each door number as she passed. Thirty-three, thirty-five, thirty-seven – this was it, thirty-nine. But then she stopped, puzzled. All the curtains were tightly closed. That was very odd, in the middle of the day. She knocked on the door and waited. Nobody came. She knocked again. Still no reply. A thin rain began to fall, grey and chill. May shivered. Her back and arms were aching from carrying the box. She got the letter out of her pocket. Yes, she did have the right street, the right number and the right day. So why was nobody here?

'You won't find nobody at home there, deary.'

May looked round. A toothless old woman in a rusty black dress and grey shawl was standing in the doorway of the house next door but one.

'W-what?' May asked stupidly.

'Died, she has. Four days ago. Fever.' The old woman gave a cracked laugh. 'Didn't help her in the end, all her praying and turning up her nose at the likes of us. Good twenty years younger'n me, she was, but she's gone and I'm still here. What d'you think of that, eh?'

'Died?' May repeated. 'You mean – she's dead?'

'Yes deary, dead, gone. What's the matter, you stupid or something? Don't you understand?'

'I, yes, of course, but–'

What was she going to do? Where was she going to go?

A younger woman appeared, trailing a couple of grubby toddlers.

'What's the matter, love?'

She sounded nicer than the old woman. May explained.

'I was supposed to be lodging here, with Mrs Chambers.'

The younger woman shook her head.

'She's dead, love. Didn't you know?'

'No,' May admitted. Her throat was very tight.

'Never mind, love. Plenty of people round here take in lodgers. I'd give you a bed meself, only I'm full to busting. Why don't you try Winnie Green over the road? Now she's got a spare room, that I do know. Tell her I sent you.'

May looked at the street. It no longer seemed exciting and bustling, but mean and grey and poverty-stricken. This was not what she had come to London for. But where else was she to go? And then it came to her. Packards. They would tell her what to do. That was it, she would go to Packards.

4

It was a slow day in the Stationery Department of Packards.

'I can't think where they've all gone,' Ruby Goss remarked to her friend Ellie Marks.

'All got something better to do than write letters,' Ellie supposed.

It was most unusual. In Ruby's sub-section of the department, Writing Papers, there was generally a steady flow of people all day.

'Just you wait, they'll be putting us on to tidying in a minute,' she grumbled. 'I hate tidying. That's why I like it here, there's always customers around. That lot up in Jewellery or Silver or Plate, they give themselves airs and look down on us in Stationery, but most of the time all they're doing is tidying stuff that's tidy already. Boring, if you ask me.'

Not that anybody did ask her, since she was a junior shopgirl with only three years at Packards under her belt. To have any authority, you needed to have been behind the counter for at least ten years.

'Watch out, Mr Lambert's looking this way,' Ellie warned.

They moved away from each other. Gossiping

between shopgirls was not encouraged during working hours. Ruby tried to look busy. To her relief, a customer appeared, wanting mourning writing paper. Ruby arranged her face into sympathetic lines.

'Certainly, sir. Do you have any particular preference as to colour?'

The man looked baffled.

'No – just show me what you have.'

Ruby made a quick assessment of his clothes and accent. This was not a Royal Saxon Superfine customer. More of a Papyrus Regia or a St Regulus. She got out samples of the middle-range papers in cream, azure and grey, and explained about the various thicknesses of black border. The man looked undecided.

'Or of course we do have a superior range,' she said, displaying the Westminster Note and the Duchess of Kent. 'These are excellent quality while still being very good value. The difference is in the thickness, you see. They're very dignified.'

The man evidently did see.

'I'll take a ream of those, with medium borders, and envelopes to match,' he said.

Ruby packed up the order and sent away a satisfied customer. She looked up to find that Mr Lambert, the buyer, was heading her way. This time she was sure she was going to be told to tidy. Not that it needed doing. She always kept her drawers and shelves immaculate.

'Ah, Miss Goss—'

'Yes, Mr Lambert?'

Ruby put back her shoulders a fraction more in order to show off her fine bust, and ventured a demure smile. Mr Lambert was really rather good-looking if you liked fair men, and by far the youngest buyer at Packards.

The smile was not returned.

'You're wanted up in Staffing. You had better go straight away.'

Ruby was immediately on the defensive.

'Staffing? What do they want me for?' she demanded, before she could stop herself. She had done nothing wrong. She was always on time, she worked hard, she achieved good sales.

'I really have no idea,' Mr Lambert said.

Ruby flushed. That was not the way to speak to a buyer. If she went on like that then she really would be in trouble.

'No sir, of course not. I'll go right now,' she gabbled.

She hurried off, burning with indignation. She had never, ever been summonsed by Staffing before. Had someone made a complaint against her? If they had, then it was just not fair. Someone must have it in for her. Who could it be? Who didn't like her? She ran through a few of the other shopgirls in her head. Bitches, the lot of them. But they didn't know anything about her that was bad enough to report, and if they'd thought of some lie, she'd deny it. Oh yes she would, and find out who did it, too. She wallowed for a few moments in pleasurable thoughts of revenge. They wouldn't do that again in a hurry.

What if it wasn't one of the other girls, though? And now that she came to think of it, it wasn't really very likely. What if it was Mr Anderson, the floorwalker, or worse still, Mr Lambert? She couldn't bear it if Mr Lambert wanted to get rid of her. He was always very correct, of course – well, he was a buyer, and she was only a junior – but she'd sort of got this feeling that he quite fancied her. She caught sight of herself in a glass display cabinet. Striking, that's how she liked to think of herself. A striking girl. With her height and her hour-glass figure and her dark colouring, she stood out from the crowd. That was good when you were off for an evening out, but not so helpful when you worked at Packards and were supposed to be part of the furniture.

Perhaps that was what Mr Lambert and Mr Anderson didn't like. But if so, why hadn't they warned her? Why just let Staffing send for her like this? It wasn't fair.

As Ruby made her way through the store, it came home to her how much she loved working at Packards. She should have gone the quick way up the service stairs to the offices on the fifth floor, but instead she mounted the beautiful red marble stairway under the great central dome that let daylight into the store in the days before electricity, and allowed herself a quick diversion through Ladies' Gowns, with its eau-de-Nil and gold decor and deep carpets and fashion plates, and Fabrics, hung about with wonderful silks and satins and brocades like a palace from the Arabian Nights, and Millinery, with its incredible creations of ribbons and feathers and flowers displayed on cream-coloured columns. She did not dare linger, of course. Staff were not there to look at other departments' stock, they were there to work. But she managed to take it all in out of the corners of her eyes, and it only served to confirm what she already knew. There was nowhere else quite like Packards. Packards staff thought themselves superior to those from any other store in London. Harrods, Liberty, Selfridges, none of them was a patch on Packards. There was something about being part of the place, an excitement, a glamour. She might only be a junior shopgirl, but she was able to handle the beautiful goods, see the wonderful displays, serve Society ladies and gentlemen whose names appeared in the papers. She couldn't bear to lose all that.

All too soon she found herself on the fifth floor. Here the luxury of the shopfloor gave way to plain cream walls and brown linoleum. Ruby knocked on the door marked Staffing and went into the outer office. Four typists glanced up from their machines just long enough to run an eye over her and register that she was a shopgirl and therefore inferior to them. Two young clerks gave her a more appreciative look but did not dare take it further, and the boy doing the filing just gaped. Ruby rolled a contemptuous lip and addressed herself to the middle-aged man behind the largest desk.

'Miss Goss. I been sent for.'

He finished what he was writing before looking up at her over the tops of his steel-rimmed spectacles.

'Goss? Yes.' He frowned at the clock on the wall. 'You were indeed sent for. Ten minutes ago.'

'I was serving an important customer,' Ruby told him. That was a rock solid reason. She knew it and he knew it. Customers always came first.

The man's mouth tightened.

'Miss Withers wishes to see you.'

Ruby's heart gave a great bound of relief. Miss Withers. She was Welfare and Accommodation. It was going to be all right. She flashed a smile at Steel Rims, bounced across the room to the door that he indicated, knocked, and entered.

Miss Withers' office was small to start with and further cramped by a huge filing cabinet and a row of wooden chairs. On one of these chairs sat a freckle-faced girl with an anxious expression and a wooden box. Ruby immediately summed her up as a new bod and introduced herself to Miss Withers, a severe woman of indeterminate age dressed all in black.

'Oh yes, Miss Goss. I believe your mother takes in lodgers?'

Miss Withers was not one to beat about the bush.

'Yes, Miss Withers.'

'And does she have a room free at the moment?'

Better and better. Ruby's mum had been saying only yesterday how they needed to get that back bedroom filled.

'Yes, she does, Miss Withers.'

'Good – well, your house does appear to be on our approved list, though we have not used your mother's services before. We generally like to give our landladies a week's notice of a new tenant, but this young woman,' – she frowned in the seated girl's direction – 'having refused a place on our list, now informs me that she needs somewhere as from tonight in order to start work tomorrow. Do you think that your mother would be able to take her in?'

Ruby knew exactly what her mother's reaction would be – delight. She would fuss around shooing cats off chairs and moving coats and flapping sheets. And as for supper, that was no problem, she would just peel a few more potatoes and spread the meat around a bit. There was always room for one more in their house.

'We-ell,' she said, 'it's a bit short notice, isn't it?'

She watched for a flicker of reaction on Miss Withers' face. Disappointment was too much to hope for. All she got was a slight tightening of the already thin lips, but that was enough.

'But as it's for Packards, I'm sure she'll make an exception.'

The lips relaxed into something near to a smile.

'Thank you, Miss Goss. Perhaps you would be so good as to convey Packards' thanks to your mother. And of course Miss Hollis will be duly grateful.'

Ruby glanced round at Freckle Face, who nodded earnestly. She began to feel quite sorry for the poor girl, stuck here waiting for old Withers to find her a place to lay her head. She must have had quite a strip torn off her when she arrived. Ruby gave her a surreptitious wink, and saw her eyes widen in surprise.

'That is settled then. You will come back here and collect Miss Hollis when you leave this evening, and escort her to your home. Thank you, Miss Goss.'

Ruby found herself dismissed. She would have liked

37

to have talked to the new girl, but knew better than to try in front of Miss Withers. So she just smiled at her, and was rewarded with a grateful grin. Walking back to Stationery, she found that what had been a boring day had now become much more interesting.

When she came back at the end of the day to pick up the new lodger, she found her in the waiting room of Staffing, where job applicants were put before interviews.

'You been here all afternoon?' she asked.

'Oh no. I been having a lovely time. They sent me off to walk round the store and get to know where everything is. Isn't Packards wonderful?' the new girl enthused. Then she blushed and looked down. 'Of course, you're used to it, I suppose.'

'Yes, well, I been here three years,' Ruby said.

'Three years! You must know everything about it.'

Ruby gave a dismissive shrug.

'Quite a lot, yes.'

'You must tell me – if you will, that is. I don't know anything, really. This is the very first time I've been here.'

Ruby stared at her.

'You mean – you didn't come for an interview?'

'No. Sir – Sir Thomas took me on.'

'You knew Sir Thomas? Sir Thomas Packard?'

'Well, not exactly. But he came into the shop where I worked at Tatwell, where I live, and – and I asked him if there were any vacancies at Packards, and he said he'd see, and then I got this letter to say I had a job here.'

'Blimey!' Despite herself, Ruby was impressed. 'You're not as green as you're cabbage-looking, are you? Asked Sir Thomas for a job! Well – if you don't ask, you don't get, do you? Good for you. I think we might get on, you and me. I'm Ruby Goss, just in case you didn't know.'

She held her hand out. The new girl shook it.

'Pleased to meet you, Miss Goss. I'm May Hollis.'

'Never mind the Miss Goss business. Call me Ruby.'

For the first time, May relaxed a little. She gave a relieved smile.

'Oh thank you – Ruby. I do hope your mother's not going to be put out.'

Ruby waved a hand.

'Oh no, not her. That was just an act what I put on for old Withers. No, my mum'll be happy as Larry to see you. Come on, let's get you home.'

Between them, they lugged May's box down to the fourth floor, but once there, Ruby looked round for suitable help. Her eye lighted on one of the young men from Carpets.

'Now you look like someone who's got nice strong muscles. How about being a real gent and helping us poor girls with this box?'

And of course he fell for it at once and carried it all the way to the bus stop for them.

'Is he a friend of yours?' May asked, when Ruby dismissed him.

'What – him? No! And don't let him take no liberties with you, neither, if you see him again,' Ruby advised. 'That's what men are for, to do things for us girls.'

She basked in May's look of slightly shocked admiration.

'You've never been to London before, then?' she asked.

'No.'

'Your first time away from home?'

'Yes.'

Better and better. Ruby patted her shoulder.

'Don't you worry, I'll show you the ropes.'

May gave her a grateful smile.

'Thank you.'

On the journey out to Holloway, Ruby found out all about May's family, her home life and what it was like in the village. Pretty boring, by all accounts. And as for all this chapel business, it sounded deadly.

'So you wanted to get away to London, did you?'

'Yes.'

'But your parents wanted you to stay at home?'

'Yes. They only let me go because Sir Thomas offered me the job. And then only if I stayed with chapel people. I don't know what they're going to say when I tell them what's happened. Your – your family's not Chapel, I suppose?'

Ruby laughed out loud. Her family only saw the inside of a church for weddings and funerals.

'Can't say as we are, no.'

'Oh dear.'

May chewed her lip.

'Don't you worry yourself, you don't have to tell your folks that, do you?' Ruby said.

May was shocked.

'I can't tell them you are when you aren't.'

'Well . . .' Ruby cast about for a way out. 'There's a chapel at the corner of the street next to ours. You can go there of a Sunday. That'd be all right, wouldn't it?'

'I suppose so,' May said. She didn't sound convinced.

'Blimey, girl, they should be glad we've taken you in. After the way your precious Chapel lot left you in the lurch, you could of been on the streets by now.'

May looked chastened.

'Oh I know, and I'm very grateful. Please don't think I'm not. It's just that my parents are very strict about these things.'

'But they're not here now, are they?' Ruby pointed out.

'No, they're not,' May had to agree.

'So that's all right.'

When they got off the bus in Holloway, Ruby looked about for possible help with the box. All she could spot was a neighbour, a gangly youth who worked as a clerk in the City and who had been hanging round her for a while without plucking up the courage to ask her out. She had no intention of agreeing even if he did, but he was handy so she pressed him into service.

'Oh Mr Firth, just the man we need. Here's us two girls with this box to carry and we just can't take it an inch further. I'm sure it wouldn't feel like more than a feather to a strong man like you . . .?'

Flushing and stuttering with pleasure at being asked to do such a service, the boy picked up the box and staggered off with it balanced precariously on his shoulder. Ruby made a derisive face at his back and grinned at May.

'Come on. It's not far now.'

They walked down a street of square-bayed houses with small front gardens and tiled paths running up to front doors with stained-glass windows, then turned into another with rather smaller houses with flimsier bays and tiny front gardens, where children were playing at skipping and football in the road. Ruby let the unfortunate Mr Firth carry the box right up to the front door of number eighty-one and sent him off before he could do anything as stupid as hope to see her again. Then she fished out her latchkey and opened the door. A smell of cabbage and stew wafted out.

'Hello, Mum! Come and see what I've brought home!' she called.

An older version of Ruby came out of the door at the end of the long narrow hall, greying black hair escaping from a loose bun on top of her head, cheeks flushed even redder than normal from cooking. When she spotted May, her face broke into a wide smile. She hurried

41

forward, wiping her hands on her apron.

'Well, and who have we got here?'

Ruby introduced May and explained the situation.

'I'm very sorry if this puts you out, Mrs Goss,' May said.

'Puts me out? Not a bit of it. Very pleased to have you here, lovey. Georgie! George! Where is the lad? My son-in-law,' she explained to May. 'Lazy great good-for-nothing. Shouldn't never have let our Iris marry him, but there you are, she said she was in love with him, and what can you do? It seemed like a good match at the time. Now he's not even around when there's something useful to be done.'

She called again, and this time a large young man in his shirtsleeves emerged from one of the bedrooms and came shambling downstairs.

'What's the matter, Ma?'

He looked May up and down. Ruby was incensed.

'That's right, get an eyeful. This is George Spratt, my sister's husband, May. And this is our new lodger, George, Miss May Hollis.'

The young man had the grace to look uncomfortable, and when Mrs Goss asked him to take the box upstairs, did so without another word.

'Come on, dear,' she said to May. 'I'll show you your room. Good thing I put some clean sheets on the bed the other day. Only needs a hot water bottle or two in there to air them out a bit.'

Ruby winked at May. Good old Mum.

'There, what did I tell you?' she said.

Ruby followed May into the small spare bedroom at the side of the house, helped her unpack and then brought her up some water to wash. At supper Ruby introduced May to her older sister Iris, her younger sister Meggie and her father. May seemed rather over-whelmed with them all. Ruby wondered if she found it a bit noisy.

'But I expect it's just as bad at your house at meal-times, isn't it? You got more brothers and sisters than this.'

'Yes, but we're not allowed to speak at table,' May said.

Ruby stared.

'Blimey! Rules you with a rod of iron, your dad, does he?'

'Sort of.'

Mr Goss guffawed.

'Per'aps I ought to do that, eh, girls?'

His wife laughed almost as loud.

'I'd like to see you try!'

Mr Goss banged on the table with his spoon.

'Silence! No more talking at this table.'

Iris saluted and said, 'Yes sir – I don't think!'

Meggie shrieked 'Talk, talk, talk!' at the top of her voice.

Mrs Goss said, 'Oh, Frank, you are a card,' and went off into peals of laughter.

Ruby noticed that May was sitting silently pushing the food around her plate.

'Don't mind us, it's just a bit of fun,' she said.

'Yes, don't mind us, we like to have a laugh,' Mrs Goss took her up. 'What's life without a bit of a laugh, eh? Supper all right, is it? I hope you like stew?'

'Yes, it's very nice,' May said politely.

This was a lie, Ruby knew. Her mum was not the world's best cook. The meat was hard and the gravy was thin.

'That's good, 'cause stew's all you're likely to get round here,' Mr Goss said.

'The cheek of it! We have as good a roast as anyone of a Sunday!' his wife retorted.

May ate up every scrap on her plate, even the watery

cabbage, then ploughed her way through a heavy bread pudding. By the end of it, she was looking very white behind her freckles.

'You tired, ducky? Been a long day for you, I expect. First day away from home, is it?' Mrs Goss asked.

May nodded.

'Yes.'

'Well, don't feel you got to stay down with us. You go straight off to bed if you want. Ruby'll look after you, won't you, Ruby?'

Ruby dutifully showed her out to the lavatory beside the scullery, then refilled one of the hot water bottles for her and left her to get changed. Once she heard the bedsprings creak, she went in and crept under the other end of the green eiderdown.

'You all right, then?'

'Yes.'

May looked even younger and more of a country girl with her hair in plaits for the night.

'Think you're going to like it here?'

'Oh yes, your family are very – er – friendly.'

'Bit different from back home, is it?'

'Yes, a bit.'

Ruby hugged her knees. She liked a cosy chat before bed.

'And have you left a young man behind you?'

'Well . . .' May blushed. She blushed at almost anything, Ruby found.

'Come on, tell us. I'll tell you about mine, then,' she said, by way of encouragement.

May hesitated.

'Well, I was walking out with Jim Dudwell, the blacksmith's apprentice. My dad liked him, and so did my mum, but – well . . .'

'He was a bit dull?' Ruby guessed. He had to be, if chapel-going parents approved of him.

44

'Yes,' May admitted. 'I know I shouldn't think like that. I mean, he's very steady, and he never misses a day's work, and he leads the Young Men's Bible Circle, but–'

'Makes ditchwater sound quite interesting,' Ruby commented.

May giggled.

'Yes,' her voice was breathless with suppressed daring, 'yes, that's just it. He's got no – no go in him. He didn't see why I wanted to come to London.'

'And why did you want to come to London?' Ruby asked.

'To see a bit of life. I didn't want to be born and get married and have children and die in the village, like everyone else.'

Ruby smiled. This was going to be good.

'You've come to the right place, then. I'll make sure you see a bit of life,' she promised.

5

Mr Arnold Meredith, senior partner of Meredith, Drew and Oldcastle, solicitors, had wisely decided that the reading of Sir Thomas Packard's will should take place at his offices. Knowing both the family and the contents of the will, he felt that neutral territory was needed for the event.

'Anyone who is of the opinion that being a solicitor is a somewhat limited and boring profession should attend one of our will readings,' he remarked to his junior. 'I sometimes find them a deal more entertaining than an evening at the theatre.'

His office was duly made ready for the occasion, with seats placed in a semicircle and teacups, sherry glasses and plates of biscuits set out on a side table.

'One would think that we were hosting an At Home,' the junior remarked.

Mr Meredith regarded him over the tops of his spectacles.

'The Packards are one of our best clients, and I would like them to continue to bring their business to us. Therefore we must do all that we can to please them. I do not want to suffer the fate traditionally meted out to the bearers of bad news.'

The junior's eyes brightened.

'Are there some fireworks in the will, then, sir? Is Mr Edward Packard not going to inherit the bulk of the estate?'

But Mr Meredith was not going to give anything away.

'Wait and see,' he counselled.

He looked longingly at the sherry decanter, but restrained himself, sending his secretary to make him a cup of Earl Grey instead. He did not want to face the Packard family en masse with alcohol on his breath.

The widow and her daughter and son-in-law were the first to arrive. He brought Lady Packard a glass of sherry with his own hands, noticing how hers had a distinct shake. She had aged much more than her late husband. Sir Thomas had kept his health and his faculties right up to the last, when he had been carried away by heart failure. Mr Meredith prayed that he would be taken like that, when his time came. In the meantime, he wondered if Lady Packard had any inkling of the shock that awaited her. Probably, since she had always struck him as being a suspicious-natured woman. He hoped she was going to have the strength to withstand it. He made sure that the sherry was a generous one.

He had never had a lot of time for Sir Thomas's only daughter Winifred, and still less for her husband Bertie. Two of life's takers, always wanting more than they were given. Bertie was disgruntled to find that neither whisky nor brandy and soda were available, while Winifred complained about the seating arrangements. Mr Meredith was not inclined to dance to either of them. They were not important players in today's drama. He slid away from them the moment the next arrivals appeared.

'Mr and Mrs Rutherford! How do you do? You are looking very well, Mrs Rutherford.'

Amelie Rutherford had always struck him as being by far the best of the bunch, the only one who resembled her grandfather in any way. Not that he approved of her having such an important role in the running of the store. Women should know their place, in his opinion, and restrict themselves to what they were best at, namely being wives and mothers. But then Mr Meredith prided himself in being a little old-fashioned in that respect. Although no one could accuse Amelie Rutherford of neglecting her duties in that department. It was all too embarrassingly obvious that she was soon going to be a mother yet again. His eyes slid away from her burgeoning figure to her husband. Fine upstanding chap, splendid sportsman and now, it was rumoured, about to enter politics. Exactly the solid and honourable type one would wish for in parliament. Everything an Englishman should be.

Out of the corner of his eye, Mr Meredith saw the next person arrive. Aha, the bastard son. He left his junior to see to him. It had often fallen to him to advise gentlemen as to the best way to proceed in these circumstances. He only wished that Sir Thomas Packard had listened to him. But then Sir Thomas had gone against his express advice on many an occasion and usually, it had to be admitted, turned out to have the better judgement in the end. In fact there were times when Mr Meredith suspected that Sir Thomas only sought his counsel in order to find out what not to do.

Edward Amberley Packard and his sour-faced wife arrived exactly when Mr Meredith expected them – just two minutes before the meeting was due to begin. Edward was not one to waste his time waiting around, especially if it meant having to speak to members of his own family. Mr Meredith hurried over to greet them, beckoning the junior to come and act as waiter.

'I trust you are going to be able to conduct this occasion in a suitable manner, Mr Meredith,' Edward said.

'I shall endeavour to do so, Mr Amberley Packard, to the very best of my ability,' Mr Meredith assured him. Then he felt compelled to add, 'But of course you realise that the contents of the will are entirely your late lamented father's business. I merely framed his wishes in the required legal form.'

'Quite. In other words you disclaim all responsibility. Just what I would expect from you, Meredith.'

Which was just the sort of remark Mr Meredith expected from him. Once more he wondered if he was going to be able to retain the Packard account.

Sylvia Amberley Packard ignored her husband. Instead she addressed herself to Mr Meredith.

'I understood that this reading was solely for members of the family?'

Mr Meredith felt the first prickles of real discomfort.

'Yes, Mrs Amberley Packard.'

'Then why is That Person present?'

They all three knew exactly who she meant. Mr Meredith applied his most unctuous tones.

'By special request of the late Sir Thomas, Mrs Amberley Packard.'

It was, he hoped, an unanswerable reason. He glanced at the clock on the wall. Eleven precisely.

'Is it necessary to wait for Mr Peregrin Amberley, do you think?' he asked Edward.

'Certainly not. If he can't be bothered to be on time, then he can take the consequences,' Edward replied.

Mr Meredith could not decide whether he disliked Edward or his wife the most. He retreated behind his desk, glad to have four feet by six of solid mahogany between him and the Packards. He adjusted his spectacles, shuffled the papers, cleared his throat. The Packards stopped chatting amongst themselves. Eight pairs of eyes focused on him, each one expecting him to

49

tell them something to their advantage. It was unnerving, even for a man as experienced as Mr Meredith. He launched into his preamble, and had just got into his stride when the door opened and Mr and Mrs Perry Amberley Packard came in, she with a face like thunder, he with an ingratiating grin. Mr Meredith quite liked Perry. He was harmless, if nothing else. His wife was a regular harpy.

Before Mr Meredith could draw breath to greet them, Edward took charge, assuming the role of Head of the Family.

'What time do you call this, Perry? Sit down, do. Not all of us have all day to waste.'

Perry did as he was bid. His wife Gwendoline saw fit to take on Edward.

'We were unavoidably delayed,' she informed him. 'I do hope we have not missed anything important?'

'You've not missed hearing how much you've been left, if that's what is bothering you,' Edward informed her.

Gwendoline stuck her nose in the air and sat down, not deigning to reply.

From her seat, Amelie saw Sylvia's thin lips tighten, as if she wanted to say that that was an uncalled-for remark, but forebore to do so in front of the rest of the family. For the umpteenth time, Amelie wondered whether she most disliked or felt sorry for her two sisters-in-law. Once upon a time, she had had a great deal of sympathy for Sylvia. True, she had gone into the marriage with her eyes open, trading her breeding for his money, but she did not deserve to find so soon after the wedding that he had been keeping a mistress, and what was more, that he had driven the poor young woman to suicide. But as time went on, Amelie had lost patience with her. She seemed to enjoy being a martyr.

Gwendoline was quite different. She was out to turn

50

Perry into the sort of husband she had always hoped for, and she was not going to let his natural indolence stop her. Amelie had not even tried to suggest that she had taken on an impossible task. Gwendoline would certainly not thank her for her advice, so she left her to make her own mistakes, which included trying to attack Edward head on. That was a dangerous and pointless way to tackle him, but after three years of being part of the Packards, Gwendoline still did not seem to realise that she might be going about things the wrong way.

Amelie's attention returned to the solicitor. He had finished his little homily about what a fine man her grandfather had been, what a loss his death was and how the best interests of both the family and the store had always been close to his heart, never more so than when he was drawing up his will. He paused, readjusted his spectacles, then addressed himself to the documents in front of him.

'This is the last will and testament of Thomas Arthur Packard, Knight, of Tatwell Court, Hertfordshire, and Hill Street, Mayfair, London . . .'

All around her, Amelie could feel the sharpening of interest. Like hounds following a scent, every one of the Packards had all their senses trained on the words that droned from the solicitor's lips.

'. . . personal fortune, I bequeath ten thousand pounds each to my daughter Winifred and my grand-children Edward, Amelie and Peregrin.'

Ten thousand pounds. Just about what she expected from Grandfather. It was not the money that Amelie was concerned about, useful though it was. What she wanted to know was how the shares in the store were to be distributed. She cast a surreptitious glance along the row of seats. Edward was looking impassive. Like her, he wanted to know about the store. Sylvia was as icy as ever, but then she was expecting to get Tatwell and the

51

town house. Gwendoline and her mother both looked as if they had sucked lemons. Ten thousand was not nearly enough for them.

'. . . to each of my great-grandchildren the sum of five thousand pounds to be kept in trust until they marry. Any future great-grandchildren are to be endowed in the same way and to the same amount from a fund to be set up for this express purpose. Any money left in this fund after all children are deemed to have been born shall be divided equally between those living.'

'Quite right too,' Hugo muttered under his breath. He would take that, Amelie guessed, as a sign of approval from Thomas for fathering a succession of perfect male children.

She stroked the bulge, which kicked in reply, as if celebrating its good fortune. This time Sylvia did look put out. No doubt she had hoped that the same amount would be given to each branch of the great-grandchildren, thus making her only daughter richer than Amelie's brood. Gwendoline, who had not so far produced any offspring, showed a glimmer of satisfaction that her future children would be provided for.

'The sum of twenty-five thousand pounds shall be put into a fund to endow the Packard Trust, a charity to educate the deserving children of Packards staff.'

Along the row, there was a definite snort of disapproval from Edward. Amelie smiled to herself. Edward regarded charity as encouraging the needy to do nothing to help themselves. He did however allow himself to be associated with certain fashionable charitable societies when it was to his advantage to be seen doing so. No doubt he would soon find a way to make the Packard Trust serve his own ends.

'To Mrs Dora Eden, mother of my son and my devoted companion of over twenty-five years I give the freehold of the house in which she is currently residing, together with an annuity of five hundred pounds per annum.'

There was an audible intake of breath. Some heads stayed resolutely still, others swivelled from Lady Packard at one end of the row to Alexander Eden at the other, to see how they were reacting. Sir Thomas's widow's hands were clasped tightly in her lap, but nothing could stop the tremor of her head. She was staring straight at the solicitor, as if willing him to say that it was all a mistake, that she had not been humiliated in front of her family. Her daughter moved to pat her arm in support, but Lady Packard gave an impatient jerk, rejecting her sympathy. Alexander Eden was also avoiding all their eyes. He was looking at a point somewhere above the solicitor's head, a flush across his cheeks betraying his moment of triumph.

For it was a triumph, Amelie realised. He had been acknowledged before all of them. So did this mean there was something else to come, something for him as well as for his mother? She stroked the bulge again. She would quite like to see Edward's place challenged, but she was not going to stand for her children being disadvantaged in any way by this usurper.

There followed a list of small bequests to long-serving staff at the store and the Tatwell estate. Amelie's attention wandered a little. What, she wanted to know, was to become of the store? How were the shares to be allocated?

The very same question was dominating Edward's mind. The allocation of the money was of secondary importance. He had to be sure that the reins of power at the store were going to pass into his hands. They ought to, by all rights. He was the one who knew how to run the place, and he was the natural successor to his grandfather. But he could not trust the old man. He had pulled some unpleasant tricks in the past. Unfair tricks, in the light of what had just been revealed. To think that the old boy had criticised his behaviour, when all the time he had been running a second household and supporting a bastard. Bloody old hypocrite. He always had suspected something of the sort. But the old man was gone now, and if that pup thought he was going to get his foot in the door, he was gravely mistaken.

'The remainder of my personal fortune, my house and estates at Tatwell and my house at Hill Street, Mayfair, are to remain the property of my beloved wife Margaret for as long as she shall survive me. Thereafter, they shall pass to my grandson Edward.'

Edward stiffened, and beside him, he heard Sylvia draw a breath in through her teeth, which was always a bad sign. Now there was going to be trouble. He knew that Sylvia had been counting on getting Tatwell and moving his grandmother out to the dower house. Come to that, *he* had been counting on getting Tatwell and moving Sylvia out there from under his feet, leaving him a free agent in town. The old man probably knew that and did it deliberately, the vindictive old sod. He never had liked him. Always preferred Amelie. Just because she made up to him with her little-girl ways. But it wouldn't be forever. The old girl couldn't have many more years left in her. And in the meantime, what was to happen to the store?

'The administration of Packards Department Store, Oxford Street, London, shall be as follows:

'Family members with seats on the board, namely my grandson Edward and my granddaughter Amelie, shall retain their present positions. The board as it currently stands shall elect a new chairman, who need not be from amongst their number.

'My shares in the company shall be distributed to make up the following percentages: twenty-five percent each to my grandson Edward and my granddaughter

Amelie–'

The old weasel! Not getting the chairmanship was bad enough, but to share equal status with Amelie was unbearable. Edward could feel the pressure of anger building up, throbbing through his veins like an over-heating engine. He had to hold on to it. He could not let them see how it was affecting him.

'–fifteen percent each to my wife Margaret, my daughter Winifred and my grandson Peregrin–'

Ninety-five. Ninety-five! So who was getting the last five? Not . . .? Surely not?

'–and five percent to my son Alexander.'

'What?'

Edward's exclamation was lost in a chorus of gasps and disclaimers. He glared across at his rival. Alexander was trying to remain impassive, but there was no hiding the glitter in his eyes, the smile that fought to spread across his face. Edward's hands clenched involuntarily. He wanted desperately to smash the whippersnapper's nose all over his face. He wanted it so much that it hurt. Then he realised that the solicitor had not finished. There was more to come.

'It was a condition of the bequest of the shares to all concerned that my son Alexander shall be taken on to the staff of Packards Department Store and thoroughly trained in all aspects of management. On his thirtieth birthday, or before that time if the board deem it necessary or advantageous, he shall be appointed to a seat on the board in whatever capacity the board decides most suitable to his talents, with a salary commensurate with that of other board members.'

'Yes!'

There was a smack as Alexander's right fist hit his left palm. Now there was no containing his grin of delight.

Edward's normally tight control snapped. He jumped up.

'That is ridiculous. My grandfather cannot have been in his right mind when he dictated that.'

His words broke through the dam of British reserve that had been stopping the Packard clan from showing its emotions. A torrent of resentment was released.

'–intolerable that I should be passed over where Tatwell is concerned. I am his daughter, his only issue. His only legal issue–'

'–not fair that Perry should only get fifteen percent when Edward and Amelie get twenty-five–'

'–to think that That Woman should be mentioned before me, and in such terms–'

'–how Grandfather thinks I'm going to live on that. I do have a certain position to keep up–'

'–to prove the unfortunate results of uncontrolled breeding–'

'–must have lost his marbles. We could contest it–'

'Ladies! Gentlemen! Please . . .' Mr Meredith raised both hands, palms outwards, and made calming gestures. 'Let us preserve a little decorum, please.'

It took several minutes for his words to cut through the uproar, and several more for the incensed beneficiaries of Sir Thomas Packard's will to subside, muttering, into their seats.

'Thank you. Now . . .' The solicitor clasped his hands in front of him and regarded them all in turn with the air of a patient but firm schoolmaster. 'Let us look at this calmly and rationally. I can understand that some of you might feel some sense of grievance, but I have to tell you that this will is a watertight legal document. Sir Thomas took the precaution of seeing a very eminent physician the day before it was drawn up, and had him testify that he was indeed of totally sound mind. I would advise that you all go back to your homes and reflect calmly on what has passed. I think that in the cool light of day, you will find that a most generous settlement has been made to everyone concerned. If any of you wish to consult with me on any matter arising, then of course I shall be only too happy to do so.'

Edward took several long breaths through his nose. The pounding of blood through his brain subsided. Of course the old vulture would be happy to be consulted. A contested will would set him up for a comfortable retirement. No, there were more ways than one to make sure he got what he wanted. Sylvia was no more than an irritant. No doubt she would be worse now that she knew she had to wait that much longer before she got her hands on Tatwell, but he had coped with her coldness and prudishness these last five years, so a few more weren't going to make that much difference. Amelie was rather more of a problem. He had made the mistake of underestimating her in the past, and he had to admit that she had turned out to be a formidable opponent, but with Rutherford obligingly keeping her breeding, she was effectively neutralised at regular intervals. The unknown factor was The Bastard. He looked along the row to where his half-uncle was sitting with a glow of satisfaction radiating from him. Let him bask in it now. It wouldn't last for long.

6

At last.

Alexander walked through the tall revolving doors and into the red marble vestibule. He looked up, slowly, taking in the sweeping curve of the red marble staircase, the glimpses of floor after floor of departments, on up to the great dome letting in shafts of winter sunlight. Packards, the most prestigious store in London, and therefore in the entire British Empire. He had come to claim his birthright.

Of course, there was nobody here to greet him. That was only to be expected. He had been informed of his new position, not by a meeting with or even a letter from Edward or Amelie, but by a curt note from the Assistant Staffing Manager, setting out the terms and conditions of employment at Packards and telling him to be at the Stationery Department at half past eight today. Nobody in the family, it seemed, was going to acknowledge his presence. But that was unimportant. What mattered was that he was here, taking the first step on the ladder that was to take him to a seat on the board. He squared his shoulders and walked in.

All through the store, shopmen and girls were getting ready for the day ahead. Dust covers were being taken off, counters polished, new stock taken out of huge wheeled baskets and put on show. Stationery was on the ground floor, along with other departments selling small, frequently needed goods, such as ties, gloves and umbrellas, hosiery, haberdashery, and of course the famous Food Halls. He took a short diversion through these now, marvelling at the glowing piles of fruit, the glittering array of fish, the amazing selection of cheeses, all in the process of being laid out on the marble counters in artistic displays by white-coated young men.

Indeed, the displays were tempting in every department, however prosaic the goods concerned. This was Amelie's doing. Gone were the days when everything was hidden away inside drawers and the shop windows were crowded with every single item on sale in the store. Since Gordon Selfridge shook the London retailing world to its foundations by bringing Chicago methods to Oxford Street, Packards had undergone a transformation. Under Amelie's leadership, Packards now rivalled or even surpassed Selfridges in the splendour and inventiveness of its displays. In the past, each buyer had been responsible for his department's window and the arrangement of its goods. Now, theatrical designers took charge of the windows, while a team of young people recruited from Art Schools planned the overall theme of the store and descended upon each department in turn to show what they had to sell to best advantage. Just now, the Autumn's Bounty displays were still in place, but Alec knew that the Christmas ones must be almost ready to go up.

Alec could find his way round the store almost as well as those who had worked there for five years. He had spent many a spare hour walking through the departments consumed with anger at the thought of his near but so distant relatives having all this while he was kept from it. Now, cutting through Gentlemen's

Accoutrements to get to Stationery, he had a sense, not quite of belonging – it was too early for that – but of it all being within his reach. He arrived at Stationery at half past eight precisely.

'Mr Eden?'

A man about ten years his senior came forward, his hand held out in greeting.

'Victor Lambert. I'm the buyer for Stationery.'

Alec shook the proffered hand and introduced himself, glad of the welcome but wondering just how much the buyer knew of the situation, and where his loyalties might lie. For now, he had to assume that everyone was going to side with the current power, and that meant with Edward.

'I've been asked to introduce you to the day-to-day running of the store, so I think the best course to pursue will be for you to spend the first fortnight in just one of our subsections learning the basic principles of how to deal with customers, wrap goods, send off orders and all the rest,' Mr Lambert proposed.

Disappointment dragged at Alec. He knew in his head that one had to start from the bottom, but in his heart, he wanted to go straight into managing the department.

'I see,' he said.

Mr Lambert was watching him closely. He had steel grey eyes that gave the uncomfortable impression of missing nothing.

'It is much easier to lead people when you know from personal experience what their jobs entail, and what is more, they know that you know. That way, you gain their respect.'

This was true, Alec had to concede. He had seen that for himself at the bank.

'Yes, I do realise that,' he said. 'And I do want to learn everything about the store.'

Mr Lambert's expression relaxed a little.

'Good. So what I propose is this: once you have been given your grounding, so to speak, I'll move you round the department so that you can form an idea of the range of goods we sell here. Then when you're familiar with what we have and what we need, I'll introduce you to some of the sales representatives when they call and take you out to see our suppliers, so that you can learn something of the buying process.'

That sounded a good deal more like what he had been hoping for.

'Thank you. I should like that very much indeed.'

Mr Lambert smiled.

'I think you will find that Stationery is a good place to start. We may not sell the large prestige goods, but we have one of the highest turnovers in the store and I believe that we are responsible for bringing in many customers who subsequently go on to make further purchases in other departments.'

'I see. You mean that people come in here to buy, say, a fountain pen and then recollect that they need a tie or a – a portmanteau.'

'Exactly. That is the reason why we have so many services and free facilities in the store. They bring people in, and once here, they are tempted to buy.'

'Of course, yes. So they are,' Alec said.

It all made sense, what Mr Lambert was saying. He had done the very same thing himself, many a time, without realising that he was being deliberately led on to part with his money. He realised that the buyer's eyes were now glinting with enthusiasm, and got the distinct feeling he had been fortunate in his first foothold in Packards. Here was someone who found retailing fascinating, and who was willing to share his knowledge.

'I hope you find me an apt pupil,' he said.

'So do I,' Mr Lambert told him. 'Now, if you will

come this way, I'll show you our Writing Papers section.'

Alec followed him across the department to where a tall dark-haired shopgirl in the regulation black skirt and white blouse was polishing the counter.

'Miss Goss.'

The girl looked up, and Alec was confronted with the most luscious pair of lips he had ever seen. He gazed at them, entranced, while the girl's eyes went rapidly from Mr Lambert to himself and back again in a swift assessing glance.

'Yes, Mr Lambert?'

She had the standard shopgirl's mock genteel accent. Alec suspected that a far more earthy and lively London one lay just underneath.

'This is Mr Eden. He has just joined Packards and has no previous experience in retailing, so I would like you to show him how we go about things.'

Alec was torn between annoyance at being handed over to what was obviously a junior and a girl to boot when he had expected the buyer himself to show him the ropes, and delight at the prospect of being in the company of the owner of that mouth for the next two weeks.

The lips curved in a bright smile.

'Certainly, Mr Lambert. Happy to oblige, I'm sure.'

'You'd better start with writing receipts and working the pneumatic tube system. Then show him where everything is.'

'Yes, Mr Lambert.'

The buyer turned to Alec.

'Once there are customers in the department, observe how Miss Goss deals with them. It is essential that our customers always go away feeling satisfied, even if they don't actually make a purchase. They must receive polite and prompt service from persons who know everything there is to know about the goods they are selling. That is every bit as important as having the right range of goods to show them.'

'I understand,' Alec said, realising that he had always known this without actually putting it into words. It was brought home to him that though he had spent many fruitless hours envying the Packards their inheritance, he had never given any thought at all to the actual process of running it. But now there was every opportunity to make up for lost time, and he intended to make very good use of it.

'Good, then I'll leave you in Miss Goss's capable hands,' Mr Lambert said.

Alec turned to the Lips.

'How do you do? I hope we are going to be friends, if we are going to be working together for the next two weeks.'

Miss Goss gave him a speculative look with her dark eyes.

'So do I, Mr Eden. Charmed, I'm sure. Your first time behind the counter, is it?'

Just in time, he stopped himself from saying something about being a virgin. He really must not start flirting with the girl, however tempting it was.

'That's right, but I think you'll find I'm quick to pick things up.'

'Where was you before this, then?'

'I was working in a bank.'

'A bank? What, a clerk? You don't sound like a clerk.'

'Oh well, you can't always judge people by how they talk.'

'Mostly you can,' Miss Goss insisted. 'What made you come here, then?'

'I've always wanted to work at Packards,' he said, truthfully. Then, not wanting to answer any more questions, 'Where do you think we ought to start?'

He listened and watched carefully as she initiated him into the skills of a shopman. None of it seemed very

63

complicated. What was incredible was the vast range of papers and envelopes that the department stocked. Miss Goss introduced him briefly to the difference between a wove and a laid paper, a glazed and a mill finish, rough and cut edges, and all the various thicknesses and sizes, as well as the different styles of envelope, until he began to feel bemused.

Opening time was signalled by an electric bell ringing through the store. Miss Goss looked round her immaculate corner of the department.

'I think we're ready all right. Now, we won't have many customers for the first hour or so, so I'll be able to serve them all and you can watch. But if we do get a little rush and you have to serve, just ask me if there's anything you need to know. If there's nobody waiting, then we're supposed to tidy, so you could be seeing where everything is. That's very important, that is. You feel a right idiot if you don't know where something is when a customer asks for it.'

Alec worked his way through the shelves and drawers, trying to memorise the difference between Imperial Sillurian, Bishopsbourne, Royal Saxon and Grenari. By the end of an hour, he was simply more confused. What was more, he had begun to see that there was far more to being a shopman than merely knowing how to write out a receipt and send the customer's money whizzing along the Lanson system to the central counting house. Listening to Miss Goss coping with the customers, he realised that infinite tact and patience were required, as well as an ability to sum up people at a glance. Miss Goss had a little game she played as each one approached, assessing them and guessing what sort of paper they would buy. Three times out of four, she was right.

'How do you do that?' Alec asked, impressed.

'I'm a witch,' Miss Goss said.

By eleven o'clock, the department was busy.

'Do you think you can manage to take the money and wrap the goods, if I do the selling?' Miss Goss asked.

'Of course,' Alec said.

It was not as easy as it appeared. His fingers turned to thumbs when trying to make a neat parcel. Customers tut-tutted with impatience and Miss Goss had to move in several times and take over, finishing the job with a few assured movements.

'You'll get the hang of it,' she told him.

Alec was beginning to doubt it.

At some point when the morning seemed to have gone on forever and his legs were beginning to ache from all the standing, there was a lull long enough for Miss Goss to revert to her questioning.

'It's a funny thing, you remind me of someone, but I can't think who. You sure you've never worked here before?'

'Quite sure.'

'And neither have none of your family?'

This was a tricky one.

'There's a customer coming. Britannia Pure Linen,' he said, pulling a brand name out of the air at random.

'Nah – more of a Bucksburn or a Charta Legalis,' Miss Goss said, unable to resist using her skill.

As usual, she was right.

Dinnertime brought a welcome break. Alec was sent with one of the shopmen, Charlie Dobbs, to the staff canteen on the fifth floor. Here, three thousand solid two-course meals were served daily in three sittings to the sales and office staff. Alec, balancing a tray loaded with shepherd's pie and cabbage and treacle pudding and custard, followed Charlie between the tightly packed rows of tables. It was a steamy, cheerful place, noisy with the clatter of cutlery on crockery and a thousand people catching up with the latest news and gossip.

'The best places are over there, by the barrier,' Charlie explained.

Alec looked where he was indicating. Across the width of the huge room was a wrought-iron divider, and on the other side were seated the female staff. The tables next to the barrier were especially animated. Above the general racket, Alec could hear the gales of laughter coming from them.

'The Powers That Be don't like us chatting to the girls, but we get round it all the same,' Charlie said.

So that was why he was sent to dinner with Charlie and not with Miss Goss. How ridiculous. When he had a say in things, Alec decided, he would see to it that the barrier came down. They sat with a group of Charlie's friends, and once more he had to explain where he had been working and why he was at Packards, and once more he had to resort to half truths. It had been very clearly spelt out to him in his letter from the staffing manager that his relationship to the Packard family was not to be revealed. He managed to steer away from it by mentioning the delectable Miss Goss.

'Oh yes, now there's a cracker,' Charlie agreed.

His pals nodded and made noises of appreciation.

'Not had much luck there have you, Charlie boy?' one of them taunted him.

'Not yet, I haven't. Won't do you much good making up to her, neither, mate. She's got ambitions, has that one. She's looking for something better than one of us,' Charlie told Alec.

'Such as what?' Alec asked.

'Oh, anyone as long as he's rich.'

'I'm going to be rich. I've got a hot tip for tomorrow,' someone said.

Talk turned to racing.

It was right at the end of the meal, when they were all about to get up and hurry back to their counters, that the quietest man in the group suddenly spoke up.

'I know who you remind me of,' he said, pointing at Alec. 'Put you in a set of side whiskers and you'd be the spit of that picture of old Sir Thomas.'

The other all gazed at Alec, mentally comparing him to the picture in the memorial windows. Some shook their heads in disagreement, but others saw the likeness.

'You're right, you know,' one said. 'Sir Thomas to a T.'

'You one of the family then, are you?' someone else asked. 'Here – I know, you're one of the old man's by-blows.'

There was a general guffaw at this.

The pain hit him with splintering force. By-blow. It was a horrible term. And the truth. Alec forced a smile.

'No such luck. If I was family, I wouldn't be behind the counter in Stationery, I'd be up here on the fifth floor with all the management, telling you lot what to do.'

They laughed again. Charlie thumped him on the shoulder.

'That's right, mate. Come on, if we don't get back we'll have old Lambert breathing down our necks.'

Alec was grateful for the trip downstairs. It gave him a couple of minutes to recover.

He needed all his wits about him, for within half an hour of his return to the department, Amelie Rutherford came in. Alec, engaged in wrapping a large purchase, followed her with his eyes. She looked round the department first, seemingly making mental notes of everything that was going on, and as she did so, their eyes met. Alec kept a wooden face, silently challenging her to recognise him. Nothing, not a flicker. Her gaze swept on, and Alec felt himself going hot with irrational anger. He knew really that she was hardly going to come running over loudly claiming him as one of her own, but still she might have done something, given some little sign that she at least knew who he was. Forgetting what he should be doing, he stared after her. Mr Lambert hurried up to speak to her. His manner was not obsequious, but still it was evident just from the way he was standing that he wanted to make a good impression, that he was pleased when Amelie smiled and nodded. They conversed for a few moments, then Amelie went to talk to the people on the pen counter.

'You finished that yet?' a voice hissed in Alec's ear.

He realised that his hands were still, the customer was waiting and Miss Goss wanted the sale concluded. He hastened to finish the task.

And then Amelie was there, in front of Writing Papers.

'Ah, Miss Goss. Congratulations – Mr Lambert tells me that you achieved the best sales in this department last week.'

Despite himself, Alec had to acknowledge that Amelie had just the right manner, pleasant but authoritative.

Miss Goss flushed and simpered.

'Thank you, Mrs Rutherford. I'm very proud, I'm sure.'

'You're certainly the best person to show a new member of staff the ropes.' She looked directly at Alec. 'Mr Eden, is it not? Packards expects very high standards from all its staff, Mr Eden. We only have the best people here, as I am sure you know. Not everybody makes the grade.'

Again that same manner, but now it grated. She was speaking as to a shopman, the very lowliest shopman, just learning the job. Alec looked steadily back at her.

'Indeed I do know, Mrs Rutherford. Getting into Packards was very difficult.'

That hit home. He saw it in her face, the shock at

having his unwanted presence in the family waved in front of her, however well disguised before others. Yet she did not falter.

'Always remember, Mr Eden, that Sir Thomas Packard himself used to say that he would rather a customer went away without buying something than feel they had been forced into purchasing goods they did not want.'

'Naturally, I have the greatest respect for Sir Thomas's opinions,' Alec assured her.

For a moment they battled it out, each silently claiming the closer kinship with Thomas Packard. Whom had he really loved the best, Alec wondered, himself or Amelie?

'I'm very glad to hear it,' she said. 'Sir Thomas's opinions were always worth adhering to.'

'I shall make it my business to adhere to all his wishes,' Alec told her.

To anyone who happened to overhear them, he sounded almost sycophantic. Only between the two of them did the words convey a different meaning.

Amelie stretched her lips into something resembling a smile.

'Splendid. Keep up the good work,' she said, and before he could say any more, changed the subject.

'Has anyone told you about the Packards Volunteer Rifle Company? Quite a number of our young men are members. Perhaps you should consider joining. My husband is looking for more recruits. The drills are held every Monday evening on Clapham Common.'

A wise new employee would agree at once. Alec kept his voice respectful.

'I'll think about it, Mrs Rutherford.'

Amelie chose to take this as assent.

'Good.'

And she went, leaving Alec fuming with resentment,

only very slightly lightened by the knowledge that he had managed to score the odd small point. It was such a ridiculous charade. Why would the family not acknowledge him? They would have to eventually, when he got his seat on the board. Perhaps they were hoping he would give up or get bored or do something so dreadful that they would be justified in getting rid of him. But if that was what they were banking on, then they were due for a disappointment. He was going to be a model employee. They would find nothing they could legitimately sack him for, and he was going to use his time well. As he calmed down, it occurred to him that he might as well join the Rifle Company. Getting to know something about Amelie's husband could be useful, and if nothing else, it might even be fun.

When he got home that evening, his mother wanted to know all about his day. Alec tried to sift through the kaleidoscope of jostling impressions – Miss Goss – Mr Lambert – the myriad types of writing paper – his own ineptitude at tying parcels – being called a by-blow – the brush with Amelie Rutherford. A sense of depression came over him, all the more devastating for being alien to his optimistic nature. For once, he could not dress things up for his mother's benefit. He dropped his head into his hands with a profound sigh.

'Oh, I'm just the dogsbody, the lowest of the low. And you can bet the Packards will make sure that that's where I'll stay.'

The moment the words were out of his mouth, he regretted it. He should keep his doubts to himself, not go upsetting his mother. But to his surprise, she put an arm round his shoulders and spoke bracingly.

'Rubbish! You'll win through, I know it. You're your father's son. It's early days yet, remember.'

'Yes,' Alec agreed.

'And the bottom is the best place to start. That way

you'll know everything about the store, far more than those others. They'll never know how it works from behind the counter; they've only ever been on the management side. Thomas did, you see. He was a shopman. He knew how to find out what the customers wanted. You keep your eyes open and when your time comes, you'll have lots of ideas to put into place.'

Alec looked at her with amazement.

'You're right,' he said.

For the first time since his father died, she smiled.

'I do know something about the store, you know. Your father talked to me about it for over twenty years. Have patience, dear. Your father always knew best.'

Alec could only hope that she was right.

7

Amelie heaved herself out of the cab and lumbered through the revolving doors. She was feeling more and more tired now that the baby was nearly due, but she was determined not to let it stop her. Out of the corner of her eye, she caught a frosty look from a stiff-backed matron of the old school. A lady in her condition should not be out in public. Only the working classes advertised their embarrassing fecundity so openly. Let her stare, Amelie decided. If she went into purdah every time she was pregnant, she would never get out at all.

She was on her way to Household, to check on the arrangements for the Homemakers' Event, one of her pet innovations, but on impulse she stepped through to Stationery just to see how Alec Eden was getting on. There he was, showing a selection of card cabinets to a middle-aged couple. As she watched, he demonstrated the flaps and drawers and pointed out the extent of the contents, subtly emphasising the qualities of the most expensive model. The couple nodded and pulled the drawers in and out and looked at the packs of cards, consulting between themselves and asking a question or two. Alec did not appear to be pushing them, but before very long they had rejected the inferior cabinets in favour of the Imperial. There were smiles all round. Alec had made a good sale and the couple went away happy with their purchase. Amelie was impressed. He had become a good salesman. She had seen his figures and wondered whether he was too pushy, but now having seen him in action she had to admit that he had completely absorbed the Packards method.

She hesitated for a moment, wondering whether to speak to him, but decided against it. Best not to let him know that he was being watched. She took the lift up to the third floor. Was Alec Eden going to pose a real threat? Edward thought not. He thought they would find a way to get rid of him long before he reached thirty and had to be given his place on the board. That was why the whole family had agreed to delay acknowledging his relationship to them for as long as possible. But Amelie was beginning to wonder if that was a mistake. Maybe drawing him in would neutralise him, for Alec was making it very clear that he was going to make sure his father's wishes were carried out. She certainly did not want another young male rival. It was hard enough trying to hold her place against Edward's efforts to be sole dictator.

But when she arrived at Household, all thoughts of Alec Eden went right out of her head. She stood and looked at the department, disbelief boiling rapidly into anger. Then she accosted the buyer.

The man's face said it all. After initial incomprehension, understanding dawned, followed by fear of being caught in a battle between two members of the Packard family. He covered it with professional blandness.

'It is all in place, as you can see, Mrs Rutherford. All exactly as I was asked to arrange it. Display have done an excellent job, don't you think?'

'Of what there is of it, yes,' Amelie had to agree. Display was one of her areas of responsibility after all,

73

and the piles of cushions, the swathes of table linen and the shelves of open cutlery canteens were very attractive. But that was not the point.

'I was under the impression that the whole of the area up to those pillars was going to be given over to the Event,' she said, indicating a space at least twice the size of that occupied by the special displays and demonstrations.

'That was not what I was told, Mrs Rutherford.'

Amelie controlled herself. It was not his fault. He only carried out orders from above.

'I see. Thank you,' she said, and enquired into the success of the Event.

With palpable relief, the buyer was able to assure her that the young couples and brides-to-be and their mothers whom she had been aiming at had been much in evidence at the Event. Almost all of them had made some use of the helpful lists of household necessities that Amelie had had made up and printed especially, and large quantities of goods had been bought. Amelie congratulated him and passed on, still fuming.

The Homemakers' Event had been very much her idea, especially the demonstrations. It had occurred to her that young couples setting up home on a restricted income would be the most likely people to buy gadgets claiming to save time and money. So she had sent Mr Purvis out to buy all the latest devices, and to her delight he had come back with such wonders as the Patent Coal Economiser, and Self-Closing Bread Bin and the Nodust Cleaner. Together with the Display team, she had planned ample space for these to be demonstrated amongst the stands and shelves of more everyday household goods. That space had been cut in half, and she knew just who to blame. She made her way up to the fifth floor.

Edward jumped up as she puffed into his office.

'Amelie. This is an unexpected pleasure. Sit down –

here, this is the most comfortable chair. I'll send for some tea, or would you prefer coffee?'

'Tea, please. Darjeeling,' Amelie said.

He always affected delight at seeing her, especially when he knew she was on the warpath. It irritated her profoundly, but she no longer let him realise this, staying outwardly calm and playing him at his own game. Losing her temper with him only proved that she was in an inferior position from the start.

For a few minutes they exchanged polite enquiries over each other's health and that of their respective spouses.

'Your Homemakers' Event seems to be going very well,' Edward said, smoothly taking the initiative.

Amelie took a sip of tea to steady herself.

'Yes, I'm rather proud of it. As I said when I first suggested it, it goes hand-in-hand with our Spring Brides promotion. Of course, it would have been even more successful if the full space allocated to it had been used.'

Edward looked mildly surprised.

'I don't recall an exact square footage ever being agreed.'

'Really? I do.'

'I think not, Amelie. One's memory can play tricks, you know.' Particularly, his tone suggested, when you are a pregnant woman. 'But I can get a copy of the minutes if you want to look it up.'

He would have looked it up already, of course, or he would not have suggested it.

'I don't think that's necessary. In any case, it's not the precise measurements I am talking about, it's the general agreement. When I discussed the idea with Display, I was working on twice the floorspace that it now takes up.'

'What you mean, in fact, is your agreement with Display, not one made by the Board.'

'The Board agreed that we should have the Event and that I should set it up. The details were my responsibility.'

'The details of what the Event should contain, certainly. And very successful it has been, too. So much so that I am sure you can see that the floorspace was more than adequate.

'More space would have meant more people and therefore more sales.'

'Not necessarily. At no time has it been uncomfortably crowded down there. In fact, had there been more space, it might have looked rather empty at times.'

Amelie could feel the argument slipping away from her. She screamed inside with frustration. Normally, she was more than a match for Edward. Heaven knew, she had had enough practice. They had been battling it out all their lives. But in these last few weeks of her pregnancy, her brain had gone to soup. Sometimes she could not even get from one end of a sentence to another.

'That's not the point,' she said, then stopped. What was the point? Then, mercifully, it came to her. 'My arrangements were countermanded, and nobody even saw fit to tell me, let alone consult with me.'

Edward assumed his sweetly reasonable voice.

'Mel, first your Peter wasn't well, and then you were ill. I didn't think you should be bothered with what was, after all, a minor detail.'

He was right, of course. She had been unwell, and her youngest had been down with a very nasty chest complaint, far too worrying to be left to Nanny to deal with. A very convenient excuse for Edward to go ahead and do just what he liked with her Event.

'One telephone call would have been all that was required, Edward. I was quite capable of understanding you. I think courtesy alone demanded that.'

She heaved herself to her feet, determined to snatch some rags of victory from the contest.

'In future, I would like to be consulted on any changes that are being made to any of my projects, whatever might be going on at home.'

Edward jumped up and went to open the door for her.

'Of course, Mel. As long as it's at all possible.'

He did not mean a word of it. He would do just the same again, and she could do nothing to stop him, because she was not here all the time like he was. Fuming, she tottered along the corridor on swollen ankles. She hated being helpless like this, big and clumsy with a head that didn't work properly. All she could see ahead of her were more pregnancies, each one taking a little more out of her, until she was no longer able to fight Edward. Then he would step in and take over completely.

The impotent fury seethed throughout the day, but there was a light ahead of her. Hugo's cousin Clement and his wife Ida were coming to dinner. In the years since their marriage, Ida had become her closest friend and Clement – well, Clement was probably her best male friend, although obviously she could not tell him how she felt about being pregnant all the time. When the men were talking over their port and cigars, she could confide in Ida. Not that Ida could wave a magic wand over the situation, but merely the prospect of airing it made her feel better.

When Hugo came in, he found her sitting with her feet up, trying to reduce the swelling in her ankles. He was instantly solicitous.

'My dear, are you all right? Shall I call the doctor? You've been doing too much again. You must rest. I'll telephone the Markhams and put them off.'

'You'll do nothing of the sort,' Amelie cried.

Hugo perched beside her on the sofa, and took her hands in his.

'My dear, you must allow me to take care of you. It's

very bad for you to be overtaxing yourself at this time. You must have a quiet evening and an early night.'

Another man trying to tell her that he knew best. Amelie looked him in the eye.

'Darling, Edward has made me so cross that if you cancel this evening's dinner, I might well have a fit of hysterics, and that would not do me any good at all.'

She saw the indecision in his face. She had him where she wanted him. He had no interest at all as to why Edward had made her so angry, but the coming baby must have the very best start in life, even before it was born, and that meant keeping its mother happy. It was one of her most useful weapons. She pushed the point home.

'I can feel it bubbling up. I am furious, Hugo. A quiet evening would drive me completely crazy. It might even bring the baby on before its time.'

That clinched it.

'If you're sure, my dear—'

'Quite sure.'

'Well then, I must say I should be sorry to miss a dinner with the Markhams. I think that of all our acquaintance they are the couple who are the most ideally matched. It's such a pity that I cannot persuade them to increase their family. To have just two children is such a waste. Such talent and physical perfection as they possess should be handed on in abundance. We need the children of their union to stem the tide of mediocrity, let alone the flood of degenerates.'

'Thank you, Hugo, but I don't feel in need of a lecture just now.'

She might just as well have saved her breath. Hugo was off on his hobbyhorse. Amelie ceased listening to him. Instead she thought of Clement and Ida and their neat little family of one daughter and one son, with two and a half merciful years between them. How she envied

Ida, active and energetic with her childbearing duties now firmly behind her, able to throw her considerable abilities into the fight for women's suffrage. And on top of that, she had Clement as well.

She looked at Hugo, still expounding his theories. If she had met Clement before she met Hugo . . . but it was no use thinking like that. In fact, it was downright dangerous. She had made her choice and she had no alternative but to stick with it. She had married Hugo in the white heat of romantic passion, thinking him little less than a god. She had no one but herself to blame if he had turned out to have a fatal flaw. She was certainly not the only woman in the world who had to live with disillusionment.

'. . . positively a duty to the future of the British race.'

'Yes, yes. You'll have to tell them that, won't you?' Amelie said. She struggled upright and accepted his strong hand to get her to her feet. 'I'm just going to check that all is well in the kitchen and then I shall change.'

It was rather early yet to put herself into the hands of her maid, but at least while she went through the lengthy ritual of dressing for dinner she would be left in peace by Hugo. She made her escape.

An hour and a half later, changed from the skin outwards and feeling rather calmer, Amelie was once more in the drawing room, waiting for their guests to arrive. The fashion for straight, high-waisted dresses was quite kind to very pregnant women, although she did not opt for a hobble skirt. They were difficult enough to wear when you could see your feet. The Ladies' Gown department at Packards had made her a silk and chiffon gown in pale green and cream, draped and layered and trimmed with cream Valenciennes lace. It made her feel elegant and feminine despite her size.

The Markhams were announced. They were a striking couple, both of them tall and good-looking, as dark as the Rutherfords were fair. Clement, an MP for a poor south London constituency, was an urbane foil to Ida's enthusiasm.

Ida erupted into the room, flew to Amelie's side and embraced her.

'Melly, darling, how are you? You're looking very well. How long is it now? Is that all? I don't know how you do it. I'm sure I wouldn't look so wonderful if I had as many babies as you. I was an utter idiot when I was carrying, wasn't I, Clem? I just lay about like a beached whale.'

'You were never an idiot, my dear,' her husband said.

Ida gave him an adoring smile.

'Isn't he wonderful? He says all the right things, and what is more I believe he really means them.'

'Of course I mean them,' Clement Markham said.

He was standing next to Hugo on the hearthrug, regarding the two women on the sofa.

'Clever devils, weren't we?' he said to Hugo. 'We married the two most beautiful women in London.'

'We did, which is why I can't understand why you two can be so pig-headed over passing your talents on to the next generation.'

Ida gave an impatient wave of the hand.

'Do spare us the eugenics, Hugo. You're not going to convince us, so you might as well give up. Besides, you and Mel are more than making up for any of our shortcomings.

'Too true,' Amelie muttered, before she could stop herself.

Ida shot her a look of sympathy and changed the subject.

'What are you giving us for dinner, darling? I'm quite famished. I've been training our new recruits to speak in public all afternoon. It's been most enjoyable, but exhausting. They're so keen, so desperate to learn and to go out there and help the cause, that it's really exciting. A couple of them are going to be very good, and the others are more than competent. I'm sure we must win through soon.'

'You've been saying that ever since I first knew you,' Hugo said.

Amelie could see that he was sulking over having been stopped from saying his piece.

'More and more people are coming to agree with the WSPU,' she said. 'Surely Parliament can't close its eyes for ever?'

Clement shook his head.

'There's still a huge amount of scepticism in the House. The great majority still think that women are too weak and butterfly-brained to be given the responsibility of choosing who should govern. And if the truth were told, I think many of the members are secretly afraid of giving women the vote. They don't know what it will lead to.'

'They're all far too comfortable as they are. They need something to stir them up,' Ida declared.

'It's the stirring up that they don't like. They're afraid that you women will take over,' Clement said.

'And a very good thing that would be, in many cases,' Amelie said. 'You're an exception, Clem. I know you work very hard for your constituents, but most MPs seem to spend more time at their clubs and at Society parties than at the House or in their constituencies. And they're such a dull lot, too. Neither side wants to make any bold moves.'

'That's very true,' Clement agreed, with a wry smile.

'The poor darling has been roundly ticked off by the Party for trying to whip up some interest in social reform. And it doesn't make it any easier for him, being married to me.'

'It may not be easy, but it is interesting,' Clement said.

Amelie looked from one to the other, envious of the palpable love and admiration that flowed between them. Once, she and Hugo had been like that, long, long ago before they were married. Where had it all gone? She was glad when the butler announced that dinner was served.

As it was a small dinner for friends, rather than a Society affair meant to impress, Amelie had not ordered the full nine courses. They started with vermicelli soup, followed by devilled whitebait, beef olives, capon with ham, a choice of iced soufflé or cabinet pudding and finally fruit and cheese. With an MP and an activist at the table, it was not long before talk turned to politics.

'Churchill's ordered a mobilisation of the Fleet for July. Fisher doesn't like it one bit,' Clement told them.

'Mobilisation, eh? That'll show the Germans a thing or two,' Hugo said. 'Damned cheek, all that building of battleships and trying to outdo us.'

'I thought you admired the Germans, Hugo?' Ida said.

'I do – up to a point. I like the way they run things. But they're getting ideas above themselves. They need putting in their place.'

'A war, you mean?' said Amelie, who had heard his opinions on this point many a time.

'That's right. A short sharp war to show them just who's who.'

'I think that's horrible,' Ida said. 'And what's more, it's totally unnecessary. The King and the Kaiser are cousins, they'll never let Britain and Germany go to war.'

'I hope not,' said Clement.

Amelie looked at him. He sounded genuinely worried, as opposed to Hugo's bluster.

'Do you think it's a possibility?' she asked.

'They're certainly out for power and territory. I would hope that in this day and age diplomacy will

82

prove stronger than guns, but there's a great deal of instability in Europe. In the Balkans, for instance, and in Russia. Russia's expanding her army almost as rapidly as Germany is.'

'The Balkans have always been unstable. They don't have to concern us,' Hugo said.

'They would if Austria stormed through them down to the Mediterranean and threatened our route through Suez to India,' Clement argued.

'But a war?' Amelie persisted. 'Surely not? It's all so far away from us.'

'Even if Germany and Russia fight each other, there's no need for us to join in. We've enough to concern us at home. Look at the Irish question,' Ida said.

'A war would do us good. It would stop us from squabbling amongst ourselves over petty issues,' Hugo said.

'Petty! I wouldn't call Irish home rule petty,' Ida exclaimed.

The evening followed a fuller pattern. Ida and Hugo argued, Amelie tried to get to the truth of the matter, Clement supplied the considered opinion and inside information.

When the women left the men to their cigars, Ida sat down beside Amelie on one of the sofas. She took Amelie's hand.

'Now, tell me how you really are,' she said.

'Oh – uncomfortable, tired, frustrated. You know how it is. I'll be glad when it's all over,' Amelie sighed.

'But will it be all over? Will Hugo be content with four children?'

'No,' Amelie admitted. 'You heard him earlier. It's a crusade with him. We must populate the country with the brightest and the best.'

'But he isn't the one who has to actually bear the children. He doesn't seem to see that it's all rather one-sided, does he?' Ida persisted.

'No, he genuinely doesn't.'

Ida looked earnestly at her friend.

'Then it's up to you, Melly. You don't have to go along with it, you know. There are ways and means now for us women.'

'I know that, Ida. I'm not stupid. But it still has to be agreed between you, doesn't it?'

'But that applies both ways. Do you want more babies just as much as Hugo does?'

'No—'

'Then do something about it. You don't have to resort to sponges and douches any more. You can get yourself a cap. It's a bit tricky fitting it and the pessaries are messy but it's more than worth it.'

The prospect hovered seductively in Amelie's imagination. No more pregnancies. Then she shook her head.

'He'd find out.'

'He might not. There isn't much to feel.'

'But if I stopped conceiving just like that then he would know I was doing something about it. And then he'd make it his business to find out. There would be the most terrible row.'

Ida tried to persuade her that it was possible, but whatever her friend said, Amelie knew it was no use.

'He won't see reason on this, Ida. It's almost like a religion,' she explained.

Ida frowned.

'I still don't think it's right. If ever you feel you can take matters into your own hands, tell me and I'll give you the name of a very good female doctor.'

Amelie promised that she would.

The men were still talking about the possibility of a war with Germany when they came into the drawing room. It gave Amelie a feeling of unease, as if a crack had appeared in her secure life. She sat with an arm wrapped protectively round the unborn baby as it moved inside her. It was Clement who seemed to understand how she felt. As he and Ida made ready to go at the end of the evening, he gave her hand a squeeze.

'Don't let all this talk of armies and mobilisation worry you, Melly. It will probably only turn out to be a lot of hot air and sabre rattling. I expect it will all settle down again by the autumn.'

'Thank you, Clem. I'm sure you're right.'

She smiled at him, grateful for his words. Clem had such a good grasp of foreign affairs. She had every confidence in him.

'That was a good evening, wasn't it?' she said to Hugo when their guests had gone. 'How I wish we could have more evenings like that where we have proper conversations instead of empty chat.'

'Conversation, is that what you call it? I don't know how Clement manages to put up with Ida. She has no conception of womanly restraint. She airs all those half-baked ideas of hers as if no other view were at all tenable. She jumps in before one has even finished one's sentence. It's like having another man at the table.'

Amelie smiled.

'I would imagine Ida would take that as a compliment.'

Hugo snorted.

'That is exactly what I mean. She is just the sort of woman I find most difficult to deal with. What she needs is another two or three babies to keep her occupied.'

Amelie was about to point out that Ida was more than happy as she was, when a horribly familiar pain gripped her. She sat down abruptly.

'Hugo,' she said. 'I think you had better send for the doctor.'

Six hours later, the daughter she had hoped for was born and named Catherine.

8

'Can I help you fold those up?'

May looked up. It was Will Foster with his anxious eyes and his round face that made him look younger than his twenty-three years.

'Thank you,' she said.

Between them they folded the heavy linen bedsheets in practised movements like a well-rehearsed dance. In half lengthwise and in half again, then ends together and ends together again before the final fold and the smoothing down.

'You couldn't get her to buy these, then?' Will asked, referring to the customer May had just been serving.

'No, nor the twilled cotton. She chose the plain, and I'm not sure whether she could really afford those, but I told her they would last and last, and she seemed satisfied. It's the truth, too. I've had ladies come in here and tell me that they've been married twenty years and they're just now replacing the sheets they had from Packards as wedding presents.'

'The truth matters to you, doesn't it, Miss Hollis?'

May flushed. It made her sound so dull.

'Yes,' she said, defensively. 'It does.'

Will gazed at her, brown eyes earnest.

86

'A lot of them round here, they don't care what they say, as long as they get a sale, but you, you're not like that.'

May opened her mouth and shut it again, not knowing what to say. Finally she managed a croaky, 'No.' She could feel the thud of her heart, but whether it was through pleasure or embarrassment, it was impossible to say.

'Mr Foster!'

The floorwalker's voice boomed across the department, commanding instant obedience. Will went to attend to the waiting customer. May kept a covert eye on him as she lifted the sheets back into their place on the high shelves. She liked Will. He had been kind to her when she first arrived and helped her through the first confusing weeks when she didn't know everyone's name and forgot where things were. What was more, she knew that he liked her. He had never admitted to it openly. Today was the nearest he had come to it. But it showed in a dozen little ways. And it had not gone unnoticed in the department.

'Doesn't miss a trick, does he, your young man?' Lily, one of the other shopgirls teased.

'He's not my young man,' May said.

Lily laughed.

'Ooh, playing hard to get, are we?'

'No.'

The continual watchfulness and gossip of the department, and beyond that of the whole store, got her down at times. It was far worse than village gossip had ever been. With everyone working all day within earshot of each other, you couldn't say a word or cast a look without someone picking it up and making something of it. When she and Ruby got together at the end of the day and chewed things over, it was different. Ruby turned everything into fun. There was a delicious intimacy between them, a sharing of secrets that she had never had with her sisters, spiced with dashes of Ruby's worldly wisdom. Ruby managed to impart knowledge without ever making May feel the country bumpkin. Unlike Lily and her kind.

To May's annoyance, she and Lily were sent off to tea together. She looked across the sea of heads in the canteen, trying to locate Ruby. There she was, waving from the middle of the vast room, and indicating the seat beside her. May trotted off to join her friend, hoping to lose Lily, but Lily stuck right behind her. They helped themselves to tea from the urn at the end of the long table and sat themselves down in front of the huge platters of bread and butter and cake. Today was Monday, so it was Victoria sponge. As usual, Ruby was full of the day's doings.

'Sorry I missed you dinnertime, I was sent early. Did you manage to get a seat at the barrier?'

May shook her head.

'No, nor me. Still, never mind, eh? You'll never guess—'

'She doesn't need to get a seat by the barrier. She's got an admirer right there in our department,' Lily broke in.

Ruby was instantly alert, her dark eyes intent.

'What, that Will Foster? Is he still after you?'

'You should see him! He's always there, picking things up for her, fetching stuff, doing the heavy lifting. Got him on a string, she has.'

'It's not like that. He's just being kind,' May protested.

Lily shrieked with laughter.

'Kind? Is that what you call it? Of course, you know he used to be after me once, but I wasn't interested. Too dull for me. I like men with a bit of go in them. But I suppose he's quite good-looking, in a way, if you like that sort of thing.'

'They're a bit of a dull lot altogether, aren't they, the men in your department?' Ruby said.

'Oh I wouldn't say–' Lily began, but Ruby was not going to let her take charge of the conversation.

'We've got some really nice men in Stationery. Take that Mr Eden, for instance. Ever so nicely spoken he is. Like a real gentleman. But a wicked tease as well. And as for our Mr Lambert – well! Nobody else has got a buyer like him. Young and good-looking. The youngest buyer in the store. They say the way he's going, he'll end up on the Board.'

They were all silenced for a moment by this amazing thought. Then Lily spoke up.

'He married, then?'

'No. Well at least, I haven't never heard nothing about it, and you know how things get about in this place. No, he's single all right. Nice catch for some lucky girl, eh?'

May ventured a little dig.

'Watch it, Rube. You've already got a young man.'

Ruby laughed, and smoothed back a stray lock of hair.

'Oh well, he's hardly going to look at me, is he? Him a buyer and all.'

'Hardly,' Lily agreed.

Ruby glared at her. She had said it to be contradicted. She changed the subject, speaking just to May.

'I just got an idea. But I'll tell you about it later. Make sure you meet me after work.'

No amount of teasing or guessing would make her reveal what the idea was, so May just had to wait. After work, she was no wiser.

'I wasn't saying anything in front of that Lily. Nosy cow, she is. You're not getting pally with her, are you?'

'Oh no,' May assured her. 'We were just sent to tea

together, that's all.'

'That's all right then. But what's all this she was saying about that Will Foster? You never mentioned he was still after you.'

'I did,' May said.

She had mentioned him during their late night discussions, when either Ruby slipped into May's room or invited May to hers. The two of them would sit in bed together, huddled up against the cold, whispering and giggling in the dark, but generally it was Ruby who did most of the talking.

'Not that he runs round after you like that, you didn't. He really keen on you, then?' Ruby sounded quite put out.

May couldn't resist it. All the young men were after Ruby, with her vital personality and her striking looks. It was nice to have an admirer of her own.

'We-ell,' she said.

'He is! What does he do? What has he said? Come on, tell.'

'He helped me to fold up some sheets today–'

'Is that all?'

'And he found a magnet to pick up some pins I dropped–'

'Anyone would do that.'

Ruby was not impressed. May found herself repeating the things Will had said that afternoon. Ruby shrugged.

'Doesn't exactly set the Thames on fire, does he?'

Ruby had put her finger right on it. When May came to London, she was expecting great things to happen, exciting things, totally different from anything she had experienced in Tatwell. Will Foster did not quite fit the picture.

'He's very nice,' May said, just to keep her end up. But she could hear the lack of conviction in her voice.

'Nice! That's all right for a start, I suppose, but does he know how to show you a good time?'

'I'm sure he does,' May said.

At Tatwell, courting couples generally went for walks. May had a niggling feeling that that could be what Will might suggest.

'Hm. The more I think about it, the more I think my idea's right.'

'What is this idea, then?'

But Ruby wasn't telling. She wore an irritating smile all the way home. It was Saturday before May found out, the best day of the week as the shop closed at one o'clock.

'That Will Foster asked you out, then?' Ruby enquired as they left work.

May had to admit that he hadn't.

'Good, 'cause I've got something much better fixed up for you.'

'Oh!'

May didn't know whether to be pleased or offended, but before she could work it out, Ruby was nagging her for a better answer.

'Is that all you can say, after all the effort I been to? I dunno why I bother.'

May hastened to placate her. Putting Ruby in a huff was not a good idea.

'I'm sorry, I was just surprised. I mean – what is it you've fixed up?'

With the air of a magician producing a rabbit, Ruby announced,

'You and me and my young man Alfie and his mate Ginger are all going to go for a night out on the town.'

This time, May did not need to try to be convincing. At last, the exciting London life she had envisaged was about to begin.

'Oh Ruby! How wonderful, but . . .' Hard on the

heels of excitement came doubt. '. . . will he like me, this Ginger? I mean, I'm not like you – I don't know how–'

Ruby swept this aside.

'Course he will. You just follow me. You'll be all right.'

Getting ready was the first hurdle. May had bought some new clothes since arriving in London. Influenced by Ruby's flamboyant taste, she had splashed out on a green hat adorned with feathers, a bright blue blouse with black spots and a couple of belts that showed off her narrow waist. But still the bulk of her meagre wardrobe was sober and sensible, so the new things had to be worn with her Sunday best black skirt and jacket. When Ruby bounced in, she shook her head.

'Blue and green should not be seen, Except with something in between,' she chanted, and produced a chrome yellow blouse and dark green cape with ruffles. May put them on, together with the hat. But Ruby was much larger in the bust than she was, and the blouse ballooned round her. Ruby got out some handkerchiefs and stuffed them down May's corset, so that her little breasts sat on top of a shelf, round and full and inviting instead of respectably laced up. Now when the blouse went on, it was nicely filled. When May gazed in the looking glass, a new person looked back at her. Gone was the country girl, gone too was the neat and obedient shopgirl. Instead there was a woman of the world, in glowing colours and sophisticated styles. She turned this way and that, enchanted and just a little frightened, totally failing to see how incongruous her innocent face looked amongst the tarty splendour. She only knew that her parents would be appalled, and that heightened both the fear and the pleasure.

Alfie and Ginger arrived promptly, both of them dressed in loud checked jackets with loud voices to match. May and Ginger were introduced, and shook hands. May blushed, feeling the eyes of the whole roomful of people upon her, and worse still, reading disappointment in Ginger's. It was as she had feared. He had expected someone dashing and fascinating like Ruby. She bit her lip and muttered, 'Pleased to meet you.'

'Me too, Miss Hollis, me too,' Ginger boomed, but she could not believe it.

While Ruby and her parents exchanged bantering remarks with the young men, May stole covert looks at Ginger. True to his nickname he had carroty hair, slicked fashionably back, and the pale complexion of the indoor worker. He stood with his hands in his pockets and his feet apart, joking with the others, a picture of confidence and sophistication. May could hardly imagine anyone more different from the village boys.

'Now then, mind you bring these girls back by eleven o'clock,' Mr Goss admonished.

'Right-ho, Guv'nor. You can trust us,' Alfie assured him, with a huge wink at Ginger. The pair of them laughed raucously and Ruby joined in.

'You, you're dreadful, you are,' she said to Alfie, giving him a push on the chest.

'Ooh, do it again,' he begged.

Mrs Goss shrieked with laughter.

'He is a one, isn't he? You just watch yourself, my girl.'

'Don't worry, Mrs G. I'll do the watching,' Alfie responded, and offered his arm to Ruby with a flourish. Ruby tucked her hand in his elbow and stood smiling at her mother. May was open mouthed with amazement. Her parents would not even allow men like these over the threshold, let alone joke with them like that. But this was London, and London manners. So when Ginger crooked his arm at her, she took it with what she hoped was the air of one who did this sort of thing all the time.

'Right-ho then, girls, what's it to be? Drink to start us off?' Alfie asked, as they reached the street.

'I thought we were going up West,' Ruby protested.

'Yeah, yeah, course we are. All in good time. Got to get a few in first, eh?' Alfie said, and he and Ginger laughed yet again.

May couldn't quite see what the joke was, but she smiled along with them.

'You like a drink then, do you, Miss Hollis?' Ginger asked.

'Oh – er – yes,' May said, as this seemed to be required of her. It didn't seem the moment to admit that her family were strict teetotallers and a drop of alcohol had never passed her lips in her life.

'Lovely! That's what I like to hear. Let's go to the Greyhound, eh, Alfie?'

Even May knew the Greyhound, since it was the pub by the bus stop. It looked just the sort of low place her father would disapprove of.

'The Greyhound's horrible. If we've got to have a drink round here before we go, let's go to the Feathers,' Ruby said.

The men groaned.

'The beer's much better at the Greyhound.'

But Ruby insisted, and in the end the men gave in.

The Prince of Wales' Feathers was a brand-new shiny pub with engraved glass, polished brass, leather benches and bright lights. May was dazzled as she went in. It was more like a palace than a public house. Was this what was meant by a gin palace?

'What's it to be, girls? Drop of the old Mother's Ruin?' Alfie asked, confirming her suspicions.

'I think Miss Hollis'd prefer a port and lemon,' Ginger said.

May smiled her gratitude. A port and lemon sounded safe enough.

'Yes please,' she said.

It looked pretty, like a sort of pink lemonade, and it

tasted nice. May sat on the edge of the bench, sipping and following the conversation of the others, if conversation was what it was, for the talk consisted of discussion of the merits of various pubs and beers, mixed with a great deal of teasing and backchat. At first May was very conscious of having nothing to contribute, but as a second drink followed the first, a pleasant warmth stole over her, a sense of hazy wellbeing, so that she was happy just to listen and to join in with the laughter. She was quite sorry when Ruby stopped Ginger from getting the next round, reminding Alfie that they had been promised a night out in the West End.

'All right, all right, don't go on,' Alfie said, 'There's plenty of time.'

'The night is yet young,' Ginger added.

'Like a blooming double act, you two are. Aren't they, May?' Ruby complained.

'Er, yes,' May said.

'Don't you like this place, Miss Hollis?' Ginger asked.

'It – it's very nice,' May said politely.

Ruby kicked her in the ankle. May gaped at her, dimly aware that she had said something wrong.

'There you are, your friend's happy to stay here,' Alfie pointed out. 'Go and get another round in, Ginge.'

Ginger wove his way through the crowds to the bar. Ruby's mobile mouth settled into a dangerous droop.

'Aren't we good enough to be taken up West, then?' she asked.

'Course you are, darling. Didn't say I wasn't going to, now did I?'

'But when? Next Christmas? We can go here any day of the week. It's Saturday night. I want to have some fun.'

'We're having fun here, ain't we? You're having fun, ain't you, Miss Hollis?' Alfie appealed.

May opened her mouth and shut it again, not knowing what to say.

'No she isn't. She wants to go up West, don't you, May?'

'Yes,' May answered obediently.

'Let the poor girl speak for herself. She likes it here, she just said so.'

'That's because she don't know no better.' Ruby lifted her arm to push back an invisible strand of hair, drawing attention to her magnificent bust. 'There's plenty of men willing to take me out to somewhere nice if you're too mean to,' she told him.

Alfie flushed.

'All right. I never said I wouldn't, did I?'

The next round was knocked back rather more quickly. When May stood up, her knees felt quite wobbly, and she was glad of Ginger's arm to hold on to. Outside, it had started to rain. As they waited at the bus stop, the men's talk began to flag. Some of May's lightheadedness evaporated and she began to fear for the feathers on her beautiful new hat. Ruby complained about the lack of buses.

'You would go up West,' Alfie reminded her.

'If we'd gone when I wanted to, we wouldn't have got caught in this lot,' Ruby retorted.

What was only a ten-minute wait seemed like an hour. May was glad, when the bus did arrive, that it was crowded and there were only two double seats left, so they could not all sit together. At least she would not be drawn into Ruby and Alfie's squabbling. But it did mean that for the first time that evening she and Ginger were left to speak to each other. Afraid of an awkward silence after all the backchatting, she cleared her throat.

'Er, what line of business are you in, Mr Logan?' she asked.

Ginger laughed.

'You're a funny little thing and no mistake.' He

adopted the same formal tone that May had used. 'I'm in the employ of Messrs Hartley and Stump, Shipping Agents, Miss Hollis.'

May flushed. She had got it wrong again. And her head was beginning to ache. But to her relief, Ginger took pity on her, and regaled her with stories of his doings at Hartley and Stump that got them easily all the way to Leicester Square. The heavens opened as they jumped off the bus, and there was nothing for it but to run into the nearest pub.

'Blimey, I hope you girls've started building an ark. Same again all round?' Alfie asked, and headed for the bar.

May could see water dripping off all round the brim of her hat, and draggled feathers drooping over the edge. There was no protection from the weather in the elegant green cape, so her upper body was soaked practically to the skin. She gave a passing longing thought to her sensible Sunday jacket, but then as she took in what the other women in the pub were wearing, she dismissed it. Even in the green cape and yellow blouse, she looked quite dull compared with some of them. The place was packed with women in skin-tight shiny satin and men in suits and even dinner jackets. There was nowhere to sit down, so they stayed in a tight little group, jostled by the continual comings and goings of the crowd. May gulped down her fourth port and lemon of the evening, and began to feel warm again.

'Better?' Ginger asked.

May nodded.

'I think I like port'n'lemon,' she said, but her tongue couldn't quite get round the word 'lemon'. All of a sudden that seemed very funny. 'Port'n'lemon,' she tried again, and giggled. Once she started giggling, everything seemed even funnier. She laughed at whatever anyone said.

Someone barged into her, nearly knocking her over.

'Oops-a-daisy,' Ginger said, and put an arm round her waist to steady her. It felt nice there, so she leaned against him, and he held her a little tighter. May gazed up at him with unfocused eyes and laughed at his smallest remark, unaware that things were not nearly so harmonious between her friend and Alfie.

'What?'

Ruby's shriek shattered her happy haze.

'What do you mean, it's too late?'

'All the shows started ages ago.'

'I know that, and whose fault is it? I never wanted to stop for a drink before we came up here.'

May gazed at her friend. It was clear that Ruby was very put out.

'We can still get in for the second half.'

'Don't think so, darling. Second halves will've started by the time we get anywhere.'

'Don't you darling me! You did it deliberate. You never was going to take us to a show.'

'Now Ruby, would I do a thing like that? You know I wanted to give you a really good night out. Why–'

But Ruby was beyond appeal.

'I think you better take us home. Right now,' she said.

After a little more wrangling, that was what they did.

It was a sorry party that made their way back on the bus. Ruby insisted that they should be escorted right up to the door, and started on Ginger when she saw that he still had his arm round May's waist.

'You can stop that, and all. Taking advantage of her. Can't you see she's three sheets to the wind? I tell you, I'm used to better than this. You two are no better than animals.'

They parted at the door of the Gosses' house, Ruby flouncing up the path with May stumbling behind her, and the two men retreating down the road, muttering.

'Well!' Ruby declared. 'Good riddance, that's what I say. Any man who gets tightfisted with me gets his marching orders. The cheek of it!'

She ran on for several minutes, while May nodded and made noises of agreement. She no longer felt happily hazy, but sick and headachy and tired. She shivered, and looked miserably at her lovely hat. It was ruined by the rain. She felt suddenly close to tears. The whole evening had been a disaster. She had not known what to say, she had got drunk and she had let Ginger, whom she had only just met, squeeze her waist.

'I think I'll go to bed now,' she said.

Half an hour later, she was lying in bed thinking what a failure she was, when Ruby came in, bearing two cups of cocoa.

'Here,' she said, handing one to May and getting carefully under the covers, 'this'll make you feel better.'

May sat up and sipped the cocoa. It was comforting, as was Ruby's warm presence beside her.

'I'm sorry,' she said.

'Sorry? What for? I'm sorry I dragged you out with such a pair of – of clowns. I tell you, May, I'm fed up with city clerks. They're so full of themselves, but it's all hot air. They don't know nothing. Like I said, good riddance. But listen, I got an idea–'

May could not suppress a low groan. She had had enough of Ruby's ideas.

Ruby laughed. All her bad humour had gone.

'No, listen. This is a really good one. You known when we was talking about what we wished for? In the future, I mean. What we wanted our lives to be?'

May did remember. They often talked about it. Ruby wanted to marry somebody with money. She had no intention of being poor all her life. Quite how she was to do this, she had not been sure.

'I know who it is I want now. It's all so obvious. I

can't think why I didn't think of it before. Guess. He's young and good-looking and I see him every day.'

May stared at her.

'Not – Mr Lambert?'

'The very one.'

Ruby was looking over the rim of her cup, smiling at the glorious vision she had of her future.

'But – you said only the other day, he wouldn't look at you.'

'Wouldn't he, though? I think I could make him. I'm going to do it, May. But I'm going to be careful. I got to plan it all out, one step at a time.' She took a sip of cocoa and ran her tongue round her full lips. 'No more cheap city clerks for me.'

9

The sudden escalation of tension between the countries of Europe seemed to catch even its leaders by surprise. In late July the Kaiser was on a yachting trip in Norway, the French President and Prime Minister were on a state visit to St Petersburg and the British cabinet left London for the country. By the time that ultimatums were being issued, the British people were going away for the August Bank Holiday, but enough of them were sufficiently worried by the situation to start stocking up on food. At Packards, the Food Halls were practically stripped by the time the shop closed at one. Still the majority of Britons did not know quite what was happening and whether it really was going to concern them directly. The Goss family went for a picnic on Hampstead Heath. May went home to visit her family. Clement and Ida Markham took a train in the opposite direction from everyone else and came back to the London house they had left only a week before. Hundreds of Londoners took to the streets on the Sunday evening, singing 'Rule Britannia' and the Marseillaise outside Buckingham Palace. On Monday they were in Parliament Square, cheering members of Parliament as they arrived for the Foreign Secretary's speech. There was such a run on money reserves that the bank holiday was extended by three days. Sellers of Union Jacks made a small fortune. The ultimatums began to run out. By eleven o'clock on Tuesday the fourth, Britain was at war.

As soon as the recruiting offices opened on the fifth, Hugo Rutherford joined up. About one in three of the Packards Volunteer Rifles followed his example, but the rest of them, like the rest of the country, went back to work, wondering just how their lives were going to change, if at all. After all, it was all going to be over by Christmas.

'Ooh, there's a band! Can you hear it?' Ruby Goss exclaimed.

Alec listened. She was right. From beyond the glass doors, out there in Oxford Street, came the thud, thud of drums, the blare of brass, the familiar, cheery tune of Tipperary. Others in the department heard it too. Conversations faltered, heads were raised, listening, some people started to sing along: 'Goodbye, Piccadilly, Farewell Leicester Square . . .' Small children tugged at grown-ups' hands.

'The soldiers, the soldiers, I want to see the soldiers!'

There was cheering. People started to leave the store, first those with eager children then sober men and women, unashamedly hurrying to catch sight of the brave boys marching off to war. The shopmen and girls, unable to leave their posts, stood up a little taller, proud to be part of a nation embarking on the glorious enterprise of defending brave little Belgium from the Hun. Alec, who was closest to the door through the entrance lobby, craned his neck to catch sight of what was going on in the street, but all he could see out there in the August sunshine were waving hats and handkerchiefs, and the occasional bobbing hat of an officer on horseback.

'It must be infantry,' he said to Ruby.

The least romantic of the forces, especially now that scarlet uniforms and plumed hats had been replaced by khaki and caps. But still Ruby's face was rapt, her eyes glowing and her full lips parted.

'Ooh, so brave!'

Once more the question that nagged at every young man rose up and challenged Alec: should he go?

The sound of the band died away, the cheering ceased, the customers drifted back into the store. Business resumed, but there was a buzz, an excitement still in the air, as if a stiff breeze had stirred the placid warmth of the department.

Mr Lambert approached, and beside him, Ruby Goss stood up a little straighter. Alec observed it with a flash of resentment. When he had first arrived, he had thought he might get somewhere with Ruby, but over the weeks her attitude had changed. She still laughed and joked with him, but it was Victor Lambert who drew her real interest. He could read it in the expression in her eyes, in the turn of her body, and it rankled. Ruby Goss was infinitely desirable, but she treated him as a mere pal, a workmate. So he was doubly glad when it turned out to be him, and not Ruby, that the buyer wanted to see.

'Ah, Mr Eden, could you come into my office for a moment?'

Office was an inflated name for the cubby that Mr Lambert worked from. There was barely room in it for the two of them and a desk and filing cabinet. Ruby Goss would, Alec reflected sourly, be very happy to be placed in here. It was impossible not to touch.

'Now, we have to make some decisions about the ordering. Mr Packard wants us to go on as near to normal as possible.'

Alec looked at him in amazement. Trade had fallen

almost to nothing since the day that war was declared. People felt it unnecessary or even faintly unpatriotic to be buying such frivolities as card cabinets or music stands. Writing paper and pens, on the other hand, had been selling in much larger quantities than usual. Everybody was wanting to communicate with friends and relations, however little they had thought about them in the past.

'But – nobody is buying,' Alec said.

'Mr Packard thinks they will come back to it once the first shock is over, in which case we must be ready. More than ready, since some of the goods we stock may not then be available. Already it's going to be hard, if not impossible, to get hold of some things.'

'Anything that's made in Germany for a start,' Alec said.

'Quite. There is also this problem with credit, and the banks, but Packards' name will stand us in good stead there. We should not have any trouble. So we have to order writing cases, newspaper stands, inkwells . . .' the list went on. 'What quantities would you consider suitable?'

Victor Lambert was an excellent tutor, Alec had to admit. He didn't just tell Alec what to do or what he was doing, but made him think for himself. Alec made some suggestions and Mr Lambert agreed with some, disagreed with others, but explained why.

'I'm going to leave you with the pens. Go and speak to Mr Page behind the counter, then check our figures against what they're holding in Stores, and then put in the orders. Don't forget that before we know where we are, Christmas will be upon us, and pens are popular presents.'

Christmas. The phrase that was on everyone's lips rose to his.

'They say it'll all be over by Christmas.'

Victor Lambert shot him a sharp look.

'All the more reason not to go off playing the hero.'

'Is that what you think?'

The buyer turned again to his lists. He was frowning over the sales of letter openers.

'If it is all over by Christmas, it will be Regulars who will have done the job. The volunteers will hardly be out of the training camps. Hardly a great deal of glory in that, only five months of lost opportunities and living on the King's Shilling.'

It was certainly the practical way of looking at things.

'I suppose you're right. It's just that—'

'You'd like all the girls to wish you luck while they wave you goodbye?'

Alec flushed. It made him sound like a stupid young fool.

'I would like to do something towards defending my King and country,' he said stiffly.

'Ah well . . .' Victor Lambert made a small gesture with his hand, conceding the point. 'There is that, of course.'

'But that is paramount, surely? To protect one's country, and all that it stands for?'

That had been the bedrock upon which his schooling had been based. God and country. Even when he fully woke to the fact that he was a bastard, and all that that meant, he knew that he was still British, and therefore superior to any other race on earth.

'Yes. Of course,' Victor Lambert agreed.

'A lot of the Volunteer Rifles have gone already. Some of them went and took the shilling on the first day, like Mr Rutherford.'

'It's different for Mr Rutherford. He's a gentleman of leisure. He doesn't have his way to make in the world,' the buyer pointed out.

Whereas Alec had everything to prove yet.

'The others weren't gentlemen of leisure. They were shopmen.'

'I expect soldiering seemed a more exciting way of life than selling.'

'And more honourable.'

'There's nothing dishonourable in trade. How do you think the Empire grew rich? Not on wars, but on trade.'

Alec hadn't thought of that. It was only the wars you read about in history books.

'But this isn't a war in some distant part of the Empire, it's on our doorstep. The Germans have to be put in their place,' he argued. He could not understand the buyer's attitude. It was almost as if he disapproved of the war. 'If you don't agree with that, then I have to say that I find your opinion somewhat unpatriotic.'

'You'll not find a more patriotic man than me. It's just that I don't see the need to rush off straight away. I'll go, if I'm needed,' Victor Lambert stated. 'Now perhaps you would be so kind as to attend to the ordering of the pens. If you are not about to march to the recruiting office, that is.'

'No. I mean, of course, Mr Lambert.'

'Your progress is being noted, you know. From above.'

'Wha–'

But the buyer had turned away, and was busy filling in rows of figures.

Alec walked through the department to the pen counter, his brain spinning. He had been given a hint, that much was clear. But what did the buyer know? Had he been informed of Alec's true relationship to the Packard family? Alec rather thought not, but in that case he must be wondering just why Alec had been singled out to have this special training. It was not the way things were usually done. His progress was being noted. Now that he came to think of it, that was not so surprising. Of course they were keeping an eye on him, especially Edward. Hoping he would make a fatal mistake, no doubt. Which he was not going to do. And to start with, he had this job ordering pens. It was the first time he had been entrusted with it on his own.

He talked to the elderly shopman behind the pen counter, gently flattering him with references to his superior knowledge, then using that knowledge to estimate the numbers needed of each of the myriad types of pen the department stocked. He was going to do this task well. Edward would have to think of some other way to dislodge him.

It all took much longer than it would usually have done. Ordering only from British firms, finding the nearest equivalent to the lines he could no longer buy, then estimating the new demand was quite a challenge. He hardly noticed it was dinnertime, until the floorwalker reminded him that it was time to go. He found a seat fairly easily in the canteen, though not one of the coveted ones next to the barrier. He sat with a group of young men from Turnery. As usual these days, talk centred on the war.

'Did you hear? Powers and Smith and Watson from Tobacco all went and volunteered this morning.'

'They didn't!'

'They did. Not a word to anyone. Just didn't turn up for work. They were in a rare old state in Tobacco, with three missing. But the store can't say anything, can they? Not when they're off doing their duty.'

'Good for them!'

'Are you going to volunteer?'

'I don't know. I'd like to . . .'

Alec put forward Mr Lambert's view that the volunteers would not get a crack at the real fighting.

'Rubbish! Why are they asking for us to join up if they don't think they'll use us?'

107

'I thought the French were supposed to hold back the Germans?'

'They can't do it on their own, can they? Not the Frogs. They need us there.'

'So, are you going, then?'

'I might.'

'I will if you will.'

The meal was finished before any real decision was taken. Alec found he had eaten two solid courses without even knowing what was going into his mouth. Even more astonishing, they had not once so much as glanced in the direction of the barrier. Thoughtfully, he made his way back to his ordering.

He had almost finished when Amelie Rutherford came bustling into the department with her team from Display. She nodded at him in the same friendly fashion that she greeted all the staff. Your progress is being noted. From above. Of course. It was Amelie who was keeping the close watch on him, and no doubt relaying it to her brother. He could just imagine the two of them plotting his downfall. She certainly looked very cheerful today, for a woman whose husband had gone off to fight for his country. He eavesdropped on her conversation with Mr Lambert, not too difficult a task as they were standing just outside the buyer's little office.

'Now, Mr Lambert, trade is going to be tricky for a while, make no mistake, but people are still going to want to buy things, so they might as well buy them at Packards, don't you think? So what I want to do is to draw attention to those things that people are particularly going to need in wartime, and we'll make a special display of them in each department, with Union Jacks and bunting. Books are having a positive run on maps of Europe, and I want to have map pins and little paper flags for sale there, but you could still make a feature of them here as well, for people who already have maps.

And then I thought that letters to and from the men were going to be very important, so we could include writing paper . . .'

She was very clever, Alec had to admit. If she was doing this in every department, then it showed an extra-ordinary grasp of what they had in the store and what people would buy under any circumstances. She was now asking Victor Lambert if he had any other ideas. The buyer looked nonplussed.

'You've covered everything I would have suggested, Mrs Rutherford. I don't know if Mr Eden has anything to add?'

Alec jumped. He had not thought that his opinion might be asked. Amelie gave him an icy smile.

'Yes, Mr Eden, have you any suggestions as to what might sell particularly well at the present time?'

It was clearly a challenge. The last thing Alec wanted was to have to admit to Amelie's face that he was devoid of good ideas.

'I . . .' he began. His mind was a horrible blank. He was going to have to back down, to admit defeat. His collar felt uncomfortably tight. He was breaking out in a sweat. He looked over Amelie's shoulder – and there they were, on the counter behind her, a gift from heaven. 'We do a very nice line in photograph mounts and frames and albums. Everyone is going to want a pic-ture of their loved ones while they're away, aren't they? In fact,' – and here inspiration really took hold – 'per-haps we should have a photographer's studio in the store? It could be a service that people would really appreciate.'

'Yes . . .'

Amelie Rutherford gave him a long, thoughtful look. 'Yes. I think that is certainly worth considering.'

It was an excellent idea, and he knew it.

'It would be certain to bring people into the store.

Room could be made in one of the departments that is not doing too well at the moment, and we could sell the frames and mounts there as well as here in Stationery.'

Amelie inclined her head graciously, refusing to get excited about it.

'I shall put it to the Board at the next meeting. Thank you, Mr Eden.'

She was about to turn away, to walk off with his idea. On impulse, he forestalled her.

'I'm sure it goes without saying, Mrs Rutherford, that you will mention from whom this suggestion came?'

Beside him, he heard Victor Lambert draw in his breath in amazement and horror. Mrs Rutherford might be friendly and approachable, but she was still The Family, and not to be spoken to like that. *Just remember that I'm Family too*, Alec said silently as he held her eyes.

'Of course, Mr Eden.' Her voice was level, with just a hint of steel. 'As you said, that goes without saying. Any idea from yourself, or Mr Lambert, or indeed any other member of staff, will always be duly credited.'

And don't ever again accuse me of being underhand, came the message.

Alec felt suitably chastened. She might be the enemy, but he had no reason to believe that she was less than fair.

'Thank you, Mrs Rutherford.'

And then she was gone, dictating notes to her assistant as she went.

Victor Lambert picked up a sheaf of papers and shuffled through them.

'There are ways and ways of being noticed, but challenging Mrs Rutherford does not on the face of it appear to be the wisest of them.'

Just how much did he know?

'What–?' Alec began.

But the buyer cut him short.

110

'I have commercial travellers to see, if they have not already been sacked or gone to join up, that is. You can show me exactly what you have done later.'

He was working in the dark, Alec reflected. The family were keeping him at arm's-length, and the other staff, if they did know about him, and some of them surely must do, were keeping quiet about it. Victor Lambert probably resented being drawn into the mire of family politics, so the odd hints he threw out were the most Alec could expect from him. If he volunteered . . . everything then would be clear cut. There would be just one purpose, to stop the onrush of the German army across Belgium. A great adventure.

On the way home he passed a recruiting office with a line of men waiting patiently outside. He could feel the pull of it, as if a rope were hauling him in. He hesitated and passed on. Once he arrived home, he began to regret it.

'My darling boy . . .'

His mother fell upon him, holding him with all her tenacious strength, weeping on his shoulder. He put his arms round her, made soothing sounds, stroked her back and head. All this emotion. Sometimes he felt as if he were nothing but a huge sponge, soaking up everything that his mother poured out on him.

He waited until her crying subsided into muffled sobs, sat her on a sofa and fetched her a brandy.

'There. Better?'

She nodded, and gripped his hand with her free one.

'You're so good to me, so good. No mother ever had a better son. You won't leave me, will you? Promise you won't leave. I couldn't bear it. Not after . . .'

Fresh tears threatened.

'What's brought all this on? What makes you think I'm going to leave?' Alec asked, picturing the queue of recruits and feeling like a traitor.

'Minnie Parsons' boy went. Yesterday. Her pride and joy. She's so brave, so brave. Says she's proud to see him go to defend his country. But I'm not brave like that, my darling. I can't manage on my own. You won't leave me, will you? Promise?'

Perhaps it would all be over by Christmas.

'Yes, yes, of course,' he said, not quite able to keep the impatience out of his voice.

A tremulous smile from his mother, a prolonged kiss on the cheek.

'Thank you, thank you, my darling. I'm a terrible, selfish woman, I know. I can't help it. I couldn't bear to lose my only boy. You're all I have.'

When she finally went to dress for dinner, Alec went out into the garden. The last rays of the sun fell on the late roses, brought the scent out from the tobacco plants. He breathed in deeply. His mother's beloved flower garden, filled with fragrant plants. She had always delighted in working in it herself. One of his earliest memories of her was of her throwing off her big leather gardening gauntlets and opening her arms for him to run into and be swung round. She had not always been this helpless clinging creature. He thought of her as she used to be, full of fun, ready to make an adventure of the most mundane incident, always looking for the good side of whatever happened. It was grief that had crushed her almost beyond recognition. Alec sighed. He must be more patient with her.

It seemed that his mother had also been making resolutions. She came down to dinner impeccably dressed and coiffed with a smile pinned to her face. Only a puffiness round the eyes betrayed her earlier tears. She patted his hand.

'Now, my dear, tell me about your day. You know how I love to hear all about what's happening at the store.'

112

Alec told her of how he had been trusted to do some ordering. His mother was delighted.

'There, you see, your talents have not gone unnoticed. You've only been there nine months and already you're being given responsibility.'

'Only to order the pens. It's not exactly an office on the fifth floor.'

'But it's a start. You must make the best of it.'

'Oh, I intend to.'

They discussed it further, then he related the incident with Amelie and his idea for a photographic studio.

'Do you think I did the right thing, saying that?' he asked.

' "Always be sure to lay claim to your ideas. Nobody else is going to do it for you." That's what your father always said,' his mother told him.

'Did he?' Alec felt considerably brighter. 'She looked very put out that I should suspect her of laying claim to my suggestion.'

'She's very ambitious, that one, but I've always thought that she was honest. Unlike her brother. Now him you can't trust an inch.'

'I know that.'

'He'll put a knife in your back if he can, that Edward. Always be careful.'

'I will,' Alec promised.

It was another good reason for not volunteering. Edward would be more than happy to see the back of him. He smiled at his mother. He wouldn't go yet, not until the country's need was greater than hers.

10

'Mama, Mama!'

Amelie braced herself as her three small sons flung themselves at her and clung to her legs.

'Steady, you'll have me over,' she laughed, stooping to kiss each one in turn.

Two pairs of arms wound themselves round her neck. Hugh, the middle one, tugged at her hand.

'You play, Mama? Come and play.'

Nanny appeared, carrying baby Catherine.

'Now then, boys, don't pull your mama about. That's not how little gentlemen behave.'

Amelie gave them each one more hug, and took her daughter in her arms. The baby chuckled and reached for her nose.

'How's my own little girl today, then?'

She nuzzled the round tummy and the baby squealed with pleasure and clutched at her hair. She breathed in the sweet baby smell. How soft she was, and warm, and infinitely wonderful. They were all wonderful, all her children, perfect specimens. Thank God. A familiar chill ran through her at the thought of what their father's reaction would be if one were to turn out to be less than first class. Nothing sub-standard was to be tolerated in their nursery. But it was all right, so far.

'You play, Mama?' Hugh insisted.

Three pairs of blue eyes and one of brown looked hopefully at her. Only Hugh, who had been named for his father, did not look like him, but more like his uncle Edward.

'I'm sorry, my darlings, but I have to go to the store today.'

She felt dreadful, disappointing them. She had been so determined when Thomas, the eldest, was born that she would not be like her own mother, only seeing them for half an hour a day, clean and scrubbed and on their best behaviour in the drawing room.

'I'll be back this afternoon, and we'll all go for a walk in the park together,' she promised.

Thomas and Hugh brightened up immediately; little Peter and baby Catherine, not quite understanding but catching the general pleasure, laughed too.

Thomas caught at her arm.

'May I come to the store with you, Mama?'

Amelie smiled down at him. He might look like a Rutherford, but inside he was a real Packard.

'When you are four, you may come and do the round with me, just like I used to with my grandpapa,' she promised.

Reluctantly, she handed the baby back to Nanny and kissed the boys goodbye.

'Till this afternoon. Be good, my darlings.'

As she left the house, there was a spring in her step. Catherine was five months old now, and Amelie had had a period since Hugo had left for his training camp. Five months without being pregnant. It was the longest respite she had had in the four and a half years she had been married, and she felt charged with energy. She had almost forgotten what it was like to have a body that was all her own, and now, with Hugo away, she was set to go

115

on being babyless for some time longer. She practically skipped down the street.

It seemed wicked, somehow, to be so carefree when there was a war on. Other young wives were putting on brave faces as their husbands donned their uniforms, and counting the hours until they returned. Her over-riding emotion as Hugo left was relief. The only alloy was the slight dragging of guilt that she should be so glad.

When she reached the store, she paused as always to take in the effect of the window displays. It had taken a while for her team to catch up with the new mood of the nation. Luxury, style and the pursuit of pleasure had been the order of the day amongst the upper classes, and looking as if you had achieved those things the goal of those lower on the social ladder. Packards had been adept at supplying everything needed to support those aspirations, and Amelie's window displays were a distillation of what the store had to offer. Now it all seemed a trifle hollow and tasteless. The main windows had been dismantled and rearranged with serviceable fabrics, camp beds, trunks, plain bedding and suchlike, all decorated with bunting and Union Jacks. It had been difficult to find appropriate items. Supplying the Services and the outer reaches of the Empire had always been the domain of the Army and Navy Stores. Now, after nearly four weeks of assessing what a nation at war wanted to buy, Amelie was ready to give them all an overhaul.

The trouble was, a nation at war was not buying a great deal. Practical goods, anything that might be used to equip a hospital, things that a man might take on campaign, these were all in demand. But as Amelie went through the revolving doors it was all too obvious that today was going to be like the rest of August and people were only coming in to buy necessities. Packards had

116

plenty of necessities to offer, but it had always been the luxuries that provided the profits. The store was very thin on customers.

Instead of going through the departments to view the depressing sight of shopmen and girls standing idle or engaged in needless tidying, Amelie went straight up to the fifth floor. Mr Mason, the director of Staffing, had asked her if she would spare him some time, and she had a very good idea what he was worried about. There was to be an emergency board meeting in two days' time on the levels of staffing within the store. Alliances were hastily being formed. Amelie marched along the corridor, eager to begin. If there was to be a battle, she was more than ready for it.

Mr Mason ushered her into his office and fussed around ordering coffee. A meticulous man in late middle age with a stoop to his shoulders, he always appeared to be slightly nervous of Amelie. Not without reason, as she and Edward had conducted many arguments over staff, with Mr Mason in the unfortunate position of being shot at from both sides. Before they got down to business, the latest developments of the war were discussed and the fate of Belgium sighed over.

'My dear wife and I enjoyed a holiday in Ostend the year before last. A very pleasant place, and such nice people. Very obliging. So sad to think that it might soon be occupied by German troops.'

'Very sad, Mr Mason. Now, what was it that you wanted to see me about?'

Reluctantly, the Staffing Director turned to the matter in hand.

'You must have noticed, Mrs Rutherford, that things have been very quiet since war was declared.'

'It would be hard not to notice it, Mr Mason.'

'Indeed. And you will of course have been informed of the emergency board meeting.'

117

Amelie decided to help him along.

'Of course. I suppose you have been asked to prepare a plan to reduce the number of our staff?'

Mr Mason took off his spectacles and began to polish the lenses with his handkerchief.

'Mr Packard has asked me to detail the number of staff in each department, and the number actually needed at present levels of trade.' He sighed, put on his spectacles and pushed some lists across the desk to Amelie. 'If I am perfectly honest, Mrs Rutherford, even allowing for those who have already answered the call to arms, I could turn away at least a third of these people. Even more in some departments. Ladies' Outerwear is a disaster. I know it is always quiet after the Season and while people are away on holiday, but this is unprecedented. The ladies are just not buying. They have weightier matters on their minds. So you see, Mrs Rutherford, I am going to find it very hard to justify keeping everyone on.'

'Mm.' Amelie frowned over the numbers. She hated the idea of putting so many loyal people out of work. Many of them were breadwinners, a lot of the young girls were supporting themselves and sending money home to help out their large families, and with other shops as well as manufacturers turning off workers, they would find it hard to secure new jobs.

'On the face of it, yes,' she agreed. 'But is this situation going to last forever? Everyone seems to be saying that it will all be over by Christmas, and then people will be buying more to make up for lost time and we shall have lost all those trained people. Tell me, how long do you think it takes to fully train a shopman or girl up to Packards standards?'

'Oh, well, it depends on individual aptitude, of course, but at least a year, I should say.'

'A whole year, and therefore a large investment, considering that time is money?'

'Yes.' Mr Mason looked at her, a tentative smile twitching at the corners of his mouth as the idea took root. 'Yes, a large investment. Too large to simply dismiss.'

'For other shops to snap up.'

'Indeed,' the director's face was becoming visibly brighter.

'And then there are people leaving anyway. More young men will be volunteering, I would imagine, and there are people leaving all the time under normal circumstances. If you allow them to go and don't replace them, that must make a fair number of reductions, surely?'

'Oh yes, there are always members of staff retiring, and young women leaving to get married, and those who leave for no specific reason. There is always a turnover.'

'Right. So if you work out how many we shall lose without any dismissals, and then emphasise just how valuable our staff are, I shall try to convince everyone that it is worth keeping them on till the war is over.'

Amelie sat back, clear now about the plan of action. It would take some doing, but they could beat Edward on this one. Mr Mason, however, had thought on. Anxiety crept back into his voice.

'But what if it isn't over by Christmas? Lord Kitchener does not seem to be of that opinion.'

A war that lasted for a year, or two years? Amelie tried to take it in. She thought of all the young men who had gone already, Hugo and his contemporaries, all the ordinary shopmen and clerks and labourers whom she had seen queuing outside the recruiting offices. If they all continued to go at that rate, there would be none left at the end of two years. A cold hand of dread slid over her. No, that couldn't happen. It was unimaginable. But in France, all the men between the ages of twenty-one and forty-eight had already been mobilised. She had read about it in the papers. Great processions of men had gathered at the mustering points and been taken off by train to join their regiments, all within days of war being declared. Who was doing their jobs? Somebody must be, or everyday life would just grind to a halt. It had to be the older men, and the women.

'In that case, it is essential that we hold on to the girls. If more and more of the men go, then eventually we shall be left with only the girls staffing the store.'

And who would be running it? Nearly all the floor-walkers and buyers were men in their forties and fifties, so most of them would still be there, but possibly not all. With a skip of excitement, she saw a chance to push through one of her dearest schemes: the employment of women buyers for goods that were specifically female, like Ladies' Underwear, Millinery and Baby Linens. There were plenty of capable women in the store, spinsters in their thirties and forties, who could take over the work. Her mind ran on, calculating how long it would take to identify and train them. Alexander Eden was already doing some of the buying in Stationery, and he had started from scratch, so women who had been working for years would be able to learn all the more quickly.

She realised that Mr Mason was speaking.

'. . . very good case, on the face of it. But of course we shall have to convince the rest of the Board.'

'Yes, that's the rub,' Amelie agreed.

The Finance Director would side with Edward, not only because the figures would undoubtedly point to dismissing the surplus staff, but also because the two of them were hand in glove. She could probably get Aimes, the Merchandising Director, on her side, since he owed her some favours from past battles. The Chairman, elected by the board after a hugely acrimonious round of infighting, was Sir Richard Forbes of Forbes Bank.

She was not sure about him, but she thought she could appeal to him on patriotic as well as business grounds. The weak point was actually Mr Mason himself.

'We could carry it if we stand firm,' she said to him.

'Of course, of course,' the director agreed. But his eyes slid away from Amelie's. They both knew that when Edward got going, Mr Mason was apt to back down. The only way to counteract Edward at his most intimidating was to heap pressure in the other direction.

'I'm going to go and speak to Mr Aimes now, so we shall both be relying on you to stick with us. It will only take one of us to give way and the case will collapse,' she told him.

'Oh yes, yes, I do understand that.'

'Then you'll have the unpleasant task of dismissing scores of loyal Packards people and condemning them to the direst poverty. It's not a deed that I should like to have on my conscience.'

'Nor I, Mrs Rutherford.'

Mr Mason looked quite pale. There were times when Amelie wondered if she was becoming like her brother, threatening people in order to make them do what she wanted. But Mr Mason had asked for her help in the first place. She gave him a friendly smile.

'Don't worry, Mr Mason. We have right on our side here, as well as commercial sense. We'll win through, I know it. It's just a question of sticking to our beliefs.'

'Yes. Thank you, Mrs Rutherford.'

'Thank you, Mr Mason. I'm very glad you told me about this.'

Half an hour later, she had the Merchandising Director in her pocket. She sat in her office and considered ways of getting at the Chairman. If she were a man, it would be easy. She could buttonhole him at his club. Normally, she relied on dinner parties to do carefully disguised pieces of lobbying, but time was too short in

this case. The board meeting was tomorrow. Then she
remembered his wife. She picked up the telephone and
asked to speak to Lady Forbes, only to be told that she
was attending a committee meeting for the setting up of
a hospital for wounded soldiers.

'I see. Would you tell Lady Forbes – no, on second
thoughts, I'll write. Just inform Lady Forbes that I telephoned.'

Amelie picked up pen and paper and wrote a friendly
note, offering the services of herself personally and the
Packards organisation in any capacity that Lady Forbes
might find useful, together with a large cheque towards
the hospital. She gave it to her secretary with instructions to have it delivered through the Packards system,
since the post was already less speedy than it used to be.
She then sat back with a satisfied smile. Lady Forbes
had her husband's ear; she rather approved of Amelie
and disliked both Edward and Sylvia. It could just swing
the vote. She had done as much as she could.

So she was in a good mood when Edward sailed into
her office.

'Ah, Mel, I'm glad I caught you. You're looking well.'

'Thank you, Edward, I'm feeling well.'

'Not missing old Hugo too much, then?'

'It's the duty of all we wives who are left behind to
keep going with a cheerful face.'

Her brother shot her an openly sceptical look.

'No more little Rutherfords on the way, then?'

'That's a very indelicate question, Edward.'

Edward smiled and dropped the subject.

'You'll be here tomorrow for the board meeting, I
take it? A mere formality, of course, but we must have
board approval for sweeping changes.'

'Of course,' Amelie agreed smoothly, thinking of the
nasty shock he was going to receive.

'Good. Now, Mel, to family matters. We ought to be

thinking about what to do next about the By-blow.'

There were other names which he used for Alexander Eden, but not in front of her.

'Well, he's certainly not going to oblige us by going away or by being totally incompetent. He's actually doing a good job in Stationery,' Amelie said. 'I've watched him myself, and he's very good with customers, and I had a word with the buyer the other day and he said that Eden was learning extremely fast.'

'Yes, well, I had hoped that a spell in Stationery would do the trick, but it hasn't happened, so I think the time has come to move him on. What do you think is the most boring department? Send him there and he might go and volunteer, seeing as your Hugo has failed to inspire him on that point.'

Amelie ignored this and applied herself to the question.

'Furniture's practically dead at the moment and so is Carpets. And China and Glassware.'

'Household Linens?'

None of the departments had ever struck Amelie as being downright boring, but even she had to admit that some were more intrinsically interesting than others. Piles of white sheets and pillowcases, towels and table-cloths were not very fascinating, especially to a young man.

'Good idea,' she said. After all, it paid to agree with Edward sometimes.

'We'll do that, then.' Edward sat forward. 'You don't think anyone knows, do you?'

'Beyond the Board? There's been the odd rumour, Edward. There's bound to be. He does look like Grandfather.'

'Damn. Good thing we made it clear that he was to keep quiet about it. I think we had better have a recruitment campaign within the store to send men to the New

Army. It is our patriotic duty, after all.'

'Very laudable,' Amelie agreed, mentally adding this to her list of reasons for not sacking people. She wondered if he included himself. She knew she could do the managing director's job just as well as he could, if not a good deal better. But perhaps that was too much to hope for. Edward always put himself first; he could not be expected to change now, even at a time of national crisis.

'Good. I'll bring that up at the next regular board meeting. Well, thank you, Mel. I think this has been a very useful talk.'

Amelie let him leave thinking he had carried everything his own way. It made the thought of beating him at the emergency meeting tomorrow all the sweeter.

The conversation lurked in the back of her mind as she went through all the routine work waiting for her. By the time she had finished, it struck her as it had done before that on the subject of Alexander Eden, she and Edward were indeed in agreement. He had to go. It had taken a threat to both of them to make them pull together.

She made her way home via Household Linens. Yes, she decided, it was a good place to put Alexander Eden. It was one of the busier departments at the moment, but it was hardly exciting. She watched as a young shopgirl dealt patiently with a difficult customer, laying out all the qualities of bedsheets and explaining each one, going over it all several times, taking some very rude and high-handed remarks and finally managing to sell half a dozen of the most expensive ones. She asked the floor-walker who the girl was.

'That's Miss Hollis. Is there a problem, Mrs Rutherford?'

'No, quite the opposite. She seems very capable.'

Hollis. The name was familiar, and painful in some

way, something to do with her grandfather . . .

'She is, Mrs Rutherford. But then she did come with Sir Thomas's personal recommendation.'

Of course, it was nothing to do with the girl herself, just that she came from Tatwell and had started just after her grandfather died. It would be worth keeping an eye on her. She might be just the sort of person who would be able to take greater responsibility if the worst happened, and all the men were called to go to war. All the men – no, that surely couldn't happen. But Edward might be right in thinking that Alexander Eden would volunteer.

Amelie made her way down to Stationery. It was not until she arrived there and saw her rival talking to the very striking dark shopgirl behind the writing paper counter that something else that Edward had said struck her. Was this what he had meant by a spell in Stationery doing the trick? Amelie looked at the two of them. Assistants were not supposed to gossip, let alone flirt. They were there to work. But the department was quiet and Alec was ostensibly working. He had a list and a pencil in his hands. It was the way they were talking that gave it away. Alec was obviously keen and the girl was playing hard to get. All Amelie's habitual disgust at her brother's way of doing things rose and choked her. He had been hoping that Alec would strike up a friendship with the girl. He might even have looked all through the departments weighing up the most likely candidate, then deliberately sent Alec there. Then when he could prove something was going on, he would invoke the rule that stated that men of the family must leave the shop-girls alone, and have Alec thrown out. Alec, she was almost one hundred percent sure, had not been informed of this particular embargo, as he was not being acknowledged as one of the family. Simple, neat and horrible. Everything that she disliked about her brother surged into her mind. His contempt of people. The way he enjoyed frightening those in his power into obedience. She felt ashamed to be associated with this tawdry way of getting rid of her rival. As usual, Edward had behaved despicably. She was not going to let him get away with it. She stepped forward.

'Might I have a word with you, Mr Eden?'

Briefly, she explained the situation.

'It was one of Sir Thomas's strictest rules,' she added.

Alexander Eden nodded.

'I see. And this applies to me even though I have to keep my parentage secret?'

'Yes.'

'And also though I'm not able to use my position to take advantage of any of our shopgirls, since I have no power over them at all?'

It really was most unfair. Amelie could see that clearly, but she could not admit it, for Edward would lose no time in using it.

'Rules are rules, Mr Eden.'

'It seems to me that I'm getting the worst of both worlds.'

As always when she dealt with him, his voice was well controlled, but anger glinted in his eyes.

'That's the price to be paid for being part of Packards,' Amelie told him.

'Oh, I'm part of Packards, Mrs Rutherford. I'm glad that you realise that I am also part of the family. I must thank you for letting me know how things stand.'

'I thought it only fair,' Amelie said.

All the way home, she thought over what had happened, still not quite believing her own total change of heart. Old habits were hard to break, she decided. She was so used to opposing Edward that she could not stay solid with him even over this threat to both of them. By the time she reached the front door of her house, she was even beginning to wonder whether working with Alexander Eden might be better than working against him. If he did become a force to be reckoned with, it was far better to have him as an ally than as an enemy. Far better certainly than having Edward as an ally.

With a sense of having made the right decision, she went to play with her children.

11

'It's going to be a funny Christmas, isn't it?' Ruby said, as she and May hurried towards the store.

'Yes. The village won't seem the same at all. Jim, my young man as was, won't be there. He volunteered almost straight away, along with some of the boys from Home Farm and the estate. And now my mum says my brother Silas is talking about going. I'm going to write to him specially and tell him how brave I think he is. I always used to think he was dull, but now I've had to think again.'

Ruby wasn't really listening.

'I hate it with the lights all dim. The West End isn't fun any more.'

'It's the war,' May said.

'I know it's the war. They said it was all going to be over by Christmas, but it doesn't look much like it to me.'

She glared at the poster of Lord Kitchener, his stern face staring straight ahead, his finger pointing. Your Country Needs You.

'I hope Mr Lambert won't go,' she said.

It was ground they had covered many an evening as they huddled up in bed, but it was reassuring to go over it again.

'I think he ought to. They all ought to, all the men, then those wicked Germans would be stopped. Look what happened to those poor people in Hartlepool and Scarborough. Seven hundred casualties! Just ordinary people in their homes. It's terrible.'

Ruby looked at her in amazement. This was not the answer she was expecting. She waved it aside.

'But just think how awful it'd be if he went now, just when I might be getting somewhere.'

'You shouldn't be thinking of that at a time like this,' May said.

Ruby was not used to being lectured by May.

'I know,' she conceded, 'but I can't help it. You know that, Maisie. I'd just die if he went.'

May gave a small sigh.

'Do you think he really likes you?' she asked.

Happy now that her friend was playing the required part again, Ruby spoke with confidence.

'Oh yes. I can tell.'

She was sure of that. She could see it in his eyes, in the slight flush that spread up his neck as he spoke to her. What she could not make out was why he did not make a move. She had never had any trouble in the past attracting men once she let them know she was interested.

'Trouble is, he's a buyer and you're only a shopgirl.'

That had to be the reason, but it infuriated Ruby.

'He was only a shopman once, and not so long ago, either,' she said.

'That's right,' her loyal accomplice agreed.

'Perhaps something will happen today,' Ruby said. After all, who knew what one more morning might bring?

Inside the store, everyone was still discussing the shocking shelling of the north-eastern seaside towns. No one had expected the war to actually reach English soil.

Ruby put in the odd remark, but her heart was not in it. Hartlepool was a long way away. She wasn't even sure where it was. She hurried down to Stationery, eager as always to be first at her post.

To her delight, Mr Lambert was already there.

'Good morning, Miss Goss. Glad to see you so keen to start.'

'Thank you, Mr Lambert.'

'Dreadful, this news from the north.'

It was the first time he had ventured a remark that was not to do with work. Ruby seized her chance.

'It is indeed, Mr Lambert. They say there was a poor girl killed as she scrubbed her doorstep.

'One reads of these awful atrocities happening in Belgium, and now our own defenceless women and children are being killed.

'I don't know what the world's coming to,' Ruby said. 'That's why I say you should enjoy yourself while you can. Who knows what might happen tomorrow?'

Mr Lambert seemed very struck by this remark. For fully a minute he stood staring into space. Then he looked at Ruby again.

'I believe you are right, Miss Goss. Yes . . .'

Ruby waited, holding her breath.

'After all, you only live once, don't you?' she said.

There were voices and footsteps coming through from Ladies' Gloves. Ruby mentally cursed. Why couldn't they have left it another five minutes?

But Mr Lambert was not put off. He spoke with quiet urgency.

'Miss Goss – would you care to come out to supper with me one evening?'

Triumph coursed through Ruby. Just in time, she stopped herself from saying yes. She feigned amazement.

'Oh, Mr Lambert, I never thought–'

She saw the confusion in his face. He might be the most successful buyer in the store, but he did not know how to judge her reactions. She picked up her rag and polish and started rubbing the counter just as the rest of the Stationery staff came in. Out of the corner of her eye, she watched Mr Lambert as he greeted the floor-walker. It was essential to act as if nothing had happened, at least until she was completely sure of him. The store existed on gossip, and she did not want to be laughed at as having overreached herself.

The day passed in an agony of suspense. Mr Lambert was closeted with manufacturers' salesmen for much of the time and said nothing more to her at all, not even in the way of instructions. Ruby wondered if she should have seized her chance while she had it, but the gambler in her knew that that was not the way to achieve the high stakes. She poured it all out to May that night, and made sure that she was first in the department again in the morning.

Mr Lambert was there before her. He stopped her before she even got as far as her counter.

'Miss Goss – have you had time to think over my invitation?'

Ruby put on a great show of reluctance.

'We-el . . .'

Mr Lambert smiled.

'Just remember, Miss Goss, you only live once.'

She just had to smile back.

'Why not?' she agreed, and rapidly found herself also agreeing to time and meeting place.

'Of course, you understand that this must be just between ourselves. I wouldn't want the whole store knowing.'

'Oh of course,' Ruby said. Not yet, anyway. Not until she had something to really boast about.

But it was extraordinarily hard to carry on as normal

all the way till Saturday. She only managed it by chewing it all over with May every night.

Saturday evening found her on the bus, heading for Charing Cross. There had been a row before she went out. Her father had wanted to know why she was not being called for at home. It had only made her all the more determined to go out, but now that she was sitting all by herself trundling through the dimmed streets of London, she had to admit that all of her previous men friends, even the roughest and readiest of them, had called for her and escorted her home, and that she really did not know anything about Mr Lambert at all. But that only made him all the more fascinating.

He was there at the bus stop as she got off, tall and distinguished in a dark coat and a bowler hat. Ruby felt a surge of excitement. He was several cuts above anyone she had ever been out with before. She was a proud woman as she took his arm and they walked along the Strand.

'There's a nice little chophouse just along here that I thought you might like. Are you feeling hungry?' he asked.

Ruby found that she was.

The chophouse was warm and welcoming after the chill December streets. Red papered walls and a roaring fire gave an immediate impression of cosiness, which was added to by the high-backed oak seats like church pews that enclosed each table. A waiter took their coats and another one showed them to their table. Ruby was impressed. Nobody had ever taken her to a place like this before. She looked about wide-eyed, forgetting for once to act.

'It's nice here, isn't it?' she said.

Mr Lambert smiled.

'I'm glad you like it. I think you'll find the food's good, too.'

She was handed a red-tasselled menu. The prices made her mouth drop open. She looked across at Mr Lambert, but he seemed undisturbed. Her admiration of him climbed even higher. She watched him as he studied the menu. He really was very handsome. The firm jaw and the neat little clipped moustache gave him a very distinguished air, and yet he had deliciously long dark eyelashes, longer even than hers. A small quake of desire shivered through her.

'The steak and kidney pies are excellent here,' Mr Lambert said.

Ruby turned her attention back to the food. She was not having steak and kidney pie. She had those at home and they were full of gristle with tooth-breaking pastry. She read down the list of dishes. Roast chicken. Now that was more like it. They only ever had chicken at Christmas.

'And what would you like to drink?' Mr Lambert asked.

Ruby hesitated. She really fancied a half of mild, but she was not sure whether that was ladylike enough. Was this the sort of place where you drank gin?

'Some wine, perhaps? White, to go with your chicken?' Mr Lambert suggested.

'Oh – yes – that'd be lovely,' Ruby agreed.

Wine! This really was turning out to be an evening to remember.

'I told my dad we'd be going somewhere ever so respectable. He didn't want me to come out at all this evening. It was a good thing my friend May stuck up for you. She said you were a proper gentleman,' she told him.

'Good for May. Is your father very strict?'

A tyrant of a father was always a good excuse to have in reserve, in case an evening turned out to be a disaster. But she did not want this one cut short.

'Dad? No, not usually, but he likes to know where I'm going and who I'm with and when I'm going to be back.'

'And the rest of your family? You've got brothers and sisters?'

Ruby sipped her wine and chattered about her family. The first glass slipped down very easily. She decided she liked wine. By the time the waiter arrived, she was well into her stride, telling Mr Lambert about the dreadful things her brothers did to each other. Enormous steaming plates of food were placed in front of them. Ruby's mouth watered. There was a whole leg, a succulent pile of breast, great spoonfuls of forcemeat and chestnut stuffing, roast potatoes, carrots, sprouts . . . and all swimming in fragrant gravy. She looked at Mr Lambert's plate. The steak and kidney pie looked a completely different dish to the one her mother served up, the meat dark and rich, the pie crust light as a feather.

'Tuck in,' he said, picking up his knife and fork.

Ruby tucked in with a will. She had never tasted such delicious food. Even the sprouts were tasty, a far cry from the soggy balls of watery greenstuff she was used to. She ate up every scrap, mashing the potatoes into the gravy to collect the last drops. When she looked up, she realised that Mr Lambert was looking at her with some amusement.

'What's the matter?' she snapped.

Had her hair slipped down, or her blouse come undone?

'Nothing, nothing at all,' he assured her. 'It's nice to see a girl with a good appetite.'

Hot already from the wine and the dinner, Ruby flushed scarlet.

'What's wrong with that, then?'

'Nothing, really. I meant it – it's lovely to see someone enjoying what she's eating instead of just pushing it round her plate.'

He reached across and refilled her wine glass. Ruby took a couple of longish sips and calmed down. She was beginning to get quite woozy and cross-eyed.

'How long has your friend May been lodging with your family?' he asked.

Ruby thought.

'Heavens – over a year now. She's like another sister to me. Well, we're closer than sisters really. I don't fight with her like I do with them. We have such laughs.'

She rambled happily on, encouraged by his attention. He watched her all the time, nodding, laughing when she did, putting in the odd remark. She did not at first notice that the waiter had come back with the menu.

'Now don't let me down. I know you can do justice to one of these puddings,' Mr Lambert said.

She had thought she was full up till she looked at what was available. Apple pie, treacle tart, queen of puddings, steamed sponge . . . she plumped for the sponge. It arrived swimming in perfect custard, neither runny nor solid nor lumpy. Her natural confidence renewed now, she attacked it with gusto. When she finally put down her spoon, she was wishing she had put on her old, saggy corset.

'That was scer-umptious!' she declared, forgetting to act the lady.

Mr Lambert laughed.

'Wasn't it? I can't remember enjoying anything so much for a long time.'

Even through her tipsy haze, Ruby recognised a compliment when she heard one.

'I thought you said you'd been here before?'

'I have, and the food is always good, but the company makes the difference.'

Ruby's insides gave a shiver of triumph. It was working. She gave a flirtatious smile.

'Ooh – get away! I bet you say that to all the girls.'

'No, not at all. I've never brought a girl here before. You're the first.'

'Oh, come on, you don't expect me to believe that, do you?'

'It's true. I come here on business or with male friends. But I've always wanted to bring a lady.'

She wanted to push him into saying that he had been waiting until he could take her, but they were interrupted once more, very gently, by the waiter.

'Would you like some brandy and coffee?' Mr Lambert asked.

Ruby had only had coffee a few times, and she was not impressed by it. A nasty, bitter taste.

'I'd rather have tea,' she said.

'Tea it shall be, then. But you'll have a cognac with it, I hope?'

Cognac? What was he talking about now?

'No, a brandy, please.'

Neither Mr Lambert nor the waiter let slip the faintest twitch of amusement at her gaffe. When the glasses of amber spirit arrived, it did occur to her vaguely that her brandy looked exactly the same as his cognac, but at that moment he began asking her about what she had done before joining Packards, and she launched into another rambling tale of her life.

She was so engrossed with reminiscing, and entranced by his absolute attention, that she hardly noticed the cheerful groups flooding into the chophouse. But Mr Lambert did. He looked quite startled.

'Good heavens, people are coming out of the theatres. It must be much later than I thought. The time's gone so quickly. I suppose I had better get you home.'

And in no time at all, the bill was paid and they were

out of the blissful warmth and into the chill dimness of wartime London. Ruby felt rather dazed. It was so sudden. It had all been going so wonderfully, and now it was nearly over. They walked to her bus stop.

'I feel a real cad not taking you home, but I have to get back,' Mr Lambert said.

'Get back?' Ruby repeated.

Out in the fresh air, her head was clearing a little. Why did a grown man, one who ordered meals and wine without turning a hair at a posh place like that, have to get back on a Saturday night?

'It's – er – it's my mother. She's an invalid, and she's taken rather a turn for the worse recently. I shouldn't really have come out at all tonight, but I didn't want to lose this chance of seeing you.'

So that was it. Ruby was satisfied.

'Oh, I see. Well, in that case you'd better not hang about here.'

'Oh no, I couldn't possibly leave you alone at this time of night. I'll wait to see you on to your bus.' He laid a hand over hers as she held his arm. 'Miss Goss, I've very much enjoyed this evening. Is there any chance that we might do this again?'

Oh yes, please.

'We-ell, I don't know . . .' Ruby prevaricated.

'Of course, I know that a girl like you must have lots of admirers, but would you possibly be free again next Saturday?'

Next Saturday? Oh yes, and all the days in between.

'I don't know. I might be. I'll have to see.'

'Will you let me know? Soon?'

'Like I said, I'll have to see.'

The bus came rumbling along the road.

'Miss Goss,' there was an urgency in his voice now. 'I would hate it if you were the object of gossip at the store. I know what people are like there. We'll keep this as our secret, shall we? We can have a little joke all of our own, knowing that they don't know.'

That appealed to Ruby. She smiled.

'Yes. That'd be fun.'

The bus stopped and the queue pressed forward. Mr Lambert handed her on.

'Goodnight. Take care. Thank you!' he called.

She made herself go inside without looking back. But as she sat down, her heart was singing. The whole evening had been like a dream. He was every bit as wonderful as she had thought. Best of all, he wanted to see her again. She gave a great sigh. She was in love. And if he wasn't yet, then he very soon would be.

12

'. . . and then he said he'd never met anyone like me before! Well! It's not the first time I've had that said to me, mind you, but when he said it – you know what I mean?'

'Mm? Oh yes,' May said.

It was really cold in her bedroom now. She and Ruby no longer sat up, even with the eiderdown round them, but snuggled right down with only the tops of their heads showing above the covers. With both of them in bed, it got nice and cosy.

'And I said, "Well, there's not many around like me," and he said, "I don't think there's anyone around like you. You're unique." What d'you think that means? Unique?'

'It's – er – like there's only one of them,' May said.

'Really? Unique! I like that. Unique. Well, anyone . . .'

May drifted off on her own train of thought. It was odd how she felt so at home here, as if she had been here all her life, and when she went to her real home, she felt strange and distant, even though they were her own family that she had grown up with. Christmas had not been a success. Just as she had predicted the village was different, subdued with a number of the young men away, and on top of that she found she no longer had so much in common with her old friends. They could still talk about things that had happened when they were at school, but their current lives were so different that there was little meeting ground. All they wanted to discuss was the latest gossip from the big house or their sweethearts. May had been forced to embroider a little on this point in order to keep up. She had elevated Will Foster to the status of a proper admirer and hinted at an interest from Mr Eden, but her old friends were not really interested since they had never met them. She had been glad to come back to the Gosses' and to work. Packards meant more to her now than the village.

'And to think that I nearly let myself get interested in that Mr Eden,' Ruby was saying.

May was instantly attentive.

'Mr Eden?'

'Yes, you remember. I was quite keen on him when he first came to Stationery. And he liked me, oh yes, that was plain to see. I had to keep giving him the brush-off. Well, I'm really glad I did now. Funny he should go to your department after mine, isn't it? I mean, funny that he should be in our two out of all the store, and funny he should have been moved so quickly.'

'Mm.'

May lay in the dark, frowning. Finally, she came out with the question that nagged at her continually these days.

'Do you think it's true, what they say?'

'About what?'

'About Mr Eden. That – that he's related to Sir Thomas. That he might be his – his natural son.'

She held her breath. She could hardly bear to hear the answer. If it was yes, then she would just die.

'Oh, I don't think so.'

140

Ruby sounded so authoritative that May let out her breath again in a huge sigh of relief.

'Really? Are you sure?'

It did not occur to her that her friend could not possibly let herself believe that she had let a member of The Family slip through her fingers.

'Yes. That's just gossip. After all, if he was, he wouldn't be keeping quiet about it, would he? But if you really want to know, I could ask Victor about it.'

There was a special proprietary note in her voice as she said his Christian name, but May did not pick it up. She was far too tied up with her own concerns.

'Yes, you're right. He'd tell everyone about it, wouldn't he? It must just be a co-whatsit. After all, some people do look like other people, don't they, without being related to them at all?'

'Anyway, why is it so important?' Ruby was suddenly alert, like a hound on the scent. 'Are you getting sweet on him?'

May hesitated.

'You are! I know it! Well, I must say he's a much better choice than that Will Foster. Much better. He's really quite handsome. Not as handsome as Victor, but nice. He'd be a very good catch, too. Anyone can see that he's going to be someone important in the store. He might even get to be a buyer, like Victor. How long have you liked him? You've kept very quiet about it.'

She sounded quite accusing. May wanted to point out that it was difficult to get a word in edgeways these days, since Ruby talked endlessly about her Victor, and where they had been and how wonderful he thought she was and how he cared so much about her that she had to keep it all a secret as he did not want anyone saying the least unkind thing about her behind her back.

'I didn't think he liked me,' she said, which was certainly the truth.

'And now you do? Why? What has he said? Come along, tell me all about it,' Ruby commanded.

With encouragement like that, May could do no less than pour out her heart.

'Oh Ruby,' she sighed, 'he's so handsome, and so clever, and so – well, it's like he's going somewhere, you know? You just know he's going to be in charge of something one day soon.'

Since Alec Eden had come to Household Linens, Will Foster had seemed very dull and ordinary.

'And then this morning, he came and asked me if I'd tell him all about the different qualities of sheets, because he could see I knew all about them,' she said.

It had been a wonderful morning. She had had him practically to herself for nearly two hours. At the end of it, he had thanked her and said he had learned a lot.

Beside her, Ruby nodded in the dark and advised her in detail as to how to proceed next.

Heartened by Ruby's interest, May felt a lot more confident when she went into work the next morning. It all sounded so easy when Ruby talked about what to do. You just looked at a man the right way and said the right things and they all came flocking round you. May kept a covert eye on Mr Eden as she swept and polished ready for the day's business. Unfortunately, he was on Table Linen, over the other side of the department from her counter in Bed Linen, whereas Will Foster was her neighbour, only a counter away in Towels. If only it were the other way round. But as Ruby had said, there are ways round anything. Her polish was nearly finished up. Determinedly ignoring Will, who would have been only too pleased to let her have a bit of his, she walked across the department. It seemed a very long way.

'Oh, Mr Eden–'

To her oversensitive ears, she sounded ridiculously squeaky and unnatural. Mr Eden smiled at her.

'Miss Hollis. What can I do for you?'

She felt quite weak at the knees. He had such a lovely voice, quite unlike Will Foster's or even the floor-walker's.

'Oh Mr Eden, can you help me out? I've no polish left at all and my counter's only part done.'

She had tried to do it the way Ruby would, looking up at him and making her eyes all big and putting a hidden suggestion into the mundane words. Somehow, it didn't come out the same. She sounded silly. She felt herself getting hot with embarrassment.

He handed her his.

'There you are. You can keep it if you like.'

A sinking sense of failure dragged at her. That wasn't how it was supposed to go. He was supposed to say something joking and flirtatious, and then she would say something else, and even though the whole conversation was about polish, it would really be about them. As it was, he hadn't even asked her to return it, giving her another chance.

'Oh, er, thank you,' she mumbled. Then, as a last desperate effort, 'I'll bring it back when I've finished.'

'There's no need. I can always get some more.'

Friendly, polite and dismissive.

'Er, right, thank you.'

May walked back to her place, rejected.

Alec watched her go out of the corner of his eye. She was a nice girl, May Hollis, but he wasn't the least bit tempted by her transparent move. Sweet, innocent little things like her were fine if you were thinking of getting married. She probably had all the qualities a man might ask for in a wife, added to which she was quite pretty in a countrified sort of way. But Alec was very far from wanting to settle down, and when he did, it was not going to be with one of the shopgirls. He had his future position to think of. In the meantime, the sort of girl he was looking for was very different from May Hollis. He wanted someone lively and amusing, someone who was out to enjoy herself and knew how to keep a man interested. Someone like Ruby Goss. He still had dreams about Ruby Goss, with her come-hither eyes and her tempting lips and her voluptuous body. But since the warning from Amelie Rutherford, he had abandoned his seige of her, and no longer looked at any of the shopgirls that way. It made him go quite cold to think how close to disaster he had come there. He had to admit that he was deeply indebted to Amelie for that hint, though he was sure she had not given it for entirely altruistic reasons. There had to be some purpose behind her throwing away a chance to get rid of him.

He turned his back on the despondent figure on the other side of the department and began tidying the already tidy piles of tablecloths and napkins. He was bored. Bored to the bone. The entire department was dull compared with Stationery, from the buyer to the merchandise. Try as he might, he could not develop any glimmer of enthusiasm for what he was selling. Writing paper in all its varieties he had found fascinating, along with pens and inkstands and letter racks and all the other hundred and one objects both useful and decorative that were sold in Stationery. Household Linens just did not have the same appeal. Even the customers were far less interesting than those on the ground floor. There was not the variety of people passing through. The whole atmosphere was worthy and useful, whereas down in Stationery it was lively and attractive. He no longer came in each day eager to start, wondering what would happen, what he would learn.

The electric bell sounded, signalling opening time. Alec sighed.

'Another exciting day,' he muttered.

'What's the matter?' one of the girls asked.

'Oh, nothing. Everything,' he said.

Edward hadn't had to do this. Neither had Amelie. He doubted whether either of them had ever spent so much as a day actually standing behind the counter. They just waltzed into jobs on the fifth floor.

'You can be sure your dear father had a very good reason for ordering things the way he did. You're learning the way he did, from the bottom up,' his mother was fond of telling him.

'But that was different. He was building his own business, not working in one controlled by people who are doing their utmost to keep me out of it,' he protested.

Despite everything, he still tried to get what he could out of his time in Household Linens. He wanted to find out as much as possible about how the department was run in the hope that he would soon be moved on. With this in mind, he went to speak with the buyer, an elderly man named Wagstaff.

'Mr Wagstaff, when I went down to Stores yesterday afternoon I found that we only have three dozen of the best quality double damask dinner napkins left, and when I checked the order book I found that the next consignment should have arrived last week. Would you like me to send them an urgent reminder?'

The buyer shot him a repressive look.

'Thank you, Mr Eden. I am well aware of the situation and a reminder has already been sent.'

In that case, as both Alec and the buyer knew, a note should have been made of it. The truth was that Mr Wagstaff was getting behindhand with the paperwork but would not admit it.

'Really? Oh well, that's all in hand then. Would you like me to check on the other stock, as it's so quiet in here at the moment?'

The buyer glared at him.

'Thank you, Mr Eden, but I don't think that will be

necessary.'

Alec groaned inwardly. Mr Wagstaff could hardly be more different from Lambert in Stationery. He seemed to see Alec as a threat, keeping him at arm's-length and only letting him do the occasional odd job about the place. The trouble was, as Alec had found out within a week of arriving at the department, that Mr Wagstaff was trying to cover up the fact that he was barely keeping up with the job. Alec changed tack.

'I really would be very grateful for the opportunity, Mr Wagstaff. If I could be allowed to try my hand at ordering, it would be very valuable experience. I have done it before in Stationery, but of course I would need your guidance as to what quantities are generally needed here.'

As if he couldn't find out for himself by looking back at previous years' figures, but he had learnt that flattery sometimes worked.

Reluctantly, Mr Wagstaff agreed.

'But under no circumstances must you do anything without asking me first.'

Alec feigned amazement.

'Of course not, Mr Wagstaff. I wouldn't dream of it. Thank you very much. I really do appreciate it.'

Which was perfectly true. He was always glad to snatch the opportunity to learn more about the store, and even gladder to escape another deadly day selling tablecloths. Taking out the pencil and notebook he always kept in his jacket pocket, he made his way down to the store rooms in the lower basement. He whistled as he ran down the service stairs. From his cursory look first thing this morning it was clear that there was plenty that needed doing. If only Mr Wagstaff would take him on a buying trip to Lancashire for the cottons or to Ireland for the linens, then he would really see how things were done. But he knew there was next to no

146

hope of that. The more useful he was, the more Mr Wagstaff resented his presence. It occurred to him that this could be used to his advantage. If the buyer felt threatened enough by his efficiency, he would try to get him transferred to another department. Anything would be better than dull old towels and pillowcases.

He spent the morning counting and making notes, then got out the past order books and looked for patterns in the sales. It didn't take long before he decided that things in Household Linens were done very much the same way from one year to the next. He wondered whether this was because nothing much came along in the way of new stock. There was not a great deal that could be done, after all, to the design of a sheet or a blanket. Only the bedspreads showed any variety of type and colour and pattern. It was quite different from Stationery, where there was always some clever innovation or original design coming on the market that had to be secured for Packards before any of the other stores got hold of it. That was all very well when everything went along much as it always had done. Mr Wagstaff just sent off the usual orders for the time of year. But now, with a war on, demands were different. Hard-wearing hospital quality single sheets were walking off the shelves quicker than they could fill them, while lace-edged pillowcases were sitting up there forgotten. Not that they could restock with them now anyway, as the supplies of Belgian and French lace had practically ceased.

As a reward to himself for his hard work, he took a roundabout route back up to Household Linens, walking through the store rather than going straight up the service stairs. The place was almost as busy as it had been a year ago. It had certainly recovered from the severe slump just after war was declared. Luxury goods, particularly Ladies' Fashions, were still doing badly, but most of the other departments were fairly full of customers. The most noticeable difference was the much higher proportion of shopgirls to shopmen behind the counters, and the number of uniformed men amongst the customers. Alec eyed them with a mixture of envy and guilt. They were not stuck providing finicky matrons with matching table linen. They were serving their country, protecting their womenfolk from the ravages of the enemy, doing a proper man's .job. And he ought to be with them, sharing in the hardship and the danger.

He had just come to this conclusion, as he did almost every day, when he met with Edward Amberley Packard. Edward usually tried to ignore him, so Alec made a point of greeting him. This time, Edward stopped. He looked at Alec as if struggling to recall who he was. Alec tried not to mind that Edward's superior height meant that he had to look up.

'Mr – er – Eden, is it not? You appear to be a long way from your department. How do you account for that?'

A question like that, delivered in Edward Packard's most quietly dangerous tone of voice, had been known to reduce the toughest of buyers to a jelly. But Alec had the cast-iron strength of his father's will behind him. He looked steadily back at Edward, refusing to be cowed.

'I am returning from Stores, Mr Packard, and I decided to see how trade was faring. It is difficult to assess matters from behind the counter in just one department. Things appear to be generally looking up, don't they?'

Edward chose not to answer this.

'If you are assigned to Household Linens, Mr Eden, then that is where you should be.'

'Of course, Mr Packard. I'm very happy to be there. I'm learning a vast amount about the store and how it functions.'

If he hoped to manipulate Edward into transferring him somewhere more interesting, he failed miserably.

'Indeed? Then you will be glad to stay there a good while longer. I must say, there has been a very disappointing reaction to our recruitment campaign from Household Linens. Fewer men have volunteered from there than from any other department.'

Alec was on the point of making excuses when inspiration struck him.

'Really? Perhaps we need someone from the top to set us a good example. Until then, as you pointed out, I must return to my department.'

He left, buoyed up with the knowledge of a point scored.

But it was a short-lived feeling. Back with his piles of towels, he was conscious again of Edward's power to keep him here kicking his heels for as long as he saw fit. One day, he thought, one day I shall get even with Edward Amberley Packard. But that day seemed a long way off.

13

'Well, Mr Mason, I think we can justly say that we have been proved absolutely right in the stand we took last September,' Amelie said.

The Staffing Director nodded, but he did not look any less harassed.

'Oh indeed yes, Mrs Rutherford. More than justified. The problem is now how to get staff, not how to lose them. Young girls of the right calibre simply do not seem to be applying to us any longer, and as for young men, well, I do not think we have had one application these last four months, despite the fact that the wages we are offering are considerably higher than they were this time last year.'

'This time last year we were not at war,' Amelie pointed out.

It all seemed a very long time ago now, peacetime, as if it were another age, and yet it was only six months since war was declared.

'Yes,' Mr Mason sighed.

'And we must be in a better position than those stores which turned off some of their staff at the start.'

Which was a point that she must slip into a conversation with Edward one of these days. He must be well aware of it himself, since he met all the other top store owners and directors at his club, but it would be very gratifying to get him to admit it.

'Oh yes, we must. But we are still in difficulties, since so many of the more experienced young shopmen have left.'

'Then we must fill the gaps with the more experienced shopgirls,' Amelie said. 'After all, Packards have a tradition of leading the way in employing females. Now we must let them take over the more responsible jobs. I am sure they are more than capable of doing so. Indeed, many of them are just waiting for the chance to show us what they can do.'

Mr Mason looked doubtful. It took a fair while for Amelie to convince him. She showed him the list she had drawn up of suitable candidates for promotion throughout the store, drawn from her observations while going about her work of display and advertising. Mr Mason, a traditionalist at heart, found it hard to conceive that the idea might work. He was of course in a difficult position to argue that the women could not manage the work as well as the men, since he was debating the case with a fellow director who was female. Amelie took every advantage of this and in the end he had to agree. He would try it in some of the departments and see how it went. Amelie was more than satisfied with this. She knew that she could rely on the girls to prove her right and lead the way for their sisters.

'I'm so glad we think alike in this matter,' she said.

Mr Mason still looked despondent.

'Of course, I still have to justify it to Mr Packard,' he said.

Amelie gave him a brilliant smile.

'Don't worry, Mr Mason. Remember, you shall have my full backing at the next board meeting.'

Somehow, this did not seem to reassure him. As she

made her way out of the store, Amelie had to feel sorry for the man. It was not easy to be piggy in the middle between herself and Edward. Looking at the shopgirls going about their work as she passed, she smiled. She had scored a victory for female labour today. On impulse, she took a cab to the Markhams' house. She had to tell Ida about it.

A footman opened the door. The mistress, he informed Amelie, was not at home, but the master had just returned. Did Madam wish to stay or would she leave her card?

'I'll stay,' Amelie decided. 'Kindly inform your master that I am here.'

And as she followed him up the stairs to the drawing room, she was aware of a fluttering excitement.

Clement came into the room almost as soon as she had sat down. He held out both hands to her and kissed her cheek. It was his normal greeting, as an old friend, but it left Amelie's face glowing.

'Amelie! What a very pleasant surprise. Ida's not at home, I'm afraid. She'll be so sorry to have missed you. How are you?'

The exchange of polite information gave Amelie a chance to catch her breath.

'I don't seem to have seen Ida for ages,' she said. 'I suppose she's very busy?'

Clement gave a rueful smile.

'I don't seem to have seen her for ages myself, and yes, she is very busy. I used to think her work for the WSPU kept her fully engaged, but now she's spending even more time in her new Government post setting up the proper working arrangements for women in industry. She says that quite apart from being a splendid contribution to the war effort, it will give women a chance to show that they really can do many of the same jobs as men, and do them just as well.'

152

'I thought that very same thing today. That was why I came to call,' Amelie said, and related the contents of her interview with the Staffing Director.

'Ida will be delighted. I'll tell her all about it when she comes in. If I can get a word in edgeways, that is.' He laughed, but Amelie thought she detected a slight reservation in his voice.

She smiled back.

'She was absolutely full of what she was doing last time I saw her. It does sound very interesting.'

'She's doing a wonderful job. She's so versatile. One day she's negotiating with industrialists or trades union leaders and the next she's addressing groups of factory girls.'

Clement's admiration for his wife was patently clear. It glowed from him. Amelie was swept with sadness. Hugo never appreciated her talents like that. When they first met he had been glad to find out that she was doing a responsible job, since it proved that she had brains to pass on to the next generation, but once they were married he resented the time she spent at the store. She had had to fight for every hour there. The only time he showed the approval that Clement so clearly felt for Ida was when she presented him with another perfect son.

'She's certainly splendid at persuading people,' she agreed.

'And all without appearing to bully them, too. She has them all eating out of her hand,' Clement said.

'Including you,' Amelie said, gently teasing to cover the pang of envy.

'She's a wonderful woman. I'm a very lucky man.'

And Ida was a very lucky woman. Amelie wondered if she realised just how lucky. Very few husbands were as enlightened as Clement. She looked at him as he sat at the opposite end of the sofa, so obviously still in love with his wife, so different from Hugo. Beneath the relaxed and tolerant exterior was a man who was determined both to make a success of his career and to make the difference to the lives of his constituents. Both men had an innate confidence, but where Hugo's was expressed in an obvious physical fitness, Clement had a quiet air of power. Amelie knew which she admired most.

'When is Hugo's next leave?' Clement asked, as if divining her thoughts.

'Next month.'

She just prayed that it would be while she had her period, as it had been last time. She had enjoyed a whole year now without being pregnant. It was wonderful, like being freed from prison, but she feared that she was not going to get away with it for much longer. Hugo was getting impatient.

'Army life suits him down to the ground, of course.'

'Oh yes, he loves it. I can't think why he didn't join up years ago. It's absolutely the life for him and in peacetime he would still have had plenty of time for all sporting pursuits. Even now, he seems to be playing a great deal of rugger, besides organising matches for the men. He says it's the ideal way to achieve both fitness and a team spirit. But he's only marking time, really. He's itching to get to the Front. I can't tell you how impatient he is.'

'You feel rather differently about that, of course.'

'Yes.'

They were both silent for a moment as she faced the unknown future. However far from perfect her marriage might be, she certainly did not want Hugo to be shipped to France. She had seen the trains arrive with the wounded, read the names of friends on the lists of those killed in action. The longer Hugo remained here in Britain, the better.

'How long is it going to last, Clem?' she asked.

He shook his head.

'I don't know, Melly. I don't think anyone does. But it isn't going to be over quickly. It's going to be a long haul, and I suspect it's going to be very hard on all of us.' He looked away, his face set. 'I must go, and soon. I shouldn't be sitting round here in London letting other men face danger for me.'

Fear clutched at Amelie, cold and swift.

'No! Not you, Clem!'

She realised he was looking at her strangely, and struggled to control her voice.

'I – I mean, you're in an essential occupation, surely? You're running the country.'

'I think I can safely leave that to the senior men, don't you? I'm one of the youngest in the House. I sit there discussing how to organise labour and increase the rate of recruitment and every day I feel more of a hypocrite and a coward. I shouldn't be talking about it and exhorting other men to go. There are plenty of men older than me to do that. I'm young and fit. I should be out there doing my bit.'

He was right, of course, and Amelie respected him for it. But it did not decrease her fear.

'Ida would miss you terribly,' she said.

Clement laughed.

'Ida would hardly notice I had gone.'

'Clem! That's not true.'

'I know, I know. But Ida knows we all have to make sacrifices. You have already. You're having to carry on without Hugo and you're doing it bravely. I'm sure Ida would be just as brave.'

'I'm sure she would,' Amelie agreed.

But the question that gripped her then and through a restless night was not how Ida would react, but how was she going to cope herself with the anxiety of Clement's going to war? As she lay sleepless in the wide bed, she

155

was shocked at the strength of her own reaction. Clement was her best friend's husband. However much she tried to reason that she was anxious for him as a friend, and on Ida's behalf, she knew in her heart that that was only part of the case. She had always been attracted to Clement. It was only now that she had been forced to acknowledge how much. One thing was very clear: neither Clement nor Ida must ever suspect.

Guilt spurred her into action. The next day she spent over an hour telephoning a string of places trying to contact Ida. Each person she spoke to said either that she had just left or that she was expected soon, and when pressed suggested a possible place where she might be contacted. Most of them offered to deliver a message, but Amelie could not rest until she had spoken to her friend herself. When she finally caught up with her, she insisted that they should meet, and refused to give up until Ida had agreed on an exact time and place. That done, she felt a little better.

Three days later, she was sitting in Packards' restaurant sipping a sherry and waiting for Ida to join her for luncheon. On the dot of one o'clock, Ida appeared in the doorway, scanned the room and waved. As always, Amelie was aware of an air of energy radiating from her, an irresistible force that was practically visible. Brown eyes bright, cheeks pink, her neat figure encased in a perfectly tailored dark green jacket and skirt, Ida made heads turn all the way across the room as she made her way to Amelie's table.

'Melly darling!'

They kissed and sat down, and a waitress was there immediately offering sherry. Ida drank it without appearing to notice what it was.

'This is such heaven, Mel. You can't imagine what a dreadful morning I've had. Those stuffy old men! They can't see past their own noses. You offer them a solution on a plate and they just make difficulties. And they're so patronising. I felt as if they had patted me on the head . . .'

She went into the details of her morning's meeting, acting out all the parts until Amelie was laughing out loud.

'But did you win them round in the end?' she asked, wiping away tears.

'I shall, don't you fret.'

She waved aside the proffered menu.

'Heavens, I don't know. You choose, Mel.'

Amelie selected vegetable consommé and Dover sole.

'You make me feel very dull,' she said. 'I should be out doing war work.

'Dull? You? Darling, you're leading the way. I use you when I'm talking to all these beastly men. "Look at Mrs Hugo Rutherford," I say. "She is a director of one of the most successful department stores in the country–"'

'The most successful store in the country,' Amelie corrected.

'Sorry, the most successful store. But anyway, I hold you up as an example of what women can do. And now Clem tells me you're promoting women to positions of responsibility at Packards. That's absolutely splendid news. Not before time, mind you.'

'I know, and you know that I would have done it before, but I didn't stand a chance of getting it past the Board. They only agreed to it now because they couldn't see any alternative.'

'They'll have cause to thank you before long. The rate things are going, I doubt whether you'll have any shopmen under the age of thirty-five soon.' Ida paused, and her bright face clouded. 'Clem's talking of going, you know.'

The worry that had never gone away wakened and

kicked Amelie in the stomach.

'Yes, I know. He told me the other day when I called.'

'I can't prevent him, of course. I wouldn't even if I could, and I'd think the less of him if he didn't volunteer. I admire him tremendously for it. At a time like this, everyone must put their country first and themselves second. Hugo went straight away, after all.'

'Hugo was made to be a soldier,' Amelie said.

'Well, maybe, but how do you stand it, Mel? Being alone?'

They looked at each other, both understanding that what she meant was, alone in bed. Amelie was choked with a wave of envy. That part of Ida and Clement's married life was evidently very important. She forced a smile, tried to turn it into a joke.

'I can stand not being pregnant very well.'

Ida allowed herself to be taken off at a tangent.

'Yes, I can understand that, but you know what I think you should do—'

Amelie interrupted her. She reached across the table and took one of her friend's hands.

'Ida, make the best of it while you can.'

Ida's pretty, round face took on a knowing look.

'Oh, I shall, darling, make no mistake. I shall. The poor love will hardly be able to march.'

Amelie swallowed down the sour taste.

'I don't mean just that,' she said, with difficulty. 'I mean, just seeing him, talking to him, finding time to be together. When – when I spoke to him the other day, he said that you'd hardly notice it when he went. He was joking, of course, but I think just a bit of him was serious. I know what you're doing is important, Ida, and I know we must all make sacrifices, but marriages are important too. Yours is one of the best I know. Don't let it suffer.'

Ida blinked at her.

'Darling! So serious.'

'Yes, I am, and I want you to be.'

'Mel, I adore Clem, you know that.'

'Yes, and he adores you. But don't take it for granted. You've made time to see me today. Make time to be with him as well.'

Ida was silent for fully a minute as she considered this. Then she squeezed Amelie's hand.

'You're right. Maybe I have been neglecting him of late. I know I do get these bees in my bonnet and I let myself get carried away by them. Oh Mel, you're such a good friend. I'm so glad you made me come here today. What would I do without you?'

Tears pricked at Amelie's eyes as she smiled back at her. She had done the best she could but somehow her conscience did not feel very much lighter.

Two days later, she received a telephone call from a highly emotional Ida.

'Oh Melly darling, it's happened–'

The fear that had gripped Amelie when she spoke to Clement came back, more fiercely, twisting in her entrails.

'Clem?' she croaked.

'Yes. He volunteered yesterday. Oh Mel, I'm so tremendously proud of him, but – oh, this sounds so feeble – I don't know how I'm going to cope with his being away. How do you survive, Mel? Hugo's been gone for seven months now, yet you always seem so calm and manage so well. How do you do it?'

By not being in love with Hugo. Amelie swallowed, easing her dry throat.

'You'll find a way, Ida. You're strong.'

'Am I? Sometimes I think I'm just very noisy.'

'Rubbish, you're wonderful.' And then it came to her, what would sustain her friend. 'And what's more, Clem thinks you're wonderful, and he'll be expecting you to carry on with your war work.'

'I'm not sure that I can, Mel. I know we weren't seeing very much of each other lately, but he was always there. I knew that if I wanted him, he would support me up to the hilt–'

'And you did the same for him.'

'Yes, of course, but how can I help him when he's in France, Mel? I shall be powerless.'

There was nothing Amelie could say to that, for she knew it was true. The huge, unwieldy machine that was the New British Army would suck him in, turn him into a soldier and eventually dispatch him to France, and nothing he or Ida or anyone else could do or say would have any effect.

'It will be months before he's sent there, Ida. He'll be training here in Britain for ages. They don't just send off raw recruits to the Front.'

'I suppose not.'

'And who knows, maybe by the time he's ready it will all be over.'

'Maybe.'

But Amelie could not believe that, and she knew that Ida did not either.

'Mel, we'll support each other through this, won't we? That's one thing, we'll be even closer friends now that we both have the same worries.'

'Of course we will,' Amelie said, and knew that Ida must never know just how much the same their worries were.

14

It was a beautiful bright April morning, with a blustery wind blowing shreds of cloud across a blue sky. A morning to feel in charity with the whole world, especially if you were young, fit and full of energy. But Alec Eden, running to catch his bus into central London, was restless and ill at ease. He made his way up the stairs and found a seat next to the only other man under thirty. Surreptitiously, he looked round, careful not to catch anyone's eye. The composition of passengers on this bus, the one he had been catching ever since he went to work at Packards, had changed dramatically over the last few months. Where once nearly half had been young fellows, now there was just himself and his neighbour. The older men were still there, but most of the empty places had been taken by women and girls, eager to release a man for the Front by filling jobs in shops, Government offices and the City. It would be the same, he knew, when he got to work. Every week a few more familiar faces went missing, and either a girl would replace them or their jobs would be covered by those who were left behind.

The conductorette came up to the top deck, a sturdy girl in a uniform hat and jacket, short skirt and leather gaiters.

'Still here, then?' she said as she took his fare.

'That's right,' Alec said.

Around him he could sense the disapproval of his fellow passengers, especially the women.

He tried to read his newspaper, but it was full of accounts of the latest battle, at the place called Neuve Chapelle. Alec knew just where it was. There was a large map of Belgium and northern France pinned to the wall of the canteen at the store, with the German and Allied lines marked in. Alongside it were charts showing how many Packards men had gone off to serve their country and the latest tallies of the inter-departmental competition to send the most knitted comforts to the Front. Shopgirls with time on their hands no longer tidied already tidy shelves. Instead they knitted – mittens, mufflers, balaclavas, all in the ubiquitous khaki. Some of the girls here on the bus were knitting, doing an extra bit towards the war effort on top of their new jobs. Alec could feel their ferocity in the clicking of their needles. He should not be here, and he knew it.

He got off at his usual stop, just past Packards, but instead of heading straight for the doors, he hesitated. Then he turned around and started off along Oxford Street. There were still plenty of fit-looking young men about, he assured himself. But somehow it did not make him feel any better. He turned down the Charing Cross Road, not even admitting to himself why he was doing this. Across Trafalgar Square and round the corner to Charing Cross station, and there in the forecourt he came up against what he needed to see: a fleet of ambulances loading up with the wounded from Neuve Chapelle.

As he watched, a seemingly unending line of grey-faced men, some on stretchers, some struggling along with the help of a nurse or supporting each other,

162

entered the ambulances. As each one drew away, another took its place. There was murmured comment from the knot of people around him.

'Poor blighters.'

'They're brave men, every one of 'em.'

'God bless them.'

A mother held her child up.

'Look, girlie, see the wounded soldiers. Brave heroes, they are.'

Alec backed out of the crowd. There were more important things in life than learning the ropes at Packards, more important than ousting Edward, more important even than claiming his birthright. There was Duty, and Honour, and serving one's country. The time had come.

Immediately, he felt a weight of guilt and confusion lift from his shoulders. All these months, since Lord Kitchener's first call for men to come forward, he had known what he ought to do and he had held out against it. Edward was not going, Perry was not going, so he was damned if he was going to go and leave them rubbing their hands with delight at getting rid of him so easily. But he knew he was being petty and self-seeking. Let Edward and Perry live with their own consciences if they could. His was now clear. He straightened his back and set his shoulders. With his head held high, Alec marched to the nearest recruiting office.

There was a buzz of speculation round Household Linens when Mr Eden did not turn up for work.

'I have always had my doubts about that young man. Full of bluster and self-importance but basically unsound,' Mr Wagstaff the buyer was heard to say to the floorwalker. 'Not surprising, considering.'

'That's only hearsay. And he has been totally reliable up till now,' the floorwalker pointed out.

'Mr Eden's late. That's not like him,' one of the girls said to May.

'No, it isn't,' May said.

'He's never late. He's always here before everyone else. He's here before Mr Wagstaff sometimes.'

'Yes, often,' May agreed again. The fear that had been growing ever since she came in and found he wasn't there caught at her heart.

'Do you think he's ill? He's never been ill before, though, has he? And if he was he would have sent in a message,' the girl said. 'Perhaps he was just late out of bed and missed his bus. Mind you, he'd've got another one by now, surely? It's gone nine o'clock.'

'He's joined up,' May said, and wondered where the words had come from.

The girl gaped at her.

'How do you know?'

'I just do,' May said helplessly. And she did, though why she could not explain. There were plenty of reasons why Alec Eden should be late: illness, oversleeping, a broken down bus, an accident. But she was convinced that none of them was the one.

'Just because you're sweet on him you think you can read his mind,' the girl said crossly.

'It's not that at all,' May said. She busied herself rewinding the already tidy string to try to put an end to the conversation. She felt hot inside with worry and pride.

All that morning, she found it impossible to concentrate. She wrote receipts out incorrectly. Customers had to repeat the simplest thing to her. The floorwalker reprimanded her for daydreaming. And then, in he came.

It so happened that the department was quiet at the time. Mr Wagstaff had gone to a meeting and only one customer was being served. Alec went to speak to the floorwalker, who pulled out his pocket watch.

'And what time do you call this, young man?' he demanded.

'I know – the morning's nearly gone. I do apologise, but what I had to do could not wait,' Alec said.

'Indeed? And what was more important than coming to work on time?' the floorwalker asked.

'I went to the recruiting office,' Alec told him.

The girl beside May squealed.

'You were right! He's joined up!' She ran across the floor to Alec. The others, hearing her words, hurried to join them. May stood staring at him, dazed. She had been right. She had known it all along. Slowly, hardly knowing what she was doing, she joined the little group round Lord Kitchener's newest recruit. There was a babble of voices, all asking what it was like and what he had done. May gazed at Alec's face. He was flushed and excited, answering the tumbling questions. Their eyes met.

'I'm proud of you,' she heard herself saying.

He smiled, and a more serious expression settled over his face.

'Thank you, Miss Hollis.'

'You've done the right thing,' she said.

'Yes, I believe I have,' he replied.

Then the moment was over and he was claimed by one of the others, but May treasured it up. For just a few seconds, it had been as if there had been only the two of them in the room.

She told Ruby all about it at length that evening.

'I shall miss him terribly, but it's such a comfort to know that he's doing his duty,' she said.

It was, too. It was not right that able-bodied young men should be doing safe, non-essential jobs when their country was in danger. She had felt that for some time. Now he had become a complete hero in her eyes.

What she had not realised was just how much she

would miss him, how he had come to fill up the spaces in her life. It had begun as a defence against Ruby and her interminable ramblings about Victor Lambert, where they had been, what he had said and what he had done. Every time Ruby mentioned something about Victor, May had a detail, however minute, to relate about Alec. But in doing that, it began to be that her days were built round noticing every little thing about him. She travelled to work each morning happy at the prospect of spending the day in the same department. She watched him covertly as she worked, strained her ears to catch what he was saying, hatched plots to get herself sent to dinner at the same time so that she might walk up to the fifth floor with him. When he left to join his new regiment life seemed horribly empty. All she had left now, when Ruby described at great lengths the play that she and Victor had been to, was the knowledge that he was doing the right thing.

'Of course, it's hard for us women who are left behind, but we're all in it together,' she said to Ruby.

Her friend exploded.

'For God's sake, May, anyone would think you was married or something. You weren't even walking out together, nor likely to, neither. It's just a crush. You'll get over it. Now, me and my Victor are quite different–'

'It is not a crush! I'm not a silly little schoolgirl. I–'

'All you ever done was look at him. When did he ever talk to you?'

'Lots of times,' May asserted, all the more fiercely for knowing that what Ruby was saying was right. She pushed home her one advantage yet again. 'And now he's gone away to protect you and me from them wicked Germans.'

Ruby stuck her nose in the air.

'Victor would go tomorrow, but he's got his sick mother to think of. He's all she's got in the world to care

166

for her,' she said.

'If it's true what they're saying about Alec, then he's got a widowed mother he's left behind,' May said.

'Ha! That's just Packards gossip. If Alec Eden really was one of The Family, then we'd know it for proper, wouldn't we?' Ruby said.

With this, May secretly liked to agree. Alec the unacknowledged son of Sir Thomas Packard was deliciously romantic, but a lot less attainable than Alec Eden, shopman, or Alec Eden, soldier.

Either way, the weeks were very leaden now with no Alec to study surreptitiously as she sold sheets or tidied shelves or knitted socks. Worse, there was nothing to hope for. Before, there had always been the chance that he might smile at her, or make a remark, making her day for her, feeding the dream that one day he would look on her the same way that she did him, start a real conversation, even ask her out. The only compensation was a sort of sisterhood with other lone women. If a chance acquaintance asked if she had a young man, now she would say that he was in the army. It was easier to lie when he wasn't there. In fact, she hardly looked on it as lying, just as an exaggeration.

It was midsummer when he came breezing into Household Linens, taking them all by surprise. May was the first to see him. She gave a little squeal, and held on to the counter. Her head felt quite strange, and her heart thudded in her chest. She wanted to run over and greet him, but was riveted to the spot with shyness. The floorwalker came forward.

'This is a surprise, Eden. I didn't think they gave you leave this soon.'

The buyer appeared from his cubbyhole.

'Eden! What are you doing here? Haven't they found you a uniform yet?'

May stood staring openly, taking in every detail about

167

him. His hair was shorter. He looked fit and brown, even rather taller than she remembered him. She felt quite weak at the knees. He was speaking now. She listened unashamedly.

'No, not a proper one, so I've come to Packards to have one made.'

He was grinning, as if that were some sort of joke.

'Made? You have to buy your own uniforms? But I thought only officers . . .' the buyer began, then broke off.

'That's right,' Alec said.

'You mean – you've been given a commission?'

'Yes. Amazing, isn't it? They must be getting really hard up.'

'Nonsense. You're a credit to the department. Congratulations.'

The buyer shook him by the hand. The floorwalker thumped him on the back. Alec went quite pink.

'Oh well, it's nothing . . .'

A couple of the other girls emerged from behind their counters and hurried up to him, braving the displeasure of their superiors. Terror that Alec might speak to them and not to her overcame May's paralysis. She dodged round the counter and fairly ran over to the knot of people that was rapidly accumulating round him.

They were all talking now, all trying to get his attention. May found herself babbling with the rest, desperate that he would look at her, meet her eyes, a smile. It was like the day he joined up all over again. Almost of its own accord, her hand reached out and touched his arm. His head turned. May's mouth went dry. He gave her a friendly smile.

'And here's little Miss Hollis. How are you, Miss Hollis?'

'V-very well, thank you.'

All the better for seeing you.

He was on the point of turning to someone else.

'What – what's it like in the army?' she blurted out, and blushed scarlet with shame at the stupidity of the question.

'It's just one long picnic,' Alec answered.

And that was it. He was distracted by the next questioner. She couldn't even be sure whether he was being serious, or sarcastic, or pulling her leg. His tone of voice gave nothing away.

All too soon it was over. He was gone, and May was left to go over and over the tiny exchange in her head, revelling in the warmth of his smile, mentally kicking herself for being so inept. Who knew when he would be back again? She had bungled her only chance. Chance of what, she did not stop to analyse.

She was still agonising over it when she was sent off for her dinner break, but when she saw that Ruby was also in the queue and bent on saving her a place at her table, she had the presence of mind to change the story. She plonked her tray down and started unloading the usual solid Packards fare.

'Oh Ruby, you'll never guess who came to see us in Household Linens today–'

'Mr Eden,' Ruby said.

May stared at her, momentarily floored. Then she recovered herself.

'Yes! Isn't it wonderful? Did he come down to see you as well? Of course he did, he must have been visiting all his old friends. Didn't he look well? So handsome–'

'Oh, I've never thought he was handsome, myself. I prefer–'

May refused to let herself be sidetracked. This was her hour. Ruby had Victor there all the time to boast about. She had this one occasion.

'And now he's going to be an officer! Isn't that won-

169

derful news? Of course, I'm not really surprised. If anyone deserves to be made an officer, he does. You could see that right from the start, couldn't you?'

Her meal cooled on the plate as she enthused on, becoming more florid with each inflated memory.

'And he spoke to me, you know. He really did. I nearly fainted. I asked him about the army and he told me all about it. He joked, of course, he said it was one long picnic. Well, he's not one to make a fuss, is he? But it's a hard life really. They're living in tents, you know, and all that training, and – and – marching and that–'

Her imagination failed her at this point.

'Yes, he spoke to me as well,' Ruby said.

Jealousy tore at her. Why had he done that? Did he like Ruby? What had he said?

'Did he?' she managed to say.

'Yes, you know, asked me how I was, that sort of thing.'

It wasn't fair. It just wasn't fair. Ruby had her Victor, and now Alec Eden was talking to her, really talking to her, asking after her. May hated her friend.

'Oh yes, he asked me that as well, of course, but I was wanting to know about him,' she lied. 'After all, he's the one who's been away.'

Ruby was looking bored. She tucked into her pudding.

'I don't know what all the fuss is about. I mean, I know you've got a pash on him, but why everyone else makes such a song and dance just because Mr Eden's got a promotion, I don't know. Anyone would think he's the only Packards man who's joined the army. There are dozens of them.'

May was seized with a desire to hurt.

'Well at least he's doing his duty. Unlike some I could name.'

Ruby dropped her spoon.

170

'And what's that supposed to mean?'

There was a dangerous cutting edge to her voice, but May was feeling too sore to heed it. She shrugged.

'If the cap fits,' she said. 'How's your Vic—'

She stopped short with a yelp as Ruby kicked her viciously on the shin, hissing at her to shut up. Only then did May remember that Victor's name was not to be spoken at work, that a pretence had to be kept up because Victor did not want Ruby to be the focus of gossip.

'I don't know why it has to be such a big secret,' she sulked.

'You're just jealous,' Ruby said.

Which was so true that May could only just manage to deny it.

The days that followed were gloomy. Ruby was depressed at the new spate of rumours about Alec Eden's being related to The Family and did not go out with Victor at all, as his mother was more poorly than usual and he could not leave her. May almost regretted being so nasty about Victor. He did seem to be a devoted son. Ruby was at first defensive, then annoyed. On the Sunday a couple of weeks after Alec's brief appearance, she came stamping down the stairs and made a declaration.

'I'm fed up with all these men! Blow them, let's go out and have some fun without them.'

The two of them took the tram into central London and walked in Hyde Park. It was a perfect summer's day. May looked up at the pattern of leaves, bright against the blue sky, and felt a sudden surge of homesickness. The countryside was so beautiful at this time of year. The London parks, lovely though they were, were nothing to fields of green corn and ripening hay. She let out a sigh.

'What's the matter?'

Ruby was all concern.

'You mustn't be sad on a day like this. We got all of London for our own! Come on, let's go and see the Sunday Parade in Rotten Row.'

'Can we?' said May doubtfully. 'I thought only toffs were allowed.'

'Just let them try and stop me,' laughed Ruby. She took May by the arm and marched down one of the paths with a purposeful step. May got caught up in her mood. When you were out with Ruby, anything could happen.

The Sunday Parade in the Season had once been one of the sights of London. Everyone who was anyone, and a great many more who aspired to join them, came to the park after morning service and walked or rode or drove in the Row, or sat upon the green painted seats and watched and gossiped. Peers of the realm and their families in gleaming carriages pulled by glossy horses, impeccably bred riders on equally well-bred mounts, elegant gentlemen and ladies dressed in the very height of fashion, all came out to see and be seen. Here the great hostesses arranged their social events, and matches and reputations were made and broken. That was before the war. What was left was a sad shadow. For just as the men had gone off to fight, so the Society ladies had thrown themselves into war work and were now too busy for the gruelling round of social events that used to fill their lives.

'What a lot of hospital blue,' May sighed, looking at the young men in their war wounded uniforms.

'Poor souls. Look at him – isn't he handsome? But so pale.'

There was still some of the cream of Society out in the Park. Elderly ladies, men home on their leave with their wives or sweethearts and of course the wounded, supported by their families.

'Aren't the fashions dull now?' Ruby said. 'It used to

be wonderful at the store during the Season. The ladies used to come sweeping in in all their finery. The gowns! Oh they were wonderful, such lovely materials and colours and trimmings. And as for the hats! Well, I could just die for a hat like some of those what they used to wear. And we'd get the debutantes coming in for their court gowns. They say the most beautiful one they ever made up in Ladies' Gowns was the one they done for Mrs Rutherford when she was Miss Amelie. A real work of art, that was. It was written about in the papers. We all bought copies and read about it.'

The day unfolded, warm and lazy and laden with possibilities. The two girls listened to the band playing and ate ice creams and commented on the relative attractions of all the uniformed men and flirted with quite a few of them. May giggled and gossiped and relaxed, all thought of Alec Eden pushed to the back of her mind. This was what she had left home for: to be a part of the big exciting world that was London, to meet new people and be in the centre of all that was happening. It was always the same when she went out with Ruby, everything became more exciting. Things happened, people talked to them. As they strolled arm in arm under the trees, she gave Ruby a little squeeze.

'I'm so glad we're friends. If I hadn't had you to show me around, I'd've missed so much.'

Ruby smiled.

'Yeah, we're good pals, you and me, aren't we? I'd be lonely without you, May. You're the only one who understands me.'

May recalled this conversation as she sat in the Gosses' little back parlour one evening darning her stockings. The house that had once been so noisy and full of the voices and feet and sheer ebullient presence of the three Goss boys seemed very quiet now that they were all down in Wiltshire training for Lord Kitchener's army. Mr Goss had gone off to the pub. Ruby was once more out with Victor, whose mother had apparently got a little better. The only sounds were the ticking of the clock on the parlour mantelpiece and the purring of the tabby cat. Mrs Goss came out of the kitchen.

'All alone, dearie?' she asked.

'Yes.'

'I know, I'll make us both a nice cup of tea and come and keep you company.'

'That'd be nice,' May said.

Mrs Goss came back with the big brown teapot with its green knitted cover and poured their tea into the thick blue and white everyday cups. She ladled in two heaped spoons of sugar for each cup and pushed May's across the table. May sipped in silence. There was something very comforting in sweet tea.

'Ruby's out with her young man again, then,' Mrs Goss remarked.

'Yes.'

'You don't mind being left here all on your own-some?'

May shrugged.

'Not really,' she said. After all, she could hardly go out and act the gooseberry to Ruby and Victor.

'It's a pity, though. You two used to have some nice nights out together, didn't you?'

'We still do,' May said.

Mrs Goss leaned forward and lowered her voice confidentially.

'To tell you the truth, dearie, I'm not at all happy about this Mr Lambert. We've never met him and we don't know anything about him, except what Ruby's told us, and that's not much. What do you think of him?'

'Well . . .' May said. 'He's, er, he's very nice.'

Mrs Goss said nothing, just sat silently waiting. May had to fill the gap.

'I don't really know him, you see. I never worked with him like Ruby does and we don't see what goes on in other departments. But – but I do know he's very highly thought of at the store. He's the youngest buyer they ever had. Everyone says he's bound to go far.'

It sounded woefully inadequate. Mrs Goss looked disappointed.

'Honest, Mrs Goss, that's all I know. I'm sorry.'

Mrs Goss sighed.

'So just how old is he, then?'

'What? Oh, I'm not sure. Thirty-three or -four, perhaps.'

'Old enough to be married.'

May stared at her, shocked.

'Married?'

'Yes.' Mrs Goss rubbed her hands over her face. 'It looks like it, don't it? All this secrecy. All this rubbish about a sick mother and not wanting it to get about at work. And this not coming and calling for her and taking her home like what any decent young man'd do. It all adds up, don't it? He's hiding something, and Ruby's too besotted with him to see it.'

'Oh, I'm sure that's not it. He wouldn't do a thing like that . . .' May started, but even as she said it, she could see what Mrs Goss meant. She had had a niggling feeling that there was something odd in his behaviour, but she had allowed herself to be swayed by Ruby's explanations.

'You ain't heard nothing about him having a wife, then?'

'No, never.'

But then she didn't know about a lot of the buyers. She assumed that most of them were married, since they were mature men, but she didn't know for sure.

Mrs Goss reached across the table and clasped May's hands in hers.

'Can you try to find out for me, May?'

'Well, I . . .' May was horrified. She cast about for a way out. 'I don't know if I can.'

'Will you try? Please? She's such a strong-willed girl, Ruby. I've spoken to her about it and her dad's spoken to her and said as she can't go out with him again unless he behaves proper and comes to the house, but Ruby, she just says if we try to stop her she'll leave home. Supposing she did, May? I don't know what'd happen. You hear such dreadful stories these days of what girls are getting up to. Just seeing some of them in the street is bad enough. Smoking and swearing and going into pubs and drinking without a man with them! I don't know what the world's coming to, really I don't. I mean, I like to have a bit of a knees-up and I'm not against Ruby enjoying herself. Not a bit of it. I'm glad for her to have a young man. But not all this hole-and-corner business. It all smells very fishy to me. So will you do what you can, May? Ask about a bit, and see what you can find out? You're her friend – you'd be doing her a big favour in the long run.'

And because she didn't know how to refuse, May agreed.

Worrying about it kept her awake that night. How was she to set about the task? Who should she ask? If Mr Lambert's private life had remained private all this time, in a place like Packards where everyone's business was everyone else's, then who would know about it? And even if she could think of somebody who might be able to help her, the moment she started asking questions, she would arouse suspicions, and word was sure to get back to Ruby and she didn't want to fall out with her. But the more she thought about what Mrs Goss had said, the more she saw that she had reason to be concerned. If she was Ruby's friend, and Ruby was being deceived by a married man, then it was her duty to do something about it. The solution finally came to her when Mrs Rutherford came in to choose a new table-cloth. Mrs Rutherford would be able to find out about Mr Lambert, and she would know what to do about it. All she had to do was to find a way to speak to her, and her task would be done.

15

Edward Amberley Packard was a man with his life well under control. Packards was doing as well as any London store under the present difficult circumstances, and his hold over it was no longer threatened now that Alec Eden had joined the army. He had experienced a slight jolt when he learnt that Eden had been made an officer, but on reflection he realised that this was not going to make any difference, since the man was still out of the way. Once the working day was over there were plenty of refuges from his sterile marriage, what with his clubs, a London nightlife that got brighter as the war grew darker, and the latest in a succession of mistresses, each one younger and more vulnerable than the last. On top of this, he now had a new business venture.

It was late one summer's evening when he first looked over the warehouse in the deeper wilds of Lambeth.

'It's the whole building you're interested in, is it, sir?' the agent asked.

'Yes.'

He certainly did not want to share space with anyone else. It was worth paying for the whole lot in order to keep others out.

'Is this floor sound?' he asked, stamping on it. There

178

were no ominous creaks, but then he would be storing considerably more than his own weight here.

'Sound as a bell, sir. You can put it to any test or examination you choose.'

'What about infestation? Are there rats? Cockroaches?'

There was a ratty smell about the place.

'I've had the ratcatcher in here myself, sir. Got every last one of 'em. What was it you was thinking of storing in here, sir?'

'That's none of your damned business.'

'No sir, of course not sir.'

He checked the bars at the windows. Not much possibility of anyone getting in there, and the doors downstairs and the loading bays on the upper floors were heavy and well locked and barred. It appeared to be secure enough.

'It's hardly a salubrious area this, is it? Are there many burglaries?'

'People round here are salt of the earth, sir. Rough, but honest.'

'Don't give me that sentimental rubbish. Everyone will steal if they get the chance.'

'If you say so, sir.'

The man was an idiot. Edward took no notice of him. The place certainly seemed to be what he was looking for. It was the right size, the rent was very reasonable and it was well out of the way of anything to do with Packards while still being within easy reach of central London. He completed the deal, taking the warehouse for twelve months under the name of Bishop, an alias that had come to him as he passed Lambeth Palace.

Then he set about moving in the first consignment of goods, a dozen cases of clocks and watches. For it had become obvious to him, as it had now to many people, that the war was going to last for some time. Both sides were dug in, the Germans had huge strength and numbers, and although the French and British combined would eventually more than match them, the New Army was still in training and not even fully equipped yet, if his brother-in-law's experiences were anything to go by. It was also obvious to anyone who bought huge quantities of goods from all over Britain and the world that certain things were going to be in short supply. To start with, the munitions industry was at last creaking into large scale production, which meant that hundreds of small engineering works were stopping making whatever it was that they had been producing and going over to weapons parts, so all the goods that they used to produce would no longer be available. Which meant that anyone having stocks of those goods would be sitting on a little goldmine. The Government could say what they liked about hoarding. To Edward, it was simply good business sense. This would be his own private venture, quite separate from Packards. The clocks were followed by carriage lamps and scissors, the speculative business was under way, and Edward looked forward to making a very nice profit out of the war.

For Sylvia Amberley Packard the war was extremely unsatisfactory. It was Thursday, her At Home day, when by convention all the friends and acquaintances on whom she had called and left cards during the last week or so should come and call upon her, drink tea and make polite conversation. Calls were the foundation upon which Society was built. A hostess could calculate exactly where she stood in the delicate and complicated hierarchy by the number and quality of calling cards left at her house each day. Until, that was, the war came along and upset it all. So far this afternoon, nobody at all had called. It was a social disaster.

She picked up her piece of sewing. She refused to knit. Knitting was such a middle-class activity. But

180

totally decorative work was considered unpatriotic these days, so instead she was engaged in embroidering the family monogram on a new set of dinner napkins, a task which in happier days she would have delegated to a parlour maid. Now, with a third of the staff gone off to do war work, there was little time for the maids to sew. She came to the conclusion, one which she reached at least ten times every day, that the war had ruined all civilised life and that it was all the fault of those wicked Germans.

Sylvia had her war work, of course. Everyone did. One had to be seen to be playing one's part. She sat on various committees for the relief of Belgian refugees and helped raise funds for the Red Cross. Many of her friends had become involved to a quite ridiculous degree, going out to provide tea at unearthly hours to homecoming troops or learning to drive ambulances or even going so far as to get jobs in munitions factories filling shells. Sylvia regarded this as tasteless bravado. A lady simply did not behave in such a way, even in wartime.

She sighed. It was obvious that no one was going to call. Perhaps she should go out and buy some more embroidery thread. She did not need it yet, but she would do at some point, so she persuaded herself that it would be a good idea to get it now. She rang for the motor to be brought round. At least they still had that, and a proper butler. It was something to be thankful for.

Sylvia chose a hat and gloves, since a lady did not even consider going out of her front door with her head and hands uncovered, and made her way downstairs. As she reached the hall, the butler opened the door. Below her in the street she could see the highly polished maroon motorcar, its door held open by the uniformed chauffeur. She walked down the flight of steps leading to the pavement, and as she did so, a roughly dressed man darted up them towards her.

'You Mrs Amberley Packard?' he demanded.

Sylvia ignored him, and took another step down. The man dodged in front of her. Resolutely, she looked over his head and tried to walk round him, but he kept in front of her.

'You are, ain't you? You're his old lady, him what ruined my little sister. What you going to do about it, eh? What you going to do? Fifteen years old and a baby on the way and him just chucked her out . . .'

Sylvia went cold. Her insides quaked. Still she said nothing, for persons of this type were not to be recognised, let alone spoken to. She knew that the nuisance would be dealt with. As indeed it was. The chauffeur and the butler both reached the man at the same moment, and dragged him on to the pavement.

'Be off with you!'

'Go before I call the police.'

The man struggled between the two of them. He was much younger than they were, and stronger. They could hardly hold him. All the while, he kept shouting at Sylvia. Try as she might to close her ears to his words, still they battered into her brain.

'What about my poor little sister? What you going to do for her? You owe her. She was a good girl. She never done nothing wrong. It was him, he ruined her. She's got nothing, now, nothing. You owe her. It's only right, after what he done.'

Sylvia reached the open door of the motorcar, stepped in, sat down, closed the door. Still the racket could be heard. The chauffeur jumped smartly into his seat and drew away, but not quickly enough to stop the dreadful creature from banging on the window. It was only when the car rounded the corner that Sylvia felt safe again.

She leaned back in the seat shaking, her heart thumping. She felt physically sick. That Edward should expose her to this! It was horrible, horrible. She had always suspected that he had never stopped the revolting behaviour she had found out about soon after their child was born, but had endeavoured to push it out of her mind. She and Edward put on an outward show of a marriage and spoke to each other as little as possible. That way, they managed to function. But now she knew he was still consorting with low women. Young ones too. Fifteen! And it had come to this, men accosting her in the street, on her very own doorstep. She felt soiled. Her husband was disgusting.

Arriving at Packards did nothing to dispel her simmering loathing. Sylvia had very ambivalent feelings towards the store. She appreciated the fact that it kept her in luxury, being honest enough with herself to acknowledge that she had married for money and for the prospect of being mistress of Tatwell. In an age that worshipped money and the show that money could buy, she made free with what Packards provided. But still it was Trade and therefore vulgar. The Packard family had come from nowhere, Sir Thomas had been a self-made man; whereas her family had lived on their land and been a power in their own small corner of England for time out of mind. She had married beneath herself.

The task of buying embroidery silk was soon accomplished. The rest of the afternoon hung heavily on her hands. Part of her wanted to march upstairs and confront Edward with his crime, but it was suppressed by the need to hold it in and let it fester. Instead she made her way towards the tea room, but before she could get there, she was accosted by one of her friends.

'Ah, Sylvia, the very person!'

Sylvia tried hard to smile.

'Hello, Kitty. How are you? You look very well.'

She knew it was a vain hope to keep the conversation

183

on neutral grounds. Kitty Brisley's husband had volunteered the day war was declared and Kitty had taken up war work the day after.

'I've no time to be ill, Sylvia dear. So much to be done. You still have time on your hands, I see?'

Sylvia assumed her most repressive tone.

'I sit on five committees, Kitty.'

'Committees, pah!' Kitty waved a hand. 'Nothing but hot air. You need to get down to something practical, Sylvia. Now, I have a dozen jobs I could offer you. The Friends of . . .'

She rattled on for some time, while Sylvia found excuses for refusing every one of her suggestions. If she was going to take up that sort of thing, it was not going to be at Kitty Brisley's behest. Kitty changed tack.

'Of course, you can't be expected to understand when your husband's still here. He hasn't volunteered yet, I take it?'

Sylvia had to admit that he had not. It was another cause of embarrassment; worse, these days, than his not being from an ancient landed family.

'Mm. Well . . .' Kitty's face said it all. Not only her husband, but her brothers and even all of her male servants had gone to do their duty. Sylvia had absolutely nothing to bring up in Edward's defence and Kitty knew it. She laid a hand on Sylvia's arm.

'No, dear, I want to ask you to do something for me. I simply have to be at Waterloo in ten minutes and I must order twelve dozen pairs of hospital quality sheets.'

Sylvia could see what was coming, but resented being sent on errands.

'Surely you could have telephoned? It's a very straightforward order,' she said.

'Oh no, dear. That would never do. Nothing replaces personal attendance. Now, you can do this little thing for me, can't you? Just have them sent round to my house. Thank you so much, Sylvia dear. Goodbye! Must dash!'

Sylvia was left knowing that she had been outmanoeuvred. The day was going from bad to disastrous. She took the lift to the third floor, where Household Linens was situated.

She was not in a mood to put up with the least laxity in services. At first, the girl behind the sheets counter was quick, efficient and deferent, showing her what was available and assuring her that the order would be delivered with the last batch that evening. Then just as she was writing down the address to which the sheets were to be taken, her mouth dropped open and her eyes focused somewhere behind Sylvia. Her hand stopped halfway through a word.

'Wake up, girl – I said Hamborough Gardens,' Sylvia said.

The shopgirl jumped and went bright red.

'Oh – oh I'm sorry, Mrs Amberley Packard. Hamborough – yes, of course. Only it's our Mr Eden, you see. He must be on leave. He's been made an officer, you know. We're all so proud . . .'

Her voice trailed away under Sylvia's cold gaze. Shopgirls should not chatter to customers in that familiar way. In cowed silence, she finished taking down the address, then apologised again.

Sylvia ignored her, but something made her turn round the moment the transaction was finished and look at the young man talking to the buyer. Alec Eden. She had not seen him since the dreadful day of the reading of the will. She had to admit that he looked extremely smart in his uniform. If she had had him by her side when she met Kitty Brisley, she would not have been at such a disadvantage. She recalled that Edward had mentioned the fact that he had been promoted. He had been very put out, as if it was a personal insult that the upstart should have been picked out to join the ranks of gentlemen. Still highly disturbed by the encounter with the man on her doorstep, she felt that anyone whom Edward regarded as an enemy must be an ally. Loathing of everything her husband stood for impelled her into action on impulse for the first time in her adult life. She crossed the floor.

'Lieutenant Eden?'

Inbred self-control kept her voice cool and steady. The young man looked at her with surprise, then recognition, then something like amazement that she should be speaking to him. It soothed Sylvia's hurt a little.

'Yes – ah – how do you do, Mrs Amberley Packard?'

He spoke well. Nobody would know, looking at him or listening to him, where he had come from. A desire to do something that would outrage Edward as much as his behaviour outraged her drove Sylvia on. She found her cardcase and drew out a visiting card.

'I'm glad to see that you are doing your duty, Lieutenant Eden. Perhaps you would care to call one day?'

For a few seconds he looked almost as dumbfounded as the shopgirl had done. Then he collected himself and took the card.

'Thank you, Mrs Amberley Packard. I should be honoured.'

As she swept out, she was conscious of a glow of satisfaction. Let Edward do what he liked. She had struck a blow.

Sylvia was slightly surprised, however, to have her offer taken up so quickly. The very next day, Briggs the butler interrupted her lonely vigil in the drawing room with the news that there was a gentleman to see her.

'A Lieutenant Eden, ma'am.'

His voice oozed disapproval. Briggs, in the way of all servants, knew everything about the family.

Sylvia gave him one of her repressive looks.

'What are you about, Briggs, keeping him waiting downstairs? Show him up. Then bring some tea.'

Alec Eden was duly announced. Sylvia received him graciously. He looked rather nervous as he sat down, which pleased her. So he should be, in her company.

'You are very prompt in calling,' she remarked.

'I have to return to my regiment this evening,' he explained.

'And which regiment is that?' Sylvia asked.

He quoted a name and number, but it meant nothing to her. It was not a Guards regiment, or even one of the old established county ones, just one more of the myriad creations of the New Army. He was stationed, it seemed, in some remote part of East Anglia.

She studied him as he spoke. He was certainly very personable. If any of her friends were to call, she would be pleased to introduce him to them, just as long as her exact connection to him did not come out.

'Do you find there are many privations to army life?' she asked.

'Well, it was pretty chilly in a tent at night in March, but now that summer's here it's all quite a lark. Like being in the Boy Scouts, you know, all this camping and drilling. Mind you, there's been a tremendous amount to learn. Take riding a horse. I'd not been on anything other than a donkey on the sands. You should have seen me the first time I got in the saddle! I must have looked like a sack of potatoes sitting there and hanging on for dear life.'

As he continued with a tale of how he had been run away with by a half-broken horse and ended up in a haystack, Sylvia had found she was actually amused. Briggs appeared with the tea tray. Sylvia poured and handed Alec a cup. He handled the delicate bone china with care.

'Do go on,' she said.

So he told her about some of his fellow officers and their foibles and she even laughed once or twice. She had not been so well entertained in this room for quite some while. She had to pull herself up short.

'Being an officer has its difficulties, then?' she said. And no wonder, considering where he came from.

'It does,' he agreed. 'I wonder . . .'

He leaned forward, his hands clasped between his knees, fixing her with his grey eyes. Then he shook his head.

'No, perhaps not.'

'Please,' Sylvia said, 'what were you going to ask?'

'Well . . .' Still he hesitated. 'You might think it a bit of a liberty, but I wonder if you could give me some advice, Mrs Amberley Packard. You see, you are the only real lady I know.'

In spite of herself, Sylvia was caught.

'When I was in the ranks, we thought it was all fun and games being an officer, but I've found that that isn't quite the case. Now, I don't mind working hard, Mrs Amberley Packard. I've enjoyed learning the riding and the shooting. I can take on any of them now. And I can absorb all the reams of information and regulations we have to learn. It's the social side that I know I'm not quite getting right. That's where I need some help.'

Nobody had asked Sylvia's advice for a very long time.

'I'm afraid there is rather more to it than learning a set of rules,' she told him. 'One has to be born a gentleman – or a lady. One cannot simply become one. But there are certain ways of doing things that are acceptable and some that are not. Those I can pass on to you.'

Alec Eden's face relaxed into an attractive smile.

188

'Would you really? Thank you very much. I would be very grateful to you.'

Sylvia proceeded to spend half an hour coaching him in how to enter a room, how to shake hands, how to sit down, how to leave again gracefully.

'I never realised how much there was to it,' he admitted. 'What a pity I have to return this evening. Could I possibly call again when I next have some leave?'

Sylvia graciously consented.

She did not admit it to herself, but she missed him after he went back to his camp. Her life seemed even flatter than it had before. Motherhood never had occupied her, since Nanny had cared for her one child since the day of her birth. Her friends were increasingly involved in war work, and although her committees filled some of the time, they hardly engaged her mind or her imagination. She found she was beginning to plan how she was going to instruct Lieutenant Eden when next he was able to get up to Town. At first she tried to distract herself, as if indulging in thinking about him was a sin of some sort, but after a while she gave in to it to the extent of writing it all down in a notebook. She spent a great deal of time refining and revising her ideas, until she had planned a complete course of etiquette. It was the only really creative thing she had done since giving birth. Looking through the pages and anticipating the delivery of the next lesson became one of the more acute pleasures of her existence.

16

'We seem to have been out every evening since I came home,' Hugo grumbled, putting on his cuff links.

'I know. Everyone wants to see you. There just isn't time to fit them all in. And now Mother expects us to be at the family dinner,' Amelie said, with a remarkably convincing show of regret. Hugo had no idea that she had telephoned all their friends when she knew he was coming on leave and made sure that they never had an evening to themselves.

'Family is family, I suppose. We really must get down to see my mother and father soon. There never seems to be enough time,' Hugo said.

Amelie took a steadying breath to hide the acceleration of her heart.

'You could still go down and see them,' she said. 'There are three days left of your leave, after all. I wouldn't be able to come, unfortunately. I can't leave the store – there's so much to be done at the moment, with the opening hours being cut – but you could go. You really ought to, Hugo. You haven't seen your poor mother in months and I know she misses you. She said as much in the last letter she wrote to me.'

'Not without you,' Hugo said firmly. 'We have little

enough time together as it is.'

He threw a reproachful look at her slim figure, now covered with a yellow dinner dress with a fashionable bell-shaped skirt in three layers.

'I know. It's this beastly war. Heavens, just look at the time! Hurry up, dear. We'll be late if we're not careful, and you know how cross Mother gets.'

Since Thomas Packard's death, Amelie's mother Winifred had taken it upon herself to hold the monthly family dinner parties. This was resented by both Margaret, Sir Thomas's widow, and Sylvia Amberley Packard. Margaret simply withdrew to Tatwell and refused to take part, issuing invitations that amounted to summonses to various members of the family from time to time. Sylvia had to grit her teeth and pretend she did not mind. The fact that Winifred's husband Bertie held no real authority and Edward was head of the store that supported all of them in luxury was conveniently forgotten, at least by Winifred. She was Thomas Packard's sole legitimate offspring and the wife of the senior male member of the family and therefore entitled to hold the gatherings. Everyone else simply had to comply.

This evening, Amelie was grateful for yet another excuse to go out. She left Hugo cursing over his tie and ran along to the nursery to say goodnight to the children – now under the sole care of Nanny since the nursery maid had gone off to make munitions – and returned just as Hugo brought the motorcar round to the door.

'There really doesn't seem to be much point in keeping the motor if we no longer have a chauffeur. It's only going to be used when I'm home on leave,' Hugo said, as they set off for Bruton Street.

Once more Amelie had to suppress a qualm. Was this the moment to tell him? At least he couldn't argue for hours about it, for it only took a few minutes to drive to her parents' house.

'Well, actually, dear, it isn't only used when you are home.'

'What?' Hugo honked the horn furiously at a newspaper seller who dared to step off the pavement. 'Are you lending it out? To whom? Not to that brother of yours, I hope?'

Amelie presumed he meant Perry, since he got on well with Edward.

'No.'

Rather than let him carry on guessing until he hit the right solution, she decided simply to tell him.

'As a matter of fact, I'm learning to drive it myself.'

'You're learning to drive a motorcar?' Hugo sounded outraged.

'Yes.' And to forestall any further comment, she said, 'Surely you would not want a wife who was so stupid that she could not drive a motorcar. Supposing the boys inherited a trait like that?'

It was, she knew, a clinching argument for one who believed so passionately in eugenics. But Hugo was not ready to give in entirely.

'That's as may be. It's still a most unwomanly thing to do,' he stated.

Amelie gave a sigh for the days of their courtship, when he professed to admire her not only for her looks and sporting prowess, but for her ability to set up and run a department at the store.

'Plenty of women are doing unwomanly things now. You should be glad I'm not being a road sweeper or a railway porter,' she said.

Hugo drew up in front of Bertie and Winifred's house.

'Don't be so silly, my dear. It is only working-class women who are taking up those types of occupation.'

As far as he was concerned, that was unanswerable. Amelie was still simmering as they were let into the house.

They were the last to arrive. Edward and Sylvia and Perry and Gwendoline were already sipping sherries in the drawing room. Winifred sailed forward to greet them.

'My dears–' she kissed both of them on the cheek. 'Hugo, I was so glad you were able to come. We all miss you, you know.'

She fussed round him, making sure he had the drink he wanted, asking after his health. Amelie knew why. With neither of her sons in the armed forces, she was glad to at least have a son-in-law who had volunteered on the first day to enable her to hold her head amongst her friends. It was the same with Amelie. Once she had been an embarrassment, holding a responsible position at the store when she should be a society wife and hostess. Now she was a brave soldier's wife, keeping her family together and doing her bit towards the war effort by working. For almost the first time in her life, Amelie had her mother's approval.

Bertie asked after army life.

'Tremendous fun, sir. Plenty of riding and shooting, y'know. And now at last we're fully equipped – uniforms, guns, pack mules, right down to the field kitchens. Can't tell you how frustrating it's been waiting for it all to arrive. It came in dribs and drabs, y'know, boots here, couple of hundred rifles there and so on, but now at last we're ready. The men are all as keen as mustard. All we need now are our marching orders and we'll be over in France to join the Expeditionary Force.'

Bertie thumped him on the arm.

'That's the spirit! We'll show those Germans a thing or two, won't we?'

'Quite so, sir. They might have a much larger standing army, but nothing beats the British fighting man.'

Conversation centred round Hugo until dinner was announced. Amelie, studying the reactions of the rest of the family, noticed that Gwendoline was looking smug and Perry had an air of suppressed excitement. Sylvia wore her usual icy air and Edward a look of polite interest. Neither of them ever gave anything away.

It was a curtailed meal that awaited them, by pre-war standards: a mere four courses with only two choices at each. Gone were the days when Winifred would have been ashamed of offering less than seven courses with up to five dishes to choose from at each one.

'We must all make sacrifices,' she remarked, as the maids served this frugal fare in place of the footmen who used to wait at table.

Bertie looked mournful.

'I suppose so, but I really don't see what's so unpatriotic about eating a decent dinner.'

'We all used to eat far too much,' Amelie said. 'All through the Season it was nothing but guzzle, guzzle, guzzle, and then off to Baden Baden to try to lose a little weight. It was disgusting.'

Bertie was not listening.

'At least I've enough good wine laid down for the duration. What d'you think of this Montrachet, Edward? Still a little young, I think, but Wilkins insisted it was all right. I suppose he's the expert. One hardly dares contradict one's butler these days in case he goes off in a huff to fill shells or something. They say there aren't enough men in France to harvest the grapes this autumn. All gone to serve in the army, y'see. Nobody left but women and old men. And the champagne region's in the hands of the Boche. Imagine that! Good thing I put in a big order at the beginning of the 'fourteen Season.'

'There's really hardly been a Season to speak of this year,' Sylvia complained. 'It's too bad. Imagine Worth's closing down!'

'Very good thing too,' Edward said. 'All their customers can come to us now. Heaven knows, we need them. Ladies' Gowns have never had such a bad year. Even with over half our seamstresses gone off to sew army uniforms, we're still not rushed like we usually are at this time of year.'

'At least the Derby and Ascot week are still on,' Perry said.

'But the hats are nothing to speak of at all,' said Gwendoline.

'Well, of course one couldn't have a proper party without a regular complement of servants,' said Sylvia. 'My cook makes the most terrible fuss when I ask her to do anything in the way of a sauce. She says she cannot manage it with only one scullery maid.'

Winifred was absolutely in agreement.

'I think it's quite disgraceful the way they're all deserting us in order to earn more money elsewhere. These high wages will be the ruination of the lower classes. They only go and spend it all on drink.'

Amelie listened to them all with growing disbelief. In the end she could stand it no longer.

'For heaven's sake! You all sit round complaining about food and servants when there are men dying out there in France!'

There was a shocked silence, as if she had uttered a swearword. Then Winifred moved in to smooth it over.

'You're under a great deal of strain at the moment, Amelie–'

'Strain? Rubbish! What about the women who have lost husbands and sons? Girls I came out with are widows. Young men I danced with are dead. All those dashing young guards officers are out in France, and you wonder why the Season isn't what it used to be! All this talk of sacrifice, yet your lives have hardly changed at all. The only person in this family who has joined up is Hugo.'

'And Alec Eden,' Sylvia added, almost under her breath. The rest of them chose to ignore her remark. Alec Eden was not a subject they wished to discuss.

'Actually, you're wrong there,' Gwendoline said, so loudly that everyone looked at her. She flushed. The smug expression that Amelie had noticed earlier returned. She looked round at all of them, evidently savouring the moment.

'I have started to train as an ambulance driver,' she said.

Everyone spoke at once. Amelie was amazed. Selfish little Gwendoline, who thought of nothing but enjoying herself, giving up her time to ferry wounded soldiers about? The war really was reaching out and touching the most unlikely people.

'Good for you,' she said, and meant it.

Gwendoline sat glowing in the exclamations and the praise. Everyone was eager to find out more. She told them about where she went for her training, what she had to do, how difficult it was, who she had met. The questions went on until the dessert was brought in.

'And I'm not the only one to be doing their bit,' she said. She turned to her husband. 'Perry?'

All eyes fixed on the dedicated man about town of the family. In a moment of group prescience, they all knew what he was going to say, and unconsciously held their breaths.

Perry was his usual nonchalant self. He leaned back in his chair.

'Well, I thought it was about time I donned the jolly old khaki. I joined up this morning.'

Amidst the cries and the praise, Hugo jumped up and shook Perry by the hand.

'Congratulations, old chap. I always knew you had it in you.'

Perry flushed.

196

'Thanks, Hugo. It's nothing, really.'

'You're doing your duty, that's what counts.'

'Well, I couldn't be the last chap in London to go, now could I?' Perry said, with a rare flash of truth.

In all the outburst, there was only one voice missing. Edward's.

Later, when the ladies withdrew, Amelie went to sit beside Gwendoline. She had never cared much for either of her sisters-in-law, regarding Sylvia as being cold and Gwendoline shallow and grasping. Even now, she suspected that Gwendoline had only decided upon ambulance driving because it was a fashionable thing to do, but whatever her motives, it was still extremely useful and probably required skill and an ability to stick at the task, however hard and tiresome, that she would never have attributed to Gwendoline.

'You must be very proud of Perry,' she said.

'Yes, I am.'

'And what you're doing is admirable, too. Are you enjoying it?'

'I think I shall, when I've mastered it. Those ambulances are such great brutes of machines. I keep on crashing the gears. I really don't seem to be able to control the pedals and stick and everything at all.'

'It is difficult. I'm learning to drive our motorcar, and I'm sure that's easier than an ambulance. It certainly must be lighter to handle. But I'm getting quite good at double declutching the gears now, so I'm sure you will. It's just a question of keeping at it.'

'Thank you, I'm sure you're right. I certainly shan't give up, anyhow,' Gwendoline said.

For a while they spoke of their experiences of learning to drive, then Gwendoline put a hand on Amelie's arm.

'Amelie, I – I wanted to ask you – about, well, when Hugo went away . . .'

Amelie remembered the last time she had been asked a similar question. Ida's face swam in front of her eyes. It had been weeks now since she had seen Clement. She tried to concentrate on Gwendoline.

'You must be worried about him. But there's no danger yet, you know. The training takes several months. Hugo joined up last August and he's still in England. Perry won't be sent straight out to France.'

'I know. It's just, well, how do you manage, with him away?'

Quite easily, really.

'You'll learn. Having your ambulance driving will help, you know. It's something of your own, something useful. It will make the days pass much faster than just frittering your time away with calls and shopping and luncheon parties.'

'Yes, I realise that, but what about –' she leaned towards Amelie until they were touching, then said in a low voice, '– the nights?'

Why did everyone have to ask her that? Amelie looked at her with envy. Despite being a superficial little thing, Gwen did really love Perry.

'You learn to cope with that, too.'

'Don't you – miss him?'

Guilt gripped Amelie in its cruel claws. When she lay awake lonely in her wide bed, it was not Hugo she imagined there beside her. It was Clement.

'Of course,' she said. 'You'll be all right, Gwen, we all bear it somehow. We have to.'

At the end of the evening, Edward and Sylvia slipped into their motorcar and drove away while the others were still lingering at the door.

'I say, the night is yet young, what? Why don't we all go over to Soho and find a nightclub? I know some very jolly ones that stay open till dawn,' Perry said.

Amelie jumped at the idea.

198

'Oh yes, that would be such fun.'

To her amazement, Hugo agreed. Only a few hours ago he would not have entertained the suggestion, but now, it seemed, Perry's standing had grown out of all recognition. He had proved himself to be a real man.

'We'll all go in my motor,' he insisted, and everyone crowded in.

The Season may have been a virtual non-event that year, but London night life was more hectic than ever. Theatres and restaurants thrived, and the new night-clubs that had multiplied in the racier areas of town provided drinks, entertainment and dancing to ragtime bands till night turned into day. Amelie was not at all sure where they went or how long they stayed there. The cellar club was hot and stuffy, the music was loud and she was sure that not all of the women were ladies, judging by the way they danced. But it all had the desired effect. By the time they got home, avoiding a dozen accidents only by sheer miracles, Hugo was hardly able to climb the stairs. As she fell into bed beside him, Amelie sent up a brief prayer of thanksgiving that this was one night at least when she would not have to creep out to the bathroom and use the douche she kept hidden from Hugo's suspicious eyes. With a large helping of luck, her precious freedom would be preserved.

17

Victor Lambert found himself singing as he got ready for work. He smiled at himself in the looking glass, brushing his fair hair into fashionable glossy smoothness on each side of his head from a ruler-straight parting. A whole day and evening of Ruby lay ahead of him like a wondrous land. After the working hours spent pretending they meant no more to each other than any other two people who happened to be in the same department, they were to meet up at an ABC for tea then go on to the Holborn Empire. Ruby adored the Halls. Victor adored taking her, drinking in her wholehearted enjoyment of the entertainment. It was going to be a wonderful evening, culminating in the moment when he would take her warm body in his arms and kiss her soft, generous lips . . .

'Victor! It's twenty-four minutes to eight!'

The dream shattered into a thousand glittering shards. Oh God, strike her dead. No, I didn't mean that. That was wicked. I don't wish death on anyone, not even her, not even though it would leave the way clear.

'Coming, dear.'

He hurried down the stairs to where his wife, Enid, was waiting in the hall, holding his stick and his freshly brushed hat. Everything he wore was immaculately prepared by her, his shoes polished to mirror brightness, his trousers pressed, his shirt crisply ironed and starched. He was the best turned out buyer in the store.

'You'll be late.'

'Not if I stride out.'

He took the hat and stick from her. She flicked a speck of dust from the shoulders of his jacket, tutting her disapproval. He had allowed the enemy, dirt, to cling to him despite the heroic efforts she put into defeating it.

'You didn't finish your breakfast,' she said.

Another sin.

'I'm sorry. I wasn't feeling hungry.'

'Wasn't it good enough for you?'

'It was perfectly delicious, dear. I just wasn't feeling hungry.'

'I got up at half past six to cook that for you, and I was feeling so ill I could hardly stand. I had to hold on to the stove to stay upright. And all you can say is that you weren't feeling hungry.'

'I'm sorry, Enid. I'll try to do better tomorrow.'

Though he knew it would be hard. Love took his appetite away. Besides, whatever he did, it was never good enough.

'I must go, I shall miss the bus.'

'Not if you stride out.'

He left this unanswered, bent his head to give her the required peck on the cheek and left. At first he walked stiffly, still feeling the dead weight of her disapproval upon him, but as he turned the corner of the street he relaxed. The daily ordeal was over. He had escaped once more. The spring came back into his stride. A day of anticipation, an evening of sheer bliss lay ahead. For fully five minutes he savoured this, keeping the dark forces at bay. For he knew that in the middle of his enjoyment guilt would strike, a self-loathing that he should so deceive a wonderful girl like Ruby. It would be even worse tonight. He would look into her bright face, her glowing eyes and hate himself for leading her on, for giving her false hopes, for making her love him when he had no right to do so.

It was a bright sunny morning. Victor climbed up to the top deck of the bus and sat apart from the gaggle of girls heading for jobs in the West End and Whitehall. Lately, he had been getting some very hostile looks from them. He knew why. They thought he shouldn't be there. He should be in uniform. He hunched his shoulders and lit a cigarette. If his country wanted him that much, it would send for him. Until then, he was staying where he was. Pretending not to notice the way they were glancing at him and muttering together, he drew the smoke down into his lungs and attempted to relax. He was forbidden to smoke in the house. That was another wonderful thing about Ruby. She liked it.

'I love a man who smokes. It's so dashing,' she said.

She sometimes would light his cigarette for him, and take a puff herself before handing it over, but though Victor thrilled to a cigarette that had touched her lips, he did not encourage her. A man who smoked might be dashing, but a woman doing the same was fast.

Ruby, Ruby . . . what was he to do about it all? How was it going to end? He ought to tell her, confess everything and give her up, but he could not bear the thought of that. A life without Ruby would be a grey fog, meaningless. He loved and wanted her so much, there must be some way out. He went over the alternatives, as he had so many times before. He could go on pretending he was free, marry Ruby and act as if Enid did not exist. But that of course was a complete pipe dream. He would never get away with it. Or maybe he could persuade Ruby to go away with him, to make a completely fresh start somewhere where nobody knew them, where they could pass for man and wife. But that would mean telling her about Enid, in which case Ruby would refuse to go. Or perhaps he could convince her to move away without telling her, and marry her, so that she thought she was a proper wife. But that would mean both deceiving her and thinking of a good enough reason to go in the first place. None of it was really satisfactory, and he knew it. There was no way out, except if he were to be free again. If Enid were to contract some sudden fatal illness . . . He played with this possibility, imagining himself telling her family, acting the brave widower, and then, as soon as he was decently able, asking Ruby to marry him with a clear conscience. The heaven of having her lie in his arms all night, every night . . .

He came to with a sick jolt. It would never happen. Enid might complain weekly of this illness and that, but she was really as tough as old boots. There was no way out. He who was lauded at Packards as a model of success, the youngest buyer in the history of the store and set to rise further, had made a complete hash of his private life.

The bus drew up in Oxford Street. As he rose to get off, there was a sudden commotion amongst the group of girls.

'Go on – quick – now, he's going!'

Two of them jumped up and ran to block his way. They glared up at him, their eyes fierce, their cheeks pink with righteous indignation.

'Why aren't you in the army?'

'My fiancé is, and my brothers.'

'Yes, and mine. You should be too. Don't you know your country needs you?'

'I – I . . .' he stuttered.

Their hands scrabbled at his top pocket, and then they retreated, as suddenly as they had attacked. The last of the departing passengers were halfway down the stairs. Victor bolted after them. It was only when he reached the pavement that he looked at his pocket. There, tucked into it, was a white feather.

He snatched it out as if it were on fire and flung it away, involuntarily looking up at the bus as it drew away. The girls were hanging over the side.

'That's right, throw it away!'

'You can't throw away your duty!'

Burning with anger and humiliation, Victor strode towards the doors of the store. All around him, Packards people were heading in the same direction. They had been on the very bus with him. They had seen it all. He could hear mutterings around him. They were turning against him. He looked neither right nor left, closed his ears to the voices, pushed through the crowd. He would not let a pack of ignorant bitches reach him. He would not.

He left his hat and stick in the staff cloakrooms, and smoothed his already immaculate hair. The churning in his gut subsided. He felt ashamed of having let it affect him so much. They knew nothing. They were nothing. It was for him to decide whether he was going to join up. He straightened his tie. He had a day of Ruby ahead of him. The thought sustained him through his walk down to the department past dozens of people who might have witnessed the scene with the white feather.

When he reached Stationery, she was already there. He followed their usual ploy, treating her just like all the other shopgirls.

'Good morning Miss Hutchins, Miss Reynolds. Good morning, Miss Goss. I trust your back is better today, Miss Arnold?'

A chorus of greetings, a quick exchange of glances with Ruby, a flash of her rich smile.

'A beautiful morning, Mr Lambert.'

'Beautiful indeed.'

Little Miss Reynolds sidled up to him.

'I think it was a disgrace, what those women did.'

'Thank you, Miss Reynolds. I don't think we need discuss it any further.'

'Of course not, Mr Lambert.'

He went to speak to the floorwalker about the day's business, but out of the corner of his eye, he saw Ruby go up to Miss Reynolds and the two of them talk together, glancing at him as they did so. Outrage filled Ruby's face and he knew that she wanted to run to him, to fling her arms round him. He glowed inside. She was a gem. She was one in a million.

The day followed its usual course. With more men departing for the Front every day, sales of writing paper, the department's staple, were up, which more than balanced out the fall in peripheral items like music racks. The greatest change, however, was that Victor could no longer wait in state for commercial travellers to come to him and try to persuade him to buy their wares. He now had to go out and locate ever more scarce supplies. Every last small workshop, it sometimes seemed, had gone over to war work.

Then, at ten o'clock, a messenger boy appeared from the fifth floor.

'Mr Lambert? Mrs Rutherford would like to see you straight away, sir.'

Puzzled, but not unduly alarmed, Victor followed him. He could not think of any reason why Mrs Rutherford should want to speak to him. In the past, whenever some new display idea was to be tried out in the department, she had come to see him so that they could discuss it *in situ*. Nowadays, with the extravagant displays of the past deemed to be rather unpatriotic, she was more concerned with the store's contribution to the war effort. Was that it? Had she sent for him to read him a lecture on joining up? If that was so then she was in for a disappointment. Packards might pay him but they didn't own him. As he made his way up to the fifth floor, Victor rehearsed dignified speeches asserting the right to his own conscience.

The boy delivered him to the secretary, who showed him straight in. Mrs Rutherford gave him an assessing look as he walked towards her, her pretty summer dress of blue and white at variance with the severe expression on her face. Victor was struck with the unpleasant certainty that he was in for a rough ride.

'Come in, Mr Lambert. Sit down.'

Her voice was cool, quite unlike the enthusiastic woman he was used to dealing with when deciding on a display. He reminded himself that she was younger than he and female. The trouble was, women were becoming rather formidable creatures these days. Also, she was one of The Family. He sat.

Mrs Rutherford clasped her hands loosely on the desk in front of her.

'Mr Lambert, I have to speak to you on a very delicate matter. It is not a task I enjoy, but I feel that it is my duty to undertake it.' She paused. Victor waited, not sure whether a reply was needed. Mrs Rutherford took a breath and continued. 'I understand that you are courting one of the girls in your department, a Miss Ruby Goss?'

Victor was dumbfounded.

'W-what?' he stuttered.

'I think you heard me.'

Anger hammered in his head. Someone had betrayed them.

'Who told you this?' he demanded.

'Never mind who told me. I take it that it is true?'

Victor tried to get control of himself. He took a steadying breath.

206

'I have been out with her once or twice,' he said.

'Once or twice? My understanding was that it was rather more serious than that, that you had been seeing her on a regular basis since Christmas.'

What now? His mind raced round a tight circuit of hopeless possibilities. Admit to it and refuse to back down. In which case it looked as if the full moral disapproval of Packards would descend upon his head. Admit to it but promise never to see Ruby again. Impossible. The very idea of it made him go cold. Lie, then. He could deny everything. But she would not believe him. She knew. She had proof, she must have, or she would not be confronting him like this. He could feel himself being backed into a corner.

'And whose business is it if I have? Packards don't have any rules about it, do they?' The words burst out of him before he could stop them.

Mrs Rutherford remained calm, but her lips tightened.

'No, Mr Lambert, we do not. But we do take the welfare of our shopgirls very much to heart. The late Sir Thomas always insisted that Packards was not to be used for a cheap pick-up.'

The shock made Victor gasp. He would never have imagined hearing a vulgar term like that from the lips of Mrs Rutherford.

She fixed him with an icy gaze.

'Is Miss Goss aware that you are married?' she asked.

'Of course not!' he exploded. 'Ruby wouldn't go out with a married man. She's not that kind of girl!'

Too late he realised he had closed the only way out. If Ruby was aware of his situation and happy with it, then it really was nobody's business but their own. Except that Packards might not see it that way.

Mrs Rutherford's expression softened just a little.

'At least you don't seek to shift the burden of blame

207

on to her. I'm sorry that she is going to be made unhappy.'

'What do you mean?' Victor demanded, but even as he said it, he knew. This was it. The end. All those dreams were just that. Dreams.

Mrs Rutherford sighed.

'Mr Lambert, I could have simply told the third party in this matter that it was as they suspected, and that you are married. They would then have broken the news to Miss Goss–'

'They?' Victor interrupted. 'Who is this person? Who's been poking their nose into my private affairs?'

He wanted to kill them, to strangle them with his bare hands.

'Somebody who is concerned about Miss Goss's welfare and her good name. What I want to know, Mr Lambert, is shall I tell this person, or shall I leave you with the opportunity to do the right thing and tell Miss Goss yourself?'

Either prospect was appalling. But he could not let someone else poison Ruby's mind against him. He had to get to her first.

'I'll do it,' he said.

'Good.'

She sounded satisfied. Perhaps he was going to be allowed to go now. But it was not yet over. Mrs Rutherford was still speaking.

'There is one other important thing. It will be very uncomfortable for both of you, working in the same department. I think you might consider doing the honourable thing.'

'Yes, yes,' Victor said, hardly knowing what he was agreeing to. All he wanted was to escape from this room.

'I'm glad we have managed to discuss this in such a civilised fashion. Thank you for being so co-operative, Mr Lambert. Packards will be very sorry to see you go.'

Victor could not understand what she was talking about. Was he being sacked?

'Does this . . .?' he began.

But Mrs Rutherford was pressing the buzzer on her desk. The secretary appeared. Before he could formulate a coherent question, Victor found himself outside in the corridor. Anger and confusion battered him from inside. He began walking without knowing where he was going, phrases from the interview churning round his brain: not a cheap pick-up . . . tell her yourself . . . do the honourable thing . . . see you go . . . what did she mean by honourable thing? Put a bullet through his head, like a character in a melodrama? And then it came to him. She expected him to join up. Very neat. Get rid of a problem and increase Packards' contribution to the war effort. Rage consumed him. He punched the wall, enjoying the pain. He would not do it. He would not roll over and give in because Mrs oh-so-pure Rutherford Packard said so. What did she know about the hell of an unhappy marriage? What did she know about anything?

He arrived at the lift. He couldn't go back down to the department and act as if nothing was wrong. He pounded down the service stairs instead, his feet ringing on the harsh stone, until he finally emerged into bright sunlight.

He blinked. Here outside the store, everything was going on just as normal. People were walking, birds were singing, delivery vans were turning into the cavernous service entrance. Victor paced up and down the street behind the store, trying to think clearly. He had been given an ultimatum, not in so many words, but it had been made clear nevertheless. Give up Ruby or get the sack. Either way he had to go, since he was expected to join up. So why had he given in like that, and agreed to everything like a lamb? Why hadn't he said just what he thought about having Them control his very life? He felt sickened by himself. He was a coward. He should have fought for what he wanted, and what he wanted was Ruby, to marry her, to be with her for always. He would not give her up. But if he did not tell her, she would be told by someone else. He was going to lose her, and he couldn't bear it. Unless . . . unless he told Enid.

Victor stood still. That was it. He would confess all to Enid, and ask her to divorce him. Then he would tell Ruby, and ask her if she would marry him as soon as he was free. There would be a scandal, his family would reject him, he would almost certainly lose his job, but he would have Ruby, and that was what mattered. It all became wonderfully clear. He felt a sudden burst of something close to gratitude to whoever had given him away. Now he could stop deceiving and lying. The way ahead was open. He went back into the store.

He met Ruby as they had arranged at the ABC teashop. He had only been at the table two minutes when she came in, tall and lovely and exuding that delight in life that so entranced him. His courage nearly failed him. Why couldn't it all just go on as it had these last wonderful months? She sat beside him breathless and laughing, and accepted his offer of tea and sandwiches and toasted buns.

'Oh, isn't it just lovely to sit down? I've been run off my feet ever since Ivy left. I never did like her much, but now I'd give anything to have her back again.'

She bit into a bun with her strong white teeth, and melted butter oozed down her chin. She licked it off.

'I'm so looking forward to tonight. Millie Delaney and Arnie Roy! That Arnie Roy, he's so funny. Last time I saw him I laughed so much I thought I was going to die. I came out with my face all aching from laughing. The jokes he comes out with, and the way he does them . . .'

It was some time before she noticed that he was hardly answering. When she did, she stopped abruptly.

'What's the matter? You haven't said a word, and you haven't eaten anything either. Aren't you well?'

He almost snatched at it. What was one more lie amongst so many? But he resisted it.

'No, it's not that. Ruby, I – I'm afraid I can't take you out this evening after all.'

It was out, and he regretted it immediately, for her lovely mouth fell into a disappointed pout.

'You can't? Why not? What's more important than me?'

'Nothing's more important than you, Ruby, nothing on earth. It's just that – there's something I have to do – say – and it can't wait. It has to be done tonight. As soon as possible.'

Ruby looked intrigued.

'What on earth is it?'

'I – I can't tell you. Not yet, anyway.'

'Why not?'

'It – it's just not the right time. I will, truly I will, but I can't now.'

He could hear how feeble it sounded. Ruby evidently thought so too. She persisted, trying to get at least a hint of what it was all about. Miserably, Victor rebuffed her. It had to wait until he could tell her of his future freedom. At length, she sat back and addressed a point somewhere above his shoulder.

'Sounds to me like you got another woman.'

'Of course not!' Victor said, then tried to sugar the lie with a huge truth. 'I could never love anyone as much as I love you.'

'Then why won't you tell me what you have to do this evening?'

He leaned across the little table and tried to take her hands, but she snatched them away and folded her arms across her chest.

'Ruby, please,' he begged. 'Try to believe me. I will tell you, I promise, but not yet, not till – after. But it is very important and it's to do with us, with our future.'

She relented a little.

'It's your mother, isn't it? It's to do with her. Are we always going to be ruled by her? If you'd just take me to meet her, she might even like me.'

'Yes,' Victor said, thinking of his mother, a sprightly and cheerful lady who lived in Bristol, a very different character from the invalid he used as an excuse. She might well like Ruby, seeing as she disliked Enid and the two of them couldn't be more different.

'So when are you going to introduce me, then?'

'Soon. Look, Ruby, can you just be patient for a little while longer? And don't listen to anything that anybody says about me, do you hear? Nothing at all.'

Ruby stood up.

'It's always tomorrow, isn't it? Well, don't think I'm giving up my night at the halls. If you won't take me, I shall go by myself.'

With which she flounced out. Victor put his elbows on the table and sank his head into his hands.

He sat there over the cold tea for more than an hour, then he went home.

Enid was in the back parlour, knitting a khaki sock.

'What are you doing back at this time? You said you were going to be out all evening. I hope you're not expecting your tea.'

The very thought of food turned his stomach.

'No – no, don't worry about that.'

'So why are you back early? I thought you had a buyers' meeting to attend. You're not neglecting your business, I hope? You must always study your business.'

'I do, Enid. Always.'

'Well, I hope so. Even these days, places like yours are hard to find.'

'Yes, I know.'

He suffered a lurch of guilt. It had been Enid who had fuelled his early success. When first he had met her at a chapel tea, he had been merely an underbuyer's assistant, with years and years of being a dogsbody ahead of him before he could think of rising to greater power and responsibility. Aspiring to her expectations had given him the extra push he needed to get on. He owed her a great deal.

'I – er – I . . .' he dithered.

Enid's lips gave a twitch of impatience. She tugged at the khaki wool and jabbed her needle into the next stitch.

'Well, don't just stand there. Go and change.'

It was her rule that business clothes should not be worn in the evenings, not for elegance, but for reasons of economy and good housekeeping. As a result, Victor's trousers never sagged at the knees from having been sat in, and his jackets showed no wear at the cuffs or elbows. Glad to delay the moment, Victor obeyed.

He reappeared in sports jacket and trousers. Enid was still knitting, the steel needles clicking and grating. Through the open window came the sweet song of a blackbird. Victor looked out to where the late evening sunshine caught the leaves of the walnut tree that grew against all the odds at the bottom of the sooty back garden. There it was, perched on the topmost twig. Its freedom gave him the courage he needed.

'Enid, I – there's something I have to tell you.'

His voice sounded unnatural to his own ears, but his wife did not appear to notice. She went on frowning at the growing sock.

'Yes?'

'Yes, I . . .'

213

All the way home, he had planned to simply come out with it, to say that he had fallen in love with someone else and wanted a divorce. But now, standing across the marital hearth from her, feeling the waves of her habitual disappointment, it was not quite that easy.

'I . . .'

'What are you standing up like that for? Sit down.'

He sat, then sprang up again. He walked the two strides across to the window and back. The blackbird was still singing.

'Enid I – I wish you'd put that damned knitting down!'

The needles stopped. She looked up at him, shock and disapproval burning cold in her grey eyes.

'Victor! Language!'

'I'm sorry, it's just – this is important. Enid, there was no buyers' meeting this evening, nor all the other evenings when I've been out late. It wasn't business at all, it wasn't the war making everything different, it wasn't that I had to work longer hours to make up for all the men who had gone away. It was – it was – I've been seeing – that is, there is somebody who – who I . . .'

Her hands were stilled in mid-knit, and her eyes bore into him, choking his babble into silence.

'Yes?' she said.

He swallowed, and continued rather more slowly.

'There is somebody at work, one of the young women, whom I have been seeing – er – out of working hours.'

'I see.'

There was a terrible silence, filled only by the blackbird. The beauty of the song tore at his nerves.

'Say something, for God's sake! I've fallen for another woman. I love her, she's everything I've always dreamed of, she's–'

'Thank you. I don't think it is necessary for you to continue.'

Enid folded the sock carefully and placed it in her knitting bag. She laced her fingers in her lap and regarded him with unrelieved severity. She looked more like a middle-aged spinster headmistress than a married woman of thirty-one.

'You will of course break off your liaison with this – this hussy immediately.'

'She is not a hussy!'

Victor thumped a fist down on the chenille-covered table. She did not understand. She had never understood.

'She's a sweet, wonderful girl. I want to marry her.'

It was out. This time the silence was complete. The blackbird had flown away.

'That is not possible.'

'It is possible, if – if you divorce me.'

'We will pretend that was not said.'

'But I did say it! That's what I want! I want to live with her, to marry her.'

Victor could feel himself rushing towards a perilous point of no control. Part of him welcomed it, wanted to smash through the restraints that hemmed him in, to burst into a new world of emotional extremes.

'You cannot. You are married to me.'

'I don't have to be.'

'You do. When we married, we vowed to be together till death. I shall not falter, even though you have proved weak.'

Her implacable calm braked him before he could jump over the edge.

'You mean – you still want to stay married to me even though I love another?'

'Love! It's not love, it's infatuation. You have fallen for the temptations of these lax times. But I am prepared to forgive you, providing you break off all contact with this – person.'

'Never! I could never do that!'

'And I shall most certainly never agree to a divorce.'

The argument went round and round, but always it came to rest on the one point of certainty. Enid was not going to let go her status as a married woman. After the most miserable night of his life going over and over what had happened and what might have been, Victor rose to find his shoes polished and his jacket brushed as usual. Like an automaton, he went through the morning routine, standing outside himself looking on, hardly believing that he was able to behave so normally when inside everything was in turmoil. He got off at the same stop as always, hardly seeing the white feather girls. It was only when he looked at the revolving doors of the store that he knew he could not go on. He could not face going into Packards. He could not face Ruby. He turned and walked down the street to the recruiting office. The Western Front seemed a haven in comparison with this insoluble situation.

Two hours later, the elderly army doctor unhooked his stethoscope and shook his head.

'I'm sorry, young man, but I cannot pass you as fit. You have a heart murmur.'

Victor was horrified.

'But – but it can't be serious. It's never stopped me from doing anything. I never knew there was anything wrong with me.'

'Maybe so, but the army cannot afford to train a man who might never get to see action. I suggest you see your own practitioner if you have any worries about it. Next!'

On leaden feet, Victor made his way back to Packards. Going inside was the bravest thing he had ever done.

18

There was a faint ringing sound in Ruby's head. It formed a protective cushion, distancing her slightly from reality. The warm summer evening, the trees and grass of Hyde Park faded, leaving just the two of them in a blurred world of their own. The words that stumbled from Victor's lips seemed to be taking an immensely long time to reach her. She stared at him, trying to make sense of it. Married . . . wife . . . divorce . . . This was not her Victor, who worshipped her and her only.

Then gradually, the words hit home and a number of things began to make ominous sense.

'You mean, it wasn't your invalid mother you was always rushing off home to?' she said slowly, unwilling to accept it.

'No,' he admitted. He avoided her eyes.

'It was your – your wife?'

'Yes.'

The pain was unbearable. It clawed down inside her, acid and raw. He had come to be the centre of her existence. She had dreamed of being his bride. But all the time . . . Anger came to her defence, sweeping her with a red tide.

'You lied to me!'

She saw him flinch. It gave her a savage pleasure.

'Yes,' he admitted, his voice scarcely more than a whisper.

'You lied to me. It was all lies. You said you loved me, and all the time it was lies.'

'That wasn't a lie, Ruby. I do love you. I love you more than anything else in the world. You've got to believe me.'

'How can I? How can I believe a word you say? You're a cheat, a dirty rotten cheat. You asked me out and courted me and gave me flowers and everything and acted like you was free and single, and all the time you was married. How could you do that? How could you lead me on like that?'

'I – I just couldn't help it, Ruby. I wanted you so much. I couldn't let you go.'

'But you knew it couldn't never come to anything. You shouldn't have started it in the first place.'

'I wouldn't have if you hadn't given me the eye.'

For a moment, Ruby could not believe he had said that. She stared at him. He glared back, guilty, defiant.

'So it's all my fault, is it? You bastard! Is that what you're saying, that it's all because of me?' she demanded.

He flushed, and started to bluster.

'No, no, not exactly, not at all. But you weren't what you might call stand-offish, were you? I mean to say, I wouldn't have even thought of you if you hadn't made it very clear that you – you liked me.'

'You didn't have to take me up on it! I didn't know you was married!'

With a howl of rage, Ruby launched herself at him, slapping his face and ears, swearing, desperate to hurt him as he was hurting her. At first he backed away, ducking his head to avoid the blows and the abuse until

he found himself backed up against a thorny shrub.
Then he tried to stop her, struggling to catch her flailing
hands.

'Ruby, please, stop . . . I didn't mean it. It was all my
fault, I'm sorry . . .'

Ruby scarcely heard him. She snatched her hand free
and caught him a stinging blow on the side of his face.
She saw his head snap round with the force of it and
laughed.

'There! Bastard! See how you like it, liar!'

She choked as the laughter changed abruptly to tears.
Victor caught both her wrists and held them tight.

'Ruby, Ruby, I'm sorry. Please – I didn't mean it to
be this way. I didn't want to deceive you. I'll divorce her,
I promise, I'll talk her round. We'll be together, Ruby,
we'll get married . . .'

Ruby looked at him, at the reddening marks on his
face where she had hit him, and saw him clearly for the
first time. He was weak, he was a liar, she hated him.

'I wouldn't marry you if you was the last man on
earth!' she hissed.

He gaped at her, his grip on her wrists slackening with
the shock. Ruby wrenched herself free and ran, sobbing
and stumbling, not knowing where she was going.

A gate was ahead of her. Ruby dashed through it,
wanting to be away from the park, away from him. She
hurried along the pavement, half running, bumping into
people. There were cries of protest. Someone reached
out to stop her. A man.

'Now then, my girl, you can't–'

She pulled away with the strength of desperation and
plunged across the road. Brakes squealed, voices roared
at her. Something hard caught her a glancing blow on
the side. She staggered, choking in a cloud of blue
exhaust fumes. More voices. Hooves clattered beside
her. She was staring at the brown flanks of a horse.

Gasping, clutching at her side, she staggered on, tripping and almost falling as she reached the kerb. People were around her, some angry, some sympathetic. They were trying to stop her. She shook them off, and began running again.

At last, her lungs heaving and aching, she stopped. She leaned against a wall, her breath rasping in her chest, her heart pounding. She became aware of a throbbing pain in her hip and shoulder, but it was nothing to the pain in her heart. She collapsed on to a convenient doorstep, wrapped her arms round her legs and laid her head on her knees. A door opened behind her.

'You – girl! You can't sit there. This is a respectable street. Move on!'

Slowly, Ruby raised her head and looked round. An outraged butler was glaring at her from the doorway.

'Make me,' she said.

He hesitated, then stepped forward.

'Go now, before I call the police.'

'Call them,' Ruby told him. 'I don't care.'

She dropped her head to her knees again, shutting out anything that might be going on around her. Gradually her breathing steadied. Snatches of Victor's words swirled round her brain, taunting her. She held her head in her hands. She couldn't stay here. She had to move, just keep moving. She stood up. The butler was still there, looking agitated. Behind him were a couple of girls her own age in maids' uniforms. She hated all of them.

'What's the matter? What are you staring at?' she demanded. 'It's all right, I'm not stopping on your precious doorstep.'

She got up and moved off, walking painfully. The bruises on her side had stiffened up with the sitting. She had no idea where she was or where she was going. She got to the end of what she realised was a posh street and turned the corner into the mews at the back. There, opposite her, was a small pub. She went in.

Ruby had never been in a pub by herself before. It was crowded with men, civilians and soldiers, young and old. She pushed through them, ignoring the remarks. Some beer slopped down her back. She rounded on the culprit.

'Look what you're doing!'

'Oops – sorry, darling.'

'I'm not your darling.'

'We could change that. Here, let me buy you a drink.'

'No!'

'Woah – not very friendly, are we? What's the matter with you?'

Ruby turned her back on him and pushed forward. A renewed burst of remarks, some mocking, some suggestive, broke out behind her. There was a crowd at the bar. Men pressed round her, coins and cigarettes in their hands. Drinks were passed over her head. The barmen and maids ignored her. It was as if she wasn't there. She caught sight of herself in the mirrors behind the rows of bottles and glasses. She had to look twice to make sure it was her. She looked dreadful, her face haggard and tear-stained, her hair straggling down from under her crooked hat. Nothing could be further from the way she liked to think of herself, bright, pretty and fashionable. Anger filled her. He had done this to her. Victor Lambert, damn him. She smacked her hand down on the bar.

'I'll have a gin and seltzer, please,' she said loudly.

The nearest barmaid looked right through her and said, 'Yes?' to the soldier who was shouldering in from behind her.

'I said, I'll have a gin and seltzer,' she repeated.

The barmaid did not even blink.

The soldier gave her an assessing look.

'And a gin and seltzer for the lady,' he said.

The drink appeared in double quick time.

'Thanks,' Ruby said. She took a long gulp, and another. Half of the drink disappeared and a warm glow started inside her. She felt very slightly better.

The soldier looked at her with amusement.

'You can sink 'em, can't you, sweetheart? What's your name?'

Hardly caring now, Ruby told him.

'Ruby. Pretty name. Pretty girl. I'm Gordon Smith, Fifth Middlesex. On forty-eight hour leave.'

'Yeah?'

Normally, Ruby would have asked questions, joked, made admiring comments. Today, she had no interest whatsoever in Gordon Smith, but he did not seem to notice. He carried on telling her about himself while she finished the drink.

'Another?' he asked.

'Yes please,' Ruby said. It seemed to deaden the pain a little. She drank it down.

Gordon Smith's arm wound round her waist.

'You going to show a serving soldier a good time, then? You got somewhere to go?'

It took a moment for the implication of his words to reach her brain. When it did, she rounded on him.

'What do you think I am? A tart? The cheek!'

Smith's face assumed a dangerous expression.

'You was acting like one right enough, sweetheart. Come on, I bought you the drinks, didn't I? What more do you expect?'

'Beast!' Ruby spat.

She thrust the empty glass at him and elbowed her way out towards the door with Smith shouting and swearing after her. Faces leered at her, arms clutched, men laughed and jeered. Somehow, she managed to make it to the outside. Without any idea as to where she was going, she bolted down the street, round the corner, up another street. At the next corner she paused and looked back. Nobody was following her. Angry and humiliated, she plodded on. Her feet were aching nearly as badly as her poor heart; the bruising down her side made every movement painful. All she wanted now, she realised, was to get home. Home, to safety and love and sympathy.

A friendly passer-by directed her to Oxford Street. She emerged at last on to her own territory. There, on the opposite side of the road, was Packards, huge, solid and impressive despite the wartime drabness of its windows. She stared at it with a mixture of relief and dread. She knew where she was now, but tomorrow she had to go back in there and work alongside That Man as if nothing had happened. She did not know whether she could bear it.

A group of sailors came ambling along. They whistled when they saw Ruby.

'All alone, darling?'

'Come along with us, we'll cheer you up.'

Ruby stuck her nose in the air and hobbled across to the bus stop. After the disaster with Gordon Smith, she was not talking to any more servicemen. But the seed of an idea entered her head. A way of surviving, of having her revenge.

She was received with cries of distress by her mother and May, fussed over, given sweet tea and shoulders to cry on and put to bed as if she were an invalid. She cried herself to sleep, physically and emotionally exhausted.

In the morning she felt cold, drained, battered. The one consolation, when she walked into Stationery, was to find that Victor Lambert looked a good deal worse than she did. His face was grey and drawn, his eyes dull; he jumped when anyone spoke to him. The floorwalker asked him if he had the influenza, whether he would be better off at home. Victor looked horrified. No, he did not think he should go home. Ruby hoped his wife was giving him hell. She hated his wife, but she hated Victor even more. The trouble was, she still loved him as well. Once he tried to speak to her, to persuade her to meet him one more time, so that he could explain everything. Ruby told him she never wanted to see him outside of work again. She then proceeded to freeze him out for the rest of the day.

The first day was the worst. That over, she knew she could survive working with him, however painful it might be. It helped to see that it was just as painful for Victor. She wanted him to suffer. Badly. Then on the Monday of the next week, she was summoned to Mrs Rutherford's office.

'Sit down, Miss Goss.'

Mrs Rutherford's voice was warm, her smile welcoming. Ruby sat, and looked at her with curiosity. It was the first time she had exchanged more than a few words with a member of The Family. For a while she answered questions about her job. Did she enjoy it? Did she like working at Packards? Ruby wondered where it was all leading. Then Mrs Rutherford leaned forward and clasped her hands together on the desktop.

'Miss Goss, I don't want you to think that I am interfering with your private life, but I did wonder whether it would be more – ah – comfortable for you if you were to move to another department.'

Ruby gaped at her. Private life? Comfortable? Her head and heart were so full of Victor that she could only think that Mrs Rutherford was referring to him.

'Do you – do you know – about . . .' she stammered.

'Yes.'

Ruby's head was in confusion. How could she possibly know, when they had taken such care, when not even the people who worked in the department suspected? She realised that Mrs Rutherford was talking, and tried to listen to what she was saying.

'. . . that he join up, and apparently he did volunteer, but he was turned down on medical grounds.'

Victor? What was wrong with him?

'And so as we cannot move him to another department, I thought you might like to be transferred. There are plenty of vacancies at the moment.'

Ruby blinked at her, attempting to think. Transfer to another department. That first day after he had told her, she would have jumped at it. Now she was not so sure.

'I – I think I'd rather stay put, if you don't mind, Mrs Rutherford,' she said slowly. 'Like I said just now, I like it in Stationery. It's busy and there's always lots going on, and I'm good at what I do, though I say so as shouldn't. There's not a lot I don't know about writing paper. If I went somewhere else I'd have to start all over again.'

'Very well, if that is what you want. We certainly don't like to move trained staff around. Thank you, Miss Goss.'

Ruby found herself outside again. She walked slowly back down to the department, turning it all over in her mind. How could Mrs Rutherford have known? Who could have told her? How many other people knew? She shuddered to think that everyone was laughing at her behind her back. But no, she would have known if they were sniggering and whispering. It always came out. There was nothing Packards liked better than a good piece of gossip, and it always got back to the people concerned.

She spent the rest of the day watching everyone in the department even more closely than usual, but even in her oversensitive state, she could not discern anything out of the ordinary in the way they behaved towards her. She looked forward to telling May all about it on the way home. May had been wonderful these last few days.

May. She stopped dead in the act of picking up a piece of string from the floor. May knew everything. Slowly, Ruby straightened up. May knew everything. Ruby stared at the piece of string, twisting it round and round her fingers. If that was so, if May had gone to Mrs Rutherford . . . She tried to imagine her friend doing such a thing. She was so quiet, so overawed by everyone, surely she would not have had the courage to actually speak to one of The Family? But still it all seemed to add up. Her friend had betrayed her.

19

It was August when Hugo Rutherford first saw what had been his objective for over a year. The Line. It was a hot day, and he was weary and dirty but in the best of spirits. At last, they were going to see some action. All the training in England and more recently in France was about to be used.

His company had reached the top of a small hill. There it was, way ahead of them, stretching away on either side as far as they could see, a jagged gouge of brown through the summer green of the French countryside. Somewhere behind it a gun was firing, a dull, unthreatening sound, to be followed a few seconds later each time by a ball of smoke on the nearside.

'That's it, Saunders, that's what we're here for,' he said to his sergeant.

The man grinned.

'They won't rest peaceful now, sir. Not now we're here.'

The word was passing down the ranks of men. Cheering broke out, and shouts of cheerful defiance.

'Watch out, Fritz, you're about to get it.'

'The Early Birds are here.'

'Keep your heads down, worms!'

They had christened themselves the Early Birds because they had all volunteered in the very first days of the war, and were proud of it. No skulkers they.

The sight of the distant Front increased their already high spirits. Sore feet and aching backs were miraculously eased. Singing, they marched on towards their goal.

Close to, the Line was gaunt and desolate. In front of the network of trenches were broken stakes, shattered and dying trees, entanglements of rusting barbed wire. Beyond that was a hideous wasteland of churned and pockmarked earth before more barbed wire marked the start of the enemy trenches. By night, it could be almost beautiful. Flares and searchlights lit the sky like fireworks except that the noises were not the harmless crackles of Catherine wheels, but the rattle of rifle and machine-gun fire, and the whistle and shattering explosion of heavy shells.

It was the noise that most struck Hugo. He had used the word 'deafening' before but had never known its real meaning until a shell exploding nearby threw him off his feet and left him deaf in one ear for three days. The noise and the mud. It rained heavily a week after they arrived, a summer storm that washed down the sides of some of the trenches.

'I thought they were exaggerating when they told us about the mud,' he said to Sergeant Saunders as they struggled knee-deep through the stuff. It clung to his legs, sucking and evil smelling, as if it wanted to pull him down. An old hand who happened to hear him gave a hollow laugh.

'If you think this is bad, just wait until winter. This is nothing.'

The Early Birds had been sent to join the 7th Division of the regular army. The 7th had suffered terrible losses in the first Ypres battle, being reduced to just over two thousand men. It had been filled out by troops from Lord Kitchener's New Army, but further weakened by months of trench warfare. The Early Birds were part of the consignment that once more brought the division up to full strength.

Hugo was in his element. All his life, he had set himself challenges, had struggled for perfection. Now he knew why. It had all been leading to this, the Great Purpose. In his mind, he saw it written like that, with capital letters. Being one of the new boys amongst seasoned professional soldiers gave an extra edge to his competitive spirit. He had to prove that he and his men were worthy of the heroes they fought with. He went about his duties in a fever of enthusiasm. His platoon had to be the best, and with the able assistance of Sergeant Saunders and the willing effort of the men, it was. Detachments carried out daring raids along observation trenches into No Man's Land. Their snipers accounted for a number of unwary enemy soldiers. Thanks to Hugo's mania for hygiene, fewer of them went down with dysentery than any other platoon in the company. Morale remained consistently high, despite their sustaining their first losses. Relatively quiet the sector might be, but it was hardly safe. During those first few weeks, the company lost three men to rifle fire and five more plus a sergeant and an officer to shells, along with a dozen wounded. Hugo had been drinking with the officer only a couple of days before it happened. They had trained together, come out to France together, kept up a fierce but friendly rivalry between their respective platoons.

'I still owe him a bottle of red wine. I can't believe it. He was such a lively chap,' he said to Sergeant Saunders.

'I know, sir. Makes you think, don't it?' Saunders said.

It did make Hugo think, but he still could not really believe that it would ever happen to him. He sat up late that evening composing what he considered to be a comforting letter to the bereaved parents.

Home, when he thought about it, seemed to exist in another world, so far away that it had little to do with reality. Letters came, and parcels, from his mother, his sisters, his wife. As the weeks went on he scanned the letters from Amelie more anxiously. He had had a fortnight's leave before embarking for France. Surely by now she should have some news of real importance for him. In early September it came. Their fifth child would be born in the spring. The company was at the rear when the news came, so he was able to treat the whole platoon to beer in celebration. One of the privates confided that he had had similar news by the same post. Hugo treated him to whisky. The working classes had risen no end in his estimation since he joined the army. The ones in his platoon were splendid chaps, the salt of the earth. By the time they received fresh orders, they were as close to his heart as a family.

The 7th Division were being moved. They were to go to the section of the Front to the north of the mining town of Loos. The old hands soon realised what was going on.

'It's going to be a big push,' went the word.

The Early Birds cheered. This was it. This was their chance to show what they were made of.

As they got nearer to their destination, Hugo could see for himself that something big was brewing. Everywhere, long columns of troops were on the move. Wagons were carting load upon load of shells. Fresh field hospitals were being erected. The countryside there had never been beautiful for it was mining country, dotted with slag heaps and winding gear and straggling pit villages. Now it was downright ugly, defaced by the traffic of war.

They passed by mountains of fresh shells protected only by tarpaulins and guards.

'Those should be in underground magazines, surely?' Hugo remarked.

'Perhaps they're all full up and this is the reserve supply,' one of the regular officers told him. 'I hope so. We've been fighting this war on rationed ammunition up till now. If the artillery do their job correctly then we can sweep in and do ours instead of getting cut up before we even reach the Boche trenches.'

The men were issued with field rations and told not to touch them until ordered. They were moved from one overcrowded trench to another, then at last found space to settle down for the night. Sleep was difficult, bordering on impossible.

The sound of the artillery doing their job was beyond anything Hugo had ever experienced. For hour after hour the boom and whistle and explosion was so constant that it formed a wall of sound, battering at the brain. Even the deep dugout that the officers were called to for briefing was no protection from the noise, though it did muffle it a little. Their part in the forthcoming battle was explained. They were to take the quarries in front of the hamlet of Cité St Elie, and then proceed to St Elie itself, which was the centre of the German position. It looked simple enough, demonstrated by jabs of a pointer on a map, but they were warned that the quarries would be trenched and reinforced and that the cottages in the village had cellars that would serve as strong points. Tactics were explained, plans were given out. Hugo stared at the map, committing it to memory. He digested his own company's part in the struggle and understood what the others would be doing at the same time. He felt keyed up and eager. It was like the night before a big race, but one hundred percent more so.

This time there was more at stake than a trophy.

Later that evening, he wrote the obligatory last letter home, but still he could not believe that it would need to be sent. He had always been lucky. As long as he trained his hardest and gave of his utmost, he always won through. He did not think that that would change now.

By dawn the troops were shoulder to shoulder in the forward trenches. A mist hung over the low land, the natural white merging with a sickly yellow. At five thirty, gas had been released to creep towards the German lines. All along the British front line, smoke bombs were let off, curling up, joining and rolling, mile after mile, drifting across the valley to the slight rise occupied by the enemy. And still the artillery was firing.

At six the whistles shrilled, the first wave went over the parapet, the Early Birds moved up the network of trenches. Wave after wave of men went over. The artillery ceased and instead there was the sound of shells landing and of machine-gun fire. Hugo looked along his line of men, waiting with fixed bayonets, their faces pale in the dirty light. Now was not the time for them to get windy.

'We'll show these Regulars a thing or two, eh, lads?' he shouted.

Some nodded or grinned, others managed a cheer.

The order came along the line. Hugo drew his pistol.

'Let fly the Early Birds!' he yelled, and scrambled up the ladder.

He ran as he never had before, following the shadowy figures in front of him, charging into the mist. The men were at his heels, roaring like banshees. Bullets whined around him. One went past his face, so close he felt it. A man in front of him stopped short as if he had hit a wall, flung his arms wide, crumpled to his knees. As Hugo dodged round him, there was a cry to his left, to his right; men were dropping by the second. He glanced to either side. The ranks were holding, closing to fill the gaps, keeping on, though they were running now amongst the fallen, and the machine-guns raked through them like deadly hail. Hugo's heart swelled with pride. They were the best.

A shell landed behind him, exploding with a splitting crack and throwing up chalk and bits of bodies. Something slammed into his thigh, making him stagger and almost fall. His foot caught against something soft and he fell forward, arms outstretched. For a moment he came face to face with the remains of a man's head, the eyes still staring above a mangled red cavern where the nose and jaw had once been. And then hands caught him one each side under the armpits and he was hauled to his feet. He croaked his thanks and ran on, limping, for one leg did not seem to be working as well as it should.

They were going uphill now, lungs labouring, eyes stinging as a lingering thread of gas caught them. Ahead of him there were shouts and orders. One of the machine-guns fell silent, then another. Through the smoke and mist he saw their objective – the quarries. The first waves had already got there, and were fighting their way in. There were barbed wire entanglements still. Hugo stared at them as he staggered along. They shouldn't be there. They were supposed to be flattened. Then someone was shouting, waving, and he realised they were being shown the way through. He yelled at his men to follow him.

They plunged into a pit of chalk to be greeted by a figure with bloodshot eyes in a smoke-blackened face. It wasn't until he spoke that Hugo recognised him as the major.

'Good show. Get round that way and help capture that damned machine-gun. For Christ's sake look where you're firing, it's like a bloody labyrinth. Don't get our chaps by mistake.'

The 7th Division were storming through the quarries, leaving a trail of dead behind them. Hugo led his men along the trench the major had indicated. Several twists and turns later they came upon two more platoons held down by fire from a machine-gun playing through an opening in the soft rock ahead of them. Hugo saw immediately what was needed – a grenade lobbed neatly through the hole. But it would have to be thrown from much nearer. There must be other ways round, inter-connecting trenches. He remembered passing one twenty yards or so back that appeared to go off at an angle. It was worth a try. From the remains of his platoon he chose four whom he remembered as being accurate when throwing grenades.

'I'm going to try to knock him out. You're in charge till I get back, sergeant,' he said to Saunders.

At first he thought he'd made a serious mistake. The side trench seemed to be leading away from the machine-gun emplacement. Then it joined with another, turned a corner and Hugo and his group were confronted with a pile of bodies, khaki and grey. But there just fifty yards ahead of them was the opening. The gun was firing on the position they had just come from.

'Stay down,' he ordered.

He stared at the opening. Now, now was the moment, before they were seen. He scrambled over the dead. In his mind's eye he saw a wicket. He pulled out the pin. The grenade fitted snugly to his hand. He limped forward, accelerated into a lurching gallop just as the machine-gunner spotted him and swung round. Back went his arm, up, round in a perfect overarm bowl. The grenade flew sweetly through the air and exploded right on the gun as the bullets came hissing towards him. Hugo was dead before he hit the ground.

20

The memorial service was to be held at Hugo's family's parish church in Herefordshire. The organising of it seemed to give Hugo's mother some comfort. She wrote countless letters, hurried about with lists in her hands and gave contradictory orders to everyone remotely concerned with the event. Her whole life seemed to revolve around making sure that the service and everything to do with it would be a fitting tribute to her dead son. Every now and again she became aware that she might be rather selfish in keeping this to herself and tried to include Amelie, asking her opinion as to who should be asked or which hymns should be sung or what food should be ordered.

Guilt drove Amelie to try to please her. She gave Mrs Rutherford her address book, though she knew that nearly all of the couples with whom she and Hugo used to exchange dinners were now apart due to the war. Several of the wives were, like her, now widows. She gave her Hugo's address book as well.

'But I would think that most of his sporting friends are at the Front, too. In fact I'm sure that they are. There are the Eugenics Society people, of course. I know very little about them . . .'

Speaking was an effort. Everything was an effort. Hugo's mother translated her grief into restless energy. Amelie felt drained. Still the letters of condolence came in. Picking up a pen to answer them was almost more than she could manage. Amelie sometimes overheard her mother-in-law murmuring excuses on her behalf to sympathetic visitors.

'She's quite overcome, poor child. It's terrible, we feel so helpless. There's so little we can do to comfort her. They were such a perfect couple.'

Twisting the knife unknowingly yet again. If they only knew. Amelie kept silent, letting it all boil inside. There was no one to whom she could confess. She sat in the morning room of the Rutherfords' lovely old manor house, looking over the fading rose garden to the woods and fields beyond. It was better here than in London. There were fewer memories.

There was no escaping other people's memories, though. Hugo's mother and his unmarried sister relived his life, his opinions, his achievements continually. Visitors came and went, people who had known Hugo from babyhood, their voices hushed, their faces saddened. It was such a tragic loss, they said. He was such a fine man, so brave, a splendid sportsman, a straight bat, an example of everything an Englishman should be. Amelie nodded and agreed and let them talk. Every now and again she left the room in the closest she could get to a hurry. The visitors shook their heads and sighed. But she was not going to weep in private, she was going to be sick. She had never felt so ill before. None of the other pregnancies had been like this. The weight was falling off her, making her pale and haggard in the unrelieved black of her mourning clothes.

The vicar, Hugo's uncle, came frequently to consult about the order of the service and the choice of hymns. Mrs Rutherford changed her mind each time. It was an ideal opportunity for another burst of remembrance.

'Fight the Good Fight seems appropriate, don't you think? Hugo used to like that one. I can picture him now, singing it out in that fine strong voice of his. And that was what the poor boy was doing, after all. The second verse, too – Run the straight race – is so right for him. He was always such a fine sportsman.'

The Reverend Rutherford nodded in agreement.

'He played to win, but he was generous in defeat. He respected someone who could beat him. He had no time for cheats. Always maintained that there was no point in winning if you did it unfairly.'

'Yes, yes, that was exactly what he believed,' Mrs Rutherford sighed, then with one of her quick flashes of conscience. 'But what do you think, Amelie dear? Are you happy with Fight the Good Fight? Or would you prefer something else?'

Amelie would have preferred almost anything else, but lacked the will to say so. For all she knew, it had been Hugo's favourite hymn. It seemed highly likely. And if his mother and the vicar, along with most of the rest of the population and Hugo himself, all believed that the war was a just one, waged against the forces of evil, who was she to argue with them?

'No, no, that's all right,' she said.

The day of the memorial service drew near. Amelie's parents arrived to support her, along with Perry, who was still stationed in England, and Gwendoline, and Edward and Sylvia. Amelie did not want to see any of them. One of her reasons for accepting the Rutherfords' invitation to stay had been to avoid her own family. Unfortunately, Mrs Rutherford thought it might be of some help to her to have her family near, so the Packards were accommodated in the manor house while visiting Rutherfords were sent to the Rectory or to the Markhams, Clement's family. It was an arrangement that suited none of them, since Mrs Rutherford would have much preferred to have her own relations around her at this time and the Packards, marooned amongst Amelie's in-laws, had to put on a show of family unity.

Winifred in particular tried to play the part of the good mother, sitting with Amelie and encouraging her to look at all the things she had left in life.

'You must be so glad now that you had all those babies so quickly. Such a beautiful family, three sturdy boys and dear little–' she stumbled as the name of her granddaughter escaped her. Amelie made no attempt to refresh her memory.

'–a dear little girl,' Winifred substituted. 'Children are such a comfort at times like these. Why don't you send for them?'

'There isn't enough room for them here. The house is full,' Amelie said, as yet another cause for guilt gnawed at her. She really ought to have the children here. However good Nanny was with them, they would be missing her. But she just could not face them yet.

'Oh, I'm sure they could be fitted in somewhere. Maude Rutherford seems to be such a good manager, and so fond of you. She would find room for them if she knew you wanted them. I'm sure it would do you good to have them about you. Childish laughter, you know, and little pranks. Children can be so charming.'

Amelie wondered whether her mother knew what a hypocrite she was or if she just conveniently forgot her own former actions or opinions in order to say whatever seemed the suitable thing at the time. It roused her from her apathy.

'Really? I can't think how you know. You never used to take any notice of us.'

Winifred looked amazed.

'Nonsense, Amelie dear. You children were the pivot of my life. You still are, in fact.'

238

'That's why you never used to see us for more than half an hour a day, then? When you were home, that was, and when you could spare us that much of your time.'

Winifred gave a tinkling laugh.

'Half an hour a day? How you do exaggerate, Amelie. I utterly devoted myself to your upbringing. And even when I wasn't there, you children were always uppermost in my thoughts.'

It quite took Amelie's breath away. The only person Winifred had ever devoted herself to was Winifred.

'That is so untrue. All you ever thought about was improving your place in Society.'

'But it was all for you, my dear. You and the boys. My one object was that you should have a good start. And see how you have benefited. You have married into this charming family. Why, I believe there have been Rutherfords in this part of the world for over a thousand years.'

Amelie hadn't the strength to argue further.

'Excuse me,' she said, and left the room to be sick.

Of all her relations, Amelie was surprised to find that Gwendoline was the least irritating. Her sister-in-law made no attempt to sympathise with her or cheer her. She simply did what she always did, and chattered on at great length about her own concerns, hardly needing a reply at all. After all the pious words and hollow emotions, Amelie found it quite restful.

The only people she did want to see were delayed in arriving. Both of Clement and Ida's children had gone down with the measles, so Ida decided to travel down to Herefordshire on the day of the service. Clement was given thirty-six hours' leave starting the day before. He arrived in the early evening and came straight over to the manor house.

Amelie had gone up to dress for dinner long before it

was really necessary. It was a useful exercise for getting away from everyone. So she was sitting in a comfortable old dressing gown with her hair down staring at the fire when she heard the sound of a motorcar coming up the drive. Unbidden, a lurch of hope stirred queasily within her. She almost ran to the window. There, crunching on to the gravel forecourt, was the Markhams' Wolsey. She peered into the twilight. The car came to a halt by the front porch. The driver's door opened. Amelie's heart beat against her ribs. A tall figure in khaki stepped out.

'Clement!'

The cry broke from her lips before she could stop it. Amelie clapped a hand over her mouth and stepped back so that the curtain hid her. For a moment, she thought that he had heard her. He hesitated and almost looked up. She could not read his expression as his face was in shadow. Then he slammed the car door and walked round to the porch. Amelie gazed down at the top of his cap until he disappeared under the canopy. She found that her legs were shaking. She was alive again.

She rang the bell with such force that her maid came running.

'What is it, ma'am? Are you poorly?'

'No, no – I must get dressed at once. Quick, the silk dress with the scalloped trimming – or, no, do you think the one with the ruffles? Which is prettier?'

The maid schooled her astonishment into the carefully bland expression of the well-trained servant.

'The scalloped one is very nice, ma'am. Let's get you into your corset and petticoats and then we'll see what's what.'

The usual lengthy transformation into evening wear complete with pinned up hair was achieved in a record half hour. Amelie was glad now of the good taste of the Packards Ladies' Gowns designer and the exquisite workmanship of the staff. She had taken no interest at all in her mourning wear, but the talented woman who had masterminded her court gown, her wedding dress and practically every other outer garment she possessed had produced a wardrobe of black clothes for her that were the epitome of restrained elegance. So her dress was fine, but when she looked at her face, she groaned. She looked dreadful. She pinched her cheeks and bit her lips. The faint colour did little to dispel her pallor. Her eyes had lost their dead look, but they were glittering feverishly rather than glowing. Her hair, though stylishly done up by her maid, was dull and lacklustre.

'Very nice, ma'am,' the maid commented.

'I look like a hag,' Amelie snapped.

But there was nothing she could do about it. The important thing was to get downstairs. The questions that had raced round her head as she got ready shouted at her yet again. Was Clement staying to dinner? Mrs Rutherford was sure to ask him, but were his own parents expecting him to dine with them? If so, how long was he staying? Was he already taking his leave, walking towards the entrance hall? She made for the door.

She hurried to the top of the stairs, put her foot on the first step, and stopped. Her head was swimming. She clutched at the banister rail. The stairs went in and out of focus. There was a pounding in her head. She hung on for dear life until the world steadied and she felt in control again. Then the doubts crept in. What was she doing, acting like a schoolgirl in the grip of a crush? This was her best friend's husband she was racing to meet. Her own husband had not been dead a month. She must be the wickedest woman on God's earth. But nothing was going to stop her from seeing Clement. Very carefully, holding on to the banister, she crept downstairs, then across the stoneflagged hall to the drawing room.

Clement and Mrs Rutherford both looked up in

surprise. From the embarrassed look on both their faces, she suspected that they had been discussing her.

'Amelie, what are . . .?'

'My dear Mel . . .'

Clement jumped up and strode over to her as she stood inside the door, swaying slightly. He took her arm.

'Come and sit down. Here, by the fire. You're as cold as ice. Are you unwell? Can I fetch you anything?'

Amelie shook her head. All she wanted was that he should keep holding her arm, but once he had settled her in a chair, he let go and sat in the one next to her.

'Are you sure you're all right? A small brandy, perhaps?'

'No, really,' Amelie insisted. 'You're very kind, but I'm fine now.'

She hated it when other people fussed round her. With him, it was different.

Mrs Rutherford was still looking puzzled.

'You're down very early, Amelie. I was only just beginning to think of going up.'

'I heard the motor, and I was ready, so I thought I would come down,' Amelie said, unable to think of anything more clever than a slight twisting of the truth.

'It is so nice to see dear Clement. Hugo and he were such good friends, you know. When they were boys, they were always together. They were more like brothers than cousins. The terrible twins, we used to call them. The mischief they used to get up to! I remember the summer they were thirteen, or was it fourteen . . .?'

Mrs Rutherford rambled on. Amelie sat clenching her teeth with impatience. Why couldn't the silly woman go away?

Clement let her talk until the tale lost direction, then he slid in as Mrs Rutherford paused for breath.

'You'll have Amelie think we were a pair of young bandits, Aunt Maude.'

242

'Ah, but you grew into splendid young men,' Mrs Rutherford sighed.

Clement stood up and held out a hand to help her to her feet.

'You go up and dress, Aunt Maude. I'll just have a short word with Amelie before I drive home. I'll see you at the church tomorrow.'

To Amelie's delight, Mrs Rutherford took this like a lamb. She kissed Clement's cheek.

'Thank you, dear boy. It was so very good of you to come all this way.'

'Nonsense, Aunt Maude. You know I would have come three times as far. Till tomorrow.'

Clement waited until she had left the room, then sat down by Amelie.

'How are you, Mel? It can't be easy, staying here with Hugo's people.'

Amelie's throat felt dangerously tight.

'No,' she said, her voice coming out as a squeak. 'Everyone's so nice to me and I don't – I don't deserve it.'

'Melly! What a thing to say. Of course you deserve it.'

'I don't. They all keep saying how wonderful Hugo was and I–'

And I was pleased when he went away. I was happy. I was happier than I had been for years.

Scalding tears of guilt welled up and spilled over. Racking sobs tore at her chest, all the more fierce for having been kept in check for over three weeks. Somehow, she found herself in Clement's arms, her head on his shoulder. She wept until she was nothing but a dry husk with a throbbing head and aching eyes. Gradually, she became aware of the damp prickly khaki beneath her cheek, the strong arms holding her.

'I'm s-sorry–' she managed to say.

Clement took her shoulders and held her a little away

243

from him.

'Mel, listen to me. You must understand this. I know Hugo. Nothing you could have said would have stopped him from going. It was what he wanted, and Hugo always stopped at nothing to gain what he wanted. You must not blame yourself.'

Amelie nodded slowly. She must not blame herself. And though she knew that there were still plenty of reasons for remorse, his words sustained her through the following difficult hours.

The service started at eleven o'clock. Amelie was glad of her heavy veil. It gave her a sense of protection, cutting her off from the prying eyes of the rest of the congregation. She stood and sat and knelt along with everyone else, while the hymns and prayers mocked her. The address was even worse. All the sincerely held platitudes that she had heard so much of in the past three weeks came rolling out again. A noble death . . . a hero's path . . . the supreme sacrifice to a just cause . . . a true son of his country . . . Amelie sat through it, crushed once more by the knowledge that everyone thought that Hugo was a paragon. Except her.

The torture seemed to go on for ever. Even when the service was over, there was still the luncheon to be endured. This promised to be even worse. At least in the church nobody spoke to her.

As she walked into the entrance hall of the manor house, she was greeted by the smell of roasting meat wafting up from the kitchens. Amelie's treacherous stomach heaved. She made a dash for the lavatory.

When she emerged, white-faced and sweating, she found Ida waiting for her. Her friend immediately took charge.

'My poor darling. Come out into the fresh air. We'll get away from all the hideous Rutherfords and Markhams.'

Amelie was only too glad to obey. Ida led her into the lime walk, well away from any curious eyes, and sat her down on a wrought-iron bench.

'It's all been too much for you, hasn't it? Clem told me how upset you were, and no wonder. I don't know what I'd do if Clem . . .'

Even her closest friend was assuming that she was the grief-stricken widow. Amelie clenched her fists and beat them on the iron struts. Something seemed to burst in her heart.

'Don't you see? Surely you of all people – do you know how I felt when Hugo volunteered? Not worried, not lost. I felt glad. Glad! The day he left home, it was as if a lead cloak had lifted from my shoulders. I felt free again. I felt like a real person. I used to walk down the street and it was all I could do to stop myself from skipping like a child. When all the other women were being strong and proud and desperately anxious, I was happy. And now – now he's gone, do you know why it is that I feel so terrible? Because I don't feel as I should, as everyone thinks I'm feeling. All my grief is for what might have been, for how it should have been, not for how it was, or how he was. There – so now you know. I suppose you're shocked. I'm wicked, I know I'm wicked, but I can't help it.'

There was a silence into which her words seemed to spin, endlessly repeating themselves. Amelie existed in a state of sick suspense. Had she ruined everything? What if Ida could not understand? What if she turned from her? Without her support she truly was lost. The silence lasted for a heartbeat, but it felt like an age. Then Ida took one of her hands in both of hers.

'My poor darling,' she whispered. 'I always suspected that you and Hugo weren't like Clem and me, but – oh, but of course it makes it all so very much worse. And now another baby as well–'

There was no stopping the words now. They all came swirling out in a poisonous stream.

'Yes, the baby. Hugo had the last laugh there, didn't he? All he ever wanted was for me to keep producing perfect babies and now he's making me do it even though he's dead. And everyone thinks it's so wonderful. They keep saying that it must be such a comfort to me to be bearing his child. I can't stand it. All those eyes and teeth staring at me, pretending they care. What do they know? I never wanted this baby. I hate it. I hated it when Hugo was alive and I hate it even more now and I know I shall hate it when it's born. It's keeping me tied to him like a ball and chain—'

Ida took her by the forearms and turned her so that they were facing each other.

'Listen to me. You won't hate it when it's born, I promise. It doesn't work like that, and you know that really, so stop scourging yourself. Once it is born, then you will be free. You'll be off that continual round of childbearing that Hugo insisted on. You're not alone, you know. You're not the only one—'

'I do know that,' Amelie protested, shocked that her friend was now lecturing her, however kindly. 'Of course I know. There are new widows being made even now as we speak.'

'I don't mean that. I mean you're not the only woman who longs to stop having children. You don't speak to working-class women the way I do – and I know you know all of your shopgirls and have their welfare very much to heart but they're none of them married, are they? I speak to married women and believe me, hundreds of them feel the same as you. Now that their men are away they can go out into the world and do jobs they never thought they were capable of and they aren't tied to continual childbearing. They feel guilty too. They love their menfolk, many of them, and they're continu-

246

ally worried about them, but at the same time they're having the first taste of anything like freedom they've ever had in their lives. So stop feeling you're uniquely wicked. You're not.'

Footsteps crunched on the gravel path. Both women looked up, suddenly silent, afraid of being overheard by one of the relatives. It was Clement.

'I don't want to interrupt–' he began, but Ida interrupted him.

'Clem, come and tell Mel what your opinion is of Hugo's eugenics theories. Honestly, mind.'

Clement sat down beside his wife, but he addressed Amelie.

'I think they are at best ill-thought-out pseudo science, and at worst a set of potentially very dangerous ideas. At the moment they're only subscribed to by a bunch of cranks, but if ever they were taken on board by a political party with any power, the effects could be quite terrifying.'

'There,' said Ida. 'See?'

'Yes,' Amelie submitted. She felt emotionally drained now, a shell with nothing but dry air inside, but a fragile shell, liable to shatter at any moment.

The three of them sat under the bent branches of the lime walk, a small knot of dissenters from the eulogy to Hugo that was going on inside the house.

'I came to warn you that they are about to send out search parties for Amelie,' Clement said. 'I guessed you'd be together somewhere. It's all getting very cloying in there. They're making old Hugo out to be a saint, which he wasn't. There are times when I hardly recognise the person they're talking about.'

He turned to his wife.

'Look, Ida, don't you think it would be a good idea if Mel were to come and stay at our house for a while? If you would care to, that is, Mel?'

A crack of light broke. Amelie nodded slowly.

'Yes. Yes, I would like that. But–'

'Don't worry about Aunt Maude. I'll square it with her. I'm in her good books at the moment. And Ida would be very glad of the company, wouldn't you?'

'Of course I would. It's a wonderful idea. I can't think why I didn't suggest it myself,' Ida agreed.

'Good. We'll smuggle you indoors now and Ida can take you straight upstairs and get your maid to pack your things, while I tackle Aunt Maude. Then you can come back with us this evening,' Clement decided. 'And just remember, Mel – you are not to blame.'

'I will remember,' Amelie promised. The fragile shell felt just a little stronger.

21

Nineteen sixteen brought the full impact of the war to bear on the British people. Conscription was at last introduced, taking away yet more men to the Front. Their places were filled by thousands of women, who took over on the farm and in the factory, in transport, the police and the Post Office, as well as in the hundreds of new government departments that were springing up all over the place and of course in the myriad hospitals and convalescent homes. Families were having to manage with fewer or even no servants; officers and city gents rode on buses as there were so few cabs; museums and galleries were closed; and drinks were weak and expensive. Prices and wages both rose steeply, but at least there was work, more work than there were workers to carry it out. Government, the recruiting offices and private employers were all competing for labour.

There were times when May wondered if she ought to leave Packards and take one of the new jobs, something that would really be doing her bit towards the war effort. Her friendship with Ruby had almost collapsed with the huge row they had had after Ruby's break-up with Victor. Ruby blamed May for the whole disaster, and accused her of being jealous and wanting to make a laughing stock of her in front of the entire Packards workforce. It had taken a lot of straight talking from Mrs Goss to make her see that since nothing could change the fact that Victor was married, the affair was doomed all along to end in tears, and that at least now she wasn't being deceived. Ruby and May made it up, but Ruby still made it very clear that she held May responsible for ruining the love of her life, and used this as a level to get May to do what she wanted.

A few weeks after Ruby's crisis, Will Foster stopped May in the corridor when they were about to go home.

'Miss Hollis?'

She didn't really want to stop and talk to him, and was about to say that she was in a hurry to get back, but he did not give her time to speak.

'You – you've got pretty strong views on chaps joining up, haven't you?' he asked.

May was caught.

'Yes I have. I think every young man ought to be out there defending his country,' she said.

'I thought so. That's why – I wanted to tell you that I went and volunteered yesterday. I did it because of you.'

The last words came out in a rush. He stood blushing and breathless, waiting for her reply. For a moment, May did not know what to think or say. Then she felt a glow of pride. She had inspired a man to do his duty. Surprising herself almost as much as she surprised him, she reached up and kissed Will's cheek.

'That's for doing the right thing. I'm proud of you,' she said.

Will's blush deepened to crimson.

'Oh – Miss Hollis – May –' he stammered. 'I wonder–'

But at that moment, Ruby came along and swept May off to catch the bus, so May never did find out what it was that he was going to ask.

250

The department was not the same after he left. It was not like when Alec Eden went, but still May came to realise that it had been nice to have an admirer, even one whom she did not actually want to walk out with. It gave her a status in the Packards gossip hierarchy.

Ruby shrugged off Will's noble gesture.

'Good riddance. He's boring. Where shall we go tonight?'

For Ruby had a new aim in life: to notch up as many different types of servicemen as possible. To meet them, she needed a girlfriend to go out hunting with, and May fitted the bill nicely. She was quieter and less pretty than Ruby, so she was no competition and gave Ruby just the right amount of respectability. On top of that, she was always available.

Ruby kept a list of her conquests on the inside of her wardrobe door. There were no names, just the branch of the armed forces that each one belonged to. Infantrymen were common as grass, of course, and she soon found more than enough cavalrymen, gunners and bombardiers. Then she branched out into Engineers and the RAMC, before setting her sights on the Navy. She soon became an expert on different grades of ship and trades within the senior service, and could tell an Able Seaman from an Ordinary at fifty paces. Airmen were a prized novelty. There weren't a great many of them around. It took her nearly three months to get one on her list, and then he was only a mechanic rather than a dashing pilot. She did not regard any of them as potential sweethearts. They were just scalps to her belt. Some she would not see again after the evening on which they met. Others she liked enough to go out with for the length of their leave. If they fell for her, so much the better. She always liked it when they begged her to write to them, to wait for when they next came home, but she never made any promises. The whole point was to be able to talk about them at work.

She would wait until Victor was within earshot, then she would tell whoever was nearest to her about her latest conquest, with embellishments, if necessary.

'Tonight I'm going to the theatre with my young man. He's a Jack Tar, you know, a gunner on a destroyer. I think they're so brave, don't you? At sea for weeks at a time in dreadful weather and great rough waves and being shot at by German ships and torpedoed by U-boats. I think a lot of a man who can do that. And he's such fun! He really knows how to enjoy himself. We're going to see *A Bit of Fluff* tonight. I've wanted to see that for ages, and I just happened to mention it to him, just in passing, like, and at once he says, "If that's what you'd like to see, then that's where we'll go." Just like that!'

Out of the corner of her eye she would watch Victor's reaction. She knew he was listening, however much he tried to appear not to be. He gave himself away by a change of colour, or an uncontrollable twitch of the mouth or eyes, or a dropping of some small item from fingers that had suddenly gone nerveless. Oh yes, he was listening all right, and he was suffering. Ruby convinced herself that it gave her pleasure.

May found she was having fun. At first she had gone along because of the pressure Ruby put on her, but after a while she gained confidence and found the hunting expeditions hugely exciting. Swept along in Ruby's wake, she learned to size up a group of men and decide on the one she was going for. The most attractive and lively one was always earmarked as Ruby's property, but after him, she could take her pick. None of them ever touched her heart, but she had a good time. She put thoughts of leaving Packards to one side.

The small concerns of the civilian population seemed odd to the returning soldiers. Everyone's lives had been touched by the war, but those at home had no idea of what it was really like at the Front. Even if he could find the words to describe it, the ordinary Tommy found it next to impossible to talk about what he had experienced. Alec Eden, home on leave, saw everything as from a slight distance. It was as if the London in which he had lived nearly all his life was a stage set. The changes in it were interesting, but irrelevant. Real life was the army, and France.

'My darling boy, what have they done to you?' his mother cried when he appeared in the front hall, lean and weather-beaten and looking five years older than the boy who had gone to France only three months ago. 'Come and sit down – here, here, in the most comfortable seat. What would you like? Tea? Brandy? Cake? Oh, where is West? That girl is never here when you want her. Did you notice how long she took to open the door? I tell you, darling, things are getting dreadful. Only two servants! And they're getting above themselves. The wages I have to pay them now. And do you know, I have to do the dusting myself? I do, really! And deliveries are becoming a thing of the past. I haven't seen an errand boy down this road in I don't know how long. It's coming to a pretty pass, I can tell you. Why, I have to send the daily woman to collect the groceries!'

Alec sank back in the floral cushioned comfort of the frilly room and let her chatter on. His own home seemed alien to him. Everything was the same, but still it was strange to be somewhere so clean and soft and pretty. He encouraged his mother to talk about her own concerns. The longer she did that, the less likely she was to fix him with a wide-eyed gaze and ask earnestly what it was really like at the Front. She was far better off not knowing. Let her keep her vague ideas of jolly camps and marching and heroics.

The first evening home was devoted to a luxurious

bath, eating, drinking and listening to his mother. Slowly, he realised that she had changed, that he need not have worried about leaving her. Now that he was not there all the time trying to take the place of his father, she was at last crawling out of the pit of grief and finding interests of her own. She had joined the Friends of the local hospital and spent a lot of time raising money and visiting the sick and wounded, and she had taken up the piano again.

'They so love a bit of entertainment, and you know I used to have a nice voice. Your father always said so. "Dora," he said, "you've the sweetest voice in the world." Well, it's a shame to waste your talents, isn't it? So I'm taking lessons. We have some lovely singsongs. It gets really jolly in the convalescent wards, and I'm sure it does them good, poor loves.'

'I'm sure you're right,' Alec agreed. His mother was a charmer when she set herself out to please. He could just picture the Tommies looking forward to her visits.

He had fully intended staying in, but by the time his mother started talking about going to bed, at half past ten, he was beyond going to sleep. He took her up her chocolate and brandy, put on his overcoat and headed for Soho. There he fell in with a bunch of other young officers, went to three different nightclubs and ended up in the bed of a young woman who claimed to be an actress.

In the cold light of the morning, she did not look quite so young, and what was more, she was engaged in going through the pockets of his jacket.

'I just wanted to find your address,' she said, when she realised that he was watching her from the bed.

Alec gave her a large tip and left. It had, after all, been a good night, as far as he could remember. He went home for a wash and a change. His mother was divided between sulking because he had gone out and pride that he was acting like her idea of a real man. He escaped by telling her that he had to go and see how his inheritance was faring.

Packards was looking just a little shabby. Oxford Street in general was definitely the worse for wear. Gone were the lavish window displays, the aura of seductive opulence. His father, Alec thought, would turn in his grave if he could see his creation now. The paintwork was dingy and the windows full of practical items, the dullness of the colours relieved only by patriotic red, white and blue draping, and even that was faded.

Nothing, though, could dim the beauty of the red marble entrance hall. Standing in the centre of it and looking up past the floors to the dome, Alec felt something like his old passion for the place stir. But it was a distant flutter, a remembered dream. He was not really part of this any longer. The feeling increased as he toured round the store. It was not the same as it used to be. There were less staff, a smaller range of goods, fewer customers. There were still pockets of conspicuous luxury. In one corner of the Food Halls, four shopgirls were kept constantly busy serving well-dressed women with fancy confectionery. There were still well-dressed women around, many of them carrying what appeared to be the latest fashionable accessory, a pampered lap dog. They managed to retain the leisured manner that used to epitomise the Packard customer, but on the whole the shoppers seemed to have a distracted air. They had not come in to spend the day, to make a pleasure out of a purchase. They needed to buy something and were doing it in between more important matters. Even more noticeable was the complete absence of the young man about town. The Perry Amberleys of Society used to stroll about the store in between getting up and going to lunch parties, or before driving out in their fast cars to friends' places in the Home Counties. Now if

255

they were here at all, it was in khaki or the hospital blue of the wounded.

The stationery department was quite busy. Alec walked round, chatting to each shopgirl, lingering by the delectable Ruby Goss. Not that it did him any good. She was cool and polite, nothing more, a marked contrast to some of the others. Piqued, he went over to speak to Victor Lambert.

'Still here, Lambert? I'd have thought they would have called you up by now.'

Lambert was immediately on the defensive.

'I did try to volunteer, actually, but I was turned down. Apparently I have a weak heart.'

'I should try again, if I were you. The MOs will often turn a blind eye. If you really want to go, that is.'

'Is that so? I shall have to see if I can persuade them. Maybe if I went to a different recruiting office it would help.'

He sounded eager enough. Alec wondered if he had a lot of people trying to persuade him to go. Civilians seemed to be even keener to send men off to the Front than they were before he joined up, and it had been bad enough then. It was all very well for them, of course. They did not have to go themselves. They did not have to – he stopped himself, deliberately pushing the crowding images to the back of his mind. He concentrated on asking Victor Lambert about how the department was doing.

As he left the department, he couldn't help looking back at the writing paper counter. To his delight, Ruby Goss was looking straight at him. As he caught her eye, her wonderful mouth stretched slowly into a knowing smile. Alec grinned back and turned away. Well.

He hardly took in anything for two floors. Was that smile an invitation? Of course it was. Did he want to follow it up? Of course he did. So what was stopping him?

His father's edict on Family and the shopgirls. He was still turning it over in his mind when he reached Household Linens.

There were no young shopmen in the department at all now. The girls that were left came flocking round him, eager to ask how he was, and had to be chased back to work by the buyer and the floorwalker, both men in their late fifties, well beyond call-up age. Just to put a spoke in their wheel, he kept them all talking. He focused on one at random, trying to remember her name. Maisie? Marion?

'That's enough, Miss Hollis. There are customers waiting,' the floorwalker said.

May Hollis. That was it. A nice little thing. She was asking the question he dreaded most: what was it like in France?

'It's not so bad, May. I'm still alive, that's the main thing,' he said, wondering as he did so at the easy words. They didn't mean a thing.

He turned his attention to the men, and asked after business, but his mind was not on what they were saying. Those dark eyes and luscious lips kept calling him. He stepped out on to the service stairs and stood for a while leaning on the iron railings and listening to the familiar echo as messengers and delivery men clattered up and down the stone steps. He was still stuck in a double bind. He was Family enough not to be allowed to take Ruby Goss out, and yet if he were to go up to the fifth floor now, nobody would acknowledge him as his father's son. Footsteps sounded, coming down the stairs towards him.

'What do you think you're–?'

He recognised the voice instantly. Edward. He made himself turn slowly, and was pleased to see the brief look of surprise on his rival's face. Still leaning on the rails with the air of owning the place, he gave what he knew was an insolent smile.

'Good morning, Edward.'

'Eden. What the devil are you doing here?'

'Just making sure you're looking after the place properly while I'm away.'

It must be most annoying for Edward to find he was still alive. With the rate at which young officers were killed in France, he must have thought there was a very good chance that he wouldn't come back.

Edward put his hands in his pockets. His initial surprise over, he was now the picture of unconcern.

'I don't think you need worry about Packards, Eden. It's functioning extremely well despite the war.'

And all the easier with the troublesome relative out of the way, no doubt.

'One wouldn't think so to look at it. My father would be shocked to come back and find it looking so shabby.'

Edward gave a patronising smile.

'You're out of touch, Eden. It's thought unpatriotic to put on a show these days.'

He had all the aces, of course. Supremely confident, he stood there in his superbly cut suit, waiting for Alec to back down. His superbly cut civilian suit. Alec flicked an imaginary speck of dust off his uniform.

'Out of touch? That's one way to put it. Still, someone has to stay behind to keep the home fires burning, I suppose.'

Along with the women and old men.

Edward caught the inference, but he was unshaken.

'Anyone can pick up a gun, Eden, but very few of us are capable of keeping the wheels of commerce going. I really don't see myself as cannon fodder.'

He started down the next flight of stairs.

'Keep up the good work out there in France.'

Alec was left steaming. He marched out of the store and into Oxford Street. It was so true what Edward had

258

said. If you had money and power, you could do what you wanted, even avoid conscription. Edward would keep his hands on Packards until the war was over, come what may. Alec was so incensed that he reached Marble Arch without noticing where he was going. He stopped at the entrance to Hyde Park. The peaceful greenery did not particularly call him. He wanted company, and he wanted to get back at Edward. He stood with his hands in his pockets, frowning through the railings at the park. And then it came to him, the perfect answer. He smiled to himself, crossed Park Lane and plunged into Mayfair.

The elderly butler opened the drawing room door and announced him.

'Lieutenant Eden, ma'am.'

Sylvia Amberley Packard put down her sewing and stood up.

'Lieutenant – this is a surprise.'

Her voice was cool, her smile polite, but her grip, when she shook his hand, was warm.

'Please sit down, Lieutenant. Briggs – some coffee and cakes, please.'

'I'm afraid I've called at quite the wrong time of day,' Alec said, remembering the lessons she taught him last year.

Sylvia gave a small wave of the hand.

'The old conventions are giving way these days, I fear. Besides, some people are welcome whatever the hour. Soldiers on leave have but little time at their disposal, so they are excused.'

'You are very kind.'

The feeling of seeing everything through a sheet of glass was back, even more strongly. What had all these rules of polite society to do with the reality of the trenches? But still Alec found himself playing his part. Edward's wife was just as he remembered her, an impeccably controlled surface beneath which anything or nothing might be going on. He mentioned that he had been to the store, that it was looking a little the worse for wear.

'Yes, it's not what it used to be, but then, everything is changing. All the old standards seem to be in the process of being washed away by this terrible war.'

Alec had a brief vision of the war as a raging flood, its muddy waters sweeping wrecked houses and broken trees along with its cargo of shattered bodies.

'Yes,' he said.

'People are not behaving as they should. This rage for tea dancing, for instance, is quite shocking. I went to meet a friend for tea at the Ritz the other day and we were astonished to see women we know, women whose husbands are away fighting, dancing the tango in a way that I can only describe as abandoned, with officers on leave. Colonials, to boot, some of them. Australians and Canadians. They saw that we had recognised them, and yet they seemed to feel no shame. They merely smiled and waved, and carried on dancing.'

'Shocking,' Alec said, storing up this information. A spot of abandoned tea dancing sounded just the thing to fill in the time before dinner.

The butler reappeared with a loaded silver tray. Sylvia poured coffee and handed dainty cakes.

'At least we have no food shortages here,' she remarked. 'Unlike Germany. Apparently the people there are nearly starving. There have been riots in the streets, with desperate people demanding food of the Government. They cannot carry the war on much longer if that is the case.'

'If that is the case,' Alec said.

'It was in *The Times*,' Sylvia said, as if she were quoting Holy Writ.

'From what I can make out, the newspapers are printing more propaganda than news if what they write about the western front is anything to go by.'

'Really? Propaganda? I find that very hard to believe.'

There was a great deal of utter rubbish written about cheery Tommies eager to go over the top. Nobody with more than a week's experience of the trenches was eager to put so much as a finger above the parapet. They went because they were ordered to.

'The powers that be want to keep up morale,' Alec said.

'Yes, I suppose so,' Sylvia said, but she was frowning. Alec sought to change the subject.

'The war must have effected a lot of changes in the family.'

'Indeed it has. You will have heard of poor Hugo Rutherford's death, of course? Amelie was devastated at first, but she does seem to be getting the better of it now. Perry was sent out to France months ago, to one of the headquarters, I believe, a château. Quite a charming place, he says.'

Trust Perry to get himself a staff posting.

'Gwendoline is still insisting on driving ambulances. Very worthy, of course, but the uniform she has to wear is too dreadful. Most unfeminine. But I am afraid one sees women in breeches at every turn these days. I really do not see that it is necessary to go to those lengths.'

'They are far more practical than a skirt,' Alec said.

'Maybe, but are they respectable wear for a lady? I rather think not.'

'I bow to your superior judgement,' Alec said.

'The greatest blow, though, has been Tatwell.'

'Tatwell? What has happened to it?'

'It has been taken over as a hospital. Naturally one has the greatest respect for the wounded and one must do everything in one's power to help at a time like this, but it was such a shame to see all those beautiful rooms denuded of their furniture and turned into hospital wards. All that is left for the family is the East Wing. There is so little space that it is almost impossible to visit.'

'I'm sure the wounded will appreciate being in such surroundings,' Alec said, thinking of his friends who had been sent home with bits missing.

'Yes, you are right, of course.'

The gilded clock on the mantelpiece struck the hour, and Alec realised that he had been there far longer than the fifteen minutes of the polite call.

'I have trespassed on your time for far too long,' he said, getting to his feet.

Sylvia rang the bell for Briggs.

'Not at all. I am always glad to see you, Lieutenant Eden. You are like a breath of fresh air about the place.'

There was a real warmth in her voice, a hint of a sparkle in her ice blue eyes. Alec took a chance.

'I should be very honoured if you were to allow me to write to you occasionally. Letters mean a great deal when one is at the Front.'

A faint colour washed over Sylvia's porcelain skin.

'I – should be glad to give some support to a serving officer.'

Alec shook her proffered hand.

'Thank you. I shall very much look forward to hearing from you.'

Once on the streets of Mayfair, Alec almost laughed out loud. Let Edward put that in his pipe and smoke it.

With a spring in his step he made his way back towards Oxford Street. He had not planned to return to the store, but as he passed Packards, he realised that after the strain of Sylvia Amberley Packard's genteel company, what he needed was a bit of fun. To hell with the unwritten rules of peacetime. Everything was different now. He walked into Stationery.

Naturally, May told Ruby all about Alec Eden's visit. Riding home on the bus, she described how he had picked her out to speak to, chattering on as she always had about each small gesture. But somehow, something was wrong. She was vaguely conscious of a flattening, of it being an artificial excitement. It was all very disappointing. Alec Eden was supposed to be the love of her life.

'He didn't say how long he was home for. I hope it's not just forty-eight hours,' she said.

'I'll have to ask him,' Ruby said.

May gaped at her, not quite understanding.

'What?'

'I'll ask him. This evening, when we go out.'

'Out? You mean – with him? You're going out with Alec Eden?'

Ruby looked like the cat that had got the cream.

'That's right. He came into Stationery twice. The second time, he asked me if I'd like to go to a club with him this evening.'

'Ruby!'

May was flabbergasted. Ruby gave an unpleasant smile.

'Don't you wish it was you?'

A sense of betrayal raged in May's heart.

'You did it deliberately!' she accused. 'You know how I feel about him. You agreed to go out with him just to get back at me.'

Ruby shrugged.

'Now you know what it feels like, don't you?'

'It wasn't my fault that Victor was married!' May protested. 'Call yourself a friend! That's no way for a friend to behave.'

It should have been the end of the world. Even as she spoke, May was aware that her heart should be breaking as Ruby's had when she found out about Victor. But somehow, it wasn't. With all the real men she and Ruby had gone out with, an unattainable Alec Eden had faded in her imagination almost without her realising it.

'. . . and another thing,' she said. 'I thought you and me were going out together this evening. You can't go letting me down just like that.'

Before either of them knew what was happening, what should have been a high drama degenerated into a squabble that lasted all the way home.

22

'She's as bonny a baby as ever I saw, now that she's over the three-month colic,' Nanny Rutherford declared.

'Yes, she seems to be doing very well,' Amelie agreed, looking doubtfully at her last born.

Eva Rose stared back at her, equally doubtfully, with her father's blue eyes. Hugo would have been proud of his daughter. Physically, she was a perfect specimen of British babyhood. It was her character that worried Amelie. Eva came into the world wailing and seemed hardly to have ceased crying ever since. It was as if she knew that her father was dead and her mother finding it very hard to love her. Now, as Amelie held her, her small features creased, her chin wobbled and a thin protest started that rapidly built into a full-scale siren scream. Amelie rocked her, jiggled her, put her over her shoulder, walked up and down, but nothing seemed to soothe her. Feeling helpless and guilty, she handed the infant back to Nanny. It must be her fault. None of the others had been like this. She had hoped that once the baby was born she would come to love it as she did the others, but somehow it had never happened. Try as she might, seeing Eva was a duty, not a joy.

'She'll quieten down once I take her out for her

airing,' Nanny said. And indeed, Eva seemed already to be making less noise now that she was back in Nanny's arms.

'You take the little ones, and Tom and Hugh can come with me,' Amelie decided. Two of them at a time were all she could cope with at the moment, though that was a vast improvement on the past months, when simply trying to sound normal when talking to them had been almost more than she could manage.

The two older boys threw themselves at her, demanding to know where they were going, while Peter, the youngest, sulked.

'We're going to the store. I want to see what it's like on a Saturday,' Amelie told them. 'Then tomorrow it's our turn to go to the Markhams for luncheon.'

Everyone looked happy at this. Sunday from nine o'clock onwards was Nanny Rutherford's day off and the Markham and Rutherford children had become firm friends during the time in which Amelie had stayed with Ida. Sunday visits to each other's homes had become a regular feature of their lives, a fixed point of calm and reassurance in a world that was becoming increasingly terrible. A fortnight ago when they had spent a few days on the south coast, they had heard the rumble of British artillery far away in Picardy. Now there came daily reports of yards of ground gained on the Somme, and daily lists of thousands of dead, missing and injured, and an almost unceasing movement of ships and trains bringing the wounded back to Blighty. Hospitals nearest to the Channel ports were filled to overflowing, and men were transported to the Midlands and the north before they could find rest and care.

It seemed all wrong to be set on assessing how trade was going when at that very moment a great battle was going on in France and men were being cut down in swathes. Amelie told herself that it really was true that the economic life of the country must keep going in order to sustain the war effort, but still it did not feel right. She sent silent sympathy to all those new widows who were still in a state of shock. She knew what they were going through.

Packards was looking shabby as they walked in at the main doors, but Tom and Hugh did not notice. Seeing the place through their eyes, Amelie realised that it was still a magic palace full of surprises.

'Now remember, you have to be good boys and not fidget and complain while I'm talking to people. Then when I have finished, we'll have a drink and a cake at the teashop and go to the Toy Department,' she told them.

'Your Toy Department, Mama?' Tom said.

'That's right, my Toy Department, the one I told your great-grandfather that he should have when I was only your age or thereabouts.'

It was a story the children loved hearing, that of her first innovation at the store. Now, she had a new and much larger plan in mind. As she moved through the departments, Amelie talked to the buyers and the floor-walkers. What they said confirmed the impression she had received since she had regained her health and enthusiasm and returned to the store.

'Oh yes, Mrs Rutherford, there is very decidedly a new sort of person shopping here,' the Soft Furnishings floorwalker told her, with a sniff. 'Not the Packards type of customer at all. It's all this new money that's going around, you know. There are persons in this store who would never have thought of coming to Oxford Street before the war.'

It was the same at Carpets, at Furniture and at China and Glassware. The war had created work and high wages. Both men and women were working long hours and taking home the sort of money they had hardly dreamt of before, and they were eager to go out and spend it. Homes that had only boasted a rag rug and a second-hand sofa in their parlours now sported Axminster carpets and pianos.

Amelie watched the new customers as they went about their purchases. Some of them seemed intimidated by the fine surroundings and condescending shopworkers, others were loudly determined not to be browbeaten, but few were at ease. She wondered how many more there were out there in the acres of new suburbs that had been thrown up in the last twenty years who had money to spend but did not feel that Oxford Street was for them.

As she sat in the teashop on the third floor sipping coffee and watching her sons demolish a plate of iced fancies, she spoke her thoughts out loud.

'Your grandfather always used to say that the secret of shopkeeping was to see a need and supply it,' she remembered.

Tom and Hugh looked at her, their mouths full, their eyes uncomprehending.

'There is certainly a need out there. Not just in household goods, either. Look at all the girls and young women you see working now. If they're not married, they will be spending their money on clothes and jewellery, and they should be spending it at Packards. The question is, do we try to attract them here, to Oxford Street, or do we go out to them? Should Mohammed go to the mountain, or the mountain to Mohammed?'

'Who is Mohammed, Mama?' Tom asked.

'He is the prophet of the Moslem people, dear. But it's just an expression. What I meant was, should we persuade all these working people that Packards is the place for them, or take the shop to where they live?'

Tom laughed.

'Pick it up and take it somewhere else? Like in Aladdin?'

'No, not quite. I don't have a magic lamp with a genie to help me, unfortunately. What I meant was that we could build a new Packards, or even a number of new Packards, in the places where our new customers live. They wouldn't be quite like this one. They wouldn't be as large, or as grand, and they would carry a much cheaper range of goods. It's possible that we might not even call them Packards. We might give them another name – the Something Household Supplies, for instance. The Empire Household Supplies! Something of that kind. On the whole, I think that's the best plan, better than trying to change Packards so that it will appeal to a whole new range of customers. If we changed Packards too much, we would be in danger of losing the people who have patronised us ever since your great-grandfather founded it, and that would never do.'

It all needed a great deal of thought and planning, but Amelie was sure she had hit on a good idea, probably the best innovation she had ever conceived. What she had to do now was to persuade the Board to finance it, and to do that she needed plenty of figures to back her up. She decided to go to the delivery department, look over the addresses to which the Packards vans were now despatched and compare them to the areas they had covered before the war started, but first she had to fulfil her promise to her sons and take them to see the toys.

The way lay through Household Linens. Amelie stopped to talk to the buyer, but conversation soon turned from the state of trade to the battle.

'It's a terrible sacrifice being made over there,' the buyer said, shaking his head. 'So many thousands dead and wounded. Young Mailer from Turnery was killed on the first day. Volunteered back in the winter of 'fourteen, he did, along with three of his pals. I just hope we're winning. They say we're gaining ground.'

'I hope so. This is supposed to be the Big Push that

269

tips the balance, so they say,' Amelie said.

She thought of the names posted in the staff dining room. To the proud lists of volunteers from each department another had been added. A Roll of Honour, detailing the fallen.

'I hope so too. Our Mr Eden is out there now, you know, on the Somme. Do you remember Mr Eden? He wasn't with us for long. A very promising young man, very promising. He was made an officer. Lieutenant Eden. We were all very proud of that, of course. Quite a feather in the cap of Household Linens. He came to us only a few weeks ago, looking very smart. I do wonder if he's all right.'

'Yes, you must do. It's a case of no news is good news, I suppose,' Amelie said, distracted. Alec Eden was out there in the midst of the battle. Alec Eden, once the unwelcome rival, now – what? She had never made an ally of him, though she had considered it. Potentially, he was still an extra barrier between her and a grip on Packards, between her children and their rights of inheritance. If he were to be killed . . .

She caught her breath, shocked at herself. She was as bad as Edward, for without a doubt that would be just Edward's reaction. She clawed at the thought, to stop it escaping, trampling it down with desperate denials. I didn't wish him dead. I wouldn't do that to anyone. I hope he gets through. I want him to get through. For a terrible fear held her, that if that ill-wish were to get loose, it might do real harm. Just as she had harmed Hugo. She had been glad when he left, and because of that he had not come back. She did not want to be responsible for another death. She sent up a brief prayer for Alec's protection, and then wondered if that were any use. God had little to do with what was going on in France. It was the forces of evil that had to be appeased.

'. . . not feeling well, Mrs Rutherford?'

'What? Yes, yes I'm quite all right. I was just thinking of – of the men out there,' Amelie said, trying to pull herself together.

Tom and Hugh were tugging at her hands, trying to get her attention. Amelie stooped and gathered them into her arms, taking strength and reassurance from their sturdy little bodies, warm and full of life. They at least were safe.

They wriggled out of her embrace.

'When can we see the toys, Mama?'

'You promised, Mama.'

'I know, I know. We'll go straight away.'

She devoted the next half hour to them, giving them her full attention as they looked and pointed and exclaimed over the wonders of the toy department.

Over the next week the list of the fallen in the Battle of the Somme detailed in the newspapers each day continued to grow. Each morning, along with tens of thousands of others, Amelie scanned the dense print. Familiar names kept appearing, husbands and sons and brothers of friends, and former Packards men. The pile of black-edged writing paper on her desk grew small. But Alec Eden's name was absent. She had been able to keep the evil genie bottled up. As the days went on, a new fear grew. Would Clement's regiment, at present at a quieter section of the Front, be thrown into the battle? Was the fight there set to go on and on, like at Verdun?

There was only one way to combat the gnawing anxiety, and that was to work. Each afternoon, Amelie set out with a selection of offspring to visit one of the many high streets in the working-class areas of London. They rode on buses, to the delight of the children, climbing up to the open-top deck and peering into gardens and open windows as they went along. On one occasion she walked, pushing the two youngest in the big pram. Catherine laughed and pointed and babbled, trying out her latest words, and even fractious Eva seemed to enjoy the expedition, sleeping soundly or watching the passing shapes and her big sister with round, wondering eyes. Occasionally she even smiled. Amelie caught herself beginning to feel that deep tug of possession towards her.

Everywhere they went, Amelie made notes of types and numbers of shops and gathered impressions of what these small shopping streets were like. If Oxford Street was looking dowdy, then the suburban ones were much worse. They never had been glamorous, and now after nearly two years of war they were drab and uninviting, while the people out shopping there were tired and drawn. Just as in central London, there was a good deal of mourning being worn, and few younger men about. Those that were out in the streets were mostly in khaki or hospital blue. But there was money around. People were buying.

At Leytonstone, she came across a former Packards employee. Daisy Miller was running their small carpet shop while her husband was away in France. She welcomed Amelie in, offered her tea, admired the boys and brought her own three children down to be admired in turn.

'Yes, we are doing well at the moment, thank you,' she said, in answer to Amelie's enquiries. 'Doesn't seem right, does it, to be making all this money when there's a war on? But I'm not going to turn business away, am I? And what they pay the soldiers doesn't keep a mouse alive, not with prices the way they are now. Of course, it's all this war work going on what's making the difference to us. Our turnover's trebled this past year. The biggest problem's keeping up supplies. We can't sell Turkey carpets any more for a start . . .'

It confirmed what Amelie had worked out already. She thanked Daisy and wished her luck, and crossed

Leytonstone off her list of possible sites. Daisy Miller had been with her when she started up her first independent venture at Packards, the Ladies' Sportswear department. She did not want to ruin Daisy's new-found prosperity by setting up in opposition.

By the end of the week Amelie had come to several conclusions, the chief of which was that her original idea was sound. All she needed to do now was to convince the Board. She contacted the Chairman and asked for the subject to be put on the agenda for the next meeting.

She thought long and hard about whether she should do some lobbying of other Board members beforehand. She was sure that Edward would oppose her on principle, and she knew that her status on the Board had gone down considerably in the last few months. They had been sympathetic, but she knew that they felt she had proved what they had thought all along – women were unreliable and ruled by their emotions, and altogether unfit for serious decision making. If she turned this new project into yet another family battle, she suspected that she would find the Board lined up against her. So no lobbying. She would present the facts and figures and let her case argue itself without any machinations behind the scenes.

The decision was no sooner made than it was tested. Edward stopped her in the corridor.

'I see you're back with a vengeance, Mel. What's this I see on the agenda about expansion?'

It was said in a jocular way that Amelie found particularly patronising. Just another of the little sister's amusing ideas.

She responded in kind, giving a tinkling Society Lady laugh.

'Ah well, Edward, I am supposed to be Head of Innovation, am I not? So I thought it was about time I began innovating again.'

'But expansion, Mel, with things the way they are? What is this idea of yours?'

If he thought she was going to give it away that easily, he must think she was slipping. She smiled up at him in as archly irritating a way as she could muster.

'Now then, Edward, you don't really expect me to answer that, do you? You'll just have to wait and see.'

And she would have to wait and see how Edward would react. Would he let her know how little he was worried by her move by ignoring her, or would he be unable to resist trying to find out more?

For two days, it looked as if Edward had dismissed her unknown idea as a piece of nonsense. Amelie was irrationally disappointed. She wanted him to be off his guard, and yet she also wanted him to be wary enough of her to want to know what she was up to. Then Mr Carter, the director of finance, came into her office as she was putting the finishing touches to a map showing the changes in delivery areas within London. Mr Carter, Edward's poodle. Amelie reined her grin of delight back to a cool smile and invited him to sit down.

'I don't often have the pleasure of seeing you in here, Mr Carter. What can I do for you?'

'Nothing in particular, Mrs Rutherford. This is more in the nature of a social call. Might I say what a pleasure it is to have you back amongst us?'

Bootlicker.

'How very kind of you, Mr Carter. Can I offer you some refreshment?'

Over cups of tea they expressed insincere interest in each other's offspring and shook their heads over the progress of the war.

'Of course, the war has made a great difference to our profits,' Mr Carter said. 'But then, you will have realised that, since you are suggesting expansion.'

'I have looked very carefully at the pattern of profits,

yes,' Amelie agreed.

'It's an interesting idea, expanding at a time like this. There are a lot of points to recommend it.'

So, he was trying to get round her by pretending to be on her side. Amelie smiled.

'I'm so glad you agree with me, Mr Carter. What points in particular were you thinking of?'

But he was too old a hand to be caught that way.

'These changes in profit, for instance. They were what gave you the idea of the direction in which we might go, I take it?'

'They gave me food for thought, certainly.'

For several minutes more they continued sparring, neither of them giving anything away. When Mr Carter finally left, Amelie laughed aloud, slapping her hands down on the desk. She was fully alive again. Her brain was engaged and her body, instead of being a leaden weight to be dragged about, was light and ready to carry her anywhere. She could practically feel the blood rushing round it. For a while now she had been creeping out from under the clouds that cloaked her for so long, but it had been an effort. Now, for the first time in months, she was walking in the sunshine. She must not be over-confident, though. The board meeting was going to be a hard fight. If any of the other members had come up with her idea, they would have found it difficult to convince the rest, and in her case she had the added disadvantage of Edward's automatic opposition. It was going to be a test of her power, and there was no way in which she could guarantee winning. But it was certainly worth trying.

23

In the old days, when Sir Thomas ran Packards in a patriarchal style, there had been no need for a Board Room. He simply made the decisions, called people to his office and gave orders for those decisions to be put into place. Since Edward had taken over as Managing Director, all that had changed. An impressive meeting room had been made out of three of the old offices, furnished with a great oak table and matching leather-seated chairs and decorated with portraits of Sir Thomas and Edward and prints of the store's various stages of development. It was an essentially masculine room, and looking around the table, Amelie felt the masculine forces gathered against her. All the other directors had solid areas of responsibility – Finance, Staffing, Merchandise. Her title, Head of Display and Innovation, had merely been tacked on the end. She was very well aware that the rest of the Board, even Mr Mason of Staffing who had often been her ally in the past, regarded her presence as a sop to the memory of her grandfather.

As the meeting took its usual course, she tried to weigh up her chances. She was convinced that her idea was sound. The question was whether she would be able to carry the various personalities along with her. Would they line up with Edward just because he held the power, or would they vote for what was best for the company?

She watched Mr Carter as he gave his report on the accounts. She knew he would side with Edward, but some of the figures he was dwelling on actually helped her case. She made some additional notes to the speech she had prepared. Mr Mason she was fairly sure she could rely on, but he was easily swayed by the others and did not like to stand alone. Perhaps she should have spoken to him beforehand and made certain of him, but it was too late for that now. Mr Aimes of Merchandise she wasn't sure of. He was in constant touch with the buyers, and they in turn respected her because she had listened to them and understood what they were doing, but Aimes himself had his position to guard, and that meant keeping on the right side of Edward. As for Sir Richard Forbes, the Chairman, he was a charming man with an excellent grasp of business, but he never had been comfortable with the idea of a woman on the Board. He would see that her idea was a good one, though, and cut through the family differences.

Mr Carter's report came to an end, was discussed and passed. Mr Mason reported on the latest staffing difficulties and the measures he was taking to reduce the drain of employees to war work and attract new people. There was an argument over whether wages should be raised yet again, which Mr Mason narrowly won. Mr Aimes reported on the problems of keeping up adequate supplies even of the restricted range of goods the shop now offered. Amelie made notes of what he said was in demand in order to quote it back at him. And then it was her turn.

She looked slowly round the table, catching each pair of eyes in turn. Their expressions ranged from polite to sceptical. Not a very encouraging start.

'Gentlemen, what I am about to propose requires the ability to seize an opportunity, the sort of daring which Sir Thomas had, and which made Packards the success it is today. I am not claiming that it is without risk, but I am sure that the potential rewards make it a risk worth taking.

'For twenty years now, Packards has been the most successful department store in London. But nothing stays still. We must change with the times, and conditions now are extraordinary. There are a large number of people who have money to spend for the first time in their lives. I think that they should be spending it with us.'

She had their interest. Even Edward, though he showed nothing, was listening intently. She went on to detail the changes in customers and the areas from which they came. She circulated figures and maps.

'Now, there are many more of this type of customer, but at the moment they are not coming to Packards to buy. They find the store intimidating, in the same way that they would find a restaurant intimidating if they saw that the menu was written in French. If we want their custom, we have to make sure that they feel comfortable and at home.'

At this point, Edward interrupted.

'So just what are you proposing, Amelie? That we should change Packards into some sort of giant penny stall just in order to attract the working classes?'

There was a rumble of alarm around the table at this. Muttered remarks were made to neighbours. Sir Richard had to restore order.

'Mrs Rutherford, I don't believe you had finished?'

'Thank you. One way to take advantage of this new market would be to change the store—'

There was open protest at this. Sir Richard quelled it,

but Amelie requested that opinions be heard. Edward and Mr Aimes were eloquent as to why Packards should maintain its fine tradition. Mr Carter pointed out the folly of aiming at a totally different market, however lucrative it might appear to be at first sight. Amelie listened with growing excitement. They were doing her work for her.

'I entirely agree with everything that has been said,' she told them, when she was able to speak again. 'We have always aimed to give people affordable luxury, and nobody loves Packards as it is more than I do. From a business point of view, it would be foolish in the extreme to desert our regular customers and start courting a new group.'

Around the table, the ruffled feathers were smoothed. Having roused and then soothed their fears, Amelie took a steadying breath, and presented them with what she really wanted to do.

'That is why I am proposing something quite different. We should take the store to the people. We should set up a chain of household goods establishments in the suburbs. They would be smaller than Packards but larger and with a much better range than anything else in the particular locality. They should be bright and inviting enough to make our new customers want to buy there, but not so grand that they don't like to come in just to look. We all know the value of having customers come in merely to look. What they see, they want, and they will be back to buy another time. I want to attract all those people who for the first time in their lives can afford a carpet or a piano. There is a market there. We should be the ones to supply it.'

She could see that they were all bursting to question or comment. Before they had a chance to do so, she went on to suggest four possible sites for the new stores, the type of departments and goods she thought they should feature and the number of staff that would be needed. As she spoke, she could see that Mr Aimes was agreeing with a good deal of what she said, but that Mr Mason was looking quite agitated. Mr Carter was still sceptical and Edward was poker-faced. Edward she was sure was against her from sheer habit. She tackled Mr Carter.

'I realise that my proposals will take a great deal of investment to start with. We have seen from this month's accounts, and from the pattern of the past year, that Packards is holding its own, but because of the war we are not making the profits we used to. There are changes within those figures, which confirm what I have been saying about people spending differently, but no major investment within Packards as it now stands is going to make a great deal of difference to our profits. We are limited by the exceptional circumstances. Of course, we all hope that the war will end soon, but we have been hoping for that for nearly two years, and it seems to be less rather than more likely as time goes on. So if we want to make progress rather than just mark time, we have to do what Sir Thomas would have done, and seize the opportunity while it is there. For if we do not, somebody else is sure to do so.'

She gave details of land and property prices in the high streets she had selected, referred to the most recent department refit at Packards and pointed out that nothing so lavish would be needed for the new stores, and gave estimates for the amount needed to stock each one. She could see Edward's eyes begin to light up at this. He thought she had just ruined her own case. The amounts involved were huge. But Mr Carter was frowning with concentration. Amelie jumped in to put what she hoped was the correct interpretation to his expression.

'I can see that our Financial Director is ahead of me here, and translating that into potential profit.'

Mr Carter was not to be caught offguard.

'It all depends on the rate of turnover,' he said.

'Naturally. But remember that we shall have the advantage of novelty in the first instance. After that, if we have judged our market correctly, we shall have loyalty and word of mouth recommendation.'

She concluded with another reference to Sir Thomas's attitude to shopkeeping and an exhortation to courage and imagination.

Sir Richard gave a courteous summing up and asked for comments. Nobody dared try to get in before Edward. Amelie silently cursed them for a bunch of cowards. They were going to take their cue from him.

Edward gave the patronising smile that Amelie knew only too well.

'I'd like to second Sir Richard in thanking Mrs Rutherford for all the hours of work she must have put into researching this idea, and also in congratulating her for a most innovative idea, and also congratulating her for a most original departure. It's pleasing to see that our Head of Innovation is striving to keep Packards ahead, even in these trying times.'

Amelie's knuckles whitened round the pencil she was holding. Pleasing, indeed. He sounded like a headmaster commenting on a moderately bright child.

'However, I am sure that it is obvious to all of us that this scheme is totally impractical. Firstly, now is not the time to be expanding. None of the top stores is doing good trade at the moment, but we are holding our own better than most. We should concentrate on maintaining that position. Secondly, if we were thinking of starting other branches, it would be in major cities such as Birmingham or Manchester, and those branches would be very much like the parent store, selling the same range of goods to the same type of person. Appealing to the lower orders like this would only drag down

281

Packards' name. It could do untold damage to our trade if we were to become associated with a bargain basement type of shop in the more doubtful parts of town.'

Round the table, heads were nodding. Amelie jumped in.

'If I might answer that point, Mr Chairman? It is not my intention to use Packards' name for these new stores. I was thinking of something solid, reliable and patriotic. The Empire Household Stores, possibly, or Hearth and Home.'

Edward brushed this aside.

'It is still entirely the wrong time for any retail business to be expanding. It would be a dangerous use of our resources.'

Sir Richard asked for Mr Carter's opinion. The Financial Director was slow in answering.

'In general, I would agree with the Managing Director,' he began. Amelie tried to stop herself from glaring at him. He was such a toady. 'These are difficult times for the retail business. But our resources are being underused at the moment, and I can see some merits in this particular idea. Acquiring property has certainly been a very successful way of investing in the past.'

He spoke cautiously, avoiding looking at either Edward or Amelie.

'The specific lines that were mentioned are our best sellers at the moment, so it does make sense to concentrate on those, and I definitely agree that Packards itself should not be changed. So that does point to diversifying into a different type of outlet. But – and this is a very large but – the costings at the moment are only very general. I would need a much more detailed forecast before I could endorse the scheme.'

Amelie could hardly contain her grin of glee. She glanced at Edward. She could tell by the set of his jaw that he was not pleased.

'I realise that the figures are only approximate. If I can draw on the expertise of your department, I should be pleased to present the Board with a much more exact set.'

Put like that, Mr Carter could only agree to help.

Mr Mason was asked what he thought about it from the staffing point of view. He too avoided Amelie's eyes, addressing his remarks to Sir Richard.

'Well, ah, Mr Chairman, I can see advantages and disadvantages on both sides of the argument so far, but I can foresee some considerable difficulties in finding sufficient staff for these shops. It is hard enough to keep the people we have here at Packards, as I mentioned earlier, let alone find more, and for a less prestigious place. Working at Packards has a certain status to it that keeps some of them here despite the better wages being offered elsewhere. I cannot see that applying to these other shops. And then there is the question of training . . .'

He carried on for some time, his voice becoming increasingly anxious. When he finally stopped, Edward endorsed his view. Amelie gazed steadily back at him as he spoke. There was still Mr Aimes to come.

The Merchandising Director was also cautious. He pointed out the difficulties in obtaining enough of the lines that Amelie had proposed offering. He then confirmed her view that there was a definite demand and that if they stocked the least expensive items that Packards now sold, together with cheaper ones that they did not touch at all, they could sell in considerable quantities.

Edward wanted to know just what he meant by 'considerable'. Mr Aimes said that it was impossible to pluck a number out of the air.

'Just how many of these stores would you envisage setting up in the London area?' Sir Richard wanted to know.

'Five,' Amelie said, using the age-old bargaining principle of starting impossibly high.

There was much sucking in of breath around the table.

'That is simply ridiculous,' Edward stated. 'The whole idea is ridiculous.'

'I am inclined to think that the idea is potentially a good one,' Sir Richard said. 'But I would disagree with starting up so many immediately. I would suggest one shop in order to test the market, and then expand if that one is a success.'

There was a murmur of agreement at this. Amelie could hardly believe her ears. They were accepting it as a definite thing.

'Now just wait a minute,' Edward said. 'We are speaking as if it were all decided. I am not ready to talk about numbers of shops. As far as I am concerned, this is still merely a proposal, and one that has not even been passed for further consideration.'

He spoke at some length about the madness of investing large sums of money in a wild goose chase of a project while the country was engaged in an all-out war that was stretching national resources to the utmost. He warned that to do so would endanger the very existence of Packards. Amelie's brief euphoria collapsed. She could see his words swaying the others. He was the wise leader, the preserver of the company, she the dangerous will-o'-the-wisp, tempting them into peril.

Everybody backed down from their last position. Opinions were revised. Amelie was furious.

'If Sir Thomas could hear you now, he'd turn in his grave,' she declared. 'Businesses have to grow and change. They have to keep up with the times. At Packards we've always done better than that. We haven't followed the leaders, we were the leaders. Packards set the standard in what a store should be. But

not any longer, it seems. You're willing to just let it stagnate. And then what will happen? We'll lose our premier
position. There are plenty of other stores ready to take
our place, stores whose directors have a sense of vision.'

Sir Richard stepped in.

'I think we're getting away from the point. Let us
consider the facts. Mr Carter, do you think the company
can finance this project?'

The Financial Director looked profoundly uncomfortable.

'It's difficult to say without more precise figures. I
certainly would not recommend opening five new
shops. That would be far too big a gamble.'

'How many, then? Two? Where would you site two
new stores, Mrs Rutherford?'

Amelie was ready for this one.

'One north and one south of the river. Southgate and
Lewisham.'

'Very well. I propose that Mrs Rutherford together
with Mr Carter prepares detailed costings for two stores.
We can then decide on whether to go ahead. All those in
favour?'

Amelie raised her hand and looked round the table.
Edward's hand, of course, did not go up. Neither did
Mr Mason's. Mr Aimes raised his, followed, rather half-
heartedly, by Mr Carter. Three to two. Sir Richard
beamed.

'And I add my vote to that. Carried. Might I say, Mrs
Rutherford, that I very much hope we shall be able to
endorse what promises to be an interesting new direction for us.'

Amelie couldn't stop a smile of triumph from spreading over her face. She had won the day, for she was certain that once she had prepared the new set of figures
nobody but Edward would be able to find a reason for
not going ahead. Then would come the exciting part,

actually setting up the new shops. It was going to be hard work, but very rewarding.

'Thank you, Sir Richard. I think I can promise you that this is going to be the start of a new period of successful expansion for Packards.'

24

The letter box rattled as the postman pushed the slim envelope through. Ruby galloped down the stairs. She snatched up the letter and held it to her breast. She could feel her own heart thumping. This was the best part of receiving a letter – the anticipation, the roller-coaster of has he/hasn't he that she went through each morning when the post was expected. The actual read-ing of the contents was often a little disappointing, though she would not have dreamed of admitting it to anyone. What she wanted was declarations of undying love. What she got was generally a bare account of parcels received and evenings spent at this or that esta-minet. Occasionally there were references to friends and comrades who had been killed or wounded, or a bare statement that his company was due back at the front line the next day. Ruby did not mind the lack of infor-mation or of a picture of what his life was really like at the Front. What she did mind was the lack of passion. Alec should be missing her the same way that she was missing him. The most she ever got was a final sentence saying that he was looking forward to seeing her again. Not that she ever admitted as much to anyone else, and she was so good at going round looking starry-eyed that she almost convinced herself that she was the love of Alec Eden's life.

Today, she stood by the front door and gave a squeal of excitement.

'It is – it's from Alec!' she cried, for the benefit of anyone who might be listening, but principally May. That was another disappointment. However much Ruby paraded her conquest in her face, May never appeared to be jealous. Ruby could not decide whether she was pretending or whether she really didn't care, in which case she thought her friend really cold. She should have been heartbroken. After all, she had been carrying a torch for Alec for ages.

Well, bother May. Ruby took a long, shaky breath, holding the letter and savouring the moment. Perhaps this time it would be a real love letter. Perhaps he was coming home on leave and would be here tomorrow. She looked at it closely, delaying the moment of actually opening it. The postmark was smudged, so she could not see where it came from. Otherwise, it was just like all the others. Except that the handwriting did not look quite so firm. She frowned at it. The bold forward slope had a definite waver to it. A terrible fear clutched at her. She ripped open the envelope, read the address. It was from a field hospital.

'Oh my God, he's been wounded!' she cried.

Behind her on the stairs there was a clatter of feet. It was May, half dressed and with her hair still down, instantly sympathetic.

'Is it bad? Where is he?'

Ruby shared the letter with her. They held on to each other as they read the brief lines. It was only a scratch, he claimed, flesh wounds up his left side. The nurses were wonderful. They would soon have him patched up, back on his feet again and back at the Front. He sounded quite regretful that it wasn't worse.

Ruby loosened her manic grip on May's arm.

'Thank God. He's not in danger.'

Then hard on the heels of relief came that sinking feeling of disappointment. He had said nothing about how thinking of her had made him feel stronger, or how much he would like to see her. Just that the nurses were wonderful.

'They want more nurses out there in France, don't they?' she mused.

'Yes,' May agreed doubtfully.

'You know, I rather fancy being a nurse. All those wounded soldiers at my mercy. The lady with the lamp, that sort of thing.'

'Wounds smell horrible, and lots of the men just die in front of your eyes and you can't do anything about it,' May said.

Ruby rounded on her.

'What do you know about it?'

'I've been talking to Betty next door. She's home on leave from France.'

'Oh well, Betty . . .' Ruby dismissed her with a wave of the hand. 'She always did look on the gloomy side. And anyway, if it's so bad, why is she still doing it?'

'Because she's needed.'

Ruby shrugged. She could not see the sense in that.

'I did think of taking it up,' May said.

'What?' Ruby was appalled, recognising May's sincerity. 'You can't do that, Maisie.'

'Why not? I think I'd be good at it. I don't mind hard work and I think I could put up with the mess and the smells. And it's really important work. Like – giving something back, for all those men who've gone out there to fight for us.'

Ruby stared at her. May really surprised her at times. She seemed such a quiet little thing, but she had a mind of her own underneath it all.

'You wouldn't really, would you? I'd be lost without you, May. You're my best friend. Nobody else understands me, you know . . .'

She went on for some time, fuelled by real fear. May was necessary to her. She did not know why, did not even think of analysing it. She just knew that she could not allow her to go away.

'Promise me you won't go and enrol,' she insisted.

'I'll think about it,' May said.

Ruby put an arm through hers.

'We'll go out somewhere nice tonight, shall we? My treat. You choose, and we'll go anywhere you like – the pictures, dancing, whatever. Just the two of us, girls together.'

'Like we used to?' May said.

'Like we used to.'

Ruby no longer pursued men with her old fervour. There was the idea of being faithful to Alec to adhere to, and besides, the main target of all her boasting was no longer there every day at Packards. Victor Lambert had at last found a Medical Officer willing to turn a deaf ear to his irregular heartbeat and was even now in training for France.

There were still the other girls at work to impress, though, and after she had got over the first shock of Alec's being injured, Ruby found it was rather romantic. He was now a Wounded Hero, and so even more useful to drop into conversations. She gathered together a special parcel for him and sent sentimental postcards. She received a couple of rather unsatisfactory letters in return. Then before she knew it, it was just as Alec had forecast – he was sent back to the reserve trenches.

The same happened to two of her brothers. They were both injured on the same day, but neither of them seriously.

The summer weeks limped by. Ruby's third brother,

who was still in England working on a project that he wasn't allowed to speak about, came home on leave, but otherwise nothing happened to relieve the gloom. The great battle that was supposed to be a turning point in the war dragged on with huge loss of life and minute gains in ground. Thousands of workers agreed to give up their August Bank Holiday in order to keep up the production of war materials. By day the streets of London were drab, peopled by an increasingly shabby and anxious looking populace. By night there was a sharp contrast. The brightly lit theatres were full and restaurants and Soho clubs crowded as people tried to forget their worries. Bored, Ruby turned to her pursuit of servicemen with renewed vigour. It was her war work. Men on leave deserved a good time before they went back to the Front. Of course, she mentioned nothing of this in her letters to Alec.

Then in the last week of August came the news she was waiting for. Alec was coming home on leave. She spent a whole week's wages on a spectacular new hat and talked long into each night to May about her hopes and fears, often not even noticing that May had fallen asleep. The day he was due home she dressed with extra care and spent ages on her hair. He had arranged to meet her at nine that evening, but there was always the chance that he might come into the store straight from the station. When he did not, she felt let down. She did not see why he had to go home and see his mother first. She put all her frustrations into loathing his mother.

At nine o'clock that evening, she was pacing up and down the hall waiting for him to call for her. By five past nine, she was in a high temper.

'He might at least be on time!' she stormed.

'I expect the buses are slow again, or one was missed out altogether,' May reasoned.

'It's all very well for you. You don't know what it's

like, waiting all these weeks and having him wounded and wanting to see him all today when he's with his flaming mother and then after all that he's late,' Ruby said, working herself up into a fine state. She was just about to fling down her beautiful new hat when there was a knock at the door. She wrenched it open.

'About time too!' she cried. 'I thought you was never coming. I got better things to do than wait around for . . .'

The words died in her mouth. A new Alec stood before her, leaner, thinner-faced, older. But there was more to it than that. There was a pinched, white look about his mouth, a hard light in his eyes. He did not smile.

'Don't start an emotional scene, Ruby. I've had enough of scenes. If you want to come out and have a good time, then come, but if not, I'm off.'

It was very obvious that he meant every word. Ruby shut her mouth, which she realised was hanging open. No man had ever spoken to her like that before.

'Oh – yes – right,' she stuttered. 'I'll just fetch my purse . . .'

After a brief word with her parents, who were rather in awe of this officer who was taking their daughter out, and May, who just gave a faint smile and a greeting, they were off. Ruby held on to Alec's arm, almost trotting to keep up with his stride. There was a slight limp to his walk, but it did not seem to slow him down.

'It's so lovely to see you again,' she enthused, being the bright amusing thing he seemed to want. 'All these weeks since we last saw each other! It seems like ages.'

'It was another world,' Alec said.

'Yes, you're so right,' Ruby agreed, not knowing what he was talking about.

'There used to be BC and AD. Now it's BS and AS.'

'What?'

'Before the Somme and After the Somme.'

Ruby swallowed. She did not know quite how to handle this. Half a dozen inconsequential answers shrivelled away.

'Was – was it very bad?' she asked at last.

'You don't want to know. I don't want to talk about it. I want to go out and get plastered. I take it that's all right with you?'

'Oh yes.' She was back on firmer ground now. 'That'll be fun. Where shall we go? Soho? You can drink all night long there. So they say.'

'Soho. Anywhere. I don't care. We'll start here.' He veered into a pub at the corner of the street, the sort of spit-and-sawdust place that Ruby would not generally be seen dead in. Alec bought her a gin and lemon and himself a double whisky, which he knocked back in two gulps.

It set the pattern for the evening. Once they got into central London, they just about had time for a couple more before pub closing time, but there were plenty of clubs open. After the first three, Ruby got totally confused and did not know where she was. But at least the alcohol gradually dissolved Alec's strange mood. He switched to being raucously noisy, singing along to the band at the top of his voice together with a bunch of other officers while Ruby sat on his knee with her arm round his neck, laughing and singing with them. None of them had ever met each other before, but nobody would ever have guessed it. Tonight, they were all the best of friends.

Alec was just waving at the waitress for a further round when another couple of officers came stumbling into the club and nearly landed on their table. There were howls of protest as glasses swayed and tipped and Ruby's gin slopped down her dress. Ruby shrieked and leaped up, dabbing at it with her handkerchief.

'Whoops – sorry, chaps – bad navigation. Sorry, miss, can I . . .?'

Then one of them focused on Alec and gave a cry of amazement.

'It isn't, is it? It is! Bunnyfoot Eden, as I live! My God – let me shake you by the hand.' He pumped Alec's arm up and down and turned to his companion. 'D'you know who this is? Bunnyfoot Eden, the man who brought the Nineteenth through. He's a legend, a veri – a verit – a legend – and then he did it again, at Hill Whatsit, and he's still with us. What's the secret, old man? We all want to know.'

Alec shrugged.

'I dunno,' he slurred. 'It was a miracle.'

'Bunnyfoot?' said Ruby, mystified by the whole conversation.

'Yes, you know, lucky rabbit's foot, a talisman. Some people have a ring or Testament or whatever, some are just plain lucky, like old Bunnyfoot here. The Nineteenth–'

'The Nineteenth doesn't exist any more,' Alec stated.

'Yes, well . . .' His new-found companion had no answer to that. 'Let's have a drink! Let me buy you all a drink. What's everyone having?'

The waitress appeared, two more chairs were found, everyone shuffled up. Other women joined them, the sort of women that Ruby would normally have had nothing to do with. She suddenly felt extremely hard done by. This was the sort of outing she had with her succession of pick-ups, not the romantic evening that she had been looking forward to spending with Alec. In fact he was paying her far less heed than her one-night stands did. She might just as well be a scarf round his neck for all the consideration he gave her. The three piece band was now playing slow numbers. She shook his shoulder to get his attention.

'I want to dance. Come on, I love this song. Let's dance.'

Alec brushed her plea aside.

'Not now.'

Incensed, Ruby stood up.

'I want to dance,' she said loudly into a chance lull in the general hubbub.

There was a mocking howl from the rest of the table.

'She's getting restive, old man.'

'The little lady's cross.'

Ruby hated the lot of them, their upper-crust voices, their drunken grins and most of all the fact that Alec seemed to prefer their company to hers. She put a hand on her hip and looked him in the eyes.

For a long moment her power hung in the balance. She was on the point of flinging out of the door. Then Alec heaved himself to his feet and draped an arm round her.

'C'mon then.'

The dance floor was minute and crowded. Proper dancing was out of the question. They put their arms round each other and swayed to the music. Ruby was on cloud nine. She had won her point, Alec was hers, she could feel his body hot against her own and the music was winding a romantic melody around them. She gazed up at him, and the mood slipped a little. He was staring over her shoulder. She reached up to stroke his face, bringing his eyes back to hers.

'Bunnyfoot,' she said, teasing.

His expression suddenly hardened.

'Shut up.'

'What's the matter?' she demanded, then changed tack, pouting and widening her eyes. 'I've waited all this time to see you again and now you're being all horrid and nasty to me. Don't you like me just the tiniest little bit?'

She ran her hands down his back.

'Of course I like you.' At last he was looking at her, really looking at her, focusing his whole attention on her. 'Lovely Ruby. Ruby with the luscious lips. Luscious – rushush . . .'

He kissed her clumsily, stumbling as another couple swayed into them. Ruby giggled and held on to him, then kissed him back with slow deliberation. His hands slid over her body and pulled her closer to him.

'Ruby, Ruby, you're a wonderful girl . . .'

With a sigh of delight, she closed her eyes and leaned her head on his shoulder. This was it, this was heaven. Her head was pleasantly swimming, her body was hollow and melting, she had him all to herself. This was what she had been waiting for. She surrendered herself to the utter pleasure of the hour.

25

Alec awoke with a raging thirst, a pounding headache and no idea whatsoever as to where he was or how he had got there. He lay for a while looking at the unfamiliar ceiling. A fly buzzed round a green parchment lampshade. He became aware of lying uncomfortably with his feet higher than his head. He was on a sofa, with a blanket over him. Daylight was oozing in round the edges of the green cretonne curtains.

The door opened, and a female head appeared and looked anxiously at him.

'Ah, you're awake then. How're you feeling?'

'Dreadful,' Alec admitted. He swung his feet to the floor and sat up, groaning as his brain seemed to rattle inside his skull. He was still fully dressed, he found, except for his boots.

'I'm not surprised,' the woman said. 'You had a bit of a skinful last night, by all accounts. I'll fetch you a nice cup of tea and some liver salts.'

Alec thanked her. He wished he could remember who she was. Now that he was upright, his stomach as well as his head felt bad. He wondered how he had come to be in what appeared to be the stiff front parlour of a small house. He remembered being out on the town the night before. He had met a lot of fellows and got drunk. There had been music, and dancing. He had danced with Ruby. Of course – how could he have forgotten that? He had been out with Ruby. And then it came to him that this was Ruby's house. When Ruby's mother reappeared, he was able to call her by her name.

'Thank you, Mrs Goss. It's very kind of you. I hope I haven't put you to too much trouble?'

'No, no trouble at all. Nothing's too good for our boys at the Front, is it? How do you like your tea? I've made it strong, with sugar. I hope that's all right.'

'Yes, wonderful. Thank you.'

He took a sip. His stomach churned.

'It's a dreadful thing, this war, ain't it? Turned everything upside down, it has. There's been some that's talked of peace, did you know that? Negotiations, they call it. Negotiations be hanged, that's what I say. We got to beat them and beat them proper. There was a German baker's in our parade round the corner, you know. I never did like them. Nasty people, I always said. Shifty, you know. Couldn't trust them. They changed their name to Brown but it didn't do them no good. Chased them out of town, we did. Wasn't having none of them round here. I've read all about what they do to people. Raping nuns. Bayonetting babies. Hardly human, they are.'

They looked human enough when they were dead. A foxhole full of dead Germans looked much the same as one full of dead Britons, but for the colour of the uniform. They smelt much the same. Alec lurched to his feet.

'Excuse me – where's the lavatory?' he asked.

He made it just in time.

When he staggered out again, white and shaking but feeling slightly better, he found that Mrs Goss had warmed some water and set out a shaving kit and towel

298

for him in the scullery. He decided that she was all right. Her opinions were only those of most of the civilians he met, after all. None of them had the first idea what it was all about.

It was habit that took him to Packards later that morning. He avoided Stationery, since he wasn't sure whether or not he wanted to see Ruby yet, and wandered about, torn between wonder and anger. All this was still going on, all the buying and the selling, as if everything was normal. Just a day's journey away a nightmare was being lived, and yet here were all these people, buying sweets and handkerchiefs and wondering whether to get brown gloves or black. Didn't they realise what was happening out there in France?

After half an hour, he had had enough. He was actually about to go through the doors from the Grocery Hall into the main entrance when the floorwalker stopped him.

'Mr Eden? I beg your pardon, Lieutenant Eden. I've just received a message that Mrs Rutherford would be glad if you could see her in her office.'

'Mrs Rutherford?' Alec repeated.

'Yes, sir. She heard that you were in the store and wants to speak to you.'

The old Packards grapevine. He had forgotten how effective it was. But why this change of heart from Amelie Rutherford? Despite himself, he was curious. He made his way up to the fifth floor.

He was received in a very friendly fashion, offered refreshments and seated in a comfortable chair. Amelie was looking full of vigour and wearing a dark jacket and a fashionably short skirt that showed her rather well-shaped legs as far as halfway up her calves.

'I was very glad to hear that you were in the store today. I have been wanting to speak to you,' she began.

'Is that so?' Alec said.

'I realise we're lucky to see you here at all. Your regiment had a very bad time of it, I understand?'

'Yes.'

He wasn't prepared to discuss the virtual wiping-out of the Nineteenth with her, or with any civilian, for that matter. It was beyond words.

'I see the store's still pulling in the profits. Nothing stops that,' he said.

'The store's ticking over. That's all that can be expected at the moment.'

'So the family – your part of the family – are not suffering at all because of the war. That must be a comfort to you all.'

Amelie put down her teacup.

'You are not the only one to put on uniform, Lieutenant,' she said.

'Is that so?' he repeated.

He still remembered his last brush with Edward. It was too much to hope that he had been swept up by the system.

'My brother Perry volunteered some time ago.'

Now that he came to think of it, Sylvia had mentioned this. She also mentioned where he was stationed.

'He's at the Front, is he?' he said, knowing full well that he wasn't.

'Er – no,' Amelie admitted. 'He has a staff post, liaising with the French.'

Liaising was one way of putting it, he supposed.

'How very nice. Whereabouts is that, precisely?'

'Some of the time he's in Paris, I believe. But of course he has to travel about,' Amelie said.

He had the small pleasure of seeing her look uncomfortable.

'Well, just as long as he's not in any danger of dirtying his hands,' he said. 'Nice to know the family's doing its bit.'

Amelie's lips tightened.

'I did lose my husband, Lieutenant.'

He had genuinely forgotten. He had never considered Hugo Rutherford as a threat, since he took no part in running the store. But he had been part of the family.

'Oh yes, of course. I'm sorry,' he said. He made an effort to remember the circumstances of Hugo's death. 'Loos, wasn't it? He was awarded a posthumous MC?'

'Yes.'

It was Amelie's turn to answer in monosyllables. He understood just why. Any number of platitudes leapt to his tongue. He had written them all in the past few months to countless bereaved relatives, meaningless phrases about dying bravely, about being proud to go doing your duty, about quick and almost painless deaths. All total hogwash. He tried to call to mind what sort of a man Hugo had been. It had all been so long ago, those practices with the Packards Rifle Volunteers. They had all been so naive then, such innocents.

'At least he died believing in what he was doing,' he said.

'Yes he did, completely,' Amelie agreed. 'Though I'm not sure whether that makes a great deal of difference to those who are left behind. His children are still fatherless.'

'It makes a huge difference to those at the Front. It would have mattered to your late husband,' Alec assured her.

They were both silent for a while, brooding. Once more, Alec was faced with the impossibility of communicating with anyone who had not been to the Front. They had no idea. Perhaps it was better that way, better for them, certainly. But it meant that there was always a barrier, a sheet of glass, between the soldier and even his nearest and dearest.

'. . . families, even families in situations like ours,

301

ought not to be at odds with each other.'

He realised that Amelie was speaking.

'Right,' he said, trying to catch up with what she was saying.

'So I was really pleased to have the opportunity of speaking with you today. I wanted to tell you about the new project that I am working on.'

She went on to speak at some length about two new stores that Packards were opening in the near future. He found it hard to concentrate. Once, the minutiae of the retail trade had fascinated him. Now it all seemed rather pointless. But from what Amelie was saying, this was a very different venture from the main Packards store. It seemed to be aimed at the artisan classes and based in the suburbs. The shops would not even trade under the Packards name.

'It hardly sounds like the sort of market my father was aiming at,' he commented.

'Not before the war, certainly, but things have changed. If Sir Thomas was alive today, he would see the advantages of what I am doing. The whole point of retailing is to provide what people want at the price they can afford. That is what I shall be doing, but to a different group of people, people with money to spend. If I'm right, and it is a success, then I envisage our expanding into other cities, especially the industrial ones. I want to see a whole chain of Empire Household Supplies extending right throughout the country.'

'Very nice, too,' Alec said. Very nice to be able to play around making lots more money for the Packard family coffers. The main part of the family, that was.

'Yes, it will be. I intend to make the Household Supplies a household name.'

Amelie leaned forward a little. Her face was eager and animated. She was, Alec suddenly realised, a very attractive woman.

'This is where you come in, Alec. I may call you Alec, I hope? All this formality is really rather silly. I'm looking ahead now to when this dreadful war is over. Household Supplies will need someone active and intelligent to take charge and direct it to take advantage of whatever conditions might then prevail. It will be a very important and demanding position, with a good deal of power to act independently from the main Packards organisation. Needless to say, the remuneration would match the responsibilities. There are a number of men working for us that I might consider for the post, but none of them have all the qualities that I am looking for. The only person whom I can see making a real success of it is you.'

For a minute or two, she almost had him taken in. She was a good saleswoman, and she was obviously very keen on the Household Supplies project, but the general sense of alienation that he felt kept the greater part of his brain set aside from anything that was going on here in the safety of Blighty. It was just a game. It was not real life.

'Is that so?' he said.

'It is,' Amelie assured him. 'Of course, I don't expect you to make a decision straight away, but I do earnestly hope that you will accept, and the sooner the better. Then I can keep you up to date with all that is happening and involve you in all the major decisions.'

So she was serious about this. She was offering him what sounded like a position of real power, a dizzying contrast to that of unofficial buyer's assistant which he had left in order to join up. There had to be a reason and it did not take long to find one. In a way, it was flattering. She and Edward knew they couldn't keep him down, so they were attempting to divert him instead. It was an insurance policy, something to keep him quiet.

'Thank you,' he said, 'but I'm not sure that I want to

be fobbed off with second best.'

'It's not like that at all,' Amelie protested. 'I want the best man for the job, and you are very obviously that person.'

Alec leaned back in his chair. His head still ached horribly and his stomach was sour. He was not sure he was even very interested in this conversation. Next week he would be back in France.

'Look, Amelie,' he said, 'I'm sure these shops of yours are a splendid idea. You carry on with setting them up and make a great success of them. Good luck to you. But don't expect me to want them.'

What did he want? Packards. He still wanted Packards, but that was for some time in the future. It had very little to do with his life now.

If Amelie was disappointed, she hid it well.

'I'll keep the offer open,' she told him.

'You do that,' Alec said.

He got to his feet and held out his hand.

'Keep Packards going for me. It's nice to know the old place will be here if ever all this is over,' he said.

Amelie shook his hand. There was a wariness in her face that he had noticed in a lot of the people he had spoken to since he came home. His mother had worn the same look, and Ruby.

'May God protect you,' Amelie said.

'Thank you,' he said, and took his leave.

He walked back down through the store. He had meant what he had said. He expected Amelie to keep Packards going for him, and he expected to be back to claim his place in it. He was not called Bunnyfoot for nothing. He was lucky. It was the only reason he could give for still being alive. He was lucky and he was going to stay lucky. He had to believe it, for the day he doubted would be the day the luck would run out.

26

Edward was at his club when the message came through. One of the waitresses came to find him. Comfortably seated in a leather armchair just the right distance from the fire that had been lit against the autumn chill and pleasantly immersed in his cigar and third brandy, Edward watched her progress across the room. He had been one of the few members of the club who had not protested at the employment of waitresses in the hitherto all-male establishment. Just because one went there to get away from one's wife and any other women who tried to make demands upon one, it didn't mean to say that one did not want to look at women at all. On the contrary, the waitresses and chambermaids brightened up the place no end.

The girl leaned over him confidentially and spoke in a low voice so as not to disturb the hushed atmosphere.

'There is a telephone call for you, sir. Your wife wishes to speak to you.'

A spurt of irritation spoilt his mellow mood. What the devil did Sylvia think she was about, telephoning him at the club? She knew he disliked it. But then that was probably why she was doing it.

'Tell her I'm not able to come to the phone at the

moment.'

The girl looked anxious. Close to, she was not very attractive.

'She did say it was urgent, sir.'

'Then tell her I'll call her later.'

A male waiter would have done exactly as he was bid, since he would have understood that what women say is urgent can always be put off for a few hours, if not days, by which time whatever crisis they had managed to manufacture invariably lost its edge of drama. But the waitress still hovered at his shoulder.

'She did sound very distressed, sir.'

Edward's irritation was rapidly turning to real anger.

'I said I'll call her later,' he repeated, in a tone that withered any further supplication. The girl went, defeated. Edward decided that maybe there was a lot to be said for male staff. He had never been pestered like that before the men all went off to war.

He shook out his newspaper, but his concentration failed him. It was not Sylvia's failed message that disturbed him, but the fact of all the younger men about the place having put on khaki. If things went on much longer, he was going to have to do something. So far, he had been safe from the call-up, and no doubt with his contacts and the liberal application of funds in the right places he could continue to stay where he was. But there was a pressure of disapproval building up that no amount of seats on war committees could withstand. Not that he cared personally about what people thought of him, but it did matter if it started to affect business.

If it came to the push, he could get himself a nice little number like Perry, who was having a whale of a time in Paris. No doubt he could turn it to his advantage and make some good business contacts out in France, but he was damned if he was going to go and let Amelie get her hands on Packards, even temporarily. If he did have to join up, he was going to have to make very sure that everything was tied up before he went. In fact it would do no harm to start doing so now, so as to be prepared. That decision made, he again tried to return to his newspaper, but still found that his brain was not taking in what his eyes were reading.

He knew what the remedy was, though even that was getting harder to find these days. Now that women were playing such an important part in the world of work, there was a new confidence about them, an assurance that he found truly repellent. What he desired most in a woman was fear and submission. To find it, he was having to seek out younger and younger mistresses. His current one was barely fourteen, but she had been worth the effort. Just thinking about the look of terror that would come into her eyes when she saw him was enough to arouse him. He threw down the paper and left the club.

So he did not get home until late that evening, and he certainly did not contact Sylvia. He was surprised to find that she was still up when he got in. What was more, her usual mask of frigid calm had slipped.

'Where have you been? I have been trying to speak to you all evening,' she said. 'I know you were at your club. I told the girl that it was of the utmost importance but she just tried to fob me off with some lie about your calling me later. Then the next time I tried they said you had left. It was most embarrassing when Amelie arrived to have to admit that I did not know where you were or how to contact you.'

Amelie? At this point, Edward actually started to listen to what she was saying.

'So of course that meant that she presumed to take charge. She sent the telegram to Perry. That should have been your responsibility. And now she's gone to be with your mother, leaving me with nothing to do but wait until you condescended to come home. I can tell you, Edward, that I consider it a gross dereliction of your duty as a husband.'

At any other time, Edward would have pointed out that since she refused to do her major duty as a wife, namely sleeping with him, she had only herself to blame. But the clues she had dropped swept all such petty recriminations aside. He assumed his coldest manner to hide the spiralling hope and excitement.

'Am I to take it that there has been some family crisis?'

When it came to exuding chill, Sylvia was his superior. She took in a slow breath through her nostrils and turned her full arctic stare on him.

'Precisely. I was informed at a quarter to nine that your grandmother had passed away.'

At last! He had begun to think that the old girl was going to hang on forever. He turned a glittering smile on his wife.

'Congratulations. You must be very happy to have finally achieved what you married me for. You are now the mistress of Tatwell.'

Sylvia did not lower herself to reply.

There was another family funeral. Compared with that of Sir Thomas, his widow's was a very low-key affair, with only twelve motorcars in the cortege. The political figures who had lent weight to Sir Thomas's demise were far too busy to attend, and many of his and Edward's business colleagues and rivals merely sent apologies or representatives. Even the family was depleted. Perry managed to arrive just in time, looking handsome in his staff officer's uniform despite having come straight from the boat train, but most of the male cousins were away, Hugo was dead and Bertie ill with pneumonia. Winifred had to rely on Amelie for support and held her husband personally responsible for falling sick just when he was needed.

The whole ceremony had a distinctly perfunctory air. There had been so many funeral and memorial services for young men cut down in their prime that the death of an old woman from natural causes could not touch the heart. Amelie, Perry and Winifred were visibly upset, but the other mourners appeared to be simply doing their duty.

The will was straightforward and held no surprises, in direct contrast to that of Sir Thomas. The inheritance of the houses and the money had already been laid down, and Lady Packard had little of her own to dispose of. Annuities were left to faithful servants and lump sums to charities. Old-fashioned but very valuable jewellery was carefully listed and distributed piece by piece to the female members of the family, right down to baby Eva Rose. This caused some bad feeling since everyone would rather have had something that had been left to someone else, and Sylvia bemoaned the fact that her branch of the family had missed out once again due to her only having one daughter to Amelie's two.

On the whole, Lady Packard's death made little financial difference to the lives of Amelie, Perry or Winifred and their partners and families. It was Edward and Sylvia who had their prospects transformed. The Mayfair house that had been closed up for several years was now theirs, but far more importantly, so was Tatwell Court. No matter that most of the house was now being used as a hospital for officers, it was now their country residence and the estate was still intact. They had been waiting for this moment for a long time.

Just two days after the will was read, Sylvia made an announcement over breakfast.

'I think we must go down to Tatwell sometime this week.'

Edward kept his usual outward restraint. Their marriage was so hollow that the careful use of formal politeness was necessary to hold up the fabric.

'Really? So soon?'

'There is a great deal that needs to be attended to.'

So she was every bit as eager to claim her inheritance as he had suspected. He threw in a little tactical opposition.

'You don't think it might be rather bad form to go there so soon?'

'I think you can leave it to me to decide upon what is good or bad form, Edward.'

He ignored what was supposed to be a thrust at his Trade as opposed to her County connections. It had been the profits from Packards that had bought Tatwell, and she knew it.

'You shall have to go by yourself, in that case. I have five committees to attend in the next three days, two of them government ones.'

She made a token protest.

'I would imagine that they will be able to function without you for once. It is important that you speak to Madderson about the estate. It was in a sad condition the last time we were down there.'

'I could speak to Madderson as much as I please, but nothing will bring back the gamekeepers. As for the farms and the kitchen gardens, they are doing very well with the help of the Land Girls.'

Sylvia gave a shudder. The very thought of women in breeches made her mouth contract into its most disapproving line. The fact that there was a war on was no excuse for such immodest behaviour.

'I suppose I shall have to handle it all myself then, as you have so much to attend to,' she conceded.

It was what they both wanted, and they knew it.

'I'm sure you will manage admirably,' Edward said,

with unusual sincerity. After all, controlling a great house was what she had been born to do.

The morning Sylvia left for Tatwell, Edward felt a thrill of release. It wasn't that he let her restrict him in anything he wanted to do, but just knowing she was there at home, exuding hostile chill and exacting the toll of politeness, was a brake on his spirit. Not that she was always there. She frequently took herself off to visit friends or relations in the country, but this time it was different. This time she was going to their own house. With a touch of luck, she would find enough there to keep her occupied for most of her time. Even after she had sorted out the running of the house and the estate, if she interested herself in the hospital she might even take up permanent residence at Tatwell. Then he would be to all intents and purposes a free man, but with the bonus of having a wife in the background to save him from the irritating attentions of husband-hunting mothers. When he took his usual walk in Hyde Park before going to the store, there was a new spring in his step.

Attending the committees made him conscious of his new status, too. Formerly, he had been aware of a certain restraint in the attitudes of the other committee members and knew that it was because he was a young man still in civilian life. However useful he might make himself as an adviser on supplying the army and various hospitals, it did not quite make up for the fact that he was not in uniform. Now it was different. Now he was not merely the managing director of an important business, but master of Tatwell Court as well. People respected land and the responsibilities attached to its ownership. It gave him an added reason to be in England instead of fighting in France.

He did not go to see his mistress that evening. The fact that he could do so without Sylvia hovering in the background tended to take the edge off his pleasure rather than add to it. Instead he drove across the river to Lambeth and went to inspect his warehouses.

It was nearly dark as he drew up, for despite the new daylight saving scheme the evenings were drawing in. Heavy rainclouds covered the sky, adding to the gloom. Just one gas lamp burned feebly some way down the street.

A group of men were making their way towards him. As they passed under the streetlamp, he could see that two were in uniform and one in hospital blue, while the rest were past call-up age. He did not wait around for them to pass him. It was not that he gave a damn for their opinion. Nothing they could say would change his conviction that he was destined for better things than having his legs blown off or his lungs eaten away in the trenches. He just did not want his mellow mood disturbed by the ignorant remarks of louts. He let himself into the building.

The nightwatchman came shuffling down to check who was there. An ancient man with only two teeth and severe arthritis, he was the best Edward could get in the current labour shortage. He looked relieved to find that it was the boss.

'Oh – it's you, Mr Bishop. Good evening, sir. It's all in order, sir, nothing missing, nothing spoiled.'

'So I should hope, Brown. That's what you're paid for, to keep vermin out, human or animal.'

Outside, the group of men could be heard passing. Their heavy boots stopped by the door and a fist thudded on it.

'Oi, you! Mr Bleeding Profiteer! We know what you're up to!'

'Yeah, and we know you're in there an' all!'

'Profiteer! Filthy profiteer!'

Edward glared at Brown.

'I thought I told you to keep your mouth shut about

312

what I'm storing in here.'

The old man looked terrified.

'I 'ave, sir, honest I 'ave. Never said a word, not a soul. I swear on my mother's grave I ain't–'

Edward cut through his babble.

'Then how do they know?'

'Everyone knows things round here, sir. Kids see the stuff come in. They see you come in, like what you did tonight with your great big motorcar an' all. Word gets around like, and people put two and two together and make five. There's a lot of bad feeling around, sir, on account of the Somme. Lot of lads all joined up together, you see, and all got killed together. Lot of bad feeling, there is.'

Edward shrugged. They were only cannon fodder, after all. The banging on the door ceased and the boots clattered off down the street. They did not even have the courage of their convictions. He asked Brown for the new paperwork that had come in with yesterday's consignment, then checked that the load matched the description. He gave a grunt of satisfaction. The final corner of the old building had now been filled with silks, satins and fine lawns. He tore back the paper sleeve of each bolt a fraction to inspect them and was met with a pastel confusion of primrose, eau de Nil, peach, pink and azure as well as virginal white. Women might be dressing in incredibly ugly clothes that were either like shapeless sacks or mock uniforms, but beneath them they still wanted fine underwear. With the demand for army shirts and hospital sheets being so high, mills were hardly producing any luxury fabrics at all. Soon the prices would begin to climb.

He prowled round the packed aisles of the warehouse, making sure that all was intact. The potential of his stock excited him in a way that was almost like sex. This was his offensive against the Establishment that he had loathed from the beginning of his schooldays. While they all went off and got themselves gloriously slaughtered, he was going to make more money than they ever dreamed of. By the time this war was over, he would be in a position to buy up anyone he chose. None of them would ever look down on him again.

Already his plans were beginning to pay off. The government had clamped down on drinking early on in the war, and imports of fine wines and brandy from France were restricted. He had bought up as much as he could lay his hands on in the last few months, and now he found himself with a regular little goldmine, for since May, brandy had been obtainable only be prescription. Now there were rumours of whisky distilleries being taken over for the supply of troops, so more of his investments would come to fruition. Such was the success of his schemes that the original one property had now been added to. He had another in the same street and two more further downriver. Edward was a happy man.

He climbed the narrow wooden stairs, checking each floor until he arrived in the loft. The old building creaked and knocked around him, the timbers protesting against the weight now resting on them. There were scutterings and scrabblings. Edward made a mental note to speak to Brown about rats. The man had promised to get rid of them, but he had clearly not done so. More traps and more poison must be put down.

So engrossed was he in contemplating his gains and planning ways in which to hide the profits in respectable investments, that he did not hear the outer door being opened or the nightwatchman being overpowered. The stealthy footfalls he put down to the natural noises of the building. It was not until there was a clatter and a muffled curse a couple of floors below that he was alerted. The voice was not Brown's. Edward marched downstairs.

314

'Who's there?' he demanded.

There were half a dozen of them, filling their pockets with his precious whisky. Some already had bottles open and were swigging from them and passing them around. In the yellow light of the hurricane lamp that had been set down on a packing case, he recognised them. It was the same group he had seen approaching him earlier.

Edward's stomach churned. He knew danger when he saw it. They were all looking at him, and their expressions were far from friendly. One of the soldiers gave an ugly grin.

'Well, if it ain't Mr Profiteer! Welcome to the party. You don't mind if we help ourselves, do you? Seeing as you've got so much.'

A couple of them laughed. But the others just glowered.

'Get the bastard,' he heard one say. 'He's seen us now.'

Edward's mouth felt very dry. They were runty looking specimens, little rats of men. One to one, he could take on any of them and win easily, but with the six of them together there was no way he could overpower them. He was going to have to reason with them, even go along with them, if he was going to get out of this. Though the words nearly choked him, he answered the soldier in something approaching a jovial voice.

'You just take as much as you like, lads. Take some cases. You'll find a handbarrow downstairs to wheel it away.'

'Oh we're going to, mate, never you fear. But we're not going downstairs yet.'

Edward glanced to where a packing case had been broken open. Beside it was a crowbar. He was filled with an overwhelming desire to set about them with it. The swines, threatening him and his money pot. He wanted to smash their revolting faces in. But first he had to get

315

to that crowbar. There was only a narrow passage in between the piles of goods, just wide enough for a man and a barrow. They could not all rush him at once. He stretched his mouth into a travesty of a smile and walked slowly forward.

'There's brandy over there in that corner, and French wines if you want them. They'll all fetch you a fine price.'

He waved at the various stacks, as if giving them a guided tour.

There were rumblings of anger. One of the older men spoke.

'Yeah, we know about fine prices. You get fat on big profits while the workers sweat and the soldiers get blown up.'

The lamplight gleamed in their eyes, giving them a demonic look. They were enjoying this. They wanted to make him sweat, to see him shrivel in front of them, to hear him beg for mercy. He loathed them with every fibre of his being. The crowbar was just feet away.

'You ain't going to make money out of the poor any more. We're going to take it, and you can't do a thing about it,' another gloated.

Just as he got within reach, the soldier saw what he was at. He made a lunge for the crowbar, but Edward was already in motion. He put his head down and butted the man in the stomach, making a grab for the crowbar at the same time. His head connected with the soldier's belt buckle, sending the man sprawling backwards. Edward hardly felt the pain, for his fingers had closed round the cold iron. Exultant, he straightened up, and as he did so, he heard the sound of splintering glass and smelled the rich scent of whisky. He might be armed, but so were his enemies. They faced each other, he with the crowbar, they with broken bottles.

'Come on, then, Mr Fat Cat. Come and get it,' one

316

of them taunted.

Edward stood his ground. They could only come at him one at a time and his reach was longer than theirs. But it did not take them long to change that. They started pulling packing cases out and climbing over them to get to him. The jagged shards of broken glass glistened in their hands.

'Get him, boys – over there – slice the bastard . . .'

One of them dropped down behind him. Edward spun round and swung at him with the crowbar, but he feinted back. A blow struck Edward on the back of the head. He turned again and hit out wildly. Everything was a blur, there was a ringing noise in his ears and a searing pain as if his head was about to split open. He flailed at the dizzying moving shapes in front of him again and again. There were shouts and crashes and then a sheet of flame.

'Fire, fire, get out!'

'Take what you can–'

'Over here, quick, you'll be cut off!'

Black figures moved behind the leaping flames. There was a crackle of tinder-dry packing cases catching light as the burning whisky licked round them. Edward fought down panic. He had to get out. Already the heat was licking at his face, making him sweat. Get out, he must get out. Where was the door? The door – the door was the other side of the fire. He put his arms over his face, made a rush for it, aiming desperately for safety. His foot caught against something. He tripped, tried to save himself and pitched forward into the centre of the fire.

Flames enveloped his clothes, his hair. In a frenzy of fear and pain, he struggled to his feet, screaming out for help. The fire was searing him, eating him. His one thought was to get out. He launched himself at what he thought was the stairway, crashed against a stack of packing cases, fell to his knees, staggered up and lurched forward. His foot missed the first step. The world spun over and over as he rolled down the steps, exploding in bursts of pain. As he hit the bottom, he felt his leg give way.

For a moment the rush of his fall doused the worst of the fire on his clothing. But as he lay dazed and crippled by his broken leg at the foot of the steps, the flames began to take hold again. Unable to move, Edward Amberley Packard burned to death.

27

The rumours were rife at Packards. Round the tables in the staff dining room, the girls argued over what had happened to Mr Edward.

'It was a motor accident, that's what I heard, and it must be true, because my mam read it in the *Daily Mail*,' a small Welsh girl asserted.

'It didn't say motor accident, it just said accident, there wasn't nothing about motors,' someone else said.

'I heard it was at some factory over on the other side of the river,' said an Eastender, to whom the south of the Thames was a foreign land. 'A fall down the steps at this factory.'

A fourth girl leaned forward and spoke in an impressive stage whisper.

'Not a factory, that's not what I heard. That's just what they're saying, to hush it up, like. It was a – ahem – you know – house of ill repute.'

There was a frisson of delighted horror all round the table, and a babble of remarks. What him? He was married. That don't make any difference. All the more reason, in fact.

'Where did you hear that?' someone asked, sceptical.

'Bert told me in the basement. He knows everything.'

'He's a filthy old man. You don't want to listen to a word he says. Mr Edward at a place like that, indeed!'

'You don't want to judge by appearances. Just because Mr Edward is – was – the boss and looked all handsome and talked like Lord Muck, it don't mean to say he's some tin god. Don't you remember that to-do there was a few years ago about him and that girl from Ladies' Sportswear?'

'What girl from Ladies' Sportswear?'

'Can't remember her name – you know, that blonde girl, very pretty, posh voice. Anyway, she left all of a sudden and then next we knew she's done herself in. Stuck her head in a gas oven, poor thing, and all because of him.'

'She never!'

'She did.'

May listened to it all with a feeling of detachment. She had finally made her mind up. She was not going to stay here, whatever Ruby might say. She had to go and do something more useful than standing behind a counter selling sheets and pillowcases. Even though she had now been given a lot more responsibility and was in charge of two younger girls and had to keep the buyer informed of what stock needed ordering, still it did not seem like much when she thought of what those nurses were doing in France and back here in Britain.

She returned to the department for the long after-noon. Customers came and went, mostly efficient look-ing women in uniforms or clothes made to look faintly military. If you went down to Confectionery or along to Ladies' Gowns, there were still some of the old type of customers left, fashionable ladies with wonderful hats, but they were few and far between. They seemed almost like foreigners now, people from the far distant land of Before-the-War, while out in the streets and in the theatres and pubs there were real foreigners. Belgians and Indians and Canadians and New Zealanders, all in their uniforms with their strange accents. And here she was, extolling the virtues of Empire Quality bath towels.

'They're a tougher fibre than Egyptian, madam, so you'll find they last longer and wash up better, though of course they're not so soft to the touch.'

She was aware of a stir in the department, of suppressed squeals, of excitement. She looked up, and saw a figure in khaki. Alec, she thought, back on leave again. Ruby would be glad. Then just a couple of seconds later her brain registered what her eye had really seen. It was not Alec. She looked again. It was Will, and he was smiling across at her, shyly. She found herself blushing.

Carefully, not rushing, May completed the sale. Then she beckoned to one of her juniors to wrap the parcel and stepped to one side. Will came over. It was odd, seeing him on the other side of the counter, like a customer. He looked strange in his uniform. Tougher, like Empire Quality fibre.

'Hello,' she said. 'This is a surprise.'

Will looked embarrassed.

'Just thought I'd come back and see the old place. How are you?'

'Much the same. It hasn't changed much.'

'No. Some different faces though.'

'I thought–'

'Were you–?'

They both stopped, both asked the other to continue, both declined. May felt her face blazing and grew hotter still at the thought of everyone noticing it. She fiddled with the shiny brass yard measure on the edge of the counter. Will looked at her restless fingers.

'That's one thing this place taught me that's useful in the army – how to polish things,' he said.

May met his kind eyes.

'Yes, you always were good at that,' she said.

321

'I wondered . . .' He paused, swallowed, went on in a rush. 'If you was free tonight – would you like to go to the pictures or a show or something?'

May looked at the rough khaki he wore. He was not an officer. Ruby got to go out with officers. Ruby got to go out with Alec Eden. Will was just an ordinary Tommy, doing his bit. May smiled at him.

'That'd be nice,' she said.

Will glowed as bright as the buttons on his tunic.

They went to the pictures. There was a Charlie Chaplin and a thriller about a robbery in a grand house and a newsreel. There was footage of soldiers embarking for France.

'That'll be me, next week,' Will said.

'You're off to France?'

'That's right. We're all keen as mustard. Been doing all this training and marching and drills till we could do it in our sleep and now we're going to show the old Boche what for.'

This was a new Will, the diffidence gone. A sturdy, determined man. Someone to be proud of. On impulse, she put a hand on his knee.

'I know you will.'

He put his hand over hers, and kept it there. When the programme was finished, he tucked it into the crook of his arm. May allowed herself to be led out of the cinema.

'We'll go for a drink before we go home. I think there's just time,' Will said. 'If you want to, that is?'

'Oh – yes,' May agreed.

They chatted easily in the crowded pub and on the bus on the way home. At the gate of the Gosses' house, they shook hands.

It set the pattern for the next week. May felt at ease in Will's company. He was not like the men she met when out on a jaunt with Ruby. He did not get drunk,

322

or show off, or try to take liberties. It was comfortable talking to him. He made her laugh with his tales of life in the army, of the men he had met and the things he had done. It all sounded very exciting.

'I wish I was a man, then I could join up,' she said, and meant it.

'It's been an education, May. I wouldn't have missed it for the world. Before I went in the army, all I knew was home, school and Packards. Now I've been to all sorts of places and met lots of different people and done things I never knew I could do. I won't say it hasn't been hard, because it has. At first, certainly. All that square bashing leaves your feet like raw steaks and at one time I thought I'd never get the hang of stripping down a rifle, but now I can do it with my eyes shut. Then soon I'll be going to foreign parts. Fancy me, Will Foster, going to France! Only rich folk get to do that normally. I tell you, it was the best thing I ever did, joining up.'

'I'm proud of you,' May said.

They did not talk about army life all the time. Because he knew all about Packards, she could pass on the latest news and know that he understood. Other men would soon lose interest in the drama of Mr Edward's sudden death, but Will was eager to know what was happening at the old place and could chew it over as if he were back in the staff dining room.

'So who's going to be the new Managing Director, then?' he asked.

'Nobody knows. Somebody was saying that it had to be Family, but I can't see how that can be. Mr Perry's in France. Of course, there's Mrs Rutherford—'

Will laughed.

'Now then, May! I know you ladies are doing wonderful things now, but a woman in charge of a great big business like Packards – come off it!'

'I suppose not,' May agreed. 'Poor Mrs Rutherford.

323

She's had a hard time of it. First her husband killed and now her brother.'

'Of course, there were all those rumours about Mr Eden,' Will said.

'Oh well, you know what it's like at the store. People will say anything. My friend Ruby's been going out with him and she hasn't found out anything about whether he's connected to The Family, so he can't be,' May said.

'I suppose not, though he might just be keeping quiet about it, even to her. But if there aren't any more Family to take the reins, it'll have to be someone else. Old Sir Thomas'd be horrified.'

'I liked Sir Thomas. It was because of him that I got my job. I might never have left the village if he hadn't recommended me,' May said. Perhaps she ought to stay on at Packards, out of loyalty to Sir Thomas.

'Things weren't the same after he died,' Will said. 'I never liked Mr Edward. I don't think anyone did.'

'I like Mrs Rutherford. And she does do a lot of work at the store,' May said. But of course he was right. Mrs Rutherford couldn't take over Mr Edward's job.

On Will's last night they went to see *Chou Chin Chow*. They sat right up in the gods. May gasped when they came through the doors.

'Ooh! It's so high, and so steep! I feel as if I'm going to fall over the edge.'

'It's quite safe. I've got you,' Will said, holding her elbow.

They slid into their places on the wooden bench.

'I'm glad we're not at the front,' May said.

'Here, open this. It'll keep your mind off it,' Will said, handing her a box of chocolates.

'Oh, you shouldn't have,' May protested. After all, soldiers weren't paid much, and he had taken her out every evening for a week. But it would have been mean not to eat them.

Once the curtain rose, she lost her fear of the height in the enchantment of the show. Everything about it was wonderful, the costumes, the sets, the songs, the acting. The box of chocolates lay in her lap unheeded. During the interval, she dared peer over the edge of the balcony, and spent a happy ten minutes staring at the people below and remarking on what they were wearing. The second half, if possible, was even better than the first. May finally emerged into the chilly autumn night dazed and pleasantly disorientated.

'That was the most wonderful evening I've ever had,' she sighed, holding on to Will's arm.

Will clamped her arm tighter to his side and put a hand over hers.

'I'm glad you enjoyed it. So did I,' he said.

They sat together on the bus back home singing snatches of the songs.

At the front gate, Will stopped and took May by the shoulders. She felt suddenly nervous, her happy mood evaporating.

'I'm off first thing in the morning, so this is goodbye,' he said.

'Oh Will . . .'

She had tried not to think about it until now. France. She had seen the lists of the killed and injured, seen the ambulances drawing away from the stations, seen the men in hospital blue.

'I want to thank you for coming out with me. It was very good of you.'

'I – I've enjoyed it,' May said, honestly.

'Really?'

'Yes. Yes, of course.'

'Then – I wondered – would you write to me, out there?'

May felt obscurely trapped. She did not exactly want to refuse, it was just that she felt she had no alternative.

'Well, yes, if you want me to,' she said. Ruby would have said no without a second thought, never mind that a man had spent his every penny on her for a week.

'Thank you.' She could hardly see his face in the dim light, but she knew that he was smiling. 'Thanks ever so much, May. It means a lot to me.'

He leaned forward and kissed her, briefly, on the lips. May was much too surprised to make a protest.

'Goodbye, May.'

'G-goodbye. God be with you and protect you.'

She ran up the front path and let herself in, not looking back. He was going to need God's help, where he was going.

The next week seemed very flat. Ruby teased her unmercifully about her conquest. The customers were all cross and difficult. The letter from Will, when it finally arrived, was stilted and formal. As luck would have it, Ruby received one from Alec the very same day and sighed over it dramatically.

'Oh, he's so romantic. He just adores me, you know.'

That evening, May sat on her bed with a notepad on her knee and began drafting a letter of resignation. It took her two and a half hours to get it right. Then she copied it out in her neat copperplate handwriting, put it into an envelope and addressed it to Mr Mason, Director of Staffing. Tomorrow, she would give it in and go and find out about enrolling as a hospital nurse.

She felt like a traitor, sitting beside Ruby on the bus with the letter in her pocket. The moment she arrived at the store, she ran upstairs to the fifth floor and slipped it under the Staffing Department's door. She spent the day in a state of nervous anticipation. Would anyone say anything? But the hours passed just the same as usual. Until nearly half past four, when a messenger came down to Household Linens. She was wanted in Mrs Rutherford's office.

Mrs Rutherford looked up and smiled as she was shown in. She was looking tired and strained, poor lady, as well she might. It was only a fortnight since her brother had been killed. It was a wonder she was at work, but then they said that work is a good medicine. May sat on the chair in front of the wide desk and looked expectantly at Mrs Rutherford.

'Well, Miss Hollis, I know how hard it is to keep anything a secret at Packards, so I expect you've heard the rumours that are flying about.'

May was appalled. Was she going to ask her about what was being said about Mr Edward's death? What on earth should she say? She certainly couldn't repeat some of the things that were being passed about.

'I – er – well – that is . . .' she stuttered.

'There's no need to look so embarrassed, Miss Hollis. I don't know just what is being said, but it is certainly true that Packards are expanding. You are going to be one of the first of the staff to know just what is being planned. In a minute I'll tell you why. Now, you might have noticed that we seem to be attracting a new type of customer to the store, people whom we did not see here before the war.'

She paused, evidently expecting a reply. May, limp with relief at not having to sort through the stories she had heard and extract the least offensive ones for Mrs Rutherford's ears, tried to sound as if she understood what was being said.

'Er, yes, there is, I mean, I have–'

She fixed her whole attention on Mrs Rutherford. This sounded as if it could be very important. Now she came to think of it, the customers were different these days.

'Packards have been planning to open shops especially for these new customers.'

May listened as Mrs Rutherford described the

327

Empire Household Supplies, and wondered why she was being told all this.

'Now, these shops will need people to serve in them, people who have been trained to Packards standards, but who are young and bright enough to learn a slightly different way of treating our customers. This is where you come in, Miss Hollis. I shall not be using floorwalkers in the Empire Household Supplies. Each department will have a buyer, who will also be in overall charge, but the day-to-day running will be the responsibility of the department supervisor. I would like you to be the supervisor of the Household Linens department of our Southgate branch, Miss Hollis.'

'Oh!' May gasped. 'Me?'

She could hardly believe it. Her – a supervisor?

'But – I've hardly been here two years,' she said.

'I know. We need to keep all our older staff here at Packards to train up the new girls who are replacing all the young men. You have proved to be quick to learn and very reliable, so you are just the sort of person I need at Empire Household Supplies.'

'Well, I – I . . .'

It was difficult to take it all in. But as the idea took hold, she began to like it. In fact she began to like it very much indeed. It was a bit daunting, but she wanted to try it.

'Thank you,' she said. 'Thank you very much.'

Then she remembered her letter of resignation.

'Oh,' she said, 'I – that is, I was going to – I wrote to Mr Mason . . .'

Mrs Rutherford held out a piece of paper.

'Perhaps you would like to have this back,' she said.

May took it hastily and stuffed it into her pocket.

'We shall start taking in stock and training staff in one month's time. You'll be told exactly when nearer the date, and someone from Staffing will go over terms and conditions with you. I hope you will enjoy being part of the team, Miss Hollis.'

The interview was over, May realised. She stood up.

'I – thank you very much, Mrs Rutherford. It's a great honour. I won't let you down.'

Mrs Rutherford smiled.

'I'm sure you won't, Miss Hollis.'

May walked down the corridor in a daze. Here was some real news to write about in her first letter to Will.

28

Amelie and the children arrived at the Markhams for the regular Sunday family luncheon to find that there was an extra person waiting in the drawing room.

'Clem! What a surprise!'

'A nice surprise, I hope?'

'Yes, of course – it's wonderful to see you. How are you?' Amelie could hear herself babbling and could do nothing to stop it. It was such a shock seeing him standing there, tall and solid and handsome in his uniform, when she had been expecting just to find Ida and the children. Her hands were shaking and her legs felt weak. What she wanted to do most in the world was to totter across the room and be folded into Clement's arms.

Ida threaded an arm through her husband's and squeezed it. Her face shone with love.

'Isn't it wonderful? He only arrived last night. I didn't know he was coming at all. His letters didn't arrive and he couldn't get through on the telephone. He just turned up on the doorstep.'

'Good thing you weren't entertaining one of your lovers.'

'I always have a rest from them on Saturdays.'

They laughed at each other, both knowing that there

was nobody else in their hearts.

Amelie forced herself to move. She took Clement's hand and exchanged a friendly kiss on the cheek.

'You should have put me off. You must want to spend your time together.'

They both cried out against this. She was part of the family. They both wanted to see her. They *were* together. Amelie could only give in.

As they drank their sherries, Clement and Ida sat on a sofa, their two children lolling against them. Amelie held baby Eva Rose on her lap and despite all the warmth of the welcome, felt excluded. They were such a perfect family. She was aware of a difference in her own children. Catherine and Peter played and squabbled much the same as usual, but Tom and Hugh seemed unnaturally quiet. They were old enough to feel it as well. Their daddy would not be turning up unexpectedly to hug and admire them. Tom set up his lead soldiers on the floor and flicked at them with his fingers to make them fall over.

It was Clement who coaxed them out of their sullen silence.

'What regiment have you there? Come and show me. Oh – the Guards. How many do you have?'

Slowly, the boys unwound, until they were chattering noisily about which soldiers they had and which they were saving up to buy. Amelie wondered if they remembered that their father had never talked to them as easily as that.

Over luncheon, talk was all of the war. Clement was frustrated at still being in Britain while the struggle was going on. Ida was glad of the reprieve. There were tales of bravery and of farce. Gradually, Amelie drew her defences about her. She was reasonably sure that to the Markhams she seemed the same as usual, whatever she might be feeling. When the meal was over and the adults were drinking coffee while the children played around and underneath the table, the conversation turned to the Packard family.

'I was very sorry to hear about Edward. It was a terrible tragedy,' Clement said.

Amelie compressed her lips.

'Thank you,' she said. Even to her two closest friends, she was too ashamed to admit to the true circumstances of her brother's death. 'I was never close to Edward, far from it. If I'm honest, I have to say that we always disliked and distrusted each other, right from when we were very small. But he was my brother, after all, and it was a dreadful way to die.'

'Awful,' Ida agreed, with a shudder.

There had been very little left to bury. Just a few charred bones that were identified as being human. It was only after hearing the nightwatchman's story that the police were able to piece together the events of that evening and finally get in touch with the family.

'I think the worst part is regretting how things should have been. I do so wish that we could have been friends. We should have supported each other, but instead we were always trying to outdo each other. Families shouldn't be like that.'

'The funeral was certainly pretty grim,' Ida said.

'It was dreadful. Perry wasn't going to come, until I wired him to say that he must, for our mother's sake. There we were, Edward's supposedly nearest and dearest, and only Mother, and to a certain extent Father, showing any genuine grief. It was a good thing Sylvia could hide behind a veil, because she could hardly be said to be stricken with sorrow. That is why it was so tragic, not because Edward had died, but because hardly anyone really mourned his passing.'

'You're right, that is tragic, but Edward himself must take most of the blame for that, surely?' Clem said.

Amelie sighed.

'I still can't think of anything much that I liked about him. But I could have made more of an effort to at least get on with him while he was alive.'

'Maybe, but it's no use looking back now,' Clem told her.

Ida had already been over the same territory with Amelie. She changed the subject slightly.

'How is Sylvia now? Is she still at Tatwell?'

Glad to stop examining her conflicting emotions over her brother's death, Amelie considered her sister-in-law. Sylvia's iron control had cracked at the thought of anyone outside of the family finding out about exactly what had happened, and she had retreated to the country.

'Yes. She seems to be happier there. In fact, she's much more approachable when she's at Tatwell. She does really love the place. I can almost warm to her when I know she'll be so good at looking after what Grandfather handed on. She's talking of giving over both the London houses as hostels for Colonial officers on leave.'

'That seems a sensible idea,' Ida commented.

'So who is going to be the new managing director of Packards?' Clement asked.

The atmosphere lightened as they turned their minds to practical matters.

'That is yet to be decided. There is to be a special board meeting on Thursday,' Amelie told him.

'So it's not a foregone conclusion? Despite the fact that you're the only family member on the Board?'

'Not at all. In fact, I'm sure they're conspiring against me. They none of them quite meet my eyes, even when I'm talking about the weather. Except for Walter Carter, that is. He treats me to his oiliest patronising smile. He obviously thinks he's going to get the job.'

333

'Is it just between you and Mr Carter?' Ida asked.

'No, Mr Aimes is in the running as well. Not Mr Mason, though. I think he finds being director of staffing hard enough. He would never be able to cope with being Managing Director.'

'And the others don't think that you would?' Clement said.

'Presumably not. But I aim to persuade them. If all this had happened in a year's time, it would have been an easier task. By then, the Empire Supplies will be open and showing a profit and they wouldn't be able to deny that I know what I'm doing. I'm sure some of them still think I'm just playing at shops, that I'm only on the Board because it was Grandfather's little weakness to let me have a place.'

'I'm afraid that the only way to persuade men that women can do a job is to prove it to them. I still come across that attitude, even now, when women are doing so many jobs so valiantly,' Ida said.

'Not all men think that way,' Clement protested.

'No, not all men. You're an honourable exception,' Ida conceded, putting her hand over his. 'But you're in the minority. I argued myself hoarse in the first year of the war. They only took women on because there were no men available, and even now they're very reluctant to admit that the women are performing as well as the men used to, and they still don't pay the women the same rate for the job.'

'I know,' Amelie sighed. 'I'm certainly not the only one. It's so frustrating! I know I'm the best person to be managing director of Packards. The others are good at their jobs, even Walter Carter, much as I dislike him. He does any number of clever things with the finances and he knows exactly the right time to do it. Even now, when it's so hard to get finance for anything outside the war effort, he's managed to fund the Empire Supplies. And

Mr Aimes has done an excellent job keeping up the selection and the standard of goods we have to offer. It's nothing like it was before the war, of course, but Packards still has more choice than any other store in London. But neither of them sees the store as a whole, and neither of them looks ahead or thinks of change. They're just interested in maintaining the status quo. That's no way to run a business. You must progress or you'll stagnate. There's so many things I want to do with Packards! Not now, of course, but after the war. And I'm sure Grandfather would have agreed with me. He was never afraid to try something new. That's how he made a success of Packards in the first place.'

'I hope you're planning to say all this to the Board on Thursday,' Ida said. 'It's certainly convincing me.'

Amelie gave an apologetic smile.

'I'm sorry, am I lecturing you? It's just that I feel so strongly about it.'

'I know, and I'm right behind you. I know you'd be simply splendid as head of Packards. You deserve it. What do–?'

They were interrupted by howls of pain and shrieks of rage from assorted members of their families.

Clement quelled the combatants while wounded knees and pride were being seen to.

'Time to take them for a route march round the park,' he said.

'And while we're doing it, we can plan Amelie's speech to the Board,' Ida suggested.

They parted at seven, as usual, to get the children home in time for bed.

'I don't know what I'd do without you two,' Amelie said, and meant it. There was nobody else she could talk to the way she did with them.

'You just go in there on Thursday and blow the Board over with your arguments,' Clement told her.

'Yes, we'll be cheering you on,' Ida agreed.

They came downstairs to say goodbye and stood on the doorstep with their arms round each other, glowing with happiness and trust. Amelie waved and smiled. She managed to sound normal all the way home. It was only after the children were all safely tucked up that she gave way and cried. And then she could only be ashamed of herself.

On the day of the board meeting, Amelie arrived early and busied herself in her office. The preparations for the opening of the first two Empire Household Supplies were well in hand. Soon she would be moving in her new staff and bringing the stock out of the warehouses. She looked over the roughs of the advertisements and made a few corrections, telephoned factories who were late delivering and frowned over the list of department supervisors. She still did not have enough experienced people to run the shops as she wanted them to be run. There were better wages to be earned in the factories, more exciting jobs to be had doing things that once used to be thought of as men's work. But none of it could really hold her attention. Her heart was still aching from the afternoon with Clem and Ida; her head was engaged with the coming meeting. She was relieved when eleven o'clock came round and she could start the battle.

Sitting at the long table under the benign gaze from the portrait of her grandfather and the hostile one of that of her brother, Amelie looked at her fellow directors, trying to guess, as she had done in previous contests, whom she could work on. It was not a very encouraging line of thought. Her old ally Mr Mason could not always be relied upon, and recently she had alienated him by poaching staff for the Empire Household Supplies. Sir Richard still regarded her as a decorative extra to the Board rather than a real working member, despite all she had achieved. And then there were Mr Aimes and

Mr Carter. The three candidates were not allowed to vote for themselves, so they could both decide for her, in theory. If they voted for each other, they would effectively cancel their own votes, which would leave Sir Richard, Mr Mason and herself deciding the winner. But she was sure that there had been promises made and deals offered behind her back. Her own efforts at lobbying had come up against a total brick wall. These men had got it all worked out already. The only point she could think of that was still in her favour was that she was the only member of the Packard family standing for the post. That surely must count for something.

Sir Richard called the meeting to order and there was the usual reading and passing of minutes and reports on the state of business at the store. It was all very perfunctory. Everyone wanted to get on to the main business of the day.

'Item number six – the election of a new Managing Director.'

Sir Richard looked over the top of his half-spectacles at the assembled directors.

'This is an unexpected task, brought about by tragic circumstances,' he began.

As he gave a speech about Edward's contribution to the store, Amelie wondered just how much he did know about the place in which Edward had died. The family had given out that it had been an accident in one of the Packards warehouses, but it was easy enough for anyone with access to the files on the company buildings to discover that they neither owned nor rented any property in Lambeth. Sylvia had been so shocked at what she had found in his papers at home that she had wanted to sell off the contents of the other warehouses immediately, so adamant was she that the label of war profiteer should not stick to her name and her daughter's. Amelie had advised a quiet redirection of the goods into Packards and the Empire Supplies over the next few months, so that it looked as if everything had been destined for legal sale in the first place. For once, Sylvia agreed with her. Half listening to Sir Richard's platitudes, Amelie decided that whatever he knew, he was going to go along with the story, as they all were. It would be too damaging to Packards to do anything else.

'. . . mindful of the family representation in the running of Packards,' Sir Richard was saying.

Amelie's attention was immediately caught. Was this a hint, even a directive, to the other Board members?

'Packards has always been a family firm, for most of its time run solely by Sir Thomas himself. When Sir Thomas decided on the constitution of the Board, he was anticipating its staying largely the same for many years more, with Mr Edward Amberley Packard at the helm. He could never have foreseen that the Managing Director would die so soon, and he would certainly have wanted to have a family member in overall charge.'

There was a stiffening all round the table. Amelie kept her face poker smooth, but she could not resist a glance at Mr Aimes and Mr Carter. They were both looking grim. Her chances were suddenly looking a good deal stronger.

'The present state of war makes for an unprecedented situation,' Sir Richard continued. 'In normal circumstances, there would be two more candidates for the position of Managing Director, Mr Peregrin Amberley Packard and Mr Alexander Eden Packard–'

'Eden Packard?'

Amelie was so shocked that she spoke before she could stop herself.

Sir Richard's neck reddened very slightly, but he kept his formal calm.

'That was the name which Sir Thomas wished him to be known by.'

'But . . .'

Amelie stuttered into silence. Mr Aimes and Mr Carter were noticeably brighter. The predatory glitter was back in their eyes.

Amelie's mind was racing. Who had put him up to this? Everyone knew that Perry was not interested in the store, but it was possible that Gwendoline had got to Sir Richard in Perry's absence, and persuaded him that they should not take away the position of a serving officer. Even her mother might have had her say in the matter, not wanting to see her daughter take on such a public post as head of Packards. But Alec – who was speaking up for him? She simply could not imagine.

'I therefore propose that today's vote should be for a temporary position, for the duration of the war. On the declaration of peace, the situation shall be reviewed.'

There was a brief argument, in which both Mr Aimes and Mr Carter pointed out, as respectfully as they could manage, the relative inexperience of Alec Eden and the total lack of interest that Perry had shown in the store to date.

Sir Richard called for a vote. The two other candidates were against the temporary appointment; Mr Mason and the Chairman himself were for it. All eyes turned to Amelie. It was a hard decision. If she were to win the directorship today, she did not want Alec coming back and taking it from her. But as things were, it did not seem likely that she was going to win, and she certainly did not want either of the others in the job for years to come. They were not the stuff of which Packards leaders were made. Either way, another vote would give her another chance, when she had had time to prove that she really could fill her grandfather's shoes. Sir Richard and Mr Mason might even be more likely to vote for her if they thought it would only be until a male member of the family took over.

'I think a temporary post is the best course,' she said.

She could feel the hostility vibrating across the table from the other two candidates. She gazed coolly back at them. That had cut them down to size.

Sir Richard sailed on, disregarding the choppy emotions eddying round the boardroom table.

'I would now like to ask the three candidates to remind us, briefly if they would be so kind, of their qualifications for the post of Managing Director. Mrs Rutherford?'

Amelie rose and gave the finished version of the speech that she and the Markhams had planned on Sunday. In discussion, and on paper, it had seemed very impressive. She had had more varied experience in the running of the store than either of the others. But she could sense that her words were falling on stony ground. Only Sir Richard looked at her, and his expression was one of polite interest. The rest kept their eyes on their agenda papers, their faces closed. Anger boiled inside her. They had dismissed her before she even began. On impulse, she added a new last sentence.

'And finally, I would ask you to look beyond the constraints of sex and ask yourselves: who is the best person for the job?'

She sat down, aware of uneasy stirrings from the men. She had moved the arguments from bald statements to the personal. They did not like it.

Mr Carter and Mr Aimes then took their turns. They recited impeccable careers with Packards, rising from humble origins in their respective departments. Sir Richard thanked them and the secretary handed out voting papers. Everyone marked and folded theirs, then there was a very short pause while they were taken away and counted. The door opened, the secretary reappeared and handed a sheet of paper to the Chairman.

Sir Richard glanced at it and nodded.

340

'Here is the result of the vote: Mr Aimes, two; Mr Carter, three. So it is my pleasant duty to welcome Mr Carter to the post of Managing Director of Packards.'

There was polite applause and backslapping and exchanging of thanks and commiserations and congratulations. Amelie went along with all the rest, but inside she was stunned. Not one vote. Not one! The swines had totally discounted her. She could not believe it.

In a daze she sat through the rest of the meeting, while it was decided that Mr Carter's deputy should be made up to Director of Finance and adjustments made through the department. At last it was over and she walked out of the boardroom, past the door that still had Edward's name on it in discreet gold lettering, and back to her own office. Her secretary took one look at her and began to make tea. Amelie felt more like a very stiff brandy.

For a while she sat at her desk with her head in her hands. After all the work she had done, all the new and successful ideas she had had and seen through, they simply overlooked her. It was not fair. Tears of anger and frustration dropped on to the blotter. She hated each and every one of the Board. They were nothing but a bunch of timeservers. They could see nothing beyond the glaringly obvious. They had no imagination, no business flair, no courage. They were not the sort of men her grandfather would have wanted in charge of Packards. If they were allowed to run it like this, the store was doomed to atrophy. She picked up the agenda sheet that she had flung down on the desk, tore it up, dropped it on the floor and stamped on it.

Then she drank the tea and scolded herself. Of course it wasn't fair. Life wasn't fair, that was the way it was. There were men out in France being killed this very minute. There were women working twelve-hour days and going home to cook and clean and care for their families. She looked at the pile of advertisement roughs.

Empire Household Supplies: Everything You Need For Your Home Sweet Home.

So Clem and Ida were happily married while she was a widow and likely to stay that way. So she was not the Managing Director of Packards. She still had her family and she still had the Empire Household Supplies. She was going to make sure that the new stores were the greatest success in shopkeeping history. That would show them.

29

The journey was a nightmare that went on and on. Day merged into night in a seesaw of pain, soaring to unbearable agony whenever his body was jolted, blurring into blessed unconsciousness with the aid of a needleful of morphine. Faces swam in and out of his wavering vision. Stretcher bearers, doctors, nurses, more stretcher bearers, ambulance drivers . . . Some of the faces had voices attached.

'All right, mate, we'll soon have you out of this.'

'Better see to this one straight away.'

'Just hold on, we're going to clean you up a bit and make you more comfortable.'

'Nobody's put a ticket on this one yet. Where's he going?'

The faces he liked best were the female ones. So soft, so beautiful, always smiling. One stayed with him for quite a while, and her voice was reassuring and kind. It brought tears to his eyes, knowing that there still was some good amongst the horror. His battered mind had a handle of sanity to hold on to.

Sometimes he knew he was on a different form of transport; an ambulance, a train. Sometimes he was allowed to be still, and became aware of a tent or a hut

343

or the sky above him, of other wounded men around him, of groans and cries, of the smell of flesh and disinfectant.

And then there were the seagulls wheeling above him, and another set of stretcher bearers, looking at the label tied to him.

'This one's for us. You're lucky, sir. You got a Blighty one. We're putting you on a ship.'

Home, he was going home. He couldn't believe it. He was getting out of all this, out of the noise and the stench and the fear. Home, and safety. Too weak now even to smile, he felt the chill sea air licking the tears on his face.

The journey was not over yet. The Channel was rough, and after that there was another train, another ambulance, more jolting. His understanding was slipping badly. He seemed to have been travelling for ever. He could not recall a time without pain. He was a mangled parcel, passing from hand to hand.

Then at last he was still. He was in a bed, a proper bed, with smooth sheets. He was clean. Someone had shaved him. There was a window, and sky, and a tree with autumnal leaves. The pain was still there, across his chest and all down his left side, but it was easier to deal with now that the rest of him was comfortable, now that he had stopped moving. For a long while he lay there just watching the leaves moving on the tree.

'Good morning, Captain Eden. How are you today?'

Captain Eden. That was him. Carefully, he turned his head. A nurse with a round shiny face was smiling at him, thermometer in hand.

'Let's just pop this in, shall we?'

Obediently, he held the thermometer under his tongue while she took his pulse. Questions were stirring in his mind. By the time she took it out again, one was of overriding importance.

344

'Where am I?'

'Well, you must be feeling better. You weren't with us at all yesterday. You're in Thornton Barford hospital, in Oxfordshire.'

'Oxfordshire.'

It was true, then. He was in England.

'I'm going to start on your dressings now.'

The nurse moved down to the foot of the bed. Alec raised his head slightly to watch her. There was a frame over his legs, holding the covers like a tent. Panic seized him, fed by vivid memories of blasted limbs. He tried to sit, but failed.

'My legs – do I still have both my legs?'

The nurse wheeled a trolley round to the side of the bed. She settled him back on to the pillows.

'Lie still, you shouldn't be moving. Yes, you have still got both your legs, but one of them is badly hurt.'

'Thank God.'

He endured the changing of the dressings with stoicism. He was home, and he was in one piece, that was all that mattered. More than anything, almost more than death, he had feared being left a helpless torso with nothing but stumps, doomed to be pushed about in a wheelchair for the rest of his days.

For the next couple of days, Alec began to settle into the routine of the ward. He got to know the men on either side of him, the nurses and the doctor. His mother came down to see him, and wept copiously over him. He was relieved when she left. He found out a little about the house he was in and even started to eat again. Then some of his wounds became infected and his temperature rocketed and he lived in a strange half world where sleep and wakefulness, day and night were confused and he had no idea of who or where he was. When he came to himself again this time, he was told that he was to be moved again, to a place called Tatwell Court.

Too weak to object, Alec found himself loaded into an ambulance once more. The name Tatwell sounded vaguely familiar, but for the life of him he could not place where he had heard of it before.

Sylvia hardly recognised him when he arrived. The young man with the restless energy and the charming smile was reduced to a heavily bandaged wraith with a face the colour of ashes. She stared at him as he lay in exhausted sleep. She was used to seeing wounded men now, but she had not known any of the others before they were injured. Now she understood why relatives looked so shocked when they first came to visit their menfolk. She was experiencing the same shock herself.

'How badly hurt is he?' she wanted to know.

A nurse looked at the case notes.

'Multiple shrapnel wounds to the chest, arm and legs. Various internal injuries. Compound fractures of the left femur, tibia and fibula. Minor head injuries,' she summarised.

Sylvia nodded sagely.

'I see. It sounds as if he might be with us for some time.'

When the nurse agreed, Sylvia was surprised and a little ashamed to find that she was glad. She stayed for a while longer, discussing his situation and his chances of recovery.

In the short time she had been the mistress of Tatwell, she found that her life had been taken over by the needs of the men staying there. At first, she had felt almost like a hostess, anxious that they should be comfortable and feel welcome under her roof, and that the service received should be nothing short of excellent. But as time went on and she got to know many of the men, she began to look on them almost as an extended family. They were her brothers or cousins, or even her sons. She wrote letters for them, read to them, found out what they needed and tried to provide it. Her cool heart was touched by these helpless men as nothing had touched it before. When one of her boys began to recover, she rejoiced; when one had a setback, or worse still died, she mourned.

The empty existence she had lived in London was transformed. She rose each day with a sense of purpose. There were people waiting for her, people whose lives she could improve. So when she heard that Alec Eden had been injured, there was only one place for him to come to recover. Sylvia used every ounce of influence she could muster to have him transferred to Tatwell. As luck would have it, there was a bed free in what had been the south drawing room. It was a beautiful room, even stripped out for use as a hospital ward, with an intricately moulded plaster ceiling, a huge marble fireplace and walls hung with yellow silk. Alec had a corner space with a window that looked out over the terrace to the park beyond. Sylvia hoped he would like it.

All of that first day, she felt disturbed. She could not settle to anything. Every time she started a task, she found she could not concentrate. People would speak to her and she lost the thread of what they were saying. Her thoughts kept straying to the man lying asleep in the corner of the south drawing room. Cross with herself, unable to understand why she was behaving this way, she forbade herself from going to see him again. In the evening she retreated to her own quarters in the east wing of the house and had dinner with her daughter, Anne, as had become her habit since moving to Tatwell. She half listened as the child chattered on about what she had been doing that day, saying 'Yes,' and 'No,' at intervals.

'Mama, you're not listening!'

'I am. But I was just thinking about one of the

officers.'

'You're always thinking about the officers. It's not fair!'

Startled out of her reverie, Sylvia turned her coolest stare on the little girl.

'You do not speak to me in that fashion.'

Anne stuck out her lip and glared at her plate.

'Sorry,' she muttered.

Sylvia scarcely noticed that the chatter had stopped. Once the maid had taken Anne off to get her ready for bed, Sylvia was alone. She tried to read the newspaper, gave up and paced about the room, then finally allowed herself to do what she wanted to. She let herself out of the east wing and into the main part of the house, stopping to check her hair in a looking glass on the way.

The night staff had come on duty and the shutters had been closed. From further along the building where the men were convalescing, there came the sound of dance music from a gramophone. In the south drawing room, one of the beds was screened off and the nurses were busy behind them, leaving the ward unattended. But still Sylvia could not get to the corner bed unobserved. The men who were not seriously ill were chatting or reading. Any distraction from the boredom of hospital life was welcome, and they were more than ready to talk to Sylvia. Getting from one end of the room to the other took her twenty minutes.

Alec Eden was awake when she finally got to his bedside.

'It is you,' he said. 'I couldn't remember why I should know of Tatwell Court. It all makes sense now.'

She had to lean down to hear him, his voice was so weak. She fetched a chair and set it by his shoulder.

'You've been very ill,' she told him. 'You were in a high fever for ten days. But they say you're over the worst now. The staff at this hospital are excellent. They

348

will make sure that you make a full recovery.'

He thanked her, a look of puzzlement on his face.

'You're not a nurse?' he asked.

For the first time, Sylvia wished she was.

'No, but I try to do all I can to help the officers here at Tatwell. If there is anything I can do for you, you only have to ask me.'

'Thank you.'

Sylvia cast about for something he might want right now. Most of the newly admitted patients were anxious to let their nearest and dearest know where they were.

'I can write letters for you, if you wish. Your – er – mother will have been contacted, of course, as she is your next of kin.' She tried to keep her voice neutral, but she could not forget that his mother had been the mistress of her late grandfather-in-law. A most distasteful situation. 'But there may be others who would be pleased to receive news of you. A friend, maybe? A young lady?'

'No.'

Sylvia felt unaccountably pleased. Until she saw the bleak look in his eyes.

'My friends are probably all dead by now.'

Sylvia made a most uncharacteristic gesture. She reached out and held the hand that lay on top of the covers.

'I'm sure they're not. When you're feeling stronger, we'll write to them in France. They'll want to know you're safe. Then they can contact you. Would you like that?'

'Yes,' he said. 'Yes, I would. Thank you.'

His voice was hardly audible now, and his eyes were closing.

'I'll let you sleep now, but I'll come back tomorrow and see how you are,' Sylvia promised.

There was no reply.

It was a slow business. Autumn turned into winter as

349

Alec gradually grew stronger and his wounds began to heal. Sylvia learned to keep away during visiting hours in the afternoon. Once she was forced to greet his appalling mother, another time there were two shopgirls at his bedside, laughing and joking. After that, Sylvia made a point of calling into his ward when the hospital was quietly going about its morning or evening routines. About a fortnight after he arrived at Tatwell, Amelie came to visit her and insisted on going to see Alec.

'After all, he is family, after a fashion,' she said.

Sylvia could not stop her. She did not even know why she wanted to. She just felt very possessive about Alec, and Amelie was the last person she wanted claiming a right to him.

'You had best not stay long. Ten minutes at the most. He tires very quickly still,' she said.

Amelie shot her an odd look.

'I don't see you wearing a ward sister's uniform, Sylvia,' she said.

Sylvia summoned her most repressive tone of voice.

'I have the welfare of all the patients very much to heart.'

'I'm glad to hear it, Sylvia. Since you seem to know all about his case, perhaps you can tell me how badly he is hurt. Will he be able to go back into active service, do you think? Or will he be invalided out?'

It was easy enough to see through Amelie. She just wanted to know whether Alec was likely to be a threat to her ambitions.

'It's far too early to say at the moment,' Sylvia told her.

'I see. Are you coming with me to visit him?'

Sylvia made an excuse. She did not want to share Alec with anyone.

Seeing him became the highlight of each day.

At first they kept to safe subjects, the progress of the

350

war, the standard of the food, the difficulty of getting help on the land. But after a while they started to talk of more personal things. It was Alec who mentioned Edward.

'It must have been a terrible shock for you when he died.'

'Yes,' Sylvia agreed. With anyone else, she would have changed the subject. 'It was – the manner of his death that was the most difficult aspect.'

'An accident at a warehouse, was it? That was what I heard. An accident and a fire.'

There was no keeping anything a secret at that store. She supposed one of his former colleagues had told him about it. Or Amelie might have mentioned it when she saw him.

'Yes. According to the nightwatchman, the place was broken into, there was some sort of an argument and the fire started. My husband was unable to escape, I don't know why. The fire had got such a hold by the time the fire brigade arrived they could only stop it from spreading to other buildings. Or so they claim. The warehouse was burnt to the ground.'

She knew that she was saying it all wrong. The words were correct, but her manner of speaking them was too stiff, too unemotional. She sounded more like a detached bystander than a recently widowed woman.

'A nasty way to go.' Alec too sounded detached, but then she supposed he had seen so much of nasty ways to go that he found it hard to summon up much sympathy for a non-combatant. 'Was that why you came to live at Tatwell?'

'I was planning to live here anyway. I've always loved this place.'

Sylvia looked out of the window at the parkland. It was no longer a decorative deerpark. Cattle grazed on the nearer part, right up to the start of the formal gar-

351

den, and the stretch beyond the lake was in the process of being ploughed up for wheat. The country needed food, and land could no longer stand idle.

'It was so beautiful here before the war. People used to come down for Friday-to-Monday, and there would be the most elegant parties, with tennis and riding during the day and music and dancing in the evenings. In the summer there would be wonderful al fresco meals under the trees and people would take boats out on the lake. They used to look so picturesque, the men in their blazers and boaters and the ladies in their pale dresses. Everyone looks so drab now.'

'Happy days,' Alec said. 'It's another age, now.'

Happy days . . . With an unprecedented flash of self-doubt, Sylvia wondered if that was just an illusion. She had been happy the day Edward proposed to her, for she had been waiting for weeks for him to come to the point, and was beginning to wonder whether he ever would. She had been happy on her wedding day as well, for that had been her chance to shine, and to triumph over all the cousins for having got a husband who was richer than any of theirs. But after that, it had been nothing but disappointment. Edward had been a loathsome husband. She had lived a sham, maintaining a polite facade to the outside world. Edward had been right when he had said that she had only married him for Tatwell. She had denied it at the time, but it was true. Having this house made the dreadful marriage worthwhile.

'And yet, it's very odd, but . . .' Sylvia spoke slowly, thinking out loud. 'I believe I have been happier here these last few months than at any time since I was a child.'

She stood up abruptly, flustered and embarrassed. She was not used to revealing her innermost thoughts to anyone, let alone young men of ambiguous parentage.

But as the weeks passed and Alec began to mend, she

found she was sharing more and more of her hidden self, even admitting to things that she had refused to admit to herself. In return, she learnt that the man who seemed so buoyant and confident harboured a confused mixture of defensive love and deep resentment towards his parents and always attacked first in order to forestall any snide remarks.

'It's such a pleasure to be able to talk to you knowing that you know the exact circumstances and are not judging me,' Alec told her. Sylvia suppressed a surge of guilt and was glad of her former self-control. Now, it truly did not matter what his background was. Alec Eden was a friend, possibly the only real friend she had.

At Christmas, Sylvia consulted with the hospital administrators and the ward staff as to the most suitable way to celebrate the festive season. The mood in the country in general was sombre. So many lives had been lost and so little ground gained and still there seemed to be no end in sight to the war. On top of this, the German U-boats were sinking merchant ships laden with precious supplies and some foodstuffs were beginning to become scarce. Yet despite all this, Sylvia wanted the men under her roof to have as cheerful a Christmas as was possible. She had a tree brought into the entrance hall and decorated it, helped put up greenery and paper decorations in the wards with her own hands, ordered fruit and chocolates from Packards and went down to the cellars to raid the wine racks. The Tatwell church choir, reduced now to old men and boys, was brought in to sing carols, but far more appreciated were the London entertainers she booked to perform on Christmas Eve. The staff were not forgotten either. Everyone, down to the kitchen porter, had a gift and a note from Sylvia telling them how much they were appreciated.

It was the biggest party Sylvia had ever arranged. She

was busy from morning till night for a fortnight before the day, and by the end of it she felt exhausted. But it was worth it. Walking round the wards with little Anna on Christmas Day seeing the smiling faces and hearing the cheerful voices brought a lump to her throat. They had all given so much, all she had done was to exert herself a little.

She left Alec's ward till last. He was in the west wing now, with the convalescents, in what had once been the music room. One of the men was sitting at the grand piano in his wheelchair, playing selections from *Die Fledermaus*. When Sylvia and Anne appeared at the door, he switched to the grand march from *Aida* and the men clapped as they processed through the room. Sylvia, flushed, delighted and more than a little embarrassed, was close to tears.

Alec was actually out of bed, sitting in a wheelchair with his still fragile leg propped up straight in front of him. He had a glass of red wine in his hand.

'This is the most marvellous Pomerol,' he said. 'It must be one of my father's.'

'It is,' Sylvia said. 'I'm sure he would be glad to know that you are drinking it today.'

'He would indeed. He always liked to share a good wine with people who could appreciate it. And we certainly are appreciating it.'

'You look so much better,' she said.

Indeed, he looked a different man from the wreck that had arrived in October.

'I feel better. In fact, today for the first time I can really believe that I might get out of here some day and lead a normal life.'

Sylvia's brief euphoria plummeted. Leave? He couldn't leave. But looking at him, she knew that it would happen. Not for a while, not till the spring maybe, but he would go. She knew she ought to be happy for him, but a small, selfish part of her wanted him always here, dependent upon her, ready to listen and to talk. When the day came that he left, a huge gap would open up in her life, one that she could not begin to fill.

30

The telegram arrived just as Amelie was coming in from a busy day at the Lewisham branch of the Empire Supplies. She tore it open with trembling fingers. Telegrams always meant bad news.

'Clem arriving Charing Cross tomorrow three days' leave stop Impossible return stop Please stand in stop Forever grateful Ida stop'

It took three readings for the sense of it to penetrate. Ida, her wonderful, dependable, trusting friend Ida, was actually asking her, as a favour, to be with Clement for three whole days. She could hardly believe it. Of course, from a practical point of view, it was an excellent idea. Ida was in Ireland where her grandmother was terminally ill. The weather was dreadful in the Irish Sea in March, and even if she managed to get an early crossing, she would hardly get back to London before Clement had to return. So who better to look after him than Amelie, their oldest friend?

Amelie stood staring at the telegram, her heart pounding. Please stand in. There was nothing in the world she wanted to do more, however dangerous it might be. Dangerous for her, that was, for her heart and her peace of mind. There was no danger for her friends, for Clement had never given the slightest hint that he felt anything more for Amelie than a brotherly affection. He and Ida were devoted to each other. But she was prepared to risk future pain for present pleasure. She wrote a reply assuring Ida of her best efforts and sent a maid off to the post office with it.

She went through the rituals of playing and dinner and the children's bedtime with only half her mind on what she was doing. Her head was spinning with plans. There were only three days. What would Clement most like to do? When the last story was read and cheek kissed, she settled down by herself with relief in the silent drawing room and gazed into the fire, trying to remember what Ida had said about Clement's leaves, trying to put herself in his shoes. He would probably want to go straight home and see the children. Then he would spend the evening at his own fireside, talking about what he had been doing and catching up with home news. Amelie could do that all right. She was as familiar with Ida's family doings as she was with her own. And then, a small voice inside her said, there would be an early night and catching up of another kind. Amelie thrust the thought away. That was not the kind of standing-in Ida had envisaged. She ignored the ache that gnawed at her body and set her mind on her job as a companion. The day after – well, there was all of London to enjoy. Even in March, and in wartime, there was plenty to do. She would make sure that Clement had the best leave possible.

Three o'clock the next day found her waiting at Charing Cross. She was not sure which train Clement would be arriving on, but she was determined to be there to meet him. All her appointments were cancelled for the next three days and the children had been warned that she would not be there to put them to bed that evening. The station was crowded with troops coming and going. Hospital trains came in and the wounded were unloaded into the waiting ambulances. Amelie reminded herself that she must go to Tatwell again and visit Alec, and Sylvia for that matter.

She frowned as she considered her trips to Tatwell. Sylvia was still Sylvia, cool and controlled, giving nothing of her personal thoughts away, but once you got her talking about the hospital and 'her' officers, a new side to her was revealed. Here was a woman who cared about people and was prepared to make considerable efforts to help them without any thoughts as to how it might benefit her. Amelie found herself almost liking this person, and did her best to locate any supplies that Sylvia needed for the hospital.

Her conversations with Alec were more problematic. She had been terribly shocked when first she saw him, so weak and helpless, and she resolved to see him often and do what she could to aid his recovery. As he slowly got better, she told him about what was going on at Packards, about the problems with staffing and stock, and the growing success of the Empire Supplies. His interest and pertinent questions made him an easy and stimulating person to talk to, but also reminded her of the fact that he was a dangerous potential rival. Now he was definitely on the mend, and if she did not go soon he would be out of the hospital and recovering at home, and she drew the line at being polite to that mother of his.

Trains came and went. There were joyful reunions and tearful farewells, sometimes whole families there to meet or wave off their menfolk. Amelie watched the little dramas with envy in her heart, even of the poor women with their drab clothes and haggard faces and flocks of sickly looking children. They had real husbands whom they loved. They weren't just pretending like she was. The hands of the big clock crept round.

Amelie scanned the faces of each stream of men making their way through the gates. They were like creatures from another world, some of them, with the mud of the trenches still clinging to their uniforms. With every officer's cap her heart turned over, but none of them was Clement. She began to wonder whether she had got it wrong, whether he was due at another station or on another day. Perhaps his ship had come in at a different port. Supposing he was waiting at Waterloo or Victoria? Perhaps she should go straight to their house. Perhaps he was already there and wondering what had happened.

And then there he was. Excitement nearly choked Amelie. She jumped up and down, waving, calling, trying to push through the jostling throng waiting for the same train. Now he was approaching the gate, scanning the crowd.

'Clem! Over here!'

He caught sight of her. Surprise, disappointment, anxiety chased across his face. He shouldered through the knots of families.

'Amelie – what are you doing here? Where is Ida? What's happened?'

His words were like a kick in the stomach. Amelie tried desperately to swallow down the pain, to sound normal.

'It's all right, there's nothing to worry about. Ida's still in Ireland. She couldn't get back in time to see you so she asked me to look after you.'

'Oh, I see . . .'

There was no disguising the fact that she was a very poor replacement. Clement took a deep breath, and his innate good manners took over.

'You must forgive me, it was a bit of a shock to have you standing there instead of Ida. For a moment I thought something dreadful had occurred. But it's

359

wonderful to see you, and very good of you to come. How are you? You're looking very well.'

'I'm tip-top,' she assured him. Tip-top in body, certainly. The state of her emotions was another thing altogether. She gathered herself together, taking up her role as hostess and organiser.

'Edward and Flora are waiting for you at home. They're so excited. They can't wait to see their daddy again. Come on, I've left the motor outside. You can't find a cab for love nor money these days.'

The trip back to the Markhams' house went well enough, as she had to concentrate on her driving while Clement remarked on the changes since he had last been home. But as they drew up the front door was flung open and Ida and Clement's two children came hurtling down the steps to throw themselves at their father. Tears pricked at Amelie's eyes and threatened to spill over as Clement swept Flora up with one arm and Edward with the other, while the children clung to him like a pair of monkeys, shouting his name over and over. At last he set them down and the three of them went into the house together, holding hands. Amelie followed behind, feeling totally excluded.

She fussed about, seeing that Clement's luggage was brought in and his clothes seen to, ordering tea and having the fire made up, just to keep herself busy. She knew very well that the servants would have attended to it all without her interference. When she finally went into the drawing room, Clement and the children were cuddled up on the sofa talking away nineteen to the dozen. She wondered whether she ought to go home.

The tea tray was brought in. Amelie poured and handed a cup to Clement.

'Now sit still,' she said to the children. 'Don't jog your daddy's arm or you'll have scalding tea all over you.'

Reluctantly, they did as they were told, while Amelie passed the plate of sandwiches.

'Ah – English afternoon tea. How very civilised. Now I know I'm really back home,' Clement said. 'Smoked salmon! My absolute favourite. Mel, you're a genius. However did you manage to get hold of that?'

'Packards magic,' Amelie said, glowing.

From that moment, there was no question of leaving before she had to.

Dinner was another success, as she had conferred with the cook to make sure Clement had all his favourite dishes. Edward and Flora were allowed to stay and share it as, like Amelie, Ida had got into the habit of having an early meal and eating with the children.

'The Nannies disapprove terribly. They think children should have nursery tea and supper, not sit with their parents having grown-up meals,' Amelie told Clement.

'Yes, so Ida said. Nanny Markham gives that sniff of hers every time she collects them for bed. But Ida ignores her. She says she's spending so much time working now that she wouldn't see anything of them if they didn't eat together.'

'Exactly. That's why I changed the routine. I don't want to be the sort of mother who only sees her children for half an hour a day. My mother was like that. We were just fitted in between all her social engagements for an inspection.'

'So was I. I'm not sure that my mother liked being reminded that she had a child. She never seemed to know what to say to me. Ida wants things to be different for our two. We may be busy, but we want them to know that we are interested in them above all things. But then Ida's so close to all her family. It's just like her to go rushing off to Ireland like this. Her grandmother was a cantankerous old lady before she was ill, and she's sure to be a good deal worse now, yet Ida is staying with her till the last.'

Ida. Whatever they talked about, Clement always came back to her. It was even more marked after the children were hauled off to bed. Ida's campaigns, her ideas, her funny ways, were taken out and fondly dwelt on. Amelie tried to get him to talk about his life in France, but he refused point blank.

'I just want to forget about it, pretend it doesn't exist. It's ridiculous, I know, but Ida and I find it's the only way to cope.'

By ten o'clock his eyes were closing and his speech was becoming incoherent. With the greatest reluctance, Amelie stood up. It was like tearing a piece of herself away.

'You're tired. I'd better go home.' Somehow, the words came out.

Clement hauled himself to his feet.

'I'm sorry, Mel, I've been a rotten host, and now I'm falling asleep on you. It's not that I find your company boring, believe me.'

Amelie nodded and forced a smile.

Clement accompanied her down to the motorcar.

'This is dreadful, sending you off by yourself. I'll come with you and see you safely home.'

With startling clarity, she knew that she could not bear that.

'No, no, don't be silly, I shall be perfectly safe. You're absolutely not to come out. I insist.'

But Clement fetched his cap, swung the starter handle and climbed into the car beside her. Amelie kept both hands clamped to the wheel and navigated the few streets back to her house more through luck than skill. Clement escorted her to the door.

'I'm really grateful to you for staying this evening. I would have been desperately lonely otherwise,' he said.

'I'm sorry I've been such a bore. You don't know how good it has been to be able to talk about Ida.'

'It's been a pleasure,' Amelie heard herself say.

She brushed his outstretched hand, and ran indoors the moment the door opened.

She ran upstairs and peered out of the drawing room window. There was Clement, walking away from her up the street. Going back to his lonely bed. She watched him out of sight, then dropped into the nearest chair and curled up, hugging herself. It was scant comfort.

The next two days were a soaring pleasure and an exquisite pain. They took their combined offspring to the zoo, to Greenwich park, to the cinema, to tea at Lyon's corner house. Anyone seeing them out together would have taken them for a large and happy family. One evening they broke the family dinner rule and dined at Romano's. The next they went to see *Chou Chin Chow*. Amelie was proud to be seen out with Clement. She had almost forgotten what it was like to be accompanied by a good-looking man until she noticed more than a few envious glances directed her way by other women, the way they used to when she went anywhere with Hugo. She stood a little taller as she walked into the restaurant or the theatre bar, knowing that they made a handsome pair. But there was far more to it than that. She and Clement talked easily, joked together, argued amicably. She found far more to discuss with him than she ever had with her late husband. There was a depth to Clement that had been entirely missing in Hugo. But then she had known that for years.

The hours flew by. She tried to live for the moment, not to look ahead, and at the same time to treasure each little event or chance remark, to hoard it up against the desert time to come. But still the minutes ticked away, bringing the parting ever closer.

'You don't have to come to the station with me in the

morning,' Clement said as he took her to her door on the last evening.

'Yes I do, and no arguing,' Amelie replied, and whipped indoors before he could answer, before she started to weep in front of him. She must not spoil it all now, when she had kept up the front of cheerful friendship so well.

They were silent in the motorcar on the way to Charing Cross. Amelie was nursing a molten stone of anguish inside her, intent on keeping it under control. If she let herself start talking now, she might well say something that she would regret. On the platform she handed Clement her farewell gift, a box of treats from Packards Food Halls.

'Does that include smoked salmon?' Clement asked.

Amelie nodded. She could hardly bear to be reminded of that first evening. It had all been in front of her then, this magical time. Now it was almost gone, never to be repeated.

'I can't thank you enough for giving me your company,' Clement said. 'It's been a very happy three days.'

'Yes,' Amelie croaked through an aching throat. 'It has.'

'Give my dearest love to Ida when she returns.'

Amelie nodded.

'And watch over her for me, should anything happen. Promise me?'

Amelie nodded again.

The guard blew his whistle. Around them, couples were embracing, men jumping on board. Clement took Amelie's face in his hands and kissed her forehead.

'Goodbye, Mel. You've been a real pal.'

She stood and waved till the train passed out of sight, the kiss burning. Then she turned and walked the length of the platform, not even noticing when she bumped into people. Almost blinded by tears, she managed

364

somehow to find the motorcar. She collapsed into the driver's seat, laid her arms and head on the steering wheel and gave herself up to sorrow. At last she need not pretend. She wept until she could weep no more.

31

'You know, I sometimes think I see less of Alec now he's home than I did when he was in France,' Ruby complained.

May sighed.

'Yes,' she said. 'I mean, no.'

'It was better when he was in hospital. At least I could go and visit him there every week. But even there I had that boot-faced Mrs Amberley Packard looking at me like I'm something the cat's dragged in. Mind you, she didn't seem to be around so much after the first couple of times. I reckon we put her off, laughing and joking and telling Alec all about what was happening in the store. She doesn't like to crack her face, that one.'

'She's only just lost her husband,' May pointed out.

They had been happy times, when she and Ruby had gone down to Tatwell. It had been a shock to see Alec looking so ill, but he had been very glad to see them, and afterwards they had gone to tea at her parents' and caught up with everything that was going on in the village. After the first few times, though, Ruby had insisted on going to the hospital by herself, leaving May at her old home. It was then that she started boasting that Alec was as devoted to her as ever, and hinting at great developments once he was discharged.

'Yeah, but I reckon she's always like that. Right sour-puss. They say Mr Edward always used to have some-thing going on the side. I'm not surprised, myself. Mind you, I reckon Alec's mother must be even worse, the way he wouldn't let me visit at all once he was home. A real dragon, I expect. Poor Alec. He sounded really glad when the medical board passed him fit for light duties.'

'They should've discharged him from the army. He's done enough for his country,' May said. 'Him walking with a limp like that, he shouldn't still be a soldier. I think it's disgraceful.'

'You've changed your tune. You used to be all for every young man joining up. Practically giving out white feathers, you were,' Ruby said.

'I know. I didn't know about what the war could do to people then,' May admitted. 'It was bad enough see-ing men in the street with legs or arms missing, but going to that hospital really brought it home to me. It's wicked what those shells can do.'

'Blimey. Next you'll be telling me you're one of those pacifists.'

May glared at her. There were times when Ruby went too far.

'You calling me unpatriotic?'

'No, no, course not. I'm only pulling your leg. Where's your sense of humour?'

May still felt ruffled.

'Of course we can't back down now. Not after all that's happened and all those men killed and injured. We got to go on and win. We've got no choice.'

'Yeah, yeah, you're right. That's why Alec's still in the army. They need everyone they can get, even lame men. At least they're not going to send him back to France now. Admin, that's what he says he's doing now. Pushing bits of paper around. I just wish I could see him more often, that's all.'

May couldn't resist it.

'He's not asked you down there yet, then?'

'Of course not. They can't invite women into the camp, can they?' Ruby said.

Which was rubbish, of course. May relented.

'I expect he'll be back in London soon. It's not that far from Dorset by train, and officers get lots of leave. Not like the ordinary Tommies.'

Ruby did not take up the lead and ask her about Will. She went on talking about Alec. May went off on her own train of thought, as she often did when Ruby was rattling on. She was still writing to Will, telling him all about her job at Empire Supplies and getting rather stilted letters in return. Seeing injured men at first hand had made her realise properly the danger Will was in. There wasn't anything she could do to keep him from ending up in hospital, but if receiving letters from her made his life a little better, then it was her duty to carry on writing to him. The trouble was, he did not make her heart turn over. She liked Will, he was a nice bloke, but that was as far as it went.

'. . . we ought to go. So I'll meet you back here after work and then we can get ready,' Ruby was saying.

'What?' May said.

'Haven't you been listening to what I was saying? We're going out with these Canadians tonight.'

May groaned.

'Oh, must we? I don't feel like it, Ruby.'

She knew it was no use. When Ruby was set on an evening out there was no stopping her.

'Don't be so daft. What's the use of sitting in every evening moping over that boring old Will Foster? These men have to be taught a lesson. They can't just go off and leave us like this and expect us to stay at home all the time just waiting for them.'

'But they're away serving their country. They're not enjoying themselves,' May pointed out.

'That's no reason for not going out with these Canadians. In fact, we're doing our bit towards the war. There's all these foreign soldiers, miles away from home and nobody to keep them company. I bet your Will doesn't say no to a bit of fun with one of those French girls.'

'Will's not like that,' May said.

'Rubbish. All men are like that. Now mind you get home in good time. You can wear that nice green dress of yours. You look quite pretty in that.'

And as it was no use arguing, May gave in. Once she got going, she enjoyed herself. The two Canadians were polite and respectful, which was more than could be said for a lot of the men that Ruby dragged her out with. They were really glad of some female company and delighted to be shown all the best places to go in London.

'We would never have found all this out for ourselves. Just wait till we tell the guys about where we've been,' they said, as Ruby led them round Soho and showed them the liveliest clubs.

'There now, that was better than sitting in the parlour doing your knitting, wasn't it?' Ruby said, as they flopped into their beds.

May had to admit that it was. She had come to London in the first place to have some fun and get away from the predictable round of village life. If she had not palled up with Ruby, she would never have been to so many places and done so many things. And if all the men they went out with were as nice as the two they had been with this evening, she would have little to complain about. Just – a feeling that all this gadding about wasn't actually getting her anywhere.

The following Monday brought a letter from Will. He

was due some leave at last and would be back in England at the end of next week.

'I suppose that means you'll be tied up with him every evening,' Ruby grumbled.

'If Alec was in London, you'd be tied up every evening,' May pointed out.

'That's different,' Ruby said, and continued to complain for the next few days.

May felt she ought to be happy and excited at the prospect of seeing Will again – he was her young man, after a fashion – but she found she was almost dreading it. She was haunted by the feeling that she was on the verge of committing herself to something that was not right for her. It was no use telling Ruby about it. She would just tell her to give Will the elbow, and how could she do that to a man who was risking his life for her? There seemed to be no way out.

She wasn't able to go and meet him at the station, as she was working. At least, that was what she told him. She could have got the time off if she had made a fuss about it. The plan was that he would go home first, see his family and spend the evening with them, then meet her from work the next day. Will had wanted her to join him at home and introduce her to his parents, but May had baulked at that.

'Your mother and father will want you to themselves. It wouldn't be right to be butting in the very first day you're home,' she wrote to him, and as the post did not travel fast enough for him to argue with her by mail, Will had to take that as the last word.

May found it hard to sleep the night he arrived, knowing that he was home and that she would see him again the next day.

'I bet you can't wait,' her friend in China and Glass said.

'No,' May said, and wished it was true.

It did not help that trade was slow that day, and she had to spend a lot of time seeing that the girls in her department were kept busy tidying. She wished that something would happen to keep her mind occupied, like a rush of customers or one of Mrs Rutherford's spot checks. Not that she needed checking on. She was always careful to keep up Mrs Rutherford's standards at all times.

'Those towels could do with refolding,' she said, pointing to a shelf of Best Egyptian Hand Size.

'Then they can have a go at the bath sheets,' said a voice behind her.

She whirled round.

'Will!'

It was unmistakably him, in a newly sponged and pressed uniform. There were the same shy smile and anxious eyes, but in a weary-looking face.

'I thought I'd surprise you,' he said.

'You did. You gave me quite a turn. I wasn't expecting you till closing time,' May said.

'I'm sorry, I didn't mean—'

'It's all right, really. You – you look tired,' May said.

'It was a bit odd sleeping in a proper bed again. Nice to have a decent bath and everything, though. I hate being dirty all the time.'

'I can't imagine you dirty,' she said, and it was true. Will was always very dapper.

There was a brief pause. May felt there ought to be lots of things she should be saying.

'It's very modern here, isn't it? Different from Packards,' Will said.

With relief, May seized on the one thing about which she could talk endlessly.

'Oh yes, that was the whole point of it. Mrs Rutherford explained it to us all. The Empire Household Supplies is a place where ordinary people

371

can go and buy nice things that are not too expensive. It's all bright and pretty and light with everything displayed nicely so it's like a real treat to come here, but they don't feel like they shouldn't be there because it's too posh. Mrs Rutherford said as we've got to be polite and helpful at all times and not make people think we were looking down on them because they're not rich. Not like in Packards, you see. Specially in departments like Ladies' Gowns, where they look down their nose at you if you haven't got a handle to your name. It puts people off, like.'

'I suppose so. You like it here, then? It always sounded like you did, in your letters.'

'Oh yes, I love it,' May enthused. She glanced over to where the Floor Manager was talking to a customer. 'Look – er – you know how it is, Will, I shouldn't really be standing here nattering to you like this. Now I'm a supervisor, I got to set a good example.'

Will was instantly understanding.

'Of course, yes, I don't want to get you into trouble. Look, when's your dinner break? I'll come back then and we could go and get something to eat at an ABC or a Lyon's or something. If you want to, that is.'

She could not very well say no.

An hour and a half later they were facing each other over plates of cottage pie and cabbage. Will tucked in with gusto.

'This is better than army grub,' he said, mopping up every last morsel.

'Is it dreadful?' May asked.

'Like pigswill. There's a saying, "If the sun rises in the east, it's stew." But it's not stew like anything you've ever seen. I mean, you can hardly tell what's been put into it, it's just a sort of watery, lumpy mess. In fact, I expect a lot of pigs'd turn up their snouts at it. But it's that or nothing, so you eat it.'

'Sounds awful,' May said. 'And – the rest of it, being in the army, I mean, what's it like? Is it awful?'

A horribly bleak expression came over Will's face, and for a moment he seemed to look right through her to something terrible. Then he shrugged.

'It's all right.'

And try as she might, that was the only comment she could get out of him, either then or at any other time during his leave. He would tell her about his friends, about the sergeant who turned out to have a heart of gold beneath his gruff exterior, about the places he had passed through in France, about an orchard they had rested in and a river they had swum in, but about life in the trenches he said nothing at all. It was as if they did not exist.

They met again that evening and went to the pictures. The next day was Saturday, half day at the shop, so in the afternoon they went to Hampstead Heath on the bus and ate sandwiches under the trees. It was a warm day, still and quiet.

'Just think, it's nearly three years since war was declared,' May said.

'Yes.' Will sat hunched up with his arms round his knees. 'Seems like a hundred years ago, doesn't it?'

'Things've certainly changed,' May said.

For her, things had changed for the better. She would never have been given her present position if it hadn't been for the men going off to fight and the women going into munitions and other war work. But it didn't seem like a very tactful thing to mention.

'That's one way of putting it,' Will said.

On the way home again, Will was silent, frowning out of the window and chewing his lip. May made several attempts to start a conversation but got nowhere, so in the end she gave up. When they reached the Gosses' house, he suddenly started speaking.

'Look, May, I wanted to ask – that is – I don't know how you're placed tomorrow, but – well, my mother's having a proper Sunday roast, that is, she always does but this is a bit different because of me being home and so she's sort of killed the fatted calf and that and – and . . .'

May looked at him. The sweat was standing out on his forehead. With total clarity she knew what was coming and what her reply would be.

'What, Will?'

'I was hoping you'd be able to come and join us,' Will said.

'That's very nice of you, and your mother. Thank you.'

'You mean you'll come?'

'Yes, I'd like to.'

Ruby groaned when she heard.

'Are you mad? You know what this means, don't you?'

'I'm not stupid,' May said.

She was only too aware of the significance of the occasion. A young man did not invite a young woman to family Sunday dinner unless he was serious about her. She was about to be paraded for family approval, or more to the point, for his mother's approval.

'But you can't want to–' Ruby began.

'Oh shut up!' May snapped. 'Why can't you let me alone?'

Ruby sniffed.

'Well pardon me for living, I'm sure. On your head be it.'

May couldn't explain that she did not have an alternative. Her feet were set on a certain road and she couldn't get off it.

It was quite an ordeal. May wore her best grey dress with the white poplin collar and cuffs, a black straw hat and a new pair of cotton gloves. She knew she looked neat and respectable, but still she was nervous. The Fosters lived in a tidy little house with a trimmed hedge round a small front garden. Inside, everything was fiercely polished. May was glad she had put a shine on her shoes that morning.

Mrs Foster was a square woman with an air of contained impatience. Mr Foster was an older version of Will, already a little stooped about the shoulders. There was a married sister and her three children, and a young brother with a bad case of spots. Mrs Foster questioned May about her family, her job and her religious beliefs; Mr Foster smiled kindly at her and found her the choicest slices of lamb; the sister was mostly engaged in making the children behave; and the brother said nothing.

'That was a beautiful joint, Mrs Foster, done to a turn,' May said dutifully. 'You'll just about have enough for some cold cuts tomorrow as well.'

For the first time, Mrs Foster's face relaxed.

'That's right. It's nice to hear a young girl with an economical head on her shoulders,' she said.

Across the table, May saw Will smile and nod. It seemed she had passed muster. After that, the rest of the afternoon was easier. When May said her goodbyes, all the family shook her warmly by the hand.

'It's been very nice meeting you, I'm sure,' Mrs Foster said.

Will was quite animated as he escorted her back to the Gosses'.

'I think Mother's taken to you. It's quite a compliment. She doesn't take to everybody. In fact, she can be quite sharp at times.'

May could believe it.

'I'm glad you didn't tell me that before I met her,' she said.

Will smiled.

'I didn't want to put you off,' he admitted.

At the front gate, he took both of her hands in his.

'Thank you for coming today. It meant a lot to me.'

'I enjoyed it,' May lied.

'Oh good. I was afraid – well, it's not easy, I know, facing a lot of strangers. I was so proud of you, May.'

A glow of pleasure started inside May. It was wonderful to be appreciated.

'Thank you.'

'Tomorrow's my last day. Shall we go somewhere special? Have a nice supper or something?'

Last day. Last day. The words rolled round her head and settled in her heart, bringing a sense of dread that was so unexpected that it left her breathless.

'I – yes – that would be lovely,' she faltered.

Will lunged forward and planted a daring kiss on her cheek. That night, May hardly slept at all.

'Has he asked you, then?' Ruby demanded.

'No,' May snapped.

'Blimey, he's going to have to get a move on, isn't he?'

May said nothing.

'Well, he's not got much time left, has he? What are you going to say? Are you going to–?'

'Oh shut up!' May shouted. 'I don't know! Don't keep going on and on.'

The trouble was, she was no longer sure whether he was going to ask her at all, and she found that she wanted him to, very much indeed.

'I still can't see what you see in him,' Ruby said.

'Well, you're not me, are you?' May said, and rushed off to catch the bus.

She spent a miserable day. She couldn't concentrate at all and kept making stupid mistakes. Some of the customers were rude to her, making her even more clumsy and forgetful, and she could feel her juniors sniggering behind her back. She wanted to just run away and cry. It seemed as if seven o'clock would never come.

At last the final customer left the shop and the weary staff could tidy up and follow them out of the door. There was Will, waiting for her. May's heart gave a leap as his face lip up on seeing her.

'I thought you'd never come,' he said, and offered his arm. May slipped her hand into the crook of his elbow and felt a surge of possessive pride. She was glad the others were there to see her.

They went to a cosy little chophouse in a street leading off the Strand. The meat was hard and the vegetables soft, but May hardly noticed. With the high wooden benches fencing them in like stalls in a stable, they were in a private little world of their own. It was exactly right for an intimate tête-à-tête. Except that Will was chatting on about his family, about Packards, about his pals in the platoon, about anything, it seemed, as long as it was not about the two of them. She had never known him so talkative. May chewed her way through her mutton chop and waited for an opening. She could see that it was going to be up to her.

'. . . they're like brothers, closer than brothers. It's hard to explain to anyone who hasn't been there. It's because we've all been through so much together,' Will was saying.

May swallowed a lump of gristle.

'I'm going to miss you when you go back to them.'

There was a brief silence. May felt quite ill with nerves. Now she has done it. Supposing she was wrong? Supposing he was only pals with her, not thinking of anything else at all?

Will pushed his cabbage round his plate.

'I – er – I'm going to miss you as well, May.'

Committed now, May took another step.

'It's been lovely seeing you. I've really enjoyed all the things we've done. And meeting your family. That was nice too.'

'Oh, I have too, enjoyed it, I mean, being with you . . .'

Will ran a finger round inside his collar, as if it was strangling him.

'In fact – I wanted – what I mean is – when I next come home, would you – could we get married?'

May looked at his scarlet face. He wasn't handsome, he wasn't tall, he wasn't ever going to be rich. Ruby thought he was boring. But May knew that he was kind and reliable, that he would look after her and appreciate her looking after him. Most of all, though he had not yet had the courage to say so, she knew that he loved her. She reached across the table and held his hands.

'Yes,' she said.

32

It was an odd sensation, realising that things were at last going the way of the Allies, yet not being there to take part. Over in France, the tide was turning. The armies had broken out of the trenches and were fighting moving battles over open country. Horribly familiar names reappeared in the newspaper reports and in letters from friends still on active service: the Somme, Ypres and even, almost unbelievably, Mons.

At his training camp in the gentle folds of the Dorset countryside, Alec veered from frustration to guilty relief. Mostly he wanted to be there with the men who were forcing back the enemy step by step, regaining the ground that had been fought over so bitterly and at such huge cost for four long years. But when he looked at the casualty lists he knew that it was no walkover. The Boche might be retreating but he was fighting every inch of the way. If he was over there now, he would be a marked man. Bunnyfoot Eden was a thing of the past, his luck quite gone. In fact he found he had acquired a new nickname. Just a couple of weeks ago he had overheard one of the new conscripts referring to him as Old Hopalong.

He felt old, too. Only a few years separated him from

the youths whom he was training, but his time at the Front had hardened him beyond his years, putting a great gulf between him and those who now might not have to endure as he had done.

'It's an odd thing,' he said to Sylvia, 'but I wouldn't have missed it for the world. Despite everything, I'm glad I was there. I just feel so desperately guilty that I'm still alive when so many decent men are dead. There's no sense to it, no reason. They deserve to be alive far more than I do.'

'You deserve to be alive just as much as anybody else,' Sylvia said.

They were sitting in cane chairs under the cedars at Tatwell by the side of the now neglected tennis courts. It was a sultry Indian summer's day with a promise of thunder in the air. Swallows and martins flew low over the lawns, catching insects, and in the fields the old men and the Land Girls were harvesting the wheat. Alec sipped tea from a Crown Derby cup, ate cucumber sandwiches and scone with strawberry jam and let the peace of the picture seep into him. There was no answering the question of why he had survived when others had not. He thrust it to one side, from where he knew it would come out and attack him again before long. Then he waved a hand at the scene before him.

'This is a wonderful place. I can see why my father bought it.'

'Yes, it is. I've come to love it more and more since I've been living here. I'm so glad it's being put to such good use now. I'm sure your father would have approved,' Sylvia said.

Together, they turned to look back towards the house. The yellow brick glowed honey-coloured in the sunshine. The French windows were open and on the terrace those of the wounded who could be moved were sunning themselves in their wheelchairs or on benches and deck chairs. Even in its present role as a hospital, Tatwell was beautiful. Everything about it appealed to him, from the proportions of the building to the trees in the park. From the moment he had been aware of his surroundings in the ward in the south drawing room, he had wanted it for his own.

'. . . come here to see Tatwell,' Sylvia was saying.

Alec realised with a jolt that his attention had wandered. He tried to catch up with what Sylvia was saying, and found to his amazement that she was actually attempting to tease him.

'Oh no,' he assured her. 'It's you I come to visit. You're one of the few people I can talk to.'

Maybe it was just the heat, but he could have sworn that a slight flush of pleasure coloured Sylvia's fair cheeks.

'Surely not. You must have lots of friends.'

'Not close to hand,' Alec said.

It was true. The only ones who really understood were still in France, or dead, or invalided out. He saw the latter as often as he could. But at his present camp they were mostly old Dugouts from previous wars or raw recruits, and civilians simply had no idea. It was odd, then, that he felt able to unburden himself to Sylvia. There was just something about her, a quality of listening, so that he had even found himself confessing to the nightmares. Sylvia had nodded, calm and matter-of-fact.

'It's all right. A lot of men have them. I'm not at all surprised, after all that you've been through. Is it the same one each time?'

'Yes–' He paused, not really wanting to drag it all out into the daylight, yet impelled to do so. 'Always the same. I'm in No Man's Land and it's after a battle. There is smoke and gas drifting about, and all around me there are the dead and the dying. I'm the only one alive, the only one on his feet, and there are so many that I don't know where to start to help. I don't even know which way our lines are. It's just fog and bodies, and I know, the way you do know things in dreams, that there isn't anyone else alive anywhere. And then out of the gloom there comes a tank, and it's coming straight for me, over the bodies, crushing them. For a while I can only stare at it, and then I try to run, but I can't get away from it because I'm knee-deep in mud and I can hardly move my legs. It gets closer and closer, and I can hear it clanking and rattling, and always just as it's about to mow me down I wake up.'

Sweating and shouting and terrified.

'How dreadful for you. But you must not dwell on it, if you can possibly help it. You'll find they will come less often as time goes on.'

He had hardly hoped to believe her at the time, but in fact she was right. Now he could go up to two weeks without the nightmare recurring.

'I should be very happy to know that I had helped in some small way,' Sylvia said.

'You have. Very much so. In fact, I really look forward to our chats over tea. My leaves wouldn't—' He broke off, distracted by a female figure walking towards them over the lawn. 'Am I mistaken, or is that Amelie?' he asked.

Sylvia jumped as if she had been stung.

'What? Amelie – here? Now?'

He had never seen her look so flustered.

'What is she thinking of coming here unannounced like this? It's really too bad.'

Alec found himself staring at her as doors of possibility he had not even considered before appeared to open up. Then the habitual resentment of the outsider reasserted itself. No, she was just annoyed and embarrassed to have Amelie discover her fraternising with the skeleton in the family cupboard. It put him immediately on the offensive. He hauled himself to his feet as Amelie approached and held out his hand.

'Amelie. This is a pleasant surprise. How are you? I was going to come and visit you tomorrow and make sure that Packards is still there.'

Amelie's quick blue eyes flicked from him to Sylvia and back again. He could almost hear the questions spinning round her head – what is he doing here, acting as if he owns the place? How often is he here? Just what terms are he and Sylvia on? How is this going to affect me?

'I'll think you'll find Packards is holding its own. Like plenty of other institutions, we find we can manage perfectly well with the men away. Better, in fact.'

'I'm so glad to hear it. I wouldn't like to think that it was going downhill in my absence.'

Sylvia, with admirable self-control, appeared to have got over her panic. She and Amelie kissed cheeks and Alec limped into the tennis pavilion to fetch another chair. More tea was ordered, and the three of them sat discussing the war with every outward appearance of harmony.

'Do you think the end might really be in sight? It seems to have gone on for so long that I hardly dare believe it,' Sylvia said.

'We're certainly gaining ground at the moment, but it's not going to be over soon. I'd hazard a guess that it will continue well into next year,' Alec said. 'The Germans aren't going to give in easily. They're good fighters, and brave. You don't want to believe all the propaganda you read about them in the papers.'

'You sound as if you admire them,' Amelie accused.

'I respect them. You should never underestimate an enemy. That would be extremely dangerous.'

He certainly shouldn't underestimate Amelie.

'The casualty lists are still making very sad reading. Were there any Packards people amongst the latest numbers?' Sylvia asked.

Amelie let herself be diverted.

'I'm afraid so. One of the van drivers was killed and one of the buyers–' She turned to Alec. 'Of course, you know him. Victor Lambert. You worked under him in Stationery, didn't you? He's been injured. I believe he's had a leg amputated.'

Alec ignored the reference to his lowly position at Packards. Victor Lambert. Poor bastard. Once he had admired his skill in his job, then resented the fact that Ruby preferred him. Now all that was wiped out.

'The war will never be over for him,' he said. 'Or for many of the chaps here. I trust that he will get his old position back when he recovers.'

If he recovers.

Amelie looked surprised.

'I'm not sure that a cripple would be able to–'

'So Packards will abandon him, will they?' Alec was outraged. 'You'll let him risk death for you, have bits of him blown away and then throw him on the scrapheap with nothing but his war pension? I think that's disgraceful.'

'Packards is a business, not a charity,' Amelie said.

'I'm not asking for charity for him, I'm asking that he has a chance to prove he can still do his job. He's not a delivery boy, for God's sake, he doesn't need two legs to be a buyer. He still has a brain in his head. Packards was keen enough to encourage men to go. They should be equally keen to welcome them back again.'

'That does seem to be fair,' Sylvia put in.

'Fair!' Amelie cried. 'I can assure you that Edward wouldn't have seen it that way.'

There was a brief, prickling silence. Alec looked at Sylvia, who was wearing her icy mask. Although Sylvia had never spoken to him directly about her late husband he had his doubts about how close they had been.

'I think that was below the belt,' he said.

'And that was hypocritical. We all know you hated Edward.'

'What I–'

'How are your mother and father, Amelie?' Sylvia cut in. 'Is your mother's hip still troubling her? I really must stir myself to travel into Town and visit her. I'm just so busy here with the hospital that time seems to fly by. The weeks are gone before I can catch my breath. Perhaps I should invite her and your father here for a week or two. Do you think that would be well received? I know she was always very fond of Tatwell.'

Alec felt rather like a schoolboy who had been reprimanded for silly behaviour. Amelie compressed her lips and lowered her voice, almost matching Sylvia's measured tones.

'I'm sure the invitation would be appreciated.'

'Then I shall certainly extend one. Perhaps you would like to be one of the party. Have you heard from Perry recently?'

'Yes, only last week. His unit is moving out of Paris, apparently. He sounded very keen to see more of the action.

When they came to the end of things to say about Perry, they moved on to some people called Ida and Clement, of whom Alec knew nothing. Clement was in the thick of the push north. Right at that moment, Alec could envy him. Warfare seemed simple compared with family rivalries.

With Sylvia's tight hand on the conversational reins, they managed to keep a surface peace until the dogcart was brought round to take Alec to the station.

'Thank you again for all you're doing for the chaps here. I know it's very much appreciated,' he said to

Sylvia, for Amelie's benefit.

'I do what I can. It hardly seems enough. You will come and visit them again, I hope?'

'Of course. The very next time I get some leave.'

He and Amelie said goodbye with exaggerated politeness. He left to catch his train, wondering just what the two women were saying to each other. The behaviour of both of them had given him a great deal to think about. Up till now, he had not been able to seriously consider what he was going to do after the war. Now he realised that he wanted far more than his old job back. He wanted Edward's place. And if Amelie thought she was going to stand in his way, then she was very much mistaken. As for Sylvia – he had always thought of her as a friend and adviser, and more recently as a confidante. Up till now he had been sure that she liked to talk to him and was pleased when he came to visit, but had never suspected there might be any more to it than that. Sitting on the slow train as it pottered its way into every tiny station on the way back to London, he began to doubt what he had seen and heard. Perhaps he had been entirely mistaken. But if he had not . . . then the dizzying prospect opened up of not just Edward's job but of everything else that had belonged to Edward as well. It was almost too much to take in. He was going to have to tread very carefully.

With relief he thought of the evening ahead. Once he had spent some time with his mother, then he was free to go out with Ruby. She, thank God, was straightforward. She was just out for a good time. He always enjoyed his nights out with her.

The same thought was in Alec's mind two months later. On the continent, things were moving fast. At the end of October Ludendorff resigned, the German fleet mutinied and Turkey signed an armistice with the

Allies. Then Austria-Hungary followed suit, and now news had come through that the Kaiser had abdicated and Germany had become a republic.

'You're a lucky devil, getting leave now. If the show ends while you're in Town you'll be in for some rare old high jinks,' one of his fellow officers said.

He wondered how imminent peace might be. If the end really was in sight, it might be better to book in at a hotel rather than to go home, as then he wouldn't have to either stay in with his mother or disappoint her by going out to celebrate. He would make it up to her later by taking her out for a meal. As for the evening ahead, who better to spend it with than Ruby?

When the train reached Paddington, it was clear that something was afoot. People were in animated groups, talking, gesticulating. On the train, passengers broke their usual silence to talk to each other.

'What's happening? Is it peace? Has it finished?'

Alec jumped awkwardly down on to the platform and accosted the first person he met. The man wrung his hand.

'Eleven o'clock, it's going to stop at eleven o'clock.'

So it really was all over, or soon would be. Alec limped along the platform. He felt he ought to be ecstatic. Instead he was numb. All this time, all those good men dead and injured, and for what? For freedom, for King and country. Just now, they seemed rather abstract concepts compared with human lives. He supposed it was worth it. It had to be worth it, or they all would have died in vain, and that would be appalling beyond comprehension. Almost oblivious to the buzz of excitement around him, he caught a bus to Hyde Park Corner and booked into the first hotel with a room free. It was just a few minutes till eleven o'clock.

He stood looking out of the window as the hour struck. His head crowded with faces and scenes. He tried to hold on to the happy ones, to see the men relaxing in a sunny orchard, singing in an estaminet, playing football. He remembered the stoical cheerfulness, the black humour, the bravery, the loyalty. But the terrible pictures kept pushing in. Friends killed by his side, men mangled almost beyond recognition but still alive, bodies blackened from lying for days out on the battlefield.

Faintly, as if from a long way away, he heard whoops and cheers and church bells ringing. With difficulty, he focused his eyes on the street outside. People were hugging and kissing each other. There was weeping and laughter. Alec stared at them. He could hardly believe it. The British did not act like this, not in public, not in the street. He felt faintly repelled, but he knew that if he stayed where he was, alone, he would end up in the abyss. Already he was at the edge, staring down. He had to get out there and join in. He would go and find Ruby.

Packards was doing a roaring trade in Union Jacks and red, white and blue ribbons and favours. Alec attributed that particular piece of commercial acumen to Amelie. She would have thought ahead and had the goods all ready. There was a party atmosphere in the store, a hubbub of joyful voices as customers and shopgirls laughed and clasped hands and congratulated each other. Just as had happened all the way down Oxford Street, complete strangers on seeing Alec's uniform shook his hands and thumped him on the back as if he had defeated the enemy all by himself. Smiling, agreeing, returning thanks, but still feeling slightly apart from the mounting hysteria, Alec made his way into Stationery.

Ruby was behind her counter as usual, though she was not serving. She appeared to be caught up in an earnest conversation with two women customers. Then she looked up, and saw him. Astonishment then delight lit up her dark eyes and mobile mouth.

'Alec! Oh Alec!'

She hurried out from behind the counter and flung herself into his arms, to much cheering and laughter from bystanders.

'Oh Alec, I can't believe it! You're actually here. Isn't it wonderful?'

He held her close, feeling the warmth and vibrant life of her body. She was looking up at him with joy glowing in every line of her lovely face. He kissed her soft lips.

'Wonderful,' he agreed, and meant it.

No more killing, no more shells, no more death and destruction. It was over. Peace.

'Wonderful!' he repeated, and lifted her off her feet and swung her round till she screamed.

'When will you finish work this evening? Are they shutting up early?'

'I don't know. Nobody—'

But even as she spoke, word came through. The shop was closing in half an hour. All the shopgirls cheered.

'I'll meet you by the main door,' Alec said.

Oxford Street was jostling with celebrating people as they went arm in arm to join the crowds. All over London, workers were flooding out of offices and shops and on to the streets. Singing and shouting and waving, they made processions and filled the roads and stopped the traffic. Ruby snatched Alec's hat and put it on her own head.

'Trafalgar Square!' somebody shouted.

'Yes, yes, let's go to Trafalgar Square,' Ruby agreed.

Alec was caught up with her buoyant mood. Swept along with the human tide, they marched down Regent Street and joined the jubilant crowd round Nelson's column. Laughing and swaying, they sang their hearts out, roaring the words of 'Rule Britannia' and 'Tipperary' and shrieking as people jumped in the fountains and splashed the water about. In the middle of the square a bonfire was lit to cheers, and strangers linked arms and danced and swayed together.

It was a great big party that lurched from afternoon to evening and on into the night. They walked up the Mall to cheer the King and Queen as they waved from the balcony of Buckingham Palace. They collapsed and drank tea and ate buns at a café while Alec rested his aching leg, then when the pubs opened they started drinking. They sang in the bars and danced in the street.

Around midnight, the pub they were in ran out of drink.

'Might be some at my hotel,' Alec said.

'Where's that?' Ruby asked.

'Er – dunno,' Alec admitted.

They leaned against each other and howled with laughter.

With the exaggerated care of the drunk, he turned out all his pockets. Finally, he found a card. They staggered to a streetlight to read it. The print went in and out of focus.

'The Car – Carf – Carfax,' he managed to make out.

By some miracle, they found a cab. They fell on to the seat and rolled into the corner with their arms round each other. Alec pulled Ruby on to his lap and kissed her passionately, thrilling as her mouth and lips and tongue responded eagerly to his. He ran a hand down her back, over her buttocks, along her thighs.

'Oh beautiful, beautiful Ruby, how I love you,' he said.

She gave a moan of delight and nestled even closer.

'Say it again, say it again.'

'I love you, wonderful girl.'

'Oh and I love you too.'

Hungrily they kissed again. Alec's hand closed round a soft, full breast. It was not another drink that he wanted. It was her.

They stumbled up the steps of the hotel and leaned against the reception desk ignoring the night porter's disapproving look and trying not to giggle as he found the key. With difficulty, Alec located the room and managed to get the key in the door.

Still laughing, they wrapped their arms round each other and kissed.

'Wonderful Ruby,' Alec sighed as he shuffled her across the room. 'Stay with me. Say you'll stay with me.'

'I want to stay with you for ever.'

They reached the bed and tumbled on to it. Between kisses and caresses, Alec tore off his clothes, undid hers. Each layer revealed more of her delicious body. He explored all her wonderful soft curves while she sighed with pleasure, trembling at his touch, eager for more.

'Tell me,' she begged. 'Tell me you love me.'

'I love you,' he promised, and plunged into her luscious depths.

33

Christmas was a subdued affair for many people that year. Now that the war was over, the future had to be faced, and for thousands of families that meant a future without a husband and father. For even more, it meant a future with a family member who was trying to come to terms with disablement. Either way it meant living on a pittance of a pension. For a lot of those households whose menfolk had survived, there was disappointment. With the first euphoria, everyone had expected the soldiers to come home the moment they laid down their weapons, but soon it became clear that this was impossible. Christmas came and went, and still a huge number of men were encamped abroad.

At the end of December there was a general election. For the very first time in Great Britain, women were allowed to vote. Ida and Amelie celebrated with champagne, even though they themselves had not been able to put their crosses on the vital piece of paper. They both fell just short of the qualifying age of thirty. The one thing that took the edge off their jubilation was the fact that Clement was not there to win back his seat.

Amelie sympathised with Ida's anger and dejection when Clement wrote to tell her that he would not be

392

home till the new year at the very earliest.

'I know it's stupid of me, I know you can't just wave a magic wand and bring everyone back to where they were before the war, but I just want him home. While the war was on I could bear being parted from him. I had to, he was needed. But now it's different, and I want him back.'

'Of course you do. It must be terrible after being parted for so long,' Amelie said, while conflicting feelings tore her heart. She both longed for and dreaded seeing Clement again. Their brief days together shone in her memory as some of the happiest she had ever spent, but were seen through a veil of guilt and rejection. She did not know how she was going to be able to cope with seeing Ida and Clement back together as a happy couple once more.

It was not so bad during the day, for there was more than enough to keep her mind occupied at work. Packards was in the throes of formulating a way to re-employ returning staff and there was the threat of the imminent return of Alec Eden. Evenings were different. There were many long hours when she could not stop herself from brooding. So she had to act hard when Ida came bounding into the room to hug her one Sunday in January.

'Oh Melly, isn't it wonderful? Clem's coming home!'

'That's splendid news. I'm so glad for you. When's he arriving?' Amelie managed to say, hugging her in return. Ida's delight was so overwhelming that she really was happy for her, but at the same time her heart was aching. While he was still away, there had been room for pretence of a kind. Now all that would be at an end. Clem loved Ida. Amelie was their best friend.

'At the end of the month. Three weeks, Mel! Just three weeks – oh, I'm planning such a homecoming for him . . .'

Ida rambled happily on. Amelie could picture it all. The tears and laughter of the reunion on the station platform, the noisy family dinner, the quiet evening together then the ecstatic lovemaking. All at once her control broke, and she burst into tears.

Ida was contrite.

'Mel, darling! Oh, how could I be so inconsiderate? I'm so beastly selfish – why don't I think first? I'm so sorry. Here I am, whittering on about Clem when – oh Mel, it must be so lonely for you. I wish there was something I could do.'

Appalled at being so close to giving herself away, Amelie tried to stop herself, but somehow the tears kept on coming, until Ida could not help weeping as well. The two women clung to each other, crying out the unbearable strain of four and a half years of fear and grief and loneliness. At last, shaken and drained, they sat talking about the past. It was not until much later that Amelie noticed her friend was alternately huddling over the fire and sitting back and fanning herself.

'Are you feeling all right, Ida?' she asked.

'Yes, yes, quite all right. I'm just a bit hot, that's all.'

Amelie put a hand on her forehead.

'Hot! You've a temperature. You ought to be in bed.'

'It's nothing. I'm fine.'

'You're not. Are you aching anywhere?'

'Well – a little,' Ida was forced to admit.

They looked at each other.

'I hope you're not coming down with flu,' Amelie said.

'Of course not, I'm never ill,' Ida retorted, shivering and stretching her hands out to the fire. 'At least they're getting the miners out of the army first. That means we'll be able to have decent fires again.'

'You are ill. You're going home to bed, right now,' Amelie insisted.

The next day when she called, Ida was in a high fever, scarcely able to lift her head off the pillow. Amelie gathered up the children and took them to her house to be cared for by Nanny Rutherford, leaving Nanny Markham free to nurse Ida. Two days after that, she began to feel ill herself.

It all happened with amazing swiftness. In the morning she was fine, sorting out problems at the Empire Supplies, at lunchtime she noticed she was aching all over and by the evening she felt so rotten she retired to bed.

There followed a time when night and day seemed to blur into one. She suffered from delirious nightmares and when she was conscious felt so weak that she was hardly able to move. Faces swam in and out of her vision, strange faces making reassuring noises.

'Where are the children?' she asked, suddenly gripped with fear as she realised the house was unnaturally quiet.

'Don't worry, my dear, they're being very well looked after. Mrs Amberley Packard has taken them down to the country for a while.'

'Sylvia?'

Her head seemed to be stuffed with sawdust. She could not take things in. Sylvia had volunteered to take the children. It did not make sense. Then another odd thing struck her.

'Who are you?' she asked.

'I'm Nurse Atkins, dear. I take over at night time from Nanny Rutherford.'

'But–'

It was all too much. Her sawdust head was throbbing. She began to shiver violently.

Nurse Atkins put an extra cover over her.

'Now then dear, don't you worry about a thing. All you've got to do is lie there and get better.'

And since she was incapable of doing anything else, lie there was what she did, for what seemed like an interminable space of time. When she finally began to feel more herself, she had lost a stone and a half in weight and found it hard work to lift a spoon to her mouth, but she did have the use of her brain back. First she wrote to the children, with much labour and a rest at the end of each sentence. Then she realised that she ought to put in a note to Sylvia, thanking her for taking them on. That was enough effort for one day.

'Must write to Ida. I'll do that tomorrow,' she said to Nanny Rutherford. Then another thought struck her. 'Are her children at Tatwell with Mrs Amberley Packard as well?'

Nanny Rutherford's face assumed a blank look.

'No, ma'am, their grandparents sent for them. Time for a little rest now, I think.'

But there were still questions nagging at her.

'Ida, how is Ida? Do you know?'

'She's been very ill, ma'am, like you. You must have caught it off of her.'

'Have I been very ill?'

'Yes, ma'am, but you're on the mend now, thank the Lord. Now you just lie back and have a nice little sleep.'

Amelie had the distinct impression that she was being fobbed off in some way, but she felt too feeble to pursue it.

The next day she was a little stronger.

'I think I could manage the stairs now, Nanny, with some help. I really must telephone Mrs Markham.'

'Oh no, ma'am. I don't think that's at all wise. Doctor said you weren't to get out of bed yet, let alone leave the room. You've got to build your strength up.'

'Nonsense,' Amelie said.

She waited until Nanny was out of the room, then shuffled round until her legs were over the edge of the high bed and slid carefully down. Her feet touched the floor. A moment later, her knees gave way and she landed in a heap on the bedside rug. Nanny came running in, scolding, and helped her back in. Amelie had to be contented with sending a note to her friend.

There was no reply.

'She's been very ill,' Nanny repeated.

Amelie gave orders for some flowers to be sent round.

She could not sleep that night. There was plenty to worry about. She was not at all sure that the children would be happy at Tatwell with Sylvia. There were problems with staff at both Packards and Empire Supplies. Alec Eden was starting back and this time there was no keeping him behind the counter. He was on the fifth floor in the Merchandising department with large areas of responsibility and very obvious designs on the Board. But all of this faded in comparison with her concern for Ida. She should be getting better by now. She had fallen ill first. Amelie had a horrible feeling that something was wrong.

By the morning she was determined to find out what was happening. Feeling like a naughty child, she waited until Nanny was out of the room and once again tried getting out of bed. This time her legs held up long enough for her to totter to a chair. From there she made her way to the door, holding on to pieces of furniture as she went. She looked down the landing. It seemed a long way to the stairs. She aimed herself at the banister rails, then supported herself on them until she reached the stairs. She stood at the top, swaying and cursing her weakness. Her head was swimming. Abruptly, she sat down on the top step. There, far below her in the hall, was the telephone. Getting to it assumed the utmost importance. Come what may, she had to negotiate the stairs.

She gripped one of the uprights of the rails with one

hand and steadied herself with the other, then carefully lowered herself on to the next step. She could do it. Slowly she made her way down on her bottom, step by step. By the time she reached the hall, she was trembling but triumphant. Now she only had to get to the chair by the telephone. She sat for a few moments getting her strength back and listening. There were sounds of cleaning going on and a clattering from the kitchen, but nobody was coming her way. Then she smiled to herself as she realised she was acting like an intruder in her own home. If she wanted to use the telephone, she would do so. She hauled herself up and staggered the last few steps.

There was a pause as the operator connected her. Amelie leaned her head against the wall. She felt exhausted. It was ridiculous. All she had done was to come down one flight of stairs. There was a click and then the dialling tone.

'The Markham residence.'

Amelie recognised the voice of the parlourmaid who had taken over most of the butler's duties when he joined up.

'Good morning, Tilson. Is it possible to speak to Mrs Markham?'

There was an odd noise at the end of the line.

'Is – excuse me, but is that Mrs Rutherford?' Tilson's voice sounded oddly high-pitched.

'Yes it is,' said Amelie.

There was a clatter and the sound of doors opening and shutting and voices. Amelie could not make any of it out. Then a different person came on the line.

'Amelie my dear.'

Amelie just about recognised Ida's mother's voice. She sounded distraught. Amelie was gripped by a premonition of disaster. 'Mrs Maudesley, is that you? What's the matter? What's happened?'

'Oh Amelie – you can't have been told. This is dreadful. I wish – my dear . . .'

Amelie held on to the arm of the chair. Her head was swimming again.

'What is it? It's Ida, isn't it? I know it is. What's happened to her?'

'She's – she's – it was the influenza . . .'

Amelie's mouth was very dry. She forced the words out.

'Ida's – dead?'

'Yes. We buried her two days ago.'

Sobs shuddered down the line, then there was a click and it went dead.

Amelie sat holding the receiver. She felt cold to the core. Ida was dead. It couldn't be true. Not Ida, so full of energy and ideas, with all her life still in front of her. But deep down she knew that it was true, that she had known it for the last couple of days, but had been trying not to admit it to herself. With startling clarity, she saw a future with no Ida to talk to and laugh with and confide in. The world that had begun to have hope at last with the ending of the war now seemed bleak and empty. She did not know how she was going to cope without Ida's courage and humour and practical common sense. She felt totally alone. A great wave of grief rolled up and overwhelmed her.

People came rushing from all over the house.

'You should have told me. Why didn't you tell me?' she demanded.

Anxious faces surrounded her.

'You shouldn't have kept it from me. I never said goodbye.'

Nanny Rutherford put her arms round her.

'Now now then. Don't take on so. We did it for the best, you weren't well enough to be told. Now come along upstairs and we'll put you to bed again.'

399

'No!'

Grief and anger lent her strength. She turned on Nanny, venting her rage.

'Don't speak to me as if I was one of the children. I am not going back to bed. I am going to the Markhams'. You can help me get dressed and I want a cab called and I want it done now!'

She overrode all their objections, finding a cruel relief in seeing their apprehensive expressions. They were not used to tantrums and unreasonable demands from her. She sat shaking as Nanny and the head parlourmaid dressed her like a doll in one of the outfits she had had made when Hugo died. By the time she had been helped downstairs again and into the waiting cab she was exhausted, but determined to carry on. She could not stay in her own home. She had to go to where Ida's relatives were. With that aim in mind, she let Nanny Rutherford come with her to help her when she arrived. As she sank back against the leather seat of the cab, she caught sight of her reflection in the window. She looked like a ghost.

Her legs would hardly hold her up as she tottered up the steps and in at the Markhams' door. Then she stopped still, riveted with shock. There in the hall was Clement.

'Clem?' she croaked, hardly able to take it in. She had not expected him to be there. She had no idea what day it was, had forgotten just how long she had been ill.

He looked dreadful, his face ashen, but he held out his arms to her.

'Oh Mel,' he said. 'How am I going to live without her?'

34

A heavy April shower started just as the bridal party arrived at the Tatwell chapel. Squealing with alarm, May and her sisters ran the last few steps to the shelter of the porch. Heavy hearted, Ruby followed. Having her new dress ruined was all of a piece with the rest of her life.

'It's all right, don't worry, you look lovely,' the other bridesmaids reassured May, laughing and breathless as they straightened their frocks and arranged the bridal veil.

May did look pretty, Ruby had to admit. Her poplin dress with its square neck, long sleeves and rows of tucks was sweet and simple, like the posy of spring flowers she carried. The dash to the chapel had put the colour back into her cheeks and given a sparkle to her eyes.

'Quiet now. Remember you're entering the house of God,' May's father admonished.

Instantly cowed, the girls stopped talking and lined up behind the bride.

It was no wonder May left home, Ruby decided. Her old man put a damper on everything, even his own daughter's wedding.

Ruby did not attend to much of the service. She was

too much preoccupied with memories of past times at Tatwell. How happy she had been then, those Sundays two winters ago when she had come every week to the little station and out to Tatwell Court. The huge house had seemed like a fairytale palace to her, a place where dreams came true. Alec had been pleased to see her then. He had looked forward to her visits and laughed at the stories she told him about what had been going on at the store. Anything had seemed possible.

How different everything was now. Now, he refused to see her.

Blinking back tears of anger and rejection, Ruby tried to concentrate on what was going on. She didn't think much of the chapel, for a start. No stained-glass windows, no fancy embroidered hangings, no carved pews. Just plain whitewashed walls and chairs. She wanted somewhere really nice when she got married, with lots of lovely colours and flowers everywhere. When she got married. If. If ever. She looked at the happy couple. Well, she didn't envy May that one, that was for sure. Will had never been much fun before the war, and now he was even worse, really quiet. May was going to be bored stiff sitting on the other side of the hearth from him every evening, darning his socks. That wasn't for Ruby, oh dear no. May was welcome to him. But try as she might, she could not quite suppress the voice that told her that at least May was safe. She was married, and respectable. Even if Will were to drop dead tomorrow, at least she would have her marriage lines, and a ring on her finger. She wouldn't have to worry day and night about how soon people were going to find out . . . Ruby looked down the line of her body to where her hands clasped her posy in front of her stomach. One thing about these modern up-and-down fashions, they hid your figure.

The sun was shining when they emerged from the

chapel. Rice was thrown, kind wishes were called and family and close friends went back to the Hollises' little cottage for tea and sandwiches. It wasn't much of a wedding party, in Ruby's opinion. No drinks, no dancing, no singsong. Whenever the group from Packards became a little noisy, they got a dirty look from Mr Hollis. It would have been better if they had all gone to the pub, but the Hollises did not approve of that. In fact, she couldn't find much that the Hollises did approve of, except praying and working. Ruby couldn't wait to get back to London. Tatwell was too full of might-have-beens.

She was surprised to find how flat everything seemed once the wedding was over. The bustle of getting everything ready had irritated her beyond bearing at times, but it had occasionally served to take her mind off the dreadful worry that gnawed at her every second of the day. She missed May terribly. There was no one to talk to after work except her family, and they didn't understand the way Packards functioned like May did. More importantly, they didn't act as a foil to her like May did. She was lost without May to impress.

Work wasn't the same these days, either. The feeling of carrying on bravely in difficult circumstances was gone. During the war, they were keeping Packards going, carrying on a great tradition for England. People would come in and say, 'Well at least Packards is still here. Civilisation isn't quite dead yet.' Now they were made to feel that they were lucky to have a job.

Victor Lambert was back in Stationery as buyer, but he wasn't the romantic figure he used to be. It was not just the way he stumped about on his artificial leg. He had lost more than a limb; he no longer had the air of a man who was on his way up. It was whispered that he was completely under the thumb of his dragon of a wife. Ruby felt no great need to bludgeon him with the number and quality of her admirers any more. In fact all she felt when looked at him was a faint wonder that once he had had such a hold over her.

It was at work that people started making remarks.

'You're putting a bit of weight on, aren't you, Rube?' one of the girls said as they stood fixing their hair in the toilets.

'Yeah, what's all this, then?' another said, poking her in the side. 'You used to have the smallest waist in Packards.'

Ruby just laughed it off, turning the insult back on its perpetrators, but it left her uneasy. Despite being dull, work became precious. The day was drawing ever nearer when it could all be snatched away from her.

Going to visit May was no help. Ruby went to tea with her on Sunday at her new home in a terraced row in Stoke Newington and found that their old roles had been reversed. She was required to trail round after her friend and admire the delights of the parlour, the dining room, the back parlour and the kitchen. Then they went upstairs.

'This is our room,' May said, blushing bright pink.

'Very pretty,' Ruby said dutifully, staring at the big iron bedstead with its white cotton bedspread that dominated the space.

The second room belonged to a lodger, so Ruby was spared that. The back one contained merely an unmade bed and a wardrobe.

'We're not going to let this. We never know when we might be needing it,' May said, blushing again.

Ruby was overwhelmed with bitter jealousy. May was looking forward to a baby as a happy event. She was unable to speak a word.

When the tour was over, the three of them, May, Will and Ruby sat down to tea. May presided over the teapot with an air of self-importance while Will passed cups and plates and gazed at her with adoring pride. It made Ruby feel quite ill.

It was only when Will went out to water his cabbage seeds in the garden that Ruby and May were able to have anything like the intimate talks they used to have.

'Don't you miss the shop at all?' Ruby asked, trying to cut through May's gluey complacency.

'Oh no. I still hear all about it from Will.'

'But you were a supervisor at Empire Supplies. I know it wasn't like being one at Packards itself, but it was still a good job. You were in charge of all those juniors. Don't you miss that?'

May laughed.

'I'm in charge of everything here. The whole house. There's so much to do, and I want everything to be just right for Will. There's all—'

'You must be lonely, though, all by yourself?' Ruby cut in.

'Lonely? No! The neighbours are nice, and then there's the lady at the grocer's and the nice family at the baker's and the butcher's a very friendly man—'

'It's hard work, though, surely, doing all that scrubbing and washing and polishing every day. And you don't have any help, not on Will's wages.'

'I don't mind. I love it, Ruby. It's our little house, our nest. I love keeping it all shiny, and scrubbing Will's shirts and doing his ironing. It's so nice to see him going out looking so smart and knowing that I made sure everything was right. And then I can always stop and have a cup of tea when I feel like it. It's not like at work. I'm in charge here, I can do things the way I want to.'

Try as she might, Ruby could not shake her. Worse than that, in the slight pause that followed, May took over.

'I hope you don't mind me saying, Ruby, but that dress doesn't suit you at all. It makes you look quite fat.'

Once, Ruby might have told her, but not now.

'It's the fashion,' she said. 'You want to watch it, May. You mustn't turn into a frump just because you're married.'

When she left, the pair of them waved her off from the doorstep. She went home feeling very lonely.

In the days that followed, she continued to refuse to face the truth. She wasn't feeling sick, or having cravings. She was just late, that was all. Very late. Every time she went to the toilet, she hesitated a moment before looking, praying to find that she had started. Every time, she was disappointed, as the rational part of her knew she would be.

Then one Sunday in May, before the rest of the house was up, her mother cornered her in the back parlour.

'I want to speak to you.'

Ruby knew, from the expression on her face, that this was it. Still, she tried to get out of it.

'Can't stop now, Mum. I'm going out.'

'Oh no, you're not. You're staying here. I been far too slack with you. Sit down.'

'No.'

Ruby made for the door, but her mother caught hold of her arm.

'Sit down. Now. You and me got to have this out before your father wakes up.'

There was a hard edge of desperation in her mother's voice that made Ruby capitulate. She sat. Her mother loomed over her, her eyes deadly serious.

'Now tell me the truth, mind – are you – are you expecting?'

It was on the tip of her tongue to deny it.

'Ruby? You are, aren't you?'

'Yes,' Ruby admitted, and all at once reality rolled over her like a tidal wave. Yes, she was carrying a baby and she had known it for weeks and weeks. The very

406

worst thing that could happen to an unmarried girl. The fate worse than death.

'Oh my God.'

Her mother plumped down on the nearest chair, her face white.

'There, you happy now? Heard what you wanted, have you?' Ruby demanded, driven by fear.

'How can you sit there and talk to me like that? You wicked girl! This is a nightmare, it's a disaster for all of us and you just sit there answering back like it's something what don't matter.'

'Happening to you! It ain't you that's carrying this kid, it's me!' Ruby retorted, her voice rising.

'Hush! Your father'll hear. You know what a mood he's been in since he got the sack. If he finds out, there'll be hell to pay.' Her mother glanced up at the ceiling, listening for movement. She clasped her head with her bony fingers. 'Calm down. Now listen – who's the father? It ain't – oh it ain't that one at work, is it? The married one? I should of known. I been too soft on you, letting you out to all hours. Me and your father, we both been too soft on you. We should of made sure you was in at a proper respectable time–'

'It's not him,' Ruby admitted.

'Then who is it, and why ain't you told him?' Mrs Goss's whole face slackened with horror as another thought struck her. 'You do know who it is – don't you?'

'Of course I do! What do you think I am? It's Alec Eden.'

'Alec? But – well, that's all right, surely? You and him was walking out for a long time, wasn't you? And you went and saw him regular when he was in hospital. What's the problem? Why ain't he doing what's right by you?'

'Because he's one of The Family,' Ruby told her, bitterness churning inside her.

407

Her mother looked confused.

'The Family? You mean the Packards?'

'What other family would it be? Yes, it's all out now. He's Sir Thomas's son. He's not one of us lot. He's up on the top floor being groomed for a post on the Board and I suppose one day he'll be in charge of it all.'

And she had thought that she would be there with him, swanning around doing nothing all day long like Lady Muck and living in a big house with servants to do all the work. How stupid she had been.

'Oh Ruby,' her mother groaned. 'Oh my God, it couldn't be worse. What did you go and let him do it for? You know that sort always gets away with it. They don't marry girls like you, not in real life. What did he say when you told him?'

Ruby stared hard at the corner of the table, trying to shut out the image of Alec's expression as he listened to her claim that day. It had been hard just getting to see him, and when she did finally get inside his office, he talked to her like a stranger, calling her 'Miss Goss'. But worst of all was the way his face changed when she told him she thought she was carrying his child. It was as if it had frozen into a mask. Try as she might to look at every detail, every loop of the green chenille tablecloth, Ruby could not get rid of the picture of that chilling expression. In front of her eyes, Alec had turned into a stranger.

'He said—' she started, and choked.

'I don't think so, Miss Goss,' he had said.

'But it is, you know it is, it's yours,' she had cried.

'I'm afraid I know nothing of the kind.'

'You do! You must! It happened on Armistice night.'

'Ah well, Armistice night. Everyone was very drunk that night. Perhaps your memory is a little hazy.'

'I remember going back to your hotel room. I remember waking up there in the morning. And I remember you giving me the cab fare back home.'

'Then your recollections are very different from mine.'

'The night porter!' she had cried, desperation coming to her aid. 'The night porter saw us. He'd back me up.'

But Alec had given a small, mirthless smile that had chilled her to the bone.

'I think you'll find that night porters are very forgetful people, Miss Goss.'

Her mother's voice broke in on her painful thoughts. 'What? What did he say?'

'That – it wasn't his,' Ruby whispered.

And more besides.

'It would be unwise of you to start spreading accusations of this nature, Miss Goss,' he had warned. 'Especially when in the past you have boasted to all and sundry of your many conquests amongst the armed forces.'

She had stared at him, unable to reconcile this hard man with the Alec she loved. In her head she heard all those stupid things she had used to say for Victor Lambert's benefit. There was no denying it. Everyone in the department had heard. She had meant them to. If only she had shut her big mouth. If only she had held out on Alec. If only . . . It had been after that terrible interview that she started deluding herself that it wasn't happening, that everything was all right and things could carry on just as they were before.

'Well of course he would say that, wouldn't he?' her mother said. 'That sort always do. Why couldn't you have walked out with one of your own kind? You got plenty of offers, heaven knows. You could of been married to some nice boy by now, like May.'

'I was trying to better myself,' Ruby screamed at her. 'There's nothing wrong in that, is there?'

'There is if it lands you up in this fix,' her mother

shouted back.

'What fix?' said a third voice.

Gasping, both women turned round. It was Ruby's father.

'What fix?' he repeated.

'N-nothing. Nothing at all. We was just having a bit of a barney, that's all,' Miss Goss gabbled. 'You know what Ruby's like. Headstrong.'

'Sounded like it was more serious than that. A lot more serious. Are you in trouble?'

Ruby's father reached out a beefy hand, gripped her by the arm and hoisted her to her feet. Ruby squealed with pain.

'Stop it! You're hurting me!'

'Stop it, Frank. She ain't–'

'Shut up.'

Still holding her arm, her father stared at Ruby's belly. Try as she might to hold it in, five and a half months of pregnancy bulged against the fabric of her loose-waisted dress. With a snarl of disgust, he thrust her away from him. Ruby staggered against the table then collapsed into her chair.

'You little whore.'

Spittle flicked from his lips.

'Frank!'

Ruby stared at him, appalled. The questions came at her: whose was it, why wasn't he standing by her, what did she think she was doing, letting them down like this? She could only shake her head, stunned by the man that had once been her easy-going, affectionate father. This was twice that it had happened now. First Alec, now her father, changed before her eyes because she was carrying a child. As if it was her fault.

'It's not my fault!' she cried.

'Then whose is it?' her father demanded.

'It takes two, Frank,' her mother pointed out.

410

Her father rounded on her.

'A decent girl says no. A man knows that. You know that. A man respects a decent girl. She can't of refused. She must of let him.'

Mrs Goss was silent in the face of this onslaught. Mr Goss turned back to Ruby.

'I don't know what the world's coming to. First I get kicked out of the job I been doing for twenty years, then my daughter turns out to be a filthy little harlot. Well, I'll tell you something, you're not staying here to shame us. We've always been a respectable household. I'm not having you parade your bastard in front of the neighbours. You'll get up those stairs now and pack your things and go.'

The world seemed to be crashing round her ears. This could not be happening. There was a roaring in her head. Faintly, she heard her parents arguing, her mother pleading, her father adamant. Then she was being hauled to her feet again, dragged up the stairs to her room. A battered old carpetbag was thrown down by her feet.

'Pack. Now.'

Incredulous, she looked at this monster who was her father.

'You can't do this to me.'

'I can and I am. You're a bad lot. You got to go.'

The gross unfairness of it shook her out of her daze.

'I am not a bad lot. It was only once. It was on Armistice night. Everyone was mad then, no one knew what they was doing. You can't throw me out because of that.'

'Once! Once was too much. Look at you! Brazen, saying it's not your fault. You're no daughter of mine no more. Get that bag packed or I'll turn you out without it.'

Her mother was weeping now, clutching at her husband and begging him to change his mind. Ruby held back the tears. She could at least hold on to a remnant of pride. She pulled open drawers, stuffed clothes and possessions into the bag at random. Before she knew it, she was in her coat and hat and out on the street with the front door of her home slammed shut behind her.

She started walking mechanically, not knowing where she was heading for.

Even the familiar streets seemed to have turned against her. They felt hostile. People were going to and returning from church, dressed in their Sunday best. There was the occasional whiff of a roast drifting out of front doors. Everybody belonged, they had homes, families, somewhere to go, something to do. She was an outcast. The weather made it worse. It was the most beautiful spring morning. Tulips bloomed in front gardens, trees were in blossom, cats on windowsills basked in the sunshine, the air was warm with promise. The war was over, the men were home, broken families were reunited. All was well. But not for Ruby.

She reached the main road and turned automatically towards central London. The shops were closed. The street that was so busy on a weekday was occupied by just one returning milk cart. The cheerful ring of the trotting pony's hooves on the cobbles grated on Ruby's ears. She glared at it.

'Cheer up, darling. It might never happen,' the milkman called to her.

That was what she had thought, but now she knew that it was untrue. It had happened. She was pregnant, unmarried and homeless. The tears that she had controlled in front of her parents welled up and spilled down her face. She wanted to sit down, to bury her head in her arms and howl, but there was nowhere to stop, just the endless pavement and row of shuttered shop fronts. So she kept on walking, and crying, wiping away the tears with her sleeves until they were soaked through.

She was not sure how long she kept plodding on, but several parades of shops and the intervening houses had separated her from home before she became aware that her legs were weary and her arms and shoulders were aching from lugging the carpetbag. Beyond caring what people thought, she sat down on a garden wall. Her feet were throbbing, her eyes swollen, her head splitting. She slumped in despair.

'Oi, you!'

Ruby ignored the voice, not connecting it with herself.

'You – miss!'

Slowly, Ruby turned her head. A middle-aged man in braces with a shiny bald scalp was standing in the doorway of the house behind her.

'Get off of my wall. Go on – be off with you! We don't have your sort round here.'

Somewhere inside her mind, a memory stirred. Another step, another voice, another time when the world had come to an end. Victor. The day Victor Lambert had told her that he was married. She had run away in tears then, but she had survived. She would survive again. She could do it. Slowly, she stood up and stared back at the man with all the contempt she could muster.

'Don't worry, mate. I wouldn't stay here if you paid me.'

And with something resembling a toss of the head, she walked off.

The action released her power to think. She need not walk the streets and sleep on park benches. There was somewhere she could go. She did have a friend. May would take her in. She would go to May's, just for now, just until she got herself sorted out.

35

Somehow, it seemed the natural thing to carry on as they had left off. Ida and Amelie had always met up on Sundays for family luncheon, a walk and then tea and games with the children. After the first terrible shock, the Markham children wanted to know when they were going to see the Rutherfords, while the Rutherfords were demanding to have the Markhams to play again. Amelie telephoned Clement.

'I think it would be good for the children to continue doing something they've always done. It might be comforting for them,' she explained.

Clement agreed, and duly turned up at the Rutherfords' house at midday the following Sunday with Flora and Edward. All three of them looked wan and strained. Amelie swept the two children into her arms and longed to do the same to Clement.

At first they were all stiff and awkward, but soon the two little girls claimed Flora to come and play and the boys wanted to show Edward their new set of lead soldiers. Clement and Amelie were left looking at each other. To cover the silence, they both started talking together.

'It was good of . . .'

'Luncheon won't be . . .'

They both stopped, gave a forced laugh. Clem waited for Amelie to continue.

'I – was only going to say that luncheon wouldn't be long. Perhaps you would like a drink? Sherry? Whisky?'

They sat on either side of the fire, glasses in hands. Overhead, there was a thud of footsteps. Amelie glanced upwards.

'How are they?' she asked.

'Oh, well, up and down. Sometimes they seem quite normal, and laugh or argue like they used to, then suddenly they'll stop–' He stopped himself, staring into the flames. Then, realising where he was, he tried to pick up the thread of what he had been saying, and failed. 'Nanny's been wonderful, of course. I don't know what we would have done without her.'

'They all see more of the nannies than they do of us,' Amelie said sadly, thinking of the hours spent away from her children.

'They ask me why, why did Mamma have to die? And I have to tell them I don't know. I want to know the answer myself. Why her? She was so good, so beautiful, so full of life – it doesn't make sense. Just as everything was about to start up again. I'd managed to get through a war with hardly a scratch, which must be a miracle, and I had my date for demobilisation. I was so longing for it, Melly. Normal life again. We were going to be a family again, all of us, all together – and then this–'

Amelie sat and listened to his anger and bewilderment, her untouched glass of sherry in her hand, until he broke off and looked at her properly without Ida's image in between them.

'I'm sorry – I shouldn't be passing my burdens on to you.'

'I'm glad to share them,' Amelie told him, with total honesty. 'I loved her too, you know.' Which was also true, but which complicated things almost unbearably.

'Yes, I know, and she loved you. She always said that you held her together while I was away.'

'Me?' Amelie said, surprised and touched. She had always thought of Ida as the stronger of the two of them.

'Oh yes. I – I was jealous, sometimes, of your friendship. You seemed so close, you two.'

And she had been jealous of their love, she who had loved both of them. Was still jealous of it.

'We supported each other. All the worries – the children, the war, her job, mine . . .' You, Clement. '. . . they all seemed less pressing if we could talk about them. And we laughed a lot, too. You need to laugh, don't you, in wartime, even more than in peace. We used to get quite hysterical, like a couple of schoolgirls. We often got tipsy, too. You'd be shocked. There's hardly any wine left in the cellar. I've got to set about restocking it.'

A brief smile lit Clement's face.

'Yes, she enjoyed life. She never did anything by half measures. She went out and grasped it with both hands. That's why I can't believe she's gone. I just can't believe it . . .'

The children kept the day running on its accustomed rails. Luncheon was followed by half an hour's enforced rest on their beds – the Markhams were so often staying at the house that they had their own beds in the night nurseries – and then a walk in one of the parks. There was even the usual argument as to which park they should go to: Kensington Gardens was eventually decided upon.

It was not a pleasant day for a walk. A grey damp enshrouded everything with moisture, leaching the colours and gnawing into the bones. The people who passed them all had pinched faces and hunched shoulders. Nobody was walking for pleasure, only for health, shaking down a heavy luncheon. The Rutherford boys ran ahead, playing a noisy game that involved hiding behind trees then leaping out and shooting each other. Catherine held on to Eva Rose's pushchair and complained that they were walking too fast; Flora and Edward stayed one on either side of their father, Flora holding his hand, Edward with both fists thrust into his pockets, his thin face tight with misery. Amelie wondered how Clement could bear to look at him, he was so like Ida.

They stayed out just long enough to make the house a haven of warmth to come back to. Once again, tradition had to be adhered to. The adults played board games with the older children while the little ones trundled round the floor with the Noah's Ark animals. Then there was bread and crumpets to be toasted on the fire and two sorts of cake for tea. The curtains were closed against the winter's evening and a domestic cosiness enveloped them.

'Thank you so much,' Clement said, when the time came for them to go. 'I don't know how I would have got through the day without coming here.'

'Then you must come again next week,' Amelie said.

'No,' Clement replied, making Amelie's heart jolt with fear of loss. 'No, you must come to us. That's how it works, isn't it? Turn and turn about?'

A huge wave of relief swept through her, making her weak and limp.

'Yes, that's how it works,' she agreed.

So the pattern was established. Unless one or other of them had family commitments, the visits were fixed points in the week. Sunday succeeded Sunday, winter rolled on into spring and then summer. The London parks blossomed then flowered. Green leaves danced against blue skies. They went to the zoo and Hampstead Heath and Greenwich, they fed ducks on various ponds and rowed boats on the Serpentine. They went as far as Hampton Court and chased each other round the maze.

The Markham children began to lose their haunted look and fought and squabbled and laughed with the Rutherfords, though there was an intense edge to Edward's reactions and Flora tended to withdraw into a world of her own at times. Clement confided his concerns about them and Amelie sought to reassure him. They chewed over her plans for Packards, the likelihood of her achieving them and the threat of Alec Eden, who was making a huge success of his new job in the Merchandising department. Nobody had yet mentioned the fact that Mr Carter's job as Managing Director had only been a temporary one until a suitable Family member could be found, but Amelie felt sure that the day would soon arrive when Sir Richard would bring the subject up again. They discussed Clement's cases as he reestablished himself in his law firm. They argued over world events and politics and the progress of the land fit for heroes. But most of all they talked about Ida.

'You're the only person I can speak to about her. Even talking to her mother is difficult. I don't know how I would have coped without you,' Clement said.

Which sort of compensated for all the times when she thought she might scream if he mentioned Ida's name again.

'That's what friends are for,' she said. 'I would have fallen to pieces after Hugo died if it hadn't been for you and Ida.'

'How did you survive it, Mel?' he asked. 'And don't tell me that time heals. Everyone tells me that, and I find it very hard to take. I don't even want it to heal. That would be betraying her. I just want it not to hurt so much.'

Amelie was silent, struggling with the turmoil of her own feelings. Finally she said,

'At least you have nothing to regret. The worst part of it for me was the guilt. I wasn't the sort of wife Hugo really wanted.'

More than that, he wasn't the sort of husband she had really wanted, and she couldn't blot out the part of her that was glad to be free, thankful there would be no more babies. That was the real source of the guilt – still was, though thank goodness it rarely rose to the surface these days. Her freedom to act as she wished had become a part of her life.

'But you two seemed such a perfect couple,' Clement said. He sounded quite shocked.

'Think back, Clem,' Amelie said. 'Think of that obsession of his with eugenics.'

'I know he was something of a fanatic. But you didn't fail him, Mel. Heaven knows, you produced what he wanted. Just look at them.'

Clement nodded towards the children. They were playing at horse races, Tom and Hugh galloping with Catherine and Eva Rose riding piggy-back, while Peter leapt up and down and shrieked with excitement. Four fair heads and one dark one bobbing along, five healthy bodies growing and developing just as they should. Five sharp little brains honed by the competitive cut and thrust of family life.

'Yes, Hugo would have been proud of them,' she said.

But that was not what she meant. She had been an unwilling partner in the task of populating the world with paragons. It was hard, bordering on the impossible, to explain just what she did mean to Clem, and she was not sure that she even wanted to try. She did not want to expose any part of herself to him of which he might disapprove.

It came as a shock to Amelie when Clement told her that he was taking the children down to Ida's parents in

Dorset for August. She had assumed that he would be going to his parents' house at the same time that she was at Hugo's family home. She had envisaged them riding through the woods and playing tennis together, relaxed and happy away from the pressures of London. She had hoped that the cousins and in-laws might see what she so clearly saw, and hint to Clem what she could not, that there was an obvious solution to the problem of what should happen to their two families. But it seemed that it was not to be. She felt cruelly rejected. She knew it was ridiculous of her, but she felt it all the same.

As usual she buried her hurt in work, and concentrated her mental and physical energies on the expansion of the Empire Household Supplies. Two more stores were opening in London suburbs and she was researching possible sites in high streets in the Home Counties.

By the time autumn started turning the colours of the leaves in the London parks and the older children were back at school, she was engaged in a battle with the rest of the Board over the new shops, and the Sunday meetings had settled back into their comfortable routine.

'Oh, I'm so cross! The Board is driving me mad. They're so stuffy and unimaginative. Sometimes I feel like putting a bomb underneath them,' she complained to Clement as they sat in his drawing room.

'What have they done now?' he asked.

'It's not what they have done, it's what they won't do. They're such a bunch of old women. I can't persuade them to put money into anything except refurbishing the main store. At least they can see that that is essential work. But they won't take the risk involved in setting up the shops in Chelmsford and Maidstone.'

'Are they a risk, then?'

'There's an element of risk, of course. Nothing is certain in retail. But given the success of the suburban stores, I'm sure they'll thrive.'

She explained at length the research she had done into the prosperity of the two towns, similar establishments in their high streets and the type of shoppers she had observed on her visits.

'You've certainly convinced me,' Clement said. 'They sound like a sure-fire success.'

'I wish you were on the Board. I've put all of this before them, together with the figures from the suburban shops and projections of what the provincial ones might make, but they won't budge. They want to give the two new suburban stores two years to prove themselves before they'll agree to any further expansion. Two years! Somebody else will have stolen my idea by then and set up Empire Supplies-type shops under another name. I could almost wish Alec Eden was on the Board. No one could say he was lacking in business sense and imagination. He'd back me, I know.'

Clement swirled his whisky round in the glass, frowning at the amber liquid as it moved. It was a gesture she had come to know well. It generally presaged a bold idea.

'Why not get him promoted to the Board, then? He'll have to be allowed on when he's thirty, and he's not far off that now.'

'Too dangerous,' Amelie said, stating her immediate reaction. 'He's a real chip off the old block, though it pains me to have to admit it. You should see the way he works in Merchandising. He's travelled all over the country visiting small factories that went over to army supplies during the war and got them producing all the things that have been in short supply, all the things people are dying to buy, like mechanical goods and curtains. Then he guarantees them a minimum order and gets rock-bottom terms and we sell them as Packards exclusive lines. He runs rings round Aimes, the

421

Merchandising Director.'

'Surely that's all the more reason to invite him on to the Board? He must want a place, and if he knows that you were instrumental in promoting him, he'll be grateful to you,' Clem said.

'It's all the more reason to keep him off it for as long as possible. I want to establish my place really firmly before he has a chance to challenge it.'

'It's always wise to make allies of your enemies,' Clement pointed out.

'I know, but I still don't want him facing me across the table at board meetings yet.' Amelie smiled and restrained the impulse to reach across and touch his arm. 'I hope I'm not being a bore. It's so good to be able to air all these problems. I can't talk about them at work, and the family all have their own interests to guard, even if it's just making sure their dividends are kept up.'

'You're not being a bore at all,' Clem assured her. 'I feel as if I'm practically one of the family, except that I don't have any shares in Packards. I look on you as an extra sister.'

It was like being kicked in the stomach. Amelie, struggling for breath, was not able to say anything at all in reply.

36

As the summer of 1920 turned into autumn, Amelie was possessed with a strong sense of things repeating themselves. Once more, the other directors seemed to be avoiding her. She was sure that something was going on behind her back, and equally sure who was responsible for it. Alec Eden.

The really alarming thing was that he was very good at his new job in Merchandising. The buyers all respected him and put extra effort into ensuring that everything at Packards was top quality, good value, original and a cut above what was being offered elsewhere. Alec had a knack of providing just what was wanted by a world longing to put the last terrible years behind them.

Packards had emerged from the war years like a butterfly from its chrysalis. The dingy exterior had been newly cleaned and painted, and Amelie's window dressing department was once again in full swing, producing displays that featured frequently in the illustrated magazines. Workmen had invaded the interior and refurbished it department by department. It was no longer considered unpatriotic to buy luxuries or look frivolous. Customers returned in their droves, loitering over their purchases and chatting in the restaurant and tea rooms. Behind the counters, the younger men who had survived the fighting more or less intact were back at their jobs, while the married women who had been so valuable in keeping the store going were sent home to their kitchens.

'I suppose that I could be accused of making one rule for myself and another for all the other women working at Packards,' Amelie admitted one Sunday afternoon as she and Clement walked in Regent's Park with their combined families. 'All the returning men were given their old jobs back and the women who had taken them over were either moved elsewhere in the store or sacked. Following the same logic, I should make way for Alec Eden, but that's the very last thing I'm prepared to do. I'd rather die than let him take what should be my position.'

'Quite right too. You hold out against him. Besides, strictly speaking, you're not keeping him out of a job. Yours is different from his,' Clement said.

Amelie laughed.

'That's the lawyer speaking. But it's future jobs I'm talking about, not current ones. We both want to be Managing Director.'

'What about the present Managing Director? Can he be forced to resign?'

'Walter Carter was only put in as a temporary measure, after Edward died. At the time, it was pointed out to Sir Richard Forbes by somebody in the family that not all of us were able to be present – meaning Alec, since Perry has no interest in taking an active part in running the store.'

'But now Alec Eden is back, and wanting a very active part?'

'Exactly.'

They were interrupted by some of the children rush-

424

ing up to show them the conkers they had found. There was a squabble over who had seen them first. Clement told them that there were plenty more and joined in the search, kicking about in the first fall of leaves. Amelie looked at him as he held Flora's hand and shared her pleasure at finding a particularly fine conker. He was looking so much better now, fit and relaxed and, when caught off-guard like this, almost happy.

Later, walking back to the gates, he took up the subject of Packards management again.

'Surely Alec Eden is far too young yet for such a responsible post?'

'I suppose the same could be said for me.'

'But you were practically brought up in the store and you've worked there for far longer than he has. What you don't know about Packards can't be worth knowing, surely?'

'True, but I'm afraid all that counts for very little when Alec has one huge advantage – he's a man.'

'I can just imagine what Ida would have said to that! Don't let them blind themselves to all your talents, Mel. You will make an excellent Managing Director.'

Ida again. Amelie squashed down the familiar jealousy and its inevitable partner, guilt, and made herself concentrate on the rest of what he had said.

'I know, and I intend to be there,' she said.

'Good, and I shall be cheering for you all the way.'

There was one good thing about the threat that Alec Eden posed, Amelie found. It gave her something to worry about other than her relationship with Clement. She set her mind and energies on finding out what her rival was up to.

It occurred to her that there was one other person who was just as eager as she was to keep Alec out of the Managing Director's seat, and that was the current man in the post, Walter Carter. He was not a natural ally of hers; in fact she had always looked on him as an enemy, hand in glove with Edward, and since he had got what she regarded as her job, she had disliked him even more. But circumstances now found them on the same side. She went to sound him out.

'I really cannot discuss these matters with a Family member,' was his first reaction.

'I may be a Family member, but I am also a Board member, and as such I am entitled to know what is going on,' Amelie pointed out, then stopped herself. This was not the way to go about it. She made herself relax and smile and appear friendly.

'Of course, I have my suspicions. That is why I'm speaking to you now. I think you're being treated very shabbily. You've done a splendid job holding Packards together during the war and now Mr Eden comes along and expects to take over.'

In fact she thought he had only done an adequate job. He had certainly held the store together, but that was all. Now Packards needed someone with flare and imagination to take it into the new decade. Someone like herself.

'I did not say that was about to happen,' Mr Carter said.

'No, but I think we both know it's so. It's obvious that Mr Eden has ambitions in that direction. The question is, how soon will he make a move? I suspect that he is doing some lobbying already.'

'I'm not in a position—' Mr Carter began.

'I know, but let's just take it as read, shall we? I don't think either of us is very happy about the idea. You certainly can't be. It seems most unfair that a man with your experience and long record of loyalty to the store should have to give way to someone who has just spent a few months behind the counter and a few more on the fifth floor. It is grossly unjust.'

426

It took a bit more flattery and digging, but in the end she succeeded in finding out what she wanted to know. There were indeed moves afoot to promote Alec Eden, but they did not originate directly from Alec himself or from the Board members. Sir Richard, the Chairman, was being pressurised by the Family.

'Really?' Amelie could not believe it. They all hated Alec. It was the one thing that united them. Then a picture flashed into her mind of Sylvia and Alec sitting under the cedars at Tatwell. Alec had looked very much at ease and had got up and found her a chair from the tennis pavilion with a confidence that showed he felt quite at home. Sylvia and Alec . . .? No, it was beyond imagination. Not Sylvia, that cold-hearted snob. A man like Alec must be anathema to her.

Bringing her thoughts back to the matter in hand, she leaned forward a little and spoke in a confiding voice.

'I think you and I have the same interest here, Mr Carter. Neither of us wants to see Alec Eden as Managing Director. I could perhaps sound out the Family and see what is going on.'

She did not spell out what she expected in return. She would call in the favour when she needed it.

'That would be very useful,' Mr Carter admitted.

Amelie started with her mother.

'I really do not know what you are talking about, Amelie,' Winifred said. 'You think I have been speaking to Sir Richard Forbes behind your back? Why would I be wanting to interfere with the running of the store? I have never wanted to do so for a moment.'

Which was quite true. Her mother preferred to forget where her money came from.

'You wouldn't like to see Alec Eden in charge, though, would you?' Amelie asked.

'That man? Certainly not! He should have had the

good taste to stay where he belonged. But I suppose that is too much to ask. His sort are notoriously grasping.'

Once, Amelie would have taken the opposite view to her mother out of principle, since her mother's opinions were based solely on the rules of social position. Now she wondered. Alec certainly had designs on Packards. Did he want to get rid of her altogether? She did not think that he was in a strong enough position to do that, not at the moment. But after a few years as Managing Director, there was no knowing what he might do. Her hold on power had always been shaky under Edward's reign, but Edward's personal unpopularity and the long shadow of her grandfather had worked in her favour. Under Alec, things would be different.

'Perhaps I should have made more effort to cultivate him before the war,' she mused.

'Don't be so ridiculous! The very idea. You, your grandfather's legal descendant, fawn over the son of his fancy woman? It's quite nauseating. I shall never forgive your grandfather for foisting his nasty little by-blow on us all, never. It's all the result of this stupid obsession with sons. It was always the same. My poor mother was made to feel a failure because she did not bear him any sons, and I was a severe disappointment to him. He never had any time for me, because I was a girl. There would have been none of this sordid jockeying for position now if I had been born male. I would have been head of Packards.

The thought of her mother in charge of the store that she had always despised was so amazing that Amelie could say nothing.

Her burst of bitterness over, Winifred calmed down a little.

'Well, he's gone now, and I suppose one shouldn't speak ill of the dead, but I'll tell you something, Amelie. I've never agreed with your playing at shops, but if it's a case of you or that Alec Eden, then you have my blessing.'

'Th-thank you,' Amelie stuttered, hardly able to believe her ears.

'I know we've never seen eye to eye, and I still don't like the idea of a daughter of mine attempting to fill a man's position, but I suppose things are different now. We do have the vote, so if women can be Members of Parliament, then presumably they can do other strange things as well. And certainly anything is better than seeing that upstart in what would have been my position.'

Amelie was moved to kiss her mother's cheek.

'You think it's all or nothing, then? Me or him?'

Winifred looked at her with all her usual caustic impatience.

'But of course. One cannot lower oneself to negotiate with that sort of person.'

Amelie smiled.

'Of course not, Mother. The very idea!'

But it was said with affection.

If only things were as clear cut as Winifred's vision of the world. You got rid of Alec Eden and you got rid of the problem. But there was far more to it than that. There were divided loyalties amongst the other Board members and Alec had rights under the terms of the will. Most important of all he was an asset to Packards. Watching him work, Amelie could see what her grandfather must have been like as a young man. If the two of them could work together, it would be to the advantage of everyone. If only she had taken Clement's advice and sought to make an ally of him, her moves now would be very much easier.

If they could work together, then the main problem was how to define the areas of responsibility. She knew how she wanted the power divided, but she was not at all sure that Alec would agree to it. It all depended upon what support he had. On the Board, Sir Richard would favour Alec, as he had always treated Amelie as Sir Thomas's little indulgence. Mr Carter and his sidekick the new Financial Director were against him, Mr Aimes of Merchandising would be for him in order to protect his own job and Mr Mason would go with whoever seemed to be the likely winner. As for the family, she had thought that they would all be against Alec, but there was the possibility that Perry and Gwendoline could be bought, especially as Gwendoline was now pregnant. Which brought her back to Sylvia.

It must be Sylvia who was seeking to influence Sir Richard. What was more, it must have been she who had been working behind the scenes when Edward's successor was being chosen. Which meant that there must have been some sort of connection between her and Alec before Edward died. The idea of Sylvia, the arch-prude, having an affair with her husband's illegitimate half-uncle was so ludicrous that Amelie laughed out loud. And yet . . . out of all the hospitals in England, Alec had landed at Tatwell. That could not have been sheer chance. And Alec had looked very much at his ease that day she came upon them under the cedars, while Sylvia – Sylvia, for a few moments, had looked almost flustered. If Alec really did have designs on Sylvia and with her, Tatwell, fortune and respectability, then Amelie was on very shaky ground indeed. She could see now that not only should she have made more effort with Alec, but she should have been better friends with her sister-in-law.

'I think you might find that it's too late to start buttering up Sylvia. From what you've told me about her, she doesn't sound like a person who admits friendship easily,' Clement commented.

'Very true. Whatever she's up to, she's not likely to tell me about it. We've never been more than distantly polite to each other,' Amelie said.

'Have you considered the direct approach? Ask Alec Eden what his ambitions are?'

'Well, no, but I suppose I could,' Amelie said doubtfully.

'It might well be the best course of action. You say you want a compromise. It could be that he feels the same. He must realise that you know far more about running Packards than he does. Why don't you sound him out? At best you'll find that you have nothing to fear, and at worst you'll know just what you're up against.'

'Yes . . .' Amelie turned the suggestion over in her mind. 'Yes, I think you could be right. In fact, you are right. Thank you. You always seem to be able to make me see things more clearly.'

'What are friends for?' said Clement.

The next day, Amelie called Alec on the internal telephone system and invited him to join her for luncheon in the store restaurant. Alec sounded surprised, but agreed.

'I like to eat here rather than in the staff dining room at least four times a week,' Amelie said. 'It was one of Grandfather's traditions.'

'Yes, I know. He told me that he used to sit right in the middle and eavesdrop on customers' conversations. He found it a very good way of finding out what people really thought about the store,' Alec replied.

Amelie mentally awarded him a point. It was not going to be any use trying to compete over how much Sir Thomas had confided in her. Whatever she said, Alec would pull out an example of his own.

'Eavesdropping isn't my aim today, however. In fact it's just the opposite. I suggested that we meet here so that we can't be overheard by anyone else on the administrative staff.'

431

'You intrigue me.'

Amelie was not sure whether or not he was being sarcastic. She considered him across the table as he studied the menu. He was a very different person from the arrogant and defensive young man who had first come to work at Packards after his father's death. There was an air of confidence about him now. He belonged. He was doing a very good job and he knew it. He was on his way up. On top of that was something that Clement had put his finger on.

'The war has left marks on everyone, mentally if not physically, though many of them find it difficult to admit to it. But for some people it hasn't been all bad. It's given them incredible strength. They feel that if they have come through all that with their minds still intact, then they can face anything.'

Amelie suspected that that was what it had done to Alec.

Over bowls of mushroom soup, they discussed Amelie's plans for Christmas displays and agreed that this Christmas must be a good one, looking forward to a new decade in a peaceful world. It seemed almost a shame to break the accord between them. With the arrival of her Dover sole and his lamb chop, however, Amelie decided that it was time to start sounding him out.

'I can see a bright future for Packards once the country has recovered from the war. This present slump must only be a temporary thing. Walter Carter has done a reasonable job in holding everything together for the duration, but now we have to look at things differently.'

'Go forward into the new age?' Alec asked.

Amelie could not decide whether there was a slight edge of sarcasm in his voice.

'Yes, if you want to put it like that. I certainly hope so. I've found it very frustrating trying to carry out my job on the Board these last few years. Innovation and display have been bottom of the list of priorities unless they were to do with the war effort. Now, it should be different; we should be looking for new opportunities.'

She paused, hoping for a reply.

Alec looked across the table at her with a pitying smile.

'If "we" means the current Board, then I wish you luck. They're a bunch of second-rate fossils.'

Amelie blinked at this blanket opinion and pulled her thoughts together.

'Walter Carter was only ever put in as a stopgap after Edward died. As I said, he's managed to hold the place together, but you're quite right, he has no vision beyond his columns of figures.'

'He's the worst, but the others are almost as bad. His toady in Finance is cut from the same cloth, Mason has no mind of his own and Aimes is stuck in the past. He doesn't inspire confidence in the buying staff.'

'And what about the final member of the Board?' Amelie couldn't resist asking.

'You managed to push through the one imaginative move Packards has made since my father died. It can't have been easy making that lot see that Empire Supplies was a good move. I take my hat off to you.'

Despite herself, Amelie was flattered.

'Thank you,' she said.

'But if you want to make any other changes in Packards, you're going to run into just the same problems every time. Until some changes are made on the Board.'

Amelie's hopes rose. He definitely seemed to be hinting at their working together.

'Changes such as a greater Packard presence?' she said.

He took the acceptance of his claims in his stride.

433

'Exactly. The family's control has slipped, and it shows.'

'And you're not prepared to wait until you're thirty?' she asked, referring to the notorious will.

'You weren't,' Alec pointed out.

Their empty plates were taken away and replaced with a rather uninspired peach Melba. Both of them ate automatically.

'You're quite right,' Amelie said. 'I wanted the chance to prove myself, and I was fortunate enough to have Grandfather there to make sure I had that chance. Though I must point out that I had Edward to contend with. Things would be very different now if he was still with us.'

She leaned forward, trying to hold Alec with her eyes.

'There's room for both of us in Packards. Together we could take it into the nineteen twenties and make it a huge success. I wanted to expand years ago, but the war prevented that. Now we could open branches of the main store in all the major provincial cities and take the Empire Supplies into every high street in the country.'

'You prove my point entirely. The present Board would blench at grandiose schemes like that,' Alec said. 'They would say that it was breaking with the proud tradition of Packards as an Oxford Street store.'

'Packards would still be an Oxford Street store. In fact, it would still be *the* Oxford Street store. If we acted together, we could carry the Board with us or replace them with people who were willing to take some risks.' She took a breath, then laid before him her pet idea. 'You could be in charge of expansion while I run the main store as the flagship of the fleet.'

There was a pause. Then Alec was shaking his head, slowly but very definitely.

'Oh no. You proposed that to me a long while ago, and I refused it then. I'm certainly not changing my mind now.'

'That was quite different,' Amelie protested. 'Then there were only two Empire Supplies, now we are all set to build a chain. But you wouldn't just be in charge of them, you'd be heading the new Packards stores too. They will be the most prestigious stores in their respective regions.'

But Alec was unmoved.

'I don't see it that way at all. I'm not going to be fobbed off with the secondary enterprise. I want the main store as well.'

37

'There has to be some way to fight him,' Amelie said to Clement. 'There must be some lever I can use to move him, but I can't for the life of me think what it might be. Oh, if only I had listened to you earlier, and tried to get him on my side.'

'It might not have worked,' Clement said. 'He could quite easily have accepted your help to a seat on the Board and still claimed the managing directorship.'

'I know, I know, but at least it would have been worth trying, and I would have had a favour to call in. As it is, the only thing I can dig up against him is the faint possibility that he might have designs on Sylvia, but that's hardly a hanging offence as far as the Board's concerned.'

Clement watched as the wind chased through the dying leaves, picking them up and whirling them round. Amelie watched him, tall and dark, his clever face masked in thought, a slight frown between his black brows. She was shot through with such an ache of love and desire that she could hardly stop herself from catching hold of him.

'If that's the only thing you have to work on, then perhaps you should use it. Once you start digging, you never know what you might turn up. Are you sure, though, that you know what you are about? Leave things as they are now, and you stand a good chance of holding on to what you have already. If you try to fight Alec Eden on a personal level and lose, then he'll find a way to get rid of you. Do you want to risk that?'

He was right, Amelie realised. Alec would be only too glad to find an opportunity to take everything. He had been quite open about it.

'Sooner or later, there is going to be a clash between us, because he won't compromise,' she said. 'So it might just as well be now.'

'I see.' Clement was using his lawyer's voice, carefully neutral. 'This means a great deal to you, doesn't it?'

'Yes,' Amelie said. Since she couldn't have him, she wanted Packards.

'Then be very sure of the strength of your position before you act.'

'I'll remember that,' she promised.

She remembered it as she walked into the store the next morning. The sense of danger sharpened her feelings for the wonderful temple to shopping that her grandfather had built. The heavy pre-war colours had been done away with and a new scheme of cream and gold gleamed from all sides. Light flooded in through the central dome, picking out the throngs of fashionable shoppers, the beautifully displayed merchandise. Amelie walked through the departments, listening to what people were saying, watching the standard of service, noting things that needed to be done, while her sense of pride, possession and sheer excitement grew. This was rightly hers. It was unthinkable that it should pass to Alec Eden. Something had to be done, and soon. It was as she passed through Household Linens that a way forward struck her. She went up to her office and telephoned through to Staffing.

'May Hollis,' she said. 'She worked in Household Linens here and then at the Southgate Empire Supplies, then left to be married. Could you send her file over, please?'

'Certainly, Mrs Rutherford. Right away.'

The file confirmed the tug at her memory. May Hollis, now Mrs William Foster, had come from Tatwell village. She must still have family there, and be in touch with any gossip that might be going about. Better still, she might have family or friends working at the big house. And Amelie had promoted her at a very young age to supervisor at the Empire Supplies. It was as good a place as any to start. She told her secretary to rearrange her afternoon appointments and ordered the car to be ready at two.

Will Foster was lacing up the shoes that May had polished for him the previous evening. He was dangerously close to being late for work.

'How much longer is she going to be here?' he demanded.

May bit her lip. From upstairs came the sound of wailing. Baby Alexandra was teething, and she was determined that everyone should suffer with her. Nobody had slept well for the last few nights.

'Ruby's my friend, Will. We can't turn her out on the street. It's only till she gets herself sorted out.'

She knew she did not sound convincing.

'You've been saying that ever since she arrived. That baby's over a year old now.'

'But it's hard for her, Will, getting lodgings and a job and someone to mind the baby.'

'Of course it is, but she should have thought of that, shouldn't she? It's not as if she's really a war widow. If she was, she'd be getting a pension and she wouldn't have to work.'

'All the more reason–' May began.

But Will cut her short.

'She's got it made here, with you to look after the baby for her. But you can't go on doing that, May. You'll soon have more than enough to do without coping with her brat. I don't want my child suffering.'

May ran a protective hand over her swollen belly. Her baby was due in another couple of weeks.

'It won't, dear.'

'I just don't think it's right, you running round after her like this. She's taking advantage of us, May. She's living here practically free.'

May did not even try to point out that Ruby was paying rent. What Ruby could afford from her wages was half of what their other lodger paid, and Will was quite right in pointing out that she looked after Ruby's baby for free.

'Besides, we'll soon be needing the space. I know you said the baby will have to sleep in with us at first so you can feed it in the night, but that's just at first. Then what happens when we want to have another? We don't want our whole family sleeping in our bedroom.'

'No, I know. I'll talk to her,' May said.

'Yes, but will you? You've said this before, and you haven't.'

'I know, but I will, I promise.'

'Well make sure you do.'

May went to see him off at the door, checking his tie and kissing him on the lips.

'Go carefully, dear.'

Will caressed her cheek.

'I'm sorry to be so cross, dear, but it's for your own good, you know. For our own good. I want my little wife to myself.'

He was right, May acknowledged with a sigh, as she shut the front door. Since Ruby moved in, their mar-

439

riage had not been the same. Their home was not their own little nest any more. Ruby and baby Alexandra were like a pair of noisy, demanding cuckoos. May was constantly having to make excuses for them to Will, her loyalty torn between her husband and her friend. She wished Ruby would go of her own accord, but she knew that she would not. As Will had said, Ruby had it made here.

She was still pondering the problem when she sat down to her mending in the afternoon. Baby Alexandra was wailing again, so she had put her out in the garden in her pram, hoping that she would cry herself to sleep.

'I hope you're going to be better behaved than her,' she said to the child inside her. It pushed its hard little heels up under her ribs in reply.

The knock at the door took her by surprise. She was not expecting visitors. Surprise was hardly the word for what she experienced when she found Mrs Rutherford on her doorstep. She stood and gaped at her, astounded.

'I do apologise for arriving unannounced like this. I wonder if we might have a little chat?' Mrs Rutherford asked.

'Y-yes. Of course. C-come in,' May stuttered, opening the door into the stiff front parlour. Thank goodness she had dusted in here this morning.

She made tea and perched on the edge of the second-hand armchair with her cup in her lap.

'Congratulations are in order, I see,' Mrs Rutherford said, nodding at her lump. 'When are you due?'

'In two weeks or so.'

'Are you hoping for a girl or a boy?'

'M-my husband wants a boy, but I don't mind, as long as it's all right,' May replied, amazed to be talking woman-to-woman with someone like Mrs Rutherford. How she wished one of her new friends would call in, and see this fashionably dressed lady in her front par-

440

lour. The neighbours would have noticed something, anyhow. The shiny motorcar parked outside would not have been missed. She was happily aware of tweaked curtains up and down the road.

They chatted for a while longer about babies and housekeeping, then Mrs Rutherford changed the subject.

'You come from Tatwell, I believe?'

Then came a series of very strange questions. Did she know anyone who worked at the Big House? Were there any regular visitors there? Was Mr Alec Eden ever seen there?'

'Alec Eden?' May repeated.

'Yes – you do know him, don't you? He worked for a while in Household Linens before the war.'

'Oh yes, I know him,' May replied. The beast. He had let poor Ruby down something dreadful. And to think that she had once preferred him to Will. She must have been mad.

'So you would know who he was if he were visiting at Tatwell Court?'

'Oh yes. I went to see him myself when he was there, when it was a hospital.'

She had been sorry for him, too, all weak and poorly-looking in bed with a cage thing round his leg. That had been sympathy wasted and no mistake.

'You went to visit Alec Eden?'

This time it was Mrs Rutherford's turn to be astonished.

'Yes. I went with my friend. She was walking out with him at the time.'

Mrs Rutherford's blue eyes fixed on May's face. There was a disturbing expression in them. May was reminded of next door's cat as it followed the movements of a bird.

'Your friend,' she said carefully. 'Would she be a

441

Packards girl?'

'She was,' May said bitterly.

'Was? She isn't any longer? But she was definitely working for Packards when she was walking out with Alec Eden?'

'Oh yes.'

Mrs Rutherford set down her teacup.

'I should very much like to meet your friend if that is possible, Mrs Foster. Do you know where she is living now?'

Faintly, from the garden, came the sound of Alexandra's wailing. May stood up.

'Excuse me just a minute,' she said.

She lumbered into the garden and picked up the baby. Alex was not a pretty sight. Her nose was running, her hair damp with sweat, her cheeks bright red. She smelt strongly of ammonia. But she stopped crying and nuzzled against May's shoulder. May laid her cheek on the baby's head and rocked from side to side.

'What shall I do, little lamb?' she said out loud.

She was racked with indecision. Should she give away Ruby's secret? If it meant that Alec Eden was made to pay, then yes, she should. Mrs Rutherford had the power to do it where poor Ruby didn't. If he could be made to support his daughter, then Ruby wouldn't have to work and could get some sort of place of her own. The prospect of having the house to themselves again, of regaining the delicious cosiness of the first few weeks of their marriage, danced before her. But what if Mrs Rutherford didn't believe her, what if she sided with Alec Eden? They were both Family, after all, and blood was thicker than water. They might stick together, and then where would she and Will be? Will's job could be in danger. She carried the baby into the kitchen, changed her nappy, cleaned her up and combed her hair.

'Poor little scrap,' she said. 'It's not right that your daddy should just abandon you like this. It's just not right, and that's the beginning and the end to it. You're coming to see your rich relation.'

She hefted the baby on to her hip and went into the parlour.

'This is Alexandra,' she announced. 'You asked where my friend was living. Well, she's living here with us since no one else will take her in. This is her daughter. Proper little Packard, isn't she?'

For a long moment, Mrs Rutherford gazed at the baby. Then a slow smile spread over her face.

'Mrs Foster, I think we might be able to help each other,' she said.

38

You never know what you might turn up.

Clement's words reverberated round her head. How gloriously, wonderfully right he was. A long shot, a stab in the dark and all this had fallen into her lap. She could hardly contain her excitement as she rode back to central London, picturing Alec's face as she revealed her knowledge to him. When the car pulled up outside Packards she practically ran into the building, itching to find Alec and rout him. It was only as she sat down at her desk and reached for the internal telephone that another of Clement's strictures flashed into her mind.

Be very sure of the strength of your position before you act.

She replaced the handset in its cradle.

Just how strong was her position? She reviewed what she had at her command. Alec Eden was the father of an illegitimate child, the mother of which was a former employee of Packards. He was denying all responsibility and the mother was existing on a small wage and the charity of another Packards employee and his wife. So far, so bad. But was it enough? Alec had broken the rule about management not taking advantage of the shop-girls which was still strictly enforced, but years ago when she had first been in competition with him, Edward had done far worse and more or less got away with it. His wings had been clipped and he had not got all he wanted, but for the sake of the family name the whole thing had been hushed up. No doubt the Board would do the same this time. Pay off Ruby Goss, keep her quiet and pretend nothing had happened. And what would be her own position then? Worse than before, because Alec would really be out to finish her.

She picked up a pencil and doodled on the blotting pad, a series of black and white squares and triangles, all meticulously fitting into each other. It all came down to whether people cared enough. Alec obviously didn't and the Board would really rather not know about it. Only she and May Foster were outraged by Alec's behaviour, and of course poor Ruby Goss herself. The men looked on it as an unfortunate mistake, something that could happen to anyone, probably the woman's fault anyway. The women were left to look after the baby as best they could in a world that turned its back on unmarried mothers. No wonder Ruby pretended to be a war widow. It gave her some degree of respectability. Of one thing she was certain, that whatever the outcome of her battle with Alec, Ruby would be provided for. She would do it out of her own purse if need be.

She stared at the pattern she made, the shapes blurring as her eyes went out of focus. Something was missing. Who else would care? Sylvia. Of course, Sylvia, whom she had gone to May Foster to find out about in the first place. She lifted the telephone receiver and asked for the Tatwell Court number.

Her sister-in-law's cut-glass voice rang down the wires.

'Amelie? This is unexpected. How are you?'

After a preliminary exchange of family news, Amelie came to the point.

'We don't see nearly enough of each other, Sylvia. I was wondering – would you like to come up to Town and stay? It would save you from having to open your London house.'

She held her breath. With a bit of luck, Sylvia would decline and instead invite her to Tatwell.

'That's very considerate of you, Amelie, but I am in fact planning to come up for a few weeks quite soon. From the twenty-fifth, to be precise. Perhaps you would care to come to dinner? What evening would be convenient?'

Damn, damn, damn.

'That would be charming, Sylvia. Let me just take a peep in my diary.'

They fixed a date and discussed the relative merits of fashionable dentists, as Sylvia needed to have some teeth seen to.

'You sound a little on edge, Amelie. Are you sure that everything is all right?'

If she would just say whether she had a romantic interest in Alec Eden, then everything would be perfectly all right.

'Yes, of course,' Amelie said, with a little laugh.

'You really work too hard, Amelie. There is no need to now, you know. It was different in wartime, but now you should be able to let go a little.'

Amelie couldn't resist it.

'And let Alec Eden take over?'

Sylvia was sweet reason itself.

'Well my dear, there comes a time when one has to bow to the inevitable. He is now acknowledged as Sir Thomas's son and there are the terms of that wretched will to be complied with.'

Amelie took a chance.

'Dear me, you amaze me, Sylvia. I would have thought that you would have been the last person to take

Alec's part. But come to think of it, you did seem to be quite friendly with him that day when I visited you at Tatwell.'

'Alec Eden was one of my former patients, Amelie. I am always happy to see any of them, especially when they have recovered so well.'

Cool as ever, Sylvia was giving nothing away. Amelie had a couple more stabs, but made no hits. She and Sylvia said goodbye with mutually insincere good wishes.

Amelie sat back in her chair. Sylvia had not been adamantly against Alec, but then she couldn't have, seeing that Amelie had reminded her that she had caught her entertaining him at Tatwell. Further than that, she just could not judge. She was as much in the dark as ever.

'What should I do, Clem?' she asked out loud.

Be very sure of the strength of your position before you act.

The trouble was, she was still not sure. Needing just to hear his voice, she rang Clement's chambers.

'Mr Markham is in court. May I take a message?' a male voice asked.

'No, thank you. It isn't urgent,' Amelie lied.

For several minutes, she sat tapping her teeth with a pencil, revolving the problem until it seemed to tie itself in knots. Did she want to make an enemy of Alec? Most certainly not. Firstly because he would be a very dangerous opponent and secondly because as an ally he was just what was needed on the Board of Packards. That much was obvious, but a third reason caught her unawares. She liked and admired him. He and she were of a piece, Thomas Packard's heirs. Potentially, he was far closer to her than either of her brothers. Amongst the group of silver framed photographs of her children on the desk, her eyes rested on one of her grandfather. This must have been what he had been hoping for when he decreed that Alec should be given a part in the business. He would have wanted them to work together, possibly even to unite to oust Edward, for how could Thomas have known that Edward was to die at such a young age? Her mind cleared. She picked up the telephone once more.

'Alec? There's something I'd like to discuss with you. Yes, now, if it's convenient. Can you come along and see me? Thank you.'

Within five minutes, Alec was sitting in her office. Once more, Amelie was struck by his resemblance to the photograph on her desk. This was just how her grandfather must have looked in his twenties, full of the same burning ambition. He leaned back in his chair and smiled at her.

'What can I do for you, Amelie?'

It was the smile of someone who was confident of his own success. Amelie smiled back, trying to project a similar air of ease.

'I've been thinking about the talk we had over luncheon the other day, Alec, and I have to admit that I'm disappointed. We should be working together, not opposing each other. We think the same way, we have the same outlook. As a team, we could take Packards into the next stage of its development. We shouldn't be enemies.'

Alec looked faintly surprised.

'I wasn't aware that we were enemies. On the contrary, I quite agree with you. We should be working together. There is only one point on which we don't agree, and that is which of us should have the Managing Director's post. However, I think we can safely leave that to the rest of the Board to decide, don't you?'

'Which means that you think you are on safe ground there,' Amelie said.

448

Alec shrugged.

'Who's to say how they might vote?'

A sinking feeling crept over Amelie. It was all too obvious how Alec thought they would vote, and he was more than probably right. She had two alternatives: to use the knowledge she had at her disposal, or to back down and let him take over.

'You leave me no choice,' she said.

Alec raised his eyebrows slightly but looked unconcerned.

'You never really got acquainted with Edward, did you?' Amelie asked.

'As much as I ever wanted to.'

'But you did not work with him as a colleague, and you certainly weren't here when Grandfather stepped down from the day-to-day running of the store and became Chairman.'

'No,' Alec conceded.

'Edward wanted overall control. He wanted to run the store in much the same way that Grandfather used to, without a board to answer to. Unfortunately for him, he made a mistake. You remember that once I warned you of the ruling that Family should not play fast and loose with the shopgirls?'

Alec nodded. Amelie thought she saw the muscles of his jaw tighten.

'Edward ignored that ruling. He took up with a shopgirl, made her leave her job and set her up in a house. One of the stipulations of the arrangement, it seems, was that she was not to get pregnant. But the inevitable happened, and the girl found that she was expecting his baby. She was so terrified that rather than face him, she committed suicide.'

Amelie paused, waiting for a reaction.

'Tragic,' Alec said.

'It was. Edward ruled by fear, you see. He enjoyed it.

Now, you would think that this episode would have harmed his chances of power at Packards. Grandfather was very disappointed in him, but he wanted someone from the family in charge, and I was recently married at the time and expecting a baby myself. So Edward got his managing directorship, though not the sole control of the store that he wanted. But he did not entirely get away with it. He was not long married himself at the time, and Sylvia was appalled at his behaviour. So appalled, indeed, that it soured their whole marriage. It might not have crossed your mind to wonder why Sylvia and Edward had just one daughter, but I can tell you now that there were no more children born to them after she learnt of Edward's betrayal of their love. Sylvia has extremely high standards. She expects those close to her to live up to those standards, and has no truck with backsliders. I'm quite certain that one of the reasons why she has never remarried is that she had not found a man she can fully trust not to let her down again.'

Alec shifted in his seat.

'This is all very interesting, but I really don't see the connection with the present situation.'

He sounded rather bored. Was it a cover? Did he want Sylvia's good opinion, or was she about to make an almighty blunder? She closed her eyes briefly, then opened them to look straight at Alec's.

'Oh, there is a connection, I assure you,' she said.

She adopted a conversational tone.

'Earlier this afternoon I went to visit one of our former shopgirls, a Mrs Foster. She is now married to Foster in Household Linens, but you might remember her as May Hollis.'

There was a flicker of recognition in Alec's eyes.

'Now, May comes from Tatwell village, where she hears a lot about what is going on at the Big House,' she lied. 'But more than that, she has a lodger staying with her, her friend, another former shopgirl. Her name is Ruby Goss.'

Alec forced a laugh.

'Oh come on, Amelie. You're not going to pin that one on me.'

Amelie looked at him sadly.

'You really should go and see your daughter, Alec. Her name's Alexandra. She's a dear little thing, you couldn't help but like her, and she's absolutely one of us, a Packard to her toes. Grandfather would have been proud of her.'

Alec looked away.

'Really?' he said. His voice was flat, but there was an undercurrent of anger to it, the anger of someone who sees that they might be about to be backed into a corner.

Amelie suddenly saw a way through. She must not threaten, she must help.

'Of course, I'm not suggesting that you should marry Ruby Goss. I can quite see that that wouldn't do. But something must be done about her and the baby. A fund must be set up, or an allowance paid so that she can make a home of her own and bring the child up properly. I couldn't bear to think that a close relation of ours was growing up in poverty when we have so much.'

She watched him, trying to make out the effect of the words 'we' and 'ours'. He did not exactly look pleased.

'I suppose you're right,' he conceded.

Amelie leaned forward a little.

'If you like, I can arrange it. I'm sure it can be done in such a way that you are not implicated. In fact, I think it would be far better that way.'

There was no disguising Alec's surprise.

'Oh – yes – well, thank you. I would appreciate that.'

Amelie took a breath. Her heart thumped in her chest.

'And of course, there's no need for Sylvia to know a

thing about all this,' she said sweetly.

'Sylvia?'

'Well, yes. I do know about your friendship. I have done for a long time, but it's really no business of mine. You're both grown-up people, after all. Mind you, I doubt if the rest of the family would see it like that. I would imagine they would have forty fits. But that is beside the point. The thing is that Sylvia would not at all approve if she heard about poor Ruby and the baby. In fact, I think she could well cut you off completely. It's a good thing that we've decided to sort this out between ourselves, isn't it?'

She paused, hoping desperately that she had struck the right note. Not blackmail, but simply a favour.

Alec looked back at her with the same level gaze that she liked to employ.

'So what's the deal?' he asked.

Damn damn damn. He was regarding it as blackmail. Amelie widened her eyes in innocent surprise.

'Deal? It's not a question of deals. Not at all. In fact, what I want to propose will probably benefit you more than it will me.'

And as the words came out of her mouth, a solution offered itself. Do what Thomas Packard had done when problems of power and control arose: reorganise the structure of the company. For a moment she hesitated, torn. She could get exactly what she wanted, by turning her favour into a threat, but to do so would make Alec her enemy. Or she could make concessions and keep him as an ally and a potential friend.

'So just what is this proposition?' Alec prompted. He sounded sceptical.

Amelie realised that a silence had developed. She came to a decision.

'It's just a question of adjusting the areas of responsibility. I think that you and I are agreed that Packards should expand?'

She paused, wanting to be sure that she was taking him along with her.

'Yes,' Alec said, cautiously.

'So it will grow into a much larger organisation. There will need to be three divisions, the Oxford Street store, the Household Supplies and the provincial Packards chain.'

She waited again for a reaction.

Alec nodded, slowly.

'That would seem to be the best way of arranging it,' he agreed. He still sounded wary.

'Inevitably, this will mean more non-family members on the Board, so it's essential that you and I are in key positions. I think that the best way for us to keep the spirit of Packards thriving is for one of us to be head of the original store, while the other oversees the whole operation as managing director.'

For a moment they looked at each other, each trying to guess what the other was thinking. Before Alec could speak, Amelie made sure he was presented with the better option.

'I think that you would make an excellent managing director.'

Alec was not fooled.

'You want the main store that much?'

'Yes,' Amelie admitted.

She could feel her pulse throbbing through her head. It could still all fall apart. The pause seemed to stretch into an aeon.

Then Alec stood up and held out his hand.

'If that's the case, then it must be yours.'

Solemnly, they shook on it.

In the sudden collapse of tension, Amelie began to laugh. Once started, she couldn't stop.

'Oh dear,' she gasped. 'It's so ridiculous – we're so

pleased with ourselves – and it's all pie in the sky. The Board can throw it out.'

Now Alec laughed, but it rang with confidence.

'Oh come now, Amelie. You know very well that you and I can make the Board do just what we want if we act together.'

It was an exhilarating thought, one which sobered Amelie with its implications.

'Yes,' she said, 'you're right. We can. What's more, we must make some changes on the Board. They've no imagination at all. We have to find some people with modern ideas.'

'We must promote likely candidates from the ranks.'

'And bring in talent from other stores.'

'And send bright young people to America to learn how things are done there.'

They grinned at each other. They had each found a kindred spirit. Packards was about to go forward with new vigour.

What Amelie wanted most of all after her meeting with Alec was someone to share her triumph with. There was no one here at Packards in whom she could confide. It would not be very tactful to drop into one of the other directors' offices and inform him that she and Alec had got the company sewn up between the two of them. She certainly didn't want to tell the family yet, since with the exception of Sylvia they were sure to be outraged. There was only one person apart from Alec himself who really understood what this meant to her, and that was Clement.

She reached for the telephone once more and left a message for him asking him to call on her as soon as possible that evening. Then she walked through the store – her store – with a new spring in her step. There were lots of new ideas she wanted to put into effect, a new department devoted to gramophones and records for a start. Now she would be able to take the store in the direction she could so clearly see was right. She went down to the Food Halls and gave a huge order for all kinds of delicacies. Never mind what her cook had planned for dinner, today was a day for celebration. As she couldn't remember whether there was any champagne left, she ordered a case of Bollinger.

When she reached the main door, she found that she could not bear the prospect of being cooped up in the motorcar again, so she walked home, scarcely able to keep herself from skipping like a child.

By half past eight, her buoyant mood had evaporated. The children were in bed, the table was laid, the champagne was on ice, but Clement had not arrived. Amelie walked to the window and looked out. Surely he must have received her message? Perhaps she should have been clearer, and invited him for dinner, but she had not wanted to leave him open to comments from others at his chambers about women commanding him to dine with them. She had assumed that he would realise what she had meant.

She leaned her head against the glass. The street was quiet. Autumn leaves lay under the trees and along the gutters. The streetlamps glowed. A motorcar came into sight. Amelie's heart leapt painfully in hope, only to be almost instantly dashed. It was not Clement's Armstrong, but a stately Bentley which pulled up at the house opposite and disgorged its passengers. Amelie watched as they went into the brightly lit hallway, and felt intensely lonely. What was the point of winning battles at Packards if there was nobody to rejoice with her? It took away most of the pleasure, leaving her achievement hollow. She looked bleakly down the years marching ahead of her. She would be a successful woman, of that she was sure. She would end up extremely rich, able to buy whatever she wanted in the way of clothes and jewels and houses, able to travel the world. But she knew that it would be empty without the man she loved.

Where could Clement be? Was he ignoring her? Was he – the thought slid in like a knife under the ribs – was he dining with another woman? The prospect was unbearable. She was just about to telephone his house when there was a knock at the door. His knock. Abandoning all dignity, she ran to open it before the parlourmaid could get there.

'Clem! Oh Clem, I thought you weren't coming.'

'I nearly didn't. I'm so sorry. I went straight home without calling in at chambers and my secretary has only just remembered that there was a message to pass on.'

'It's all right, it's all right, you're here now.' In her relief, all her high spirits returned. 'I suppose you've dined already? Never mind, come upstairs, I've some very important news.'

She led the way into the drawing room and stopped dramatically under the central light.

'I've done it, Clem! I've come to an agreement with Alec.'

She told him about their meeting and what they had planned between them.

'So you see, it was worth giving up the managing directorship. Alec's now my friend and I've got the store,' she concluded, smiling up at him, her face alight, waiting for his pleased reaction.

Clement's mouth stretched into a forced smile.

'I see. Well, that's splendid news. Congratulations.'

Amelie stared at him.

'What's the matter? You don't sound very pleased. I thought you'd be delighted for me.'

'I am. Of course I am. It's what you've always wanted, isn't it?'

'It is. Ever since I was – oh, very young.'

456

'Then I'm glad you've achieved it.'

It was said with such obvious effort at warmth that Amelie stepped across the space that divided them and laid a hand on his arm.

'What is the matter, Clem?' she repeated.

He took her hand in his.

'Don't let this change you, will you?'

Amelie felt oddly breathless. She looked up into his anxious face.

'I won't, I promise.'

'You'll have a lot more power from now on. It has to make a difference.'

She felt the urgent pressure of his fingers on hers, the warmth of his breath. There was a pulse beating in his neck. Slowly, feeling her way, she said, 'That's the last thing I would want to happen. I'll still be the same person, Clem. I'll still need you to talk to, more than ever. You understand better than anyone else. Today when I was in such a quandary, I needed so much to speak to you, and then when it all finally worked out, you were the first person I thought of. I'll always want to share things with you.'

'I hope so, Mel. You mean so much to me. I couldn't bear it if you were to grow away from me now.'

Scarcely daring to believe what she was hearing, Amelie reached up and kissed his lips, and read the same dawning wonder in his eyes.

'I won't ever grow away from you, whatever happens. I know I seem to be so independent and strong, but you know that's only the outside. You're my anchor, Clem. I love you.'

'Oh Mel – my darling . . .'

Clement drew her into his arms and with a sense of coming home, she held his strong body, drowned in the sweetness of his kiss. At last, cradled against his shoulder, she admitted, 'I've wanted to do that for so long.'

Clement stroked her cheek, kissed the top of her head.

'I never thought I'd feel like this again. I thought of us as friends, close friends, and I valued your friendship – but then I saw that you could get taken over by Packards and I realised that you meant so much more to me than the closest friend. I love you, Amelie. I think I have done for quite a while. I couldn't imagine life now without you.'

Amelie sighed.

'I thought I was destined never to have what I really craved for. It was as if I'd been given success, and children, and that had to be enough. But it all seemed so empty. I thought I would never have love as well.'

Clement held her tighter, kissed her again.

'We all deserve love as well.'